THE CUSTODIAN AND THE CRUCIFIX

JOHN JOSEPH

Copyright

The Custodian and The Crucifix

ISBN: 978-0-578-70738-9

Cover Design Art by Rocco Scary; www.roccoscary.com

With Special Acknowledgements and Heartfelt Thanks to the following:

Michael Cooper of
Cooper Graphics
for cover production.

Liam Krauss; eagleeyedproofing@gmail.com

Interior formatted by NoBullJustPublishing.com

Dedicated to the kindest, most gentle and patient man I knew, my dad, John 'Jack' Scary. It was far too short a time.

Table of Contents

1

It was miles of unrelenting landscapes, horizontal proportions unequaled by any I had ever experienced before. Dusty boredom rode shotgun, as I made my trek across country. I traveled aimlessly through the backwash of American towns, most of which are just a blur to me now. At times, all I had to keep my mind occupied were my haunting thoughts of prior days and the bevy of tunes that emanated from my car radio.

But with every mile I traveled, with every city and small town forever disappearing in my rear-view mirror, I knew that I had to press on, having to forgo any inclination of turning back.

The thought of moving forward without really knowing where my final landing spot would be, was incidental. Stopping to eat only when hunger beckoned, stopping to sleep when my brain was summoned by slumber, or just pulling off to the side of the road to break the routine of the continuous miles lying before me. I headed west, away from a life that was once full of promise and prosperity.

I drove endlessly, persistently, in my 1954 red Nash Rambler. Once bright and shiny as I distinctly remember her to be, now, looking as if the paint had been peeled away in large sections on the hood and roof exposing swatches of unprimed surfaces that would eventually turn to rust. It was a four-door afterthought of a GM automobile marvel with a slant six engine and a no-frills package. The interior was black vinyl and in heat of the day, or night for that matter, I could feel my thighs sticking to the synthetic hide, peeling away ever so slightly each time I readjusted my position.

In the trunk were three suitcases of assorted sizes, my worldly possessions, packed neatly inside. Three canvas and straw bags stuffed with all that would suffice for my immediate future, as I left the past behind with a sense of urgency.

The monotony of the entire journey gave me time to think, to think about the unkind blows that life can sometimes deliver. To think about relationships that were never meant to be in the first place. I needed a way to relieve myself of the painful memories and if my only recourse was to drive west, then driving it would be.

I maneuvered ghost-like, silently, intentionally encountering as few people as possible. The occasional service station attendant for a gas fill, the night manager at some sooty roadside motel, or that worn-out waitress at a secluded truck stop, who only seems to take the late shift to escape her own personal demons.

I drove for days on end, passing through extreme examples of rural and middle America. All told, I believe I crossed the boundaries of nine states during my quest, at times spending only a night or two, in any one of them.

I managed approximately twenty-two hundred miles that summer, a major accomplishment for someone who had only lived in just two places his whole life. I had become a drifter, cutting off ties with everyone and anyone from my past.

Difficult at times, the stillness of sitting behind the constant drone of my engine was a part of a long tireless journey. As it turned out, it was only the beginning.

I arrived in Mara Del Santos, on the 15th of July 1954 at precisely 11:17 pm. At first glance, I was certain this town was as far removed from any city I had known in my earlier days. And it was here that an inner voice didn't just whisper, it shouted at me, telling me it was time to stop. It was at that juncture, on that fateful night, I decided that my journey should come to a halt. Besides, my car, which I had playfully named Denise, seemed to be also saying that if I didn't stop pushing her, she would inevitably make that decision for me. So, in the humid and tepid air of a clear New Mexico evening, I quietly coasted down the main road of this seemingly isolated town, with the windows rolled down and the radio playing, listening to The Chords spilling out their hit *Sh-Boom*, crooning how life could be a dream.

Slowly cruising through the silent avenues, the streets themselves looked as if a lame attempt had been made to pave over certain sections, consenting the rest to the extended gravel beneath. The first and most glaring thing I immediately noticed, and partly because my stomach seemed as though it was growling louder than my radio, was a small shack-like structure at the far end of the main boulevard. There under a dimly lit yellow light, a sign noticeably hanging off-center was perched above its front door, which simply read, 'The Diner'. I pulled into one of the unmarked parking spaces in front and turned off my engine.

Leaving Denise to cool off in the night air, I snatched up my keys and headed inside. The building was weathered-looking with an elongated front porch leading the way in. I made my way towards the entrance as I stretched my limbs longingly. Upon entering, a creaky screen door slammed behind. Mounted inside was a 12-foot counter aligned with stationary stools, a faded top with glass covered cake plates sitting on it, and adjacent booths which faced the windows on the south and west sides, allowing patrons to sit and view the comings and goings outside.

A small 2-foot chalkboard hung on the wall with handwritten letters spelling out the title, "special of the day", along with remnants of words that were written beneath, looking as if they had long been erased. Two coffee pots sat side by side on shiny stainless-steel hotplates which were surrounded by a rectangular four-foot open cutout window that lead to the kitchen area in the rear. From there I could hear sounds of pots clanking, and silverware being aligned, a thankful indication that there was still some activity at this late hour.

An elderly gentleman sitting at the end corner booth quietly sipping from what looked to be a bowl of soup was the only patron at that hour. Exhausted and famished, I just plopped myself down in the first seat I came upon and sat there for a few minutes rubbing my eyes and brow, not realizing someone was hovering over me.

The first thing I noticed as I squinted looking up was a name tag pinned to her blouse. My eyes teary and red, slowly ascended and before I could see who was standing before me, they ran into the bold letters distinctively spelling out the word F R A N K I E .

Her full name was Francesca Cordova, as I later found out. Wearing a plain white top and a pair of denim shorts with a frayed, off-white apron tied around her waist, she stood ready to take my order. Looking to be somewhere in her late twenties, possibly early thirties, she stood approximately five feet four inches tall, lean and very fit. She possessed glowing tanned skin, amber straight hair with golden sun-kissed streaks mingled throughout pulled back into a ponytail, and striking green eyes.

I think it was those eyes that held my gaze for a few minutes longer than I dared. They were piercing, but also seemed to possess a subtle loneliness. She was not like most waitresses I had encountered in my travels, not worn out at all, not resembling an uninspired version of life, Frankie seemed different. And for the first time in a very long time, in some obscure moment, in some obscure place, I took notice. This was not only to be remembered as the night I rolled into Mara Del Santos for the first time, but it would be also the night, I met Frankie.

At first, our encounter was brief and strictly business.

"Hi, what can I get you? And before you answer, let me give the long and the short of it", she said.

"It's late, you look like you're just passing through and we close in about an hour, the food is good, but besides Mr. O. down in the back booth," she motioned with a tilt of her head towards his direction as she continued,

"It's just me and junior back there in the kitchen, so we would appreciate it, if you don't order a four-course meal or something like that."

"Well, what do you recommend?" I said in a weary tone.

She hesitated for a moment and then, in a slightly more congenial manner, replied.

"Junior can whip up a mean omelet with fresh eggs that were just delivered a couple of hours ago, from the Jaco farm homestead just outside of town, if that's to your liking?"

"Tell you what, throw in some home fries, and an omelet sounds great," I responded, perking up a bit.

"Coffee?"

"Yes please."

"Ok, be up in a few." She plainly stated as she turned to the kitchen window and directed the order towards the cook.

And true to her word, within less than ten minutes she approached my table with a heaping pile of home fries and an oversized appealing omelet. Placing the plates down before me and returning quickly, poured me a steaming hot cup of coffee, as she smiled and went on matter-of-factly.

"Anything else I can get you?"

"No, this is great. Thank you."

I ate contently while noticing she was keeping a watch over me, stopping only once to offer me more coffee. And just as I was finishing, she came over to gather up the dirty plates and looked at me as if to imply that the lights were about to go out.

"Everything was great, freshest omelet I have had in quite some time." I said looking up at her while she scribbled out my check.

I stood and headed towards the diminutive cash register at the end of the counter where she was waiting. Reaching for my wallet, I handed her six dollars and advised her to keep the change. For a moment her eyes widened, and a half-smile became evident. I thanked her again and headed for the exit.

Pushing open the screen door and suddenly realizing I needed to find a place to spend the night, I hurriedly turned back. I noticed she was nearer than I thought, as she was coming over to lock the door behind me. I stopped suddenly and asked with a mild sense of panic in my voice.

"Uh excuse me, can you tell me if there is a place where I can get a room for the night?"

"Try the Winchester, two blocks south, down on your right. It doesn't look like much, but the sheets are clean!"

"Ok, thank you............ Frankie." I stated politely.

I turned toward the exit and noticed that my response elicited another half-smile as I called her by her advertised name. Then, off I went, two blocks south on the right just as I had been instructed.

Slightly energized from my farm fresh omelet, and my late-night banter, I came to the front of the location that Frankie had directed me towards. It was an older looking three-story structure, which seemed to have a Victorian flair about it. Too tired to study it further within the blackness of the night, I lifted one of my three suitcases from the trunk of my car, made my way up a wide set of stairs which were bookend by two tall fluted columns, and ventured inside in the hopes of meeting those clean sheets as quickly as possible.

A white-haired, middle-aged gentleman with round wired rimmed glasses was perched behind the front desk thumbing his way through a magazine. Peering up at me through the upper portion of his spectacles, he paused his reading material as I leaned forward on the desk directly in front of him.

"Looking for a room?" He unenthusiastically muttered.

"Yes sir, I am. How much for the night?"

"You're in luck, mister." He said with a slightly sarcastic tone.

"Just happen to have one available, ten dollars paid in advance, but it's on the top floor, just at the end of that flight of stairs." He said pointing to his left.

"If you can please sign this card." He added as he placed a key on the counter in front of me.

Doing as he asked, I placed the cash immediately before him as I scooped up the key in one hand, and my bag in the other. Then giving him a thankful nod, I began the climb the staircase ahead of me. The staircase was carpeted in a worn, faded violet rug and creaked and groaned ever so slightly as each step felt the pressure of my weight. Room 305 was just to the left on the third floor. Entering, I could see that the view overlooked the entire town.

"Tomorrow, tomorrow, I'll get a good look." I whispered to myself.

And with that, turning towards the bed, I slipped off my trousers and shirt and crawled between those crisp comfortable clean sheets, just as Frankie had described.

* * *

Boston was as big a city as I have ever encountered. Partially transplanted there from New Jersey, I had learned to love it, it was to become my home away from home. I didn't ascend there until the ripe old age of nearly 17 and it was music which was not only was responsible for elevating me, but also for delivering me there. It was music which was to offer me the chance of a lifetime.

I was reared to believe that this innate ability was something that came naturally and often effortlessly. From my days in grade school, all through my teen years, I was known for my musical proficiency. Singing was my core strength, it was something that I quickly became known for. And when I instinctively began to distinguish the keys on my Aunt Nell's piano at the age of 5, my parents, as well as my teachers, professed a sense of astonishment. Several years went on with me taking impromptu lessons from my dear aunt, which found me to demonstrate my proficiency rather quickly. But it was my vocal range which set me apart from others, my voice became my trademark.

A gift they called it, a gift which was a bit baffling as both my parents, grandparents, aunts, uncles, and generally everyone up and down my family tree were the most musically uninclined people I knew. Yet I, Angelo Vincent Scardosa, the son of working middle class, devout Catholic, God-fearing parents with just a high school diploma to their credit, emerged from obscurity to be accepted at one of the most prestigious institutions around, The Boston Conservatory of Music.

My parents, who had educated and disciplined me early by enrolling me at a hard-tasked Catholic grade school, and who had made sure we attended Sunday mass each week, had sacrificed and paid handily for this opportunity. My dad, an ex-navy man worked as a photoengraver for a local newspaper, while my mom (after attending secretarial school) procured a job in an administrative position in our local high school's guidance department. But here I was, after succeeding in several voice auditions, permitted to skip my senior year of high school, to become the youngest member of the current class enrolled in such a prized establishment.

The seduction of the bright lights and bustle of the big city was overwhelming at first, but with an immediate comradery of other incoming students, I felt somewhat at ease. This was it, music education personified, and

I had landed right smack dab in the middle of it. Yet, the sheer magnitude of where I was and what I was doing, felt almost transparent due to the bonds I forged from first days there.

Johnny 'Magnifico' Lupora, a.k.a. Johnny 'Mags', truly magnificent on the guitar, a magician when it came to his accuracy manipulating those strings. He was from the Midwest, Chicago to be exact, two years my elder, he had jet black, slicked-back hair, wore sunglasses most of the time and possessed a calm, cool demeanor. I knew, we all knew, that we were there for the classical element, but his look combined with the way his polished guitar was strung behind his back, just oozed the essence of one cool cat. Johnny was the first person I really met or even dared to speak to during orientation, but from the onset of our introduction, he assured me a sense of comfort as he simply referred to me as "the kid".

And look the part I did. Tall, lanky and baby-faced, I was the quintessential picture of innocence. I latched on to Johnny, as he didn't seem to mind much, I could even say he took me under his wing. And when the time was to come, he would also become my guide to the nightlife which surrounded our campus and those conservatory walls.

Johnny was suave and smooth, socially he could connect with inspired ease and knew had to sway the women in his direction. But what thrilled us the most was his guitar playing. From the very first day, in a secluded orchestra room, Johnny won over the student body that witnessed his abilities. And he did it handily, without ever breaking a sweat or his composure.

I was in awe as I watched him run his fingers up and down those strings with blistering precision. If he could court swing and jazz like this, I couldn't wait to hear him get serious with a classical rendition. We became friends from the start, and it was no accident his dorm room was right next to mine, as close as roommates could get without sharing the same space, but for that matter, our doors were always open, like most of the occupants in our building.

Walking through the halls you could get the sense that this common thread of music held us all together. You could hear the constant criticism we gave each other, musical sounds, echoing Benny Goodman and Glen Miller swirling for many nights became routine and expected. But the most enchanting element of these living arrangements was the added dimension of our dorms being co-ed. Divided by floors, males and females were separated in that respect, which in turn was a very progressive manifesto for the times. It didn't always entirely stop the co-mingling, but the R.A.'s (resident advisors) kept it at a minimum. That's when things became interesting, paving the way to something more, that's when Johnny and I went from being a duet to eventually becoming a trio.

The cello is a magnificent musical device, but within its splendor, it is rather large and sometimes cumbersome to carry, and there, attached to one, was the most captivating, petite cellist I had ever met. She maneuvered her apparatus effortlessly, with grace and care, as if it obeyed her every command. The first time I laid eyes on Elizabeth Brundige, or just "Lizzy" for short, I knew that I had to get to know her.

From New York City, the daughter of a superbly talented concert violinist, she had left the neon lights of Broadway, by the bequest of her mother, and as fate would have it, made her way north to these lovely confines just outside the back-bay area to join us here in Boston.

She was hypnotizing, long thick wavy dark hair, chestnut eyes, and armed with simply unfettered self-confidence. It was on my third day while having lunch in our usual spot, towards the back of the cafeteria (but as I later was to find out, this section was previously relegated for the new incoming freshman), that she caught my eye. She passed by, not noticing me or even Johnny, for that matter, but it was at that precise moment that I knew music was not to be my only passion here in Boston.

* * *

I awoke from a long and much-deserved slumber. It had been a while since I last remembered sleeping so soundly, and for a better part of the morning. But the noise level here at the Winchester didn't compare in the faintest notion to my previous habitations. From the open window in my room, I could hear a dog barking somewhere in the distance, the occasional sputter of an automobile passing and frequent muted sounds of voices making their way on the streets below. I laid in bed for several minutes with my body in a thankful state of relaxation. I thought about all the situations I endured to arrive here, and I was overcome for the moment with a feeling of exoneration to think that the slate could be wiped clean, liberated from any presumed expectations. I wanted to make the past only a fading memory, and here, perhaps, I was in this place to do just that.

But where is here? The sign on the outskirts of town some 2 ½ miles back said WELCOME TO MARA DEL SANTOS, pop. 850e. I arose with a purpose and pulling my suitcase out and laying it upon my bed, I flipped the latch and sprang it open. Thankfully in my haste, it was the correct one which I removed from my trunk the night before. In it were the immediate necessities, a change of clean clothes and some toiletries. The bathroom was a shared one and was located at the end of the hall. Seeing that the entire third floor looked unoccupied, I had the luxury of having it all to myself. I grabbed my shaving kit, a toothbrush, and toothpaste, discarded the clothes I had been wearing, wrapped a clean towel which I found in the closet, around my waist, and shutting my room door behind me, ventured down the hall. Some twenty minutes later, refreshed, and feeling clean and invigorated, I dressed for my morning explorations. Pulling on a clean pair of khaki pants, a simple white tee-shirt, white socks, and penny loafers, I headed down the steep flight of stairs to the lobby. This time I was greeted by a much younger man from the previous night's encounter. In his early twenties, he was full of enthusiasm.

I looked at him wide-eyed and before I could say a word, he flashed a welcoming smile with a very upbeat tone in his voice.

"Morning, Mr., uh Mr.........,what exactly is your name sir, can't seem to read the writing on the card you filled out last evening". He stated as he squinted at my penmanship.

"Good Morning." I responded.

"You can call me Vincent, it's fine." I decided to go with my middle name at that point, seemed like as good a place as any to start with a new alias.

I whisked past him before he could continue as I scooted through the lobby and out the double front doors eager to start my new adventure.

The day was brightly shining on this small out-of-the-way town, but as I stood on that grand front porch looking out onto the sun-drenched landscape before me, there was a certain serene presence that enveloped the area for miles around. First stop, breakfast, destination, 'The Diner', and the faint hope that there could be a continuation of my encounter with Frankie. But before I took another step, pausing for just a moment, I stood there with my arms outstretched wide, as if to say, I am here, and you are mine. And with a rejuvenated sense to my existence, I galloped down the stairs and out into the road.

Stopping briefly when I got to where Denise was parked, I took the keys from my pocket, thought twice about driving over, then sliding them back into my trousers, decided to continue walking about as I assessed my new surroundings. After all, it was only a short distance, to be precise, two blocks, just as Frankie had so mindfully stated.

For a Saturday morning, activity seemed to be just as it should, I passed a general store which was getting most of the activity. A pale blue-green pickup truck parked right in front was being loaded with what looked like large canvas sacks of grain. I stopped to peer into the oversized windows and noticed a woman with two young children scampering about her while eating ice cream cones. There were partly empty shelves of dry goods and tools at one end, and a counter where cleaning supplies were kept.

There were four large glass jars on shelves filled with several types of colorful candy behind a tall lean gray-haired man wearing a long white apron over his overalls with his sleeves rolled up beneath it. As I continued my stroll in a leisurely fashion, looking down towards one end of the strip and then back towards the other, I took note of several other establishments this town had to offer. A tiny barbershop, barber pole included, and a bench outside, directly in front where folks could sit and mingle. Two older, weathered-looking men were sitting there, who's conversation stopped abruptly as I passed with a friendly nod. I made my way down the sidewalk of the main street towards the diner, and in doing so felt the penetrating look that a newcomer would so happen to appropriate in a small town such as this. I supposed that a population 850e as the gateway sign read on my way in, would make for a community where everyone would know each other quite well.

There was a one window building with a single door entrance with familiar lettering stenciled on it which read, US Postal Service. And like most towns, centrally located, there was a local pub called The Daisey Mae, of course, closed during the early hours of the day. Two doors down from there I noticed a brown brick building with a more professional looking sign attached to a deep dark red colored door which read, Office of Doctor Melvin J. Coots, who also had the distinction of handling the towns dentistry matters as well, as indicated just below his name.

So, without much more immediate exploration necessary, I found myself rather quickly back at the diner. It looked significantly different in the light of day, as one might suspect. Now, appearing without the yellowish glare of the porch night light, it was much more inviting. The atmosphere was conducive to human interaction at this hour, even the screen door's creak seemed less noticeable as I ventured in.

Four of the booths were occupied, parents with children in one, three teens in another, and a pair of couples in the others. I quickly scoured the interior looking for my waitress from the night before, but she was nowhere in sight. A young Mexican girl wearing a brown waitress uniform appeared and asked me if I would like a booth or a counter seat, I chose the counter this time.

There were two waitresses that morning, but neither one was Frankie and not wanting to be presumptuous, I thought better not to ask. Breakfast consisted of habaneros and eggs, coffee, and toast, the morning special as listed on the black chalkboard. I sat at the counter keeping to myself as I devoured this southwestern delight, but all the while I could once again feel the unmistakable weight of being an outsider as residents would turn to see the stranger sitting there among them. Having a refill of coffee and generously tipping my waitress, I made my way out to decide on where and how, I would settle down in Mara Del Santos, pop 850e.

The southwest and New Mexico to be precise, in 1956 was home to a melting pot of American and Mexican occupants, along with descendants of Native American Pueblo Indians and Spanish conquistadors. And in this serene, but surreal environment, this peaceful co-existence of its inhabitants was something that seemed refreshingly at ease. The simple life is what I was searching for, and here, I believed I found it. All the necessary components were accounted for.

I decided to walk as far I could manage that first day, encircling the town in a northeasterly direction. There was a small unassuming movie house, where the marquee read: now showing; *Seven Brides for Seven Brothers*. They were decidedly in arrears, as I do remember seeing the same movie posters some years prior back east. Beyond that and down the road a bit was what looked to be a rather larger building surrounded by a makeshift fence, a school and playground. A smaller adobe structure that housed the Sheriff's office was just adjacent to it. A section of an open-air pavilion, where a couple of local craftsmen and women were selling handmade goods, mainly clay earthenware and woven blankets, beneath large tents amidst the rising temperature of the mid-morning sun , stood beyond that.

But, off in the distance, one building stood out which looked somewhat out of place. It seemed to be well established within the landscape, far enough from the town itself, yet close enough where all roads led to it. That very first day, I couldn't help but notice it as I turned the corner.

It was unquestionably a church.

Dust balls and tumbleweeds swirled past it in the dry heat of the mounting temperature, portraying an abandoned or ghostly fashion. But there it was, for all to seek out. Not grandiose by any means, but possessing an architecture which made it appear as if it belonged to another time and place. At first glance, I thought it to be minimal in size, although it had spires around its façade which jutted upward into the vast southwestern sky, giving it an undeniable presence.

It was orange in complexion, possibly from the native clay soil reflecting its hue upon it. But standing there on the northernmost tip of this community, it beckoned me instantly. Stopping in my tracks, I stood and stared at it for several minutes feeling a bit apprehensive as I began to head towards it. Pausing, contemplating, stopping again, staring, then stepping towards it once more, I decided, today was not the day. I thought it best to explore the rest of the town and possibly acquire firsthand information about it from some of the friendlier folk who had greeted me in passing.

Introducing myself as I went about, I gained in my outwardly confidence as I earned that of others. The stories that were transcribed to me during my first days there would live for years to come. The elders, with all the accumulation of the past embedded within their memory, were particularly interesting and more than willing to offer their insight. I have heard it said that true history is not acquired from a textbook, but from those who have either experienced it firsthand or have had it passed down from generation to generation, and here, I was finding that to be true.

In a sense, I was to them, a distraction from their daily routines, and they were as equally entertaining to me. With each person, I met and with each history lesson I learned, I felt like I was slowly being indoctrinated into their community, into their way of life. Everyone I encountered, although generally guarded at first, became more welcoming and accommodating and eventually seemed to accept this mild-mannered, yet inquisitive stranger from the east.

These were hard-working people, they toiled and endured the hardships of a difficult ecosystem, the harsh scolding rays of the sun during the day, and weeks upon end without precipitation. The rain was the most prominent factor, it all but dictated their way of living. When it did come, it came as a deluge, and they were as appreciative of a society as I have ever witnessed.

And faith, this was a land occupied by deep devotional faith, Christian-based faith, brought here many generations ago by the conquering Spanish settlers and instilled throughout each succeeding generation. It was a land which endured the hellfire of a manmade kind when some ten years earlier the United States government partook in the testing of the world's first nuclear weapon nearby. It was a land also filled with superstitions ranging from Native American Indian tribal sources to the strange and peculiar tales of sightings of extraterrestrials.

But this is where I had ventured and this is where I was to remain. The east coast had provided me with all the modern conveniences I could afford, it was a haven of culture, entertainment, and exhilarating nightlife. And within only a few short days here, I was quickly swept up in its curiosities, and profound tales.

* * *

The Conservatory and its musical embellishments had become a normal way of life for each student. It was as if we were in a city within a city, feeling extraordinary within its confines and protected by its walls. Each of us knew the other's talents, strongpoints, and personalities. Some were virtuosos on their chosen instruments, some could write music in their sleep, some had perfect pitch and still, others were music theory geniuses. We were there not only because we were the privileged few, but also because from deep within, we knew we had no choice.

Freshman year became an inoculation of sorts, a ritual of order. We were not only expected to carry our course loads but also carry the equipment of the upperclassman, literally, upon demand. It was a code which was exercised without words or objection. If you walked down the hall and an upperclassman was standing there with a baritone horn at his feet, you were expected to pick it up and follow him or her to their destination, even if it meant you were going to be late getting to yours. This practice was seen several times daily, with me falling prey on numerous occasions.

Bart Oppenheim, rather large in stature, and a bit clumsy, always looking somewhat disheveled in his general appearance with his clothes possessing more than an obvious wrinkle or two, was my decided antagonist in this regard. Bart was fully capable of carrying his double bass around, but as any power struggle would dictate, he was determined to maintain a steady flow of underclassman to undertake this chore. The double bass, the much larger cousin to the cello and grouped within the string family, was probably one of the bulkiest instruments to handle, and Bart had the market cornered on it. He had the prime distinction of being the sole proprietor of such. I do believe that I must have witnessed just about every person in the freshman class at one time or another lugging his case around, with Bart and his sheepish grin rumbling close behind. He even managed, much to my surprise, to enlist Johnny on one occasion. And even though this was the protocol, I did notice a look of disdain in Johnny's eyes when called upon. But as for me, I do believe I was Bart's favorite target and must have broken the record that freshman year for the most conveyances.

At times, the torment which we must endure ends up being a blessing in disguise, and in the strangest of ways, it was Bart Oppenheim that I did owe a debt of gratitude for affording me just that.

And so, it came to pass, an impromptu meeting which to my avail was completely unexpected. As it happened, it was a typical Friday morning, the end of another grueling week closing in and I felt more exhausted than usual. The recital and practice rooms were housed in Sachar hall, a one-story brick building approximately a short, one-minute stroll from the dormitories. It was comprised of one large-scaled band room with rows of tiered seating and a small stage. This was where individual senior recitals and smaller performances were mainly held. The corridors surrounding it were lined with six-foot by six-foot practice rooms, each one containing an upright piano and completely soundproof.

It was there, in that band practice room that many of us, at least the underclassman, would find ourselves at all hours of the night, most notably on Thursdays. If you were lucky enough to be of age or had that elusive false I.D., you found your way off campus and meandered downtown for a taste of 'real' nightlife. But for us, still, within our innocence, it was either the lounge in the dormitory or Sachar Hall where we caroused on Thursday evenings. It was on those occasions where we would be uninhibited, with no teachers in sight, the building was occupied by just the musical energies of our adolescence.

On these nights, musical freedom was ours to bargain with, far from the general curriculum we had to adhere to. We played jazz, experimented with show tunes, jostled with each other's instruments, and for the most part had hours of fun, as musical drips would. But the true testimony to those raucous hours was the screaming improvisational jazz and swing tunes. You wouldn't even breathe a mention of it within earshot of any teacher for fear of epic condemnation. So, after the nine-pm hour, we took turns posting a lookout, just to be on the safe side, and our sounds came together in a free-for-all which seemed endless. The early days of this energetic shift in music were filled with spontaneity and our renditions of T-Bone Walker, Cab Calloway, and The Mills Brothers were ours to be had. It was that hard edge that we craved, and in time would find it downtown, outside of our campus boundaries. But for now, we were content to make it happen here at our home base.

For some unknown reasons, some Thursday evenings were more energetically charged than others, with one night which particularly stood out. My spirit was soaring and my voice as well. There was Tony Matone on drums, Jake P. on Sax, (we only used his last initial since he had a long European name with many silent letters in it) and Clive Van Vreeland, aka, The 'Vree' man, on piano. We broke out into an awe-inspiring rendition of *Move It on Over,* that would have made the immortal Hank Williams proud. And as we built that harmony into a growing crescendo, the crowd around us continued to expand. I looked out at faces moving and grooving to that number, some I barely recognized, but one which I did immediately relish.

There to my far right, caressing the edge of the makeshift circle which emerged around us, she stood, gazing at us with a smile, one which is still etched in my memory today. Lizzy, wearing tight blue jeans and an oversized gray sweatshirt, long dark locks cascading down, was there swaying within the momentum we had created. A vision that was hard to look away from, but one that I couldn't help to be coy with. It was my nature to be shy, unless of course, I was performing, then and only then, in those moments on stage, in my element, I felt free. I could adapt to any beat, could modulate without involving any thought. As onlookers danced spontaneously around us, they erupted into a wild cheer as we ended, it was a breakout moment for all, and especially for me.

Many others would perform in this unannounced forum, some very spirited and some very methodical. But it was those of course which added their unique element which seemed to get the most attention.

I will never comprehend how the cello, can be an instrument that is so soothing, yet can cut to the heart in the same breath. And I believe that after Lizzy saw us perform, she decided to immerse us in a composition of her own which brought the room to a silent halt.

She gracefully elevated her instrument across the stage, now with her hair pulled back into a loose ponytail with several single strands falling forward, gently stroking her cheek, she projected an intense look. Lowering herself onto a stool and slowly began to embrace her instrument. In the single stroke of her bow, she managed to turn the room from a maddening moving frenzy to the subdued softness of a ballad. The overtones were such as they tugged at your heartstrings. We all stood and accepted it, there was no judgment among us, just pure appreciation for the music, for each other's talents. It was on these special nights we all felt connected, bonded together in a common cause, we felt alive.

By morning, the events of the prior evening quickly became a passing happenstance, except for an adoring comment or two as people passed me in the hallway. I was in a lackluster t due to my depravity of sleep, from the adrenaline high of my performance and the vision of Lizzy which stayed with me until the wee hours of the morning. I wanted to just get through my classes, find something to eat, and head back to my room as early as possible to take a very needed nap. But alas, as fate would have it, no sooner did I turn the corner in Henderson Hall with music theory 101 as my destination, that I felt a large slab of a forearm land squarely on my breastbone.

"Not so fast there, Mr. movin' on over," his voice bellowed throughout the hallway.

And as I peered, looking up at his sinister yet non-descript grin, it was none other than the grandmaster of misery, Oppenheim, himself. But this day was to produce an occurrence which shifted my life's course at the conservatory, it was one where a relentless, over-inflated ego landed me right in the sights of the most striking cello player I have ever come to know.

"Whatya' say there Oppy! Its Friday, the day after Thursday night, how about being a pal and cutting a guy some slack?" I pleaded in a mildly indulging way.

He ignored me as usual, as I have tried this tactic before with no resolution. And without speaking a word, he puffed up his chest to make him look more bloated than usual, and just looked sternly at me with his double bass perched on the ground. I turned with a sigh and lifted the case with my right hand while juggling my books. Instead of heading in my original direction to my appointed classroom, I succumbed to Oppenheim once again, turned, and followed him abruptly to his destination. It was orchestra practice for the seniors, and I kept pace into the practice hall where I dutifully set down the large case just as I felt my hand becoming numb. I promptly left Oppenheim and several other stray seniors, then made haste as not to be late for my own assignment. It was at that moment, as I scurried back down the hall, when an unfamiliar, but soft voice reached out to me.

"Hey, loved the show last night." She blurted out in my direction.

And upon hearing that momentous statement, I halted immediately. Yes, there she stood, no more than three feet from me, it was the first actual communication that Lizzy and I ever had on a personal basis. And it was assuredly, not to be the last. The fact that Oppenheim was his ever-present repugnant self once again, had unexpectedly turned the tide in my direction.

"Thanks," I managed to say as I cleared my throat nervously.

"You were great too." I clamored on.

We stood awkwardly quiet for a moment, then she gave me one of her patented endearing smiles.

"I've seen you around, you're the 'kid', right?"

"Uh.... uh, yeah, I mean yes, that's what they call me around here." I said quite nervously.

“Where’d you learn to sing like that, you sounded better than that Hank Williams guy himself.”

"Thanks, can't really say......... my parents, tell me that I came into the world singing instead of crying."

As she giggled at my response, we both were aware it was to time to get to our respective classes. But being already behind schedule, any sense of urgency had seemed to already pass. She turned to her left and started to head off in the opposite direction, and just before doing so, she looked over her shoulder and softly shouted,

“Hey kid, what’s your real name?”

“Uh.... Angelo, Angelo Scardosa from Jersey,” I yelled out, as there was now more space separating us.

“I’m Lizzy, see you around Angelo Scardosa.... from Jersey.”

Feeling like my feet were immersed in concrete, I just watched as she walked away, smiling to myself and sensing a debt of gratitude towards, towards .... Oppenheim?

Gathering my thoughts, and with a new revived energy, I sprinted down the now empty hallway to get to class just as Mrs. Chapman was closing the door.

“Glad you could join us, Mr. Scardosa. Please see me after class, thank you,” she gravely stated.

It wasn’t the first time I was late for her class, the frequent Oppenheim encounters made sure of that. And although I knew I was doomed to pay the ongoing price by doing some menial tasks for Mrs. Chapman and other teachers to make up for it, I do believe they were aware of the reason for my tardiness and that of other underclassmen as well. I think the instructors saw it as growing pains which we had to endure, a sort of rite of passage. But on this day, it didn't matter, on this day, whatever Mrs. Chapman wanted me to do was fine with me. Polish the flugelhorns, yeah sure, give me the cleaner...... dust the inside of the pianos, just hand over the rag, I will even move all the music stands and wash the floor if you want me too, I thought to myself. Today, none of that mattered, I even forgot how hungry and tired I was. The thought that I had broken through with Lizzy, the fact that we even spoke was more than enough for me to contemplate, and I couldn’t wait to, as she said, ‘see you around’.

2

Not at all accustomed with the heat of the southwest, I could feel my shirt becoming moist with perspiration rather quickly. The distractions of finding my way around were quickly melting away as the thermometer continued its steady upward climb. Making my way back towards the center of town I decided to detour through the open pavilion I had passed earlier. There I met a couple of locals who didn't speak English too well but were more than willing to tend to my needs. Seeking cover from the sun's persistent rays, I picked out a woven straw hat with ragged ends, from among the articles for sale. It looked authentic enough and would more than suffice. I also selected a concoction of juices served to me from a large clay pot by an elderly woman wearing a kerchief around her head, exposing only her sun-withered and wrinkled face. She delivered a hearty smile while motioning and trying to mimic the words eluding to the amount of two bits. Her glow widened to even greater lengths as I laid out two wilted singles on a faded plaid blanket at her feet.

"Thank you." I exclaimed, as I motioned with my hand across my brow in a halfhearted salute.

She recoiled and backed away rather unexpectedly as if my gesture was severely inappropriate, her smile vanished while she scooped up the money from beneath her and hurried off in another direction. Not knowing if I offended her in any way or what was the cause of her kneejerk reaction, I watched her take her leave behind a makeshift tent that was set nearly twenty feet apart from where we stood.

Approaching the borders of town where the streets turned from dirt and dust, back to thin layers of asphalt and cracked hardened roadway, I could hear the clip-clop of horses fast approaching behind me. Two men rode directly up and pulled back on their stirrups easing their steeds to a slow stop as I turned in a startled motion.

They looked as if they were in their late twenties, the first one being broad-shouldered with a ruddy complexion, wearing a black vest and a wide-brimmed cowboy hat. Together with his sidearm loosely attached to the belt around his waist, he displayed all the true characteristics of a typical cowboy figure. The second was much slighter in stature, with fair skin, almost as if he were new to cowboy territory. He wore a white collared shirt, and a sizably smaller hat, coinciding with his less imposing presence.

"Good day there, stranger," said the first one, as he tipped that large suede hat slightly towards me.

"Didn't mean to come up on ya' so fast like that, but we saw ya' from over yonder and, well, it isn't every day we see a new face new around here."

"That's quite alright. I was just doing some investigation of my own and taking in the sights." I responded.

They seemed friendly enough, but my inner spirit felt as if it was sensing some unreasonable apprehension towards me. Not the kind of just being leery of that 'new' face in town, but something more, something I couldn't quite put my finger on at that moment.

"The name's Mic and this here is Jake," the first said, as he motioned towards his partner.

"Good to make your acquaintance, I'm Vincent," I said rather sheepishly.

The mood settled a bit as they sat up high in their saddles and seemed to size me up.

"Don't want to take up much of your time seein' as we got to get back to the ranch, just wanted to say howdy. Oh, and if you are needin' any work, that is, if your planning to stay a spell, we could always use an extra hand out at the Jaco spread. Although you look more like the learned schoolboy type, you a college boy mister?"

"The Jaco spread!" I fired back as I ignored his last comment.

"Had the most delicious omelet made from your eggs last night at the diner, that Frankie recommended."

I remembered hearing Frankie mention the Jaco homestead just the night before as she promised the best omelet in the southwest.

"Oh, Frankie recommended that, did she? Yes, the diner gets most of their supplies fresh from us." He mumbled as he turned to look at his partner, making obvious eye contact with him.

The prospect of finding employment was one that would soon need to enter my consciousness, as the small cache of money I had in my possession would not last forever, but after meeting these two individuals, I would almost rest assured that the Jaco ranch was not the type of employment I would venture to entertain. For now, I was more than happy to just explore and digest whatever information I obtained.

"Okay, thanks for the news, I will keep it in mind." I said as I began to step away.

"Oh, and by the way, I noticed you just rode in from the west," as I pointed out to the horizon behind them.

"I was wondering if you could tell me what that unusual looking building out there is. Has all the makings of a church, is it one?" I stated, referring to the structure with its signature spires and orange tint, which I had seen just moments earlier.

"What do you mean…. unusual?" said Mic, as Jake just laid back a bit, not speaking a word and looking off into the distance.

"Well I didn't get the opportunity to go in and get a closer look yet, but the architecture just seems so out of place for these parts."

"Don't know much about any arch-texture," he stammered slowly.

"But you are correct, that there is the church of San Sebastian." Pointing outwardly as his voice turned sternly.

And with that, they pulled back on their reins and swung their horses' full circle as they spiraled away, galloping and kicking up a trail of dust in their wake. I watched for a moment as they disappeared into the distance, reminding me of scenes from some old black and white western movie I vaguely can recall as a young boy. Not thinking too much of the introductions which had just taken place, I continued back towards town, as the imposing heat tends to keep you moving along. Now armed with my new head cover, I was a bit more comfortable as I ventured on.

Circling back and around the eastern side of town, I came upon the second unusual sight of the day. There to my left were rows of boarded-up buildings, up one side of the street and down the other. They resembled boarding houses, ones that I experienced down on Hannity street on the south side of Boston. Only these were different, very different. The ones from my past were always full of life, children playing outside, teenagers clustered together on the front stoops, windows wide open with overseeing mothers sitting and peering out of them continuously watching the nearby activities and trying not to miss out on any gossip that they may come across. No, this was a very different sight, a woebegone reminder of something gone astray.

They were clearly unlike the church building at all. That design, as out of place as it was, looked permanent and planted (or possibly even transplanted). These appeared makeshift and hurriedly assembled but newer than the rest of the general make-up of the town. Abandoned and boarded up, they sat there rather conspicuously random, on the far side of town, quiet and still.

The wind swirled about, kicking up tumbleweeds, just as it did in much of the southwest. But here, among the stillness of these buildings, an eerie feeling abounded. I had already skirted the thought of investigating an odd structure, but here I now stood, in the center of what seemed to imply a forgotten neighborhood. I questioned the possibilities. How could housing such as this exist only five hundred yards from a town which is lively? How come no one is utilizing such valuable setups for homes and families? The questions continued to multiply in my thoughts as I proceeded along.

With my inquisitiveness getting the better of me this time, I decided to get a closer look. There was no street sign, or if there was, it was now nowhere in sight. All the other streets and roads I had already taken were marked in some respect, but this one was not distinguished in any way. There was, although, unmistakable evidence that this area was inhabited at one time. The dwellings themselves didn't seem at all in ill repair, they looked to be of solid construction, mainly brick and mortar, which was out of place for this part of the country, and they seemed to be stained with a greenish hue. Two-story flats, some attached directly to each other and others completely free-standing, creating alleyways between them.

The immediate landscape was desperately overgrown, weeds, and dozens of wild white flowering bushes, shrubs, and ground covering cacti were rooted randomly in the dust. Some even crawling and extending up the sides of the buildings giving the impression that the overgrowth would swallow them up completely in ample time. And at the near end of the street, as if to mark its designation, was the remnants of a large ineligible billboard, tattered and faded, covered with thick desert dust.

Slowly studying them as I moved past, I couldn't help but notice the ever-present reminders of past life. A child's tricycle turned on its side, its large front wheel missing and a trace of noticeable metallic red paint, lay dormant against the side of one of the buildings. Broken parts of clotheslines hanging on pullies still attached to the side of another. An old dusty hairbrush left atop one of the steps, a deflated truck tire sitting in a front yard, and so it went as I strolled down to the end of the block. And even more of a mystery were the tracks evident in the road a short distance from where I stood. These were tire tracks, very large tire tracks, the kind that you would see caused by heavy type construction equipment. These were deep and prominent, forming ravines that were now baked solid in the adobe and mud soil.

Mustering up enough courage, I decided to go even further.

Looking over my shoulders several times just to be sure there was no in the area, I approached a set of stairs, cautiously I began to climb towards the front entrance of a building situated somewhere in the middle of the block. There was a large solid wooden door, with a corroded and rusted round handle attached. I knocked. I surmised there was no one inside, but I knocked again anyway, after all, I was the new guy in town and had no business trespassing.

Not a stir came from within, just as I had expected. Trying to turn the handle as I pressed myself against the door, I found neither to be movable. Several attempts using more force still produced the same results. Having no luck, I decided to at least try and get a glimpse inside through the adjacent window. Climbing onto a brick ledge, I shimmied myself over towards one of the front windows. It was covered in a thick film of dirt and grime, producing a haze that was almost impossible to see through. Nearly losing my footing, I tried feverishly to get a grip on it and lift the window open, but as expected, it wouldn't even budge slightly. Tugging the bottom of my shirt out of my pants, using it as a rag to wipe just a small opening on the glass to peek through, I managed to clear an area about the size of a lemon. Bending over in an awkward position, I tossed my hat to the ground to get my face up as close to the pane of glass as I could. There, pressed up tightly against it, I squinted into the darkened room. The first thing I noticed was a chest of drawers in the corner and a large padded armchair perched within its middle. There was peeling wallpaper, flowered yellow and moldy. Dust bowls, beer bottles, cigarette packs, empty cereal boxes, and a varied smattering of trash were thrown about, including some yellowed newspapers, which were not legible from my vantage point. The interiors were no different from what the outside view had projected.

Why no one seemed to have cared enough to police this area or attempt to try and reuse it, was my initial response. My findings left me to wonder, and more so, drove me yet again to find someone to satisfy my curiosities. Perhaps if I could have another chance encounter with Frankie, she would indulge me in some sort of a more meaningful conversation. The morning desk clerk at my hotel, who I so rudely hurried away from, might be of service, or possibly the two elderly men I passed sitting on the bench in front of the barbershop. They appeared to be in no hurry at all to leave their posts, so engaging them in a morning talk might be beneficial. Most town news is always discussed at the barbershop anyway. In any event, I knew that I had the gift of time on my hands. For the first time in my life, there were no deadlines, no audiences to conform to, no pressure to outdo my last performance, and most of all, no general hurriedness which had become such a large aspect of my life once before.

Those first days in Mara Del Santos were days of revelation, I had spent the time encircling the town several times over, becoming visible to its residents and familiarizing myself with its histories. My encounters within this strange novel environment were refreshing and at the same time tantalizing. It was the complete and utter opposite from whence I came. Confident in my ability to feel as though I had always been an uncanny judge of character, I knew the people here were genuine enough for me to possibly want to lay down roots. And as I also knew, there was much more to uncover, many more inquiries to be made. I realized that I had the rest of my life to see it through. It was just the beginning, and other than the newness of my surroundings, I was content to make my way around and find peace with the fact that something not only led me here, but something was encouraging me to stay.

* * *

Weekends around the conservatory were generally quiet, routine, with the occasional exception of a student being picked up by parents to retreat home for a couple of days. For me, I preferred to be here in this environment, where I could focus on my studies and block out any distractions. And now the motivation to be here was even greater, knowing that there was a spark of a different kind somewhere on campus that I couldn't deny.

Part of my usual schedule included Sunday service at our campus chapel, which I attended regularly. After all, my roots were established as such. Growing up in the Scardosa household, Sundays were centered around attending mass as a family unit, before we would come home to a very large Italian dinner. Each week my mother diligently made sure we would pile into my father's big old Buick, adorned in clean pressed clothes. I didn't mind it much due in part that the church was located directly across the street from the grammar school where my parents had us enrolled. So being there on an off day allowed me to run into friends for a couple of additional hours without the burden of school controlling us. And those friends and I were a close-knit bunch. Bonds were formed there at a very early age that I do believe will endure for life, even though the years have sent us on our separate paths.

It was there that I had first publicly became known for my talent. And it was there that my mother enjoyed hearing how gifted her son was. Many times, during mass as the congregation sang the scheduled hymns, I would glance over and see her nudging my father to look over at me, while my voice resounded dramatically as I followed along. There was a look of pride about her as she noticed others turning to see that the voice they were witnessing was coming from her eleven-year-old son. My sister, sitting in between us, would just slouch in embarrassment.

After mass was over, as many mingled on the church steps, she would be smiling emphatically and shaking hands in her white gloves, as other parishioners, some even strangers, would come up to offer their praise. But my parents always managed to remain humble and stressed upon us humility in the gifts we received. It even got to the point where they were asked if I would be obliged to sing a solo or two at an upcoming wedding. And after much deliberation, they agreed. Afterward, I often witnessed the father of the bride handing my dad an envelope, which contained a certain amount of retribution. Coming from that background had a profound effect on me and prepared me for my time at the conservatory. It taught me how important family and true friendship was and to never take for granted my talent or an opportunity when it does arise.

Sunday evenings in a Boston dormitory were usually quiet until I would hear the adjacent door in the hallway slamming shut. I knew immediately it was that familiar sound which indicated my compadre had returned from wherever his outside excursion had recently led him. It surely signaled Johnny was home. And each time he got back from his evening jaunts it would take approximately two minutes after hearing that door shut that I would hear it abruptly open again. He would rush into my room, without knocking (we had that kind of understanding) and plop himself down on my bed to rehash his current events at an unmistakable frantic pitch.

Right on cue, Johnny came barreling in, animated as usual. I don't know if it was the openness we shared or just his presence alone that made me feel at ease. In a sense, I felt protected when he was around.

"What's cookin', kid?" He said as I heard my mattress springs squeak slightly from his flop.

"What a night, I gotta get you downtown and introduce you to the fellas, they are going to love that golden throat of yours." He continued.

I remained silent for the moment as I waited for him to ask again in his normal fashion.

"So, what's been cookin' around here? And what's that smirk about, huh kid?" he said as his eyes opened widely peering at me.

"Yeah, well, while you were off making new friends out there, I guess, I was doing just about the same thing here."

Ok, spill it, kid, what the hell are you talking about? With that look you have tonight, I could tell it's gotta be something big!"

I slid over to the foot of the bed and proceeded to give Johnny the details of what had transpired for me within the last forty-eight hours. He listened with a focused gaze, paying close attention to every word as I ran through the events which catapulted my world towards Lizzy's. And when I finished, I eagerly awaited his reaction as he sat silently staring at me. Then after a few moments of awkwardness, and not knowing what to expect, he tackled me onto my bed in a sort of brotherly congratulations, jokingly punching me a few times in the arm for good measure.

"Kid, I knew you had in you!"

Then punching me one last time in my upper arm, he skirted out the door before turning briefly.

"Seeya' in the morning, Oh, and kid, she is a cutie!"

I knew she was, Johnny knew it, and I do believe, so did everyone else. I had rehashed all the important points of the last couple of days, including the odd twist of fate that had occurred with Oppenheim. It was that divine providence that not only broke the ice with Lizzy but what occurred next would go down in the annals of The Boston Conservatory of Music as one of the greatest tales of my legacy there.

I was so thankful for what had transpired, that the first person on my agenda to seek out the next morning was non-other than good old Oppenheim himself. I made my way through the corridors with an extra spring in my step. In advancing to my first class, a bit earlier than usual, I spied Oppenheim only twenty feet in front of me. Without thinking, I swooped down on him with his back turned to me and coming up from behind him I proceeded to grab the handle of that larger than life case of his.

"Top of the morning to you, Oppy, don't worry I got this, where we headed?" I ironically grinned picking up his with delight, while waiting for him to lead the way.

Oppenheim stood there in a perplexed state of silence. So, did most of the other students who were meandering in the hallway at that moment and noticed my interaction. It became sinisterly quiet, as everyone had abruptly stopped their morning conversations to try and decipher what they had just witnessed. Never in the history of the conservatory did any freshman, voluntarily offer to carry an upperclassman's load. But I, Vincent Scardosa from Jersey, a.k.a. 'the kid', had plunged right in and wistfully conquered Oppenheim and every other upperclassman who had ever professed that ritual. From that moment on, others followed my lead. Freshmen were vying for the right to carry all they could, as often as they could. It became so glorified that a fight over carrying a French horn nearly broke out between two individuals the next day.

The lure that once was at its height for so long had now seemed to be slowly and steadily wearing off. The fact that underclassmen acted as if they wanted to perform this act of their own volition did not have the same impact as it did before. Now, each time Oppenheim passed me in the hallway, he just clung to his double bass so emphatically, that no one, especially myself, would be able to pry it from his hands. That patented smirk of his was gone and I do believe, even though he despised me for the rebellion I created, he respected me even more for it. And if I didn't know any better, I noticed teachers themselves also understood what had taken place, as I seemed to have gained a little latitude in their classrooms. Tardiness was a bit more tolerated and the humble tasks that were handed to me occasionally had now befallen on others. The rite of passage had finally died and my legend had been born.

I had a bit of a swagger from then on, proud of myself for what I had accomplished, and perhaps not really understanding the gravity of what it truly meant. Each time I would see an upperclassman carrying their own instruments as freshman circulated freely among them, a smile would come to my face along with a sense of inner amusement. As my confidence grew, so did the relationships with many of my peers. The notoriety that I attained in my prior schools and neighborhoods was now being surpassed and I took no reluctance to embracing it.

And Johnny and I, well, we were becoming prominent associates that everyone was looking up to. Performing together on those Thursday nights, (as Johnny disappeared less frequently into town) became our calling card, the applause from our classmates became mesmerizing while I had garnered a sense of self-confidence as I never knew before. We had gained the respect of our peers musically as well as with our general guidance and direction for them. Many nights in our rooms, a knock would come to either myself or Johnny's door from a student seeking advice. Most of the time they could find us both in the same place. And they would usually enter quietly, soft-spoken and with a sense of reverence. Johnny knew it and made the most of it, as often as he could.

"Excuse me, sirs." A faint voice uttered in the hallway as a timid knock came to our door.

Johnny loved it when anyone called us sirs.

"Yes, who is it that seeks us this evening!" Johnny responded resoundingly, as I did all I could to contain my laughter.

"ENTER, and be quick about it, man, we have business to tend to," he continued, grinning wildly at me.

Even though Johnny was glorified by such visits, he did possess a huge heart and would always have the best intentions at hand when giving out advice. Besides most of the time, he would glance over at me to interject or get my nod of approval.

And as our friendship grew, so did our recognition. The impact of his virtuoso guitar playing on the classical side of things was impressing not only students but teachers as well. Together with myself at his side, we challenged the notions of traditional lessons which we were being taught and began to improvise taking elements from jazz, classical, big bands, and a new sound which was just coming over the horizon, referred to as, rockabilly. We collaborated on writing original programs and were fast becoming a team that was headed to new heights. I had overheard many a teacher's conversations concerning us and the talent we displayed. We were out playing, outperforming, and outdistancing ourselves from older students.

Johnny was as cool as ever, he loved the limelight and knew how to use his suave demeanor to his advantage. Wearing those trademark sunglasses whenever he could, didn't hurt either, in fact, as time went on, many teachers would not object to them being worn in the classroom. The only glaring exception was orchestra class, taught by that one teacher who was grossly revered and exceedingly feared at the same time.

During a full ensemble of the entire freshman class, our conductor, Mr. Zachary Klein, would never allow it, he was that teacher which everyone was terrified of, including, in his own subtle way, Johnny.

'Z' Klein as we referred to him, was a stocky man with reddish cheeks and wide thick-rimmed classes. He wore his hair in a short crew cut which inferred a strict military look. The story out there was that Z Klein was a world war two veteran, who earned a medal of valor for his heroics when he saved three of his men while a grenade went off in his foxhole. It also caused him to supposedly lose the hearing in his left ear. We never understood how a music conductor could hear, read, and understand music so efficiently with having hearing in just one ear. But there he was, and he would make no bones about it, he would single you out in public without warning if you didn't perform to the best of your abilities. He expected perfection and if you did not deliver it, whether it was during rehearsal or a performance, you would hear about it....... LOUDLY.

Z Klein's classes may have been difficult, but his practice sessions were unique, as well as torturous. The orchestra room was his domain and had to be treated as such. It didn't matter whether you were there as a vocalist or adept at playing an instrument, he insisted that we would all come together, even just to listen and learn, while he belted out his commands. Once you entered through that doorway, the mood became one of strictly business. Whatever standing you had obtained, or how talented you were known to be, was not of any concern. You were not allowed to crack a smile or interact at all with your fellow students unless it was under his direct tutelage. Sheet music and scores were given out and they were yours to own, and protect. And if anyone inadvertently misplaced or lost them, you were better off leaving school than facing his wrath. He would not think twice about calling your parents and recommending that you be removed.

Practice periods were known to become especially intense when the school was gearing up for either the Christmas concert or the spring concert, which of course marked the end of an academic term. And as the infamous cold New England winter months were fast approaching, the holidays would soon be upon us, unleashing Z Klein's four-hour-long, four-day-a-week punishing sessions.

* * *

In the days that followed, I became a mainstay in this small southwestern town. Word spread quickly, as it usually does within a community of this size. My room at the Winchester was getting quite comfortable and content, although I knew it was only a matter of time before I would have to find more permanent living arrangements. The staff was also getting used to having me there and from time to time, I would lend a helping hand whenever possible with required chores. Hanging laundry, unloading supplies, and performing other miscellaneous tasks when asked.

The place always had the vacancy sign hung, although, it did suffice enough for visitors passing through on their way further west. I began to make friends with the residents of the hotel, as well as the town itself and became familiar with their way of life in a seemingly short amount of time. My daily habits would take me to the diner each morning and the early shift waitresses began to treat me as a regular.

I got to know most all the clientele there too and sometimes would strike up a casual conversation with them. I purchased a new wardrobe that shifted my style to a more appropriate feel for the region. It included a cowboy shirt, three pairs of brown lightweight pants (brown was the predominant color here), several plain white t-shirts, and work shoes that were more adaptable to the rough southwestern terrain. I even made a deal to park Denise in an old stable located around back of the Winchester which was being used as a makeshift garage and storage area. Talk of the stranger from the east had simmered down and a feeling of acceptance firmly and quickly began to appear. I was no threat to this forlorn community and my mild-mannered and courteous ways made most feel at ease.

Many people started to refer to me by my first name, some would use the prefix Mr. before it, especially the children, but either suited me just fine. The oddities that I had encountered were becoming less of a concern, after all, every town has its skeletons, its high-end parts, as well as its undesirable areas. I had lived long enough and had traveled far enough through several different cities and towns to now know that it should be no different here. It was true of the town I grew up in, and was certainly evident in a big city like Boston. But besides the questions which piqued my curiosity, more pressing issues were becoming a priority, and I needed to address them first.

I was living a life unencumbered, one that didn't have much responsibility attached to it, one that I wasn't used to, and one that I knew would have to eventually change. My finances were beginning to run thin and if I was going to make the most of my new life here, I would need to be gainfully employed.

I thought about my earlier encounter with the two cowboys, Mic and Jake. I thought about their 'offer' to become a ranch hand out at the Jaco spread, but I contemplated it only as a last resort. There seemed to be other alternatives right here in town. My only concern was that my work experience left much to be desired. I was very limited in any single skill, but determined to move forward. I would make every attempt to find something I would be a good fit for. I saw the possibilities for several opportunities and decided to take the fast approach and be upfront with my intentions.

First stop, the general store. The grey-haired, apron donning, middle-aged gentleman who was a fixture there, was my primary target. I had frequented the store just a couple of times for some small items such as toothpaste and shaving cream, but never really found him to be much of a conversationalist. Nevertheless, I would wave at him through his window each morning as I passed by and each time, he would politely wave back.

The general store was open for business nearly every day, except Sundays most businesses here shut down on Sundays. But it was mid-week and this time as I approached his window, our exchange of waves would turn into something more.

Instead of passing on by, I stopped at his front door and jutted right in. The bell which had been strung at the top of the entrance rang slightly, alarming him that someone had entered. Cautiously maneuvering in and about the freestanding shelves, I found him sweeping a pile of cornmeal which looked as if came from a bag that had fallen from where it was perched. He paused, looked up at me, and spoke in the most congenial tone.

"Morning Mr. Vincent, something I can help you with today?"

"Morning to you too, and I do apologize, I never caught your name."

"Oh, it's Ed, Ed Martinez," he responded with a faint smile.

"We never officially met," I said as I held out my hand.

And transferring the broom he was holding to his left hand; he graciously shook mine with his right.

"Good to meet you Mr. Martinez," I warmly responded.

"Please, call me Ed, everyone does."

The store traffic was quiet as he continued sweeping up slowly, and luckily for me, it gave us a chance to exchange pleasantries and get better acquainted. He was a very hospitable man, well balanced with an even keel about him. Although I couldn't imagine much happening here that would rattle him. The store was always clean and organized and he was very attentive about keeping it that way. But as I stood there engaged in our dialogue, it seemed obvious there was no need for additional help, there was no employment to be found here. He had this place well in order and under control. Feeling a bit dismayed, I strolled over to the candy jars that were placed on a shelf behind the counter and reluctantly asked for five licorice sticks, which he gently lifted from a large glass bowl and handed to me in a small white paper bag.

"I'll be back again, Ed, I'm sure…... good talking to you." I said as I took my parcel, paying him as I made my leave.

I wasn't very keen on licorice, but it was colorful and not wanting to be rude, it was the only thing I could think of purchasing at that moment. The next stop, the one I was most familiar with was, of course, the diner. As I made my way there, a fanciful thought crossed my mind. I was a pretty good cook. I did learn some things from the best Italian cook I ever knew, my mother. But I wasn't sure how Italian recipes would fare in this region. The thought of possibly getting a job at the diner and becoming Frankie's co-worker was enticing. I had all but given up on running into her again, as each time I was there, she was nowhere in sight. I presumed it was because I had become an early riser and perhaps she didn't work the morning shift, but there were a couple of nights when I couldn't sleep and ventured down to see if she was around, much to no avail. I didn't feel comfortable asking about her just yet, especially after the reaction I noticed from cowboy Mic at the sheer mention of her name.

Determined to see things through as it was my nature to do, I decided to move on down to the diner for my usual morning fare, only this time I did have an ulterior motive. It was quieter than normal, as I was there later than my presumed normal hour, and sure enough, the other waitresses, which I have now come to be acquainted with, Tessy and Rita took notice.

"Overslept a bit, Mr. Vincent?" Rita yelled over as I sat in my usual booth.

"Just got a late start today," I managed to shout back.

And with that, she promptly delivered my usual cup of piping hot coffee as she stood waiting for me to place my order. This time, breaking routine, my conversation would be of a different nature.

"Hey, uh, can I ask you a question?" I hesitantly conveyed as my statement immediately produced a puzzled look from her.

"Do you guys ever cook up any Italian food here? I mean does anybody ever ask for it? Or does anyone here know any Italian recipes?" I rambled on.

"That's more than one question," she quipped back.

"And the answer is no, no and no."

Even the slightest indication of me entering the foodservice business was promptly dashed. I placed my order solemnly, but before she turned away, I blurted out.

"Just one more thing.............. whatever happened to Frankie?"

She paused with a sigh, as my question seemed to mildly irritate her. And before she could give me any type of answer, she shouted over to the other waitress now wiping off a booth, two tables down from where I sat.

"Tessy, another one wants to know where Frankie is!"

Feeling completely embarrassed, I slouched down a bit and tried to make it sound as if my question was nothing more than a mere curiosity.

"Well yes, it's only because she was the first one I met when I arrived here, and I haven't seen her since?"

She ignored me as she went towards the kitchen to hand over my order. And within ten minutes, breakfast was served. Placing the plate down in front of me, and automatically refilling my coffee cup, she smiled and said in a tone barely above a whisper,

"She is in Albuquerque and will be there for at least three more weeks."

Before I could ask anything further, she continued.

"Taking care of her brother, who is ill, we are all praying for him....and her."

She tore off the check from the small paper pad she was holding and placed it face down on the table, giving me an uncharacteristic wink just before she walked away. I suppose the gesture had something to do with Frankie, and as I sat there, I hoped it did. On the other hand, one of my questions had now been answered, this explained why I had not run into her since. I felt a certain sense of empathy for what she must be enduring and hoped to see her again, only if to offer my services and compassion. I even deliberated, but only for a moment, about hopping into Denise, filling the tank with gas, and driving to Albuquerque. The urge passed quickly as better judgment prevailed seeing that I had only met her once.

The job hunt continued, I approached several other sources in the following days, the local branch of the first national bank, where, even though the manager and mostly all the tellers (there were only two) found me to be easy to get along with. I was told since I had no previous experiences handling money, it wasn't something I should consider. The post office was very standoffish, saying it was a government post and I had to pursue it with the official state office in Santa Fe only. The movie house, well, it had a total of three employees, a projectionist, a ticket-taker, who doubled as an usher, and an eighty-year-old woman who ran the very limited snack bar. The doctor's office, I didn't even try, as well as with the local sheriff's office, neither of them was ever going to be a fit. At the schoolhouse, I thought I had a good chance of catching on in some capacity, as most of the town's peoples' children were fond of me. They would always gather round in clusters, clamoring.

"Mr. Vincent, Mr. Vincent, tell us some stories about the east!"

But the classroom sizes were accordingly small, and they encompassed most age groups mingled together. And the idea of having a male teacher was one that was absurd at present, besides, I wasn't very qualified to fill such a role.

I found just how different things would be for me now, some time ago the issue of work did not even warrant a concern. Back then, I had taken a path that I believed would lead me to fame and fortune, and for all intents and purposes, it did in some respect. That was a different time and place. Circumstances had led me here, and for some unexplainable reason, I felt I was where I should be. Sometimes in life, certain lived experiences happen in a moment's notice, but once a connection is made, it can linger a lifetime.

And it was precisely a connection I felt, which had me believe that things would just work themselves out.

3

I practiced long and hard for many a night, as I would not let anything stand in the way of exceeding my expectations. It was just I, the piano and little Jim, the night janitor. He would sweep the hallways using a broom that seemed immensely out of proportion for his body as he pushed it along in front of him. The preface 'little" fit accordingly, standing approximately five feet two inches tall and missing a noticeable number of front teeth, he was a warm unassuming man, with thinning hair, a round face, and known for consistently wearing the same old worn-out beige cardigan sweater. Each night after all my required classwork was complete, I would head out to the orchestra hall to spend the next few hours practicing in solitude. While most of my peers were nestled in a cozy practice room, I felt it better to project in a much larger space.

Two heavy black metal doors led into McKenna hall where the large performance orchestra platform was located, and each night as I would pass through them they made a resounding clanking echo when they slammed shut, and each time they did, they were announcing to Little Jim that I had arrived. He became accustomed to my presence, as it became habitual. I would make my grand declaration in the same fashion every night when I would first see him.

"Jimmy boy!!!" I would shout out.

"Whatya say there kid!" he would reverberate back to me as I made my way to the piano seated on the darkened stage at the head the hall.

And so, our mutual greeting went night after night for the next several weeks. On some occasions, I would take a break, giving my throat a respite, and stop in to visit little Jim in his small and secluded cubby tucked away at the back end of the building. There I would find him usually having his dinner, sitting aside a small washed out pink Philco radio tuned in to the local Boston Braves game. I would sit with him for a short spell and follow along as we discussed many issues, including life at The Conservatory, baseball, and local Boston eateries which he always seemed to know about.

The upcoming performance date was to be my first full one with an orchestra. It was a magnitude I had not yet experienced, albeit it was the Conservatories' best assemblage, and it was to be led by our infamous conductor, Z Klein. Families would be attending, as well as public invitees. Anxieties were high and we all felt the pressures mounting. Each one of us wanted to show the incoming audience that this was the best talent to be had in the greater northeast area. The Thursday night roustabouts were put on hold, no one dared to venture off-campus for any extracurricular activity, even the church choir (which I had not yet officially joined) was down to a skeleton crew. Everyone was focusing on just one cause, the approaching holiday performance. Constant musical resonations were swirling wherever you would go, dormitory halls, vacant classrooms, even the cafeteria, it continued whenever someone had some free time, and as late-night as could be tolerated. The stir was everywhere, and it was contagious.

I was so focused that I wouldn't allow any outside interference to come into play. Working strenuously began to take a toll and I became panic-stricken as I found myself suddenly in the midst of battling a cold. When your passion takes over and suddenly nothing else matters, you find yourself not paying attention to the trivial things. Wearing a coat in twenty-degree weather as you run across campus or eating and sleeping the right way, and mainly general care for your own well-being, all become secondary notions. Tea with honey was my addiction for the next two weeks as I battled congestion and the sniffles, while trying not to let it show during the Z Klein rehearsals which was the most unnerving part of all.

Sitting at the piano long and intensely into the evening hours and struggling with the effects of feeling ill, I persisted to exercise my vocal range practicing tunes of my own composition as best I could. It was a rigorous feat, trying to push out the notes while being cut off by an intermittent cough. Each time I would get into a rhythm, I would be forced to sip some hot tea, which was quickly turning luke-warm, or grab at a tissue for my runny nose. But unconcerned of the immediate outcome, I pressed on, only looking towards the near future.

Everything in life has its exception and mine was imminent. I tried desperately to convince myself, that by the time opening night arrived, I would be fine. That type of convincing needed some extra coaxing.

On one memorable evening, Jimmy had stopped in to say goodnight, poking his head through the backstage door, he waved and motioned that he was leaving for the night. In the middle of a vocal modulation, I waved back in acknowledgment without stopping. Feeling alone and tired some moments later, I decided that I would pack it in a bit earlier and get to sleep at a decent hour for once. Then, as I sat at the piano making some last-minute chord changes on the sheet music perched in front of me, I heard the distinct sound of those two outer metal doors down the hallway clanging shut again. Thinking Jimmy had forgotten something, which had been the case on occasion, I ignored it. Moments later, managing to slink in stealthy and silent, Lizzy appeared, coming over and suddenly sharing the piano bench, sitting right next to me!

She sat there with a mischievous smile on her face, holding a brown paper bag. I looked over at her with a feeling of immense surprise and much-stunned amazement. For a moment, I thought it wasn't real, perhaps, my cold had culminated in a fever and I was delirious. I could barely speak.

Trying to be as calm as one could be in that position, I thought about Johnny, and how he and his cool demeanor would handle this.

"Hi, what brings you out at this hour in such frigid weather?" I calmly asked, as my insides were trembling.

She reached into the paper bag and removed a white Styrofoam cup with the tag of a tea bag dangling from one side of its lid.

"I heard you weren't feeling well, Angelo Vincent Scardosa, from Jersey, and thought this might be of some help." She stated playfully, as she placed the cup on the notepad I had laid out atop of the piano.

I sat there and heard her speak those words, I hoped that she would not notice how nervous I had become, feeling as if my heart was pounding loudly.

"Hey, that was really nice of you, but how did you……I mean why…. I mean, I never expected…." I stuttered embarrassingly trying to form a coherent sentence.

"I have been looking for you, I see you all the time at rehearsals, but we never get a chance to talk, you know, with Z Klein's rules and all, and besides if this plays out the way I think it will, your voice needs to be in top shape, if you are going to be a star that is."

"Well, thanks for saying that, but I don't really think of myself as any kind of star," I responded.

Feeling suddenly a bit more at ease I reached for the cup of tea and slowly removed the top to take a sip.

"You see, Angelo (I was not used to anyone calling me by my real first name at the conservatory, but it did have a nice tone coming from her) you just need to step up your confidence level and you will be tremendous," she said as she looked meaningfully into my eyes.

"I know, it's always been a problem of mine, that's one of the things I admired about you the first time I heard you play the cello," I responded as I adjusted sitting sideways, locking our gazes.

This was the first extended dialogue that Lizzy and I had, and it was not to be the last. We talked for hours as we discussed many subjects, from my triumph over Oppenheim to possibly collaborating together on a score or two, to jamming on some Thursday night. I felt a strong connection beginning to abound.

But with the late hour creeping up quickly, we both knew that the night had to soon come to an end. I proceeded to pack up my music, finished my tea, and thanked her again. Helping her with her coat, then grabbing mine, we walked out into the deadening cold night air and headed towards the dormitory. Reaching our destination rather briskly, I clumsily held the door open for her and followed inside. Her room was located on the second floor, while mine was on the third. We climbed a lowly lit stairwell, as now most of the lights had been shut off that hour, and reaching the second landing we stopped.

"This is where I get off," she jokingly whispered, as she stood smiling.

I paused there for a moment longer, then hopped up on the next set of stairs to make my way up.

"Okay, see you tomorrow then," I awkwardly stated as I held tightly onto the metal arm rail while looking down at her before I continued.

"You know, we usually sit at the back table in the cafeteria during lunch, you could sit with us if you like?"

"Yes, I know about the back table," she said as she seemed to hold back her smile as she went on.

"Well then, I guess you may just see me there one of these days."

"Uh, okay, good night then," I said as I started to climb two more stairs.

"Hey, wait," I whispered loudly leaning way over the rail above her.

"Yes?" She retorted with anticipation.

"You never told me how you knew I was in the orchestra room tonight, or how you knew to bring over hot tea?"

"Let's just say a little birdie told me……. a really cool little birdie," she said, giggling to herself before heading through the stairwell door.

I laughed all the way to my room. The night had been one I would never forget, and 'that cool little bird', I knew exactly who she was referring to as I laughed about it until I got in bed and fell into one heavenly sleep.

Over the next several nights, I was visited quite a few more times during my solitary practices. And as shy as I was, I began to feel extremely comfortable with her and believed she was feeling the same towards me. We would playfully perform duets, take turns playing the piano while the other person pretended to be in a Broadway musical. If Z Klein ever found us here and discovered what we were doing, we would both be banned from the concert, or even worse. The danger of that possibility existed and we both knew it, perhaps it added to the excitement of the whole experience.

I found Lizzy to be much more than a gifted cellist, she was very adept at other instruments as well, including the piano.

"Your piano skills are almost as good as mine……almost." I jokingly claimed.

"Oh, you think so, I'm so glad you approve." She sarcastically fired back.

"Yeah, stick with me and I'll make sure you can perfect it." I uttered while trying to contain my laughter, as I slid closer to her on the piano bench.

"Oh, really now, you think you can do that, I mean perfect my piano skills, that is?"

The moment turned awkward as we found ourselves surrounded by the quietness of our environment, looking longingly into each other's eyes.

"Uh, let me find a duet we can both agree on." She stated, interrupting the moment, as she abruptly stood up and scrambled through the sheet music piled atop of the piano.

"Hold on a second, can I ask you a question?"

"Angelo, you can ask me anything you like."

"Well, I think I have so many questions, I don't know where to begin."

"How about you just start with one, and if I can answer, I will."

"Ok, how is it that someone like you....uh, I mean someone so talented......someone so, uh nice, with a great personality and all.....doesn't have a, or maybe you do....uh doesn't have a ...."

I embarrassingly stammered as I felt my cheeks fill with warmth while beginning to blush.

"A boyfriend? Why Angelo, I'm so glad you think so many nice things about me, but let's concentrate on our music for now, shall we?"

Taken back, I felt even more embarrassed as I sunk down in front of the piano, then before I could position my hands on the keys, she reached over with the sheet music she was holding and intentionally stopped me from playing.

"What's wrong?" I asked.

"Nothing, let's take it from the second verse ....oh and the answer is no, I don't have a boyfriend."

As our sessions continued the ease of comfort in our relationship began to grow. Night after night, we laughed, we sang, we shared secrets. We opened up to each other and learned about one another's upbringing and family life. She shared with me how her parents put a lot of pressure on her to succeed. How they were upright and conservative and expected her to make her studies the first and foremost thing in her life. How her father was a big supporter of Franklin Delano Roosevelt and even worked on his campaign for a while, and her mother's persistence for her to practice nearly every day for two hours was continuous.

Our bond was becoming stronger, but I still felt a sense of uncertainty to where it was all headed, I wasn't sure if Lizzy was looking for just a confidant or something more. My general knowledge of the members of the opposite sex was very limited and having an introverted demeanor towards women didn't help either. All I knew was that I felt some kind of joy and happiness whenever she was around and wanted it to continue. And being very attracted to her didn't hinder my cause in the least.

Our midnight rendezvous were something I began to look forward to, but at the same time wondered what would happen when the holiday concert was over, after all, we still had a few years ahead of us here. In the meantime, I tried to stay focused on my mission and enjoyed every minute of her late-night visits.

It was about ten days before the main event was closing in, and it seemed like the excitement level, as well as the musical soundings being heard had been turned up to new heights. I made my way to the orchestra hall, as usual, waiting with baited anticipation for the doors to clang. I was playing the piano in full swing, a champion Jack Dupree rendition of *Let's Have a Ball*, when a bit later than normal, they finally sounded.

This time it wasn't Lizzy at all, it was Johnny.

"What's shaken', buddy?" He announced as he strutted in with his guitar strapped in its usual place.

"Johnny! Here to get in some last-minute intense practice time with me?" I nonchalantly answered.

"C'mon kid, it's me, I know you weren't expecting me, we both know who you were waiting for."

And of course, he was right. People were becoming aware of the newly formed attachment that had been created between Lizzy and me. This was a close-knit campus, and word spread quickly.

"Kid, I gotta talk to you," he said with a serious tone as removed the guitar from around his neck and leaned over the piano getting a good look where I sat.

"Ok Johnny, what's going on?"

"Kid, I know how much you like her, I know how much you got a thing for her, and I also know you, or her, haven't crossed that line yet."

"And what line are you referring to?" I added.

"That line that says you are more than just friends."

"No, we haven't crossed that line, but, I was going to, I mean when the moment is right, I plan to, uh, you know what I mean."

"Yeah well, you better hold up on that one for now."

Johnny looked at me with great concern. The need to protect me was once again evident in his voice.

"I just found out kid, that she has been dating that sax player from California, you know the one, that blonde guy, looks like he is a surfer or something, seems as though they have been keeping it quiet so her parents wouldn't find out. But people are beginning to whisper about you and her, and I just wanted you to know before he catches wind of it. Not that he worries me....... I, uh I mean, we can handle him if we have to."

I knew Johnny wouldn't lie, he was my best friend, and I also knew he wouldn't be telling me this if he hadn't made damn sure it was true. I hung my head in despair, not knowing how to respond. I had spent many nights feeling like we had become kindred spirits, Lizzy and I, but now confusion reigned on what to do next.

I thanked Johnny, as once again he offered his sage advice on the situation. Maybe I was reading too much into it, maybe Lizzy was just looking for a nighttime escape, or perhaps just a friend, a sympathetic ear, and I was a very good listener. Discouraged and deciding to not overstate the meaning of things, I thought best to treat the whole idea as it appeared, friendship, and only that.

I packed up early and left with Johnny. He knew I was discouraged by this news and could see right through me as I did my best to hide my emotions. We headed back to our rooms without much more discussion on the matter. Opening night was fast approaching, and Johnny gave me some tough advice before retiring for the evening.

"I know how you feel about her kid, but you better keep your head in the game, we got a big night coming up, you got a big night coming up! My guess has it, you are pegged for a solo, maybe two."

He placed both hands on each of my shoulders and anchoring me there in the hallway, his gaze grew stern as he repeated,

"You keep your head in the game....... right?" Staring intently at me as he waited for me to agreeably nod.

As the days grew closer, so did the degree of pressure. Rehearsals became unbearable as Z Klein stretched every inch of our musical ability extracting the best we had. Thankfully my cold had resided, and I was perched to be in prime condition. It was difficult to concentrate knowing that Lizzy was only several feet away from me during our practice sessions. Located in the string section towards my left, I could see her, Johnny, and others (unmistakably, also the large imposing figure of Oppenheim), in the very near distance. It took every ounce of discipline to keep myself from looking over, although on two instances my glance uncontrollably ventured towards her. She was looking in my direction both times.

I was shaken towards the end of one of our last rehearsals when Z Klein announced that I should stay afterward and see him privately. All eyes turned in my direction at that notification, as I began to feel a cold sweat emerge. Not knowing what to expect, as was the case anytime Z Klein requested a private audience, my mind began to race. Did he notice my casual glimpses towards Lizzy? Worse than that, was he informed about my nighttime adventures during the last couple of weeks? Or perhaps Johnny's intuition was correct once again, and this meeting was to be of a more positive nature. I prayed for the latter.

Approaching the podium with a storm brewing in my gut. I clenched my teeth in apprehension.

Standing there right in front of him, with my legs feeling like elastic bands, I waited as he was immersed in the paperwork before him. Being this close to him for the first time, I could even notice minute sweat beads that had formed on his brow. He truly worked hard up there. Eventually, he peered up over the outer edge of his thick glasses and stared at me for less than a minute. It was probably the longest thirty seconds of my life.

"Mr. Scardosa," he said with a raspy voice which probably came from constantly shouting out instructions.

"Yes, Mr. Klein?" I timidly responded.

"Mr. Scardosa," he repeated to confirm my identity.

"How are you feeling these days?"

At first, I thought this to be an odd question, did Z Klein have a human side?

"Feeling fine sir," I mumbled back.

"That's good because I thought I was detecting a frog in your throat these past couple of days. I have a solo I need you to perform Saturday night, you up for it son?"

"Uh, Uh………"

"Come now, are you up for it or not?" He harshly asked again.

"I am, I am sir…. you bet I am," I answered back trying to fend off an unmistakable look of apprehension.

"That's just what I wanted to hear, that is as long as you think that cold you were fighting has subsided."

"Oh, it has, it definitely has sir," my enthusiasm was heightening.

"Come to my office, tomorrow at lunchtime, and we will go over the logistics of the whole thing."

I was about to walk away and find Johnny to tell him the news when Z Klein stopped me short.

"One more thing Mr. Scardosa, keep drinking all that tea with honey and lemon, late at night, ALONE, …….it does wonders, right?"

And at that moment I could have sworn he gave me a quick wink and a faint……….... very faint smile.

* * *

The days in the southwest were much different than those back east. They seemed to linger more slowly. Daylight transformed seamlessly into night, emphasizing a rather peaceful transition of color and temperature. I enjoyed the laid-back attitude which existed here. Worry over the incidental things in life was not so important. The post-war era that surrounded me, that surrounded the country, was in full revival. With our victory overseas and Truman in office, the country's tough times were in retreat and a promise of a better life was in motion. An economic boom was transforming the country. With automobiles becoming more affordable and plentiful, families began to migrate to the suburbs with more frequency. Televisions quadrupled in number overnight and popular shows featured the likes of *The Lone Ranger* and *Howdy Doody*. But for me, it was a time to release the immediacy that had gripped me in my prior experiences and just accept life as it unfolded.

I hadn't much success finding a job right away, but perhaps I was trying too hard, perhaps, there was a job here that would eventually find me. And if I continued to help out around the Winchester, the manager agreed to reduce my room rate accordingly. Besides, the word had begun to spread that I wasn't planning on leaving anytime soon, so somewhere, somehow, I believed that assistance would come my way.

For the most part, I had settled into this new life rather quickly, the congeniality which grew from nearly everyone I had encountered made it easy for me to dismiss events in my past. Painful thoughts that once plagued me were beginning to subside. Many of the sleepless nights that I had fought through were now relinquishing to the aromatic desert air and howling coyotes far off somewhere in the desert landscape. I learned to appreciate the beauty of my natural surroundings. It was just the way of life in the southwest, and one that I was finding more welcoming with each new day.

Certain nights I would take Denise out, and drive a stretch through the flat, dry terrain, each time venturing a bit further. Often, I would pull over to the side of the road and just take it all in, exhaling the past and embracing all the peace and tranquility that mother nature had to offer. Sometimes, moving too fast and trying to make a name for yourself doesn't always allow for the simplicity of things to shine through.

The filling station, with its non-descript large hand-built wooden sign that simply read *GAS+Plus* surrounded by enormous 12-foot-high cacti, was located on the outskirts of town. There I would stop and share a soda pop from time to time with Otto, the only gasoline and auto repair attendant for miles around. We would sit on the front stoop of his shop with his dog, a German Shepard-Collie mix, Zeke, and watch the kaleidoscope of hues in the southwestern sky rotate around us. Many times, we even witnessed several shooting stars streaking across the enormity above us.

This was not an unusual occurrence, particularly in this magnificent state of never-ending deserts, hidden lakes, and sudden elevations. In the 1940s, New Mexico had been known to become the most secretive state in the country, it was not only home to one of the largest air force bases, but strange observances in the sky overhead were regarded as commonplace. Some twelve years before my arrival, the town of Roswell, approximately fifty miles from Mara Del Santos became the center of the world's attention. The infamous sighting of an alleged alien flying saucer's crash landing dominated the news and the airwaves. And even though the topic still reigns as one of controversy and highly contestable debates, most folks around here are convinced of its authenticity.

Back east I could remember reading about it for weeks in the newspapers as it was a constant heated area of discussion. The fervor did die down eventually as the military reported that the object which was found was nothing more than a weather balloon. On the east coast, no one thought much about it after that, but out here, the news lives on. After all, Boston had the Braves, New York had The Yankees, Giants, and Dodgers, and Roswell, well Roswell, it had, its aliens.

Otto was a devout supporter of such and would swear by the occurrence which took place in July 1947. Each time a shooting star would cross our field of vision, he would begin to tell the tale of how he drove to the actual crash site, the Brazel homestead, to hunt for alien debris. He once found a shiny thin piece of aluminum that he swears came from that specific location. It was hung like a trophy in his small shop with a handwritten wooden sign mounted just below it that read 'Found from the alien ship in Roswell, NM, 1947'.

His lore would seem to be outlandish at times. He would go on for hours describing how he had several encounters with military personnel forbidding him to enter the restricted area, and how he would eventually find a way in, penetrating their defenses in the middle of the night. It was during these times that I would just sit back and let him continue in a slightly boastful manner. I wasn't sure if I really believed any of it, I think he just wanted someone to listen with a sense of admiration, which I happily did. He even introduced to me some of his friends that would sporadically stop by his shop sharing in his stories while interjecting their own speculation.

The existence of alien life had never really occurred to me before relocating here. And hearing testimonies first-hand from those who had such staunch beliefs about it was yet another new revelation which I encountered. Otto like so many others were under the assumption that it not only existed, but that extraterrestrial life still occupied the same land as we do now. He would go on to add, that since that world-changing moment of 1947, several hundred witnesses have come forward claiming to have undeniable evidence regarding it. And it was precisely this event which brought him here.

Otto Krauss was of Irish descent, he was an ordinary-looking soul, standing at a medium height with short brown hair and a small mustache to match. At first sight, everything about him read as just ordinary, but Otto proved to be much more than that.

He wore a plain blue mechanics jumpsuit with his first name printed in white thread script over the upper left-hand pocket. He had told me how, as a young boy, he discovered an early fascination with the planets and stars. And how he was not allowed to entertain the idea of becoming educated in astronomy as it was labeled as foolish, but was forced to work in his father's garage, learning the trade of car repair. He thrived under his father's strict guidelines for all his teenage and young adult years earning a reputation as a top-notch mechanic before long. But when the news broke about Roswell, he could no longer resist the urge. Packing all he could in his black 1942 Chevy coupe he left his home in Duluth, Iowa, and escaped right to the center of his universe. And here is where he has remained ever since.

I believe we became friends on some level, as we both seemed to find this common destination for one reason or another. The truth of the matter was that they were both loners in some respect, Otto, and Zeke, that is. And I do think I became a bit of a loner myself after my own exodus. The only difference was that he believed he knew exactly what his purpose was from the start, what he had come for was evident. I, on the other hand, had yet to know mine.

But it was good to befriend them both, they lived in the one-room cottage which was attached to the back of his shop and only ventured into town when necessary. Besides, the townspeople, as well as myself, respected his talents, and on occasion, when their vehicles would need service, Otto was the best around. Otherwise, it was a 2-hour drive in the opposite direction to find a good car repair service.

One evening, I pulled into the *GAS+Plus* needing a new tire for Denise, and to have my usual meeting with Otto. This time he was not to be found wearing his standard blue jumpsuit, this evening he was donning a clean pair of grey khaki pants and a blue denim shirt, this evening he had on a pair of dress loafers and his hair was combed in precise order. Zeke was in his normal place, sitting outside the front door with his head down. I parked in my customary spot and went over to give him my usual pat on the head, and scratch behind his ears, as his tail wagged generously.

"Where's Otto? huh Zeke," I said expecting as if he could respond.

"Oh, hey there Vincent," Otto proclaimed as he emerged through the front door of his shop in his neat and clean state.

"Wow, looking good there, Mr. Otto, did I come at a bad time?" I asked.

"Well I'm on my way out tonight, something you need in a hurry?" he stated with his familiar concern.

"Think Denise could use a new tire but is not imperative....... I mean it's not an emergency."

"Say, do you have anything planned tonight?" He strangely asked.

"Just coming to spend time with you and Zeke and watch the stars." I humbly replied.

"How about coming with me and Zeke for a spell, we're headed over to meet up with some friends and I would love to introduce you to them, that is if you don't mind."

"Ok, I'm game," I said as we climbed into his Chevy, with Zeke following along and jumping into the back seat.

We rode off on CR-b007, the local highway at top speed with the radio on and Otto grinning contently. Paul Anka was crooning his new hit *Diana*, as our tires spun over the loose gravel, peeling away. The night was dry, and the air heated as we shot down that road with the windows wide open and Zeke trying desperately to stick his head out of either side of the car. On the way, Otto told me about the friends we would be meeting. They were a group who all shared the same experience as he. They each had a common story, or two, about the Roswell incident, swore on the fact that their stories were true.

It took about thirty-five minutes for us to arrive. It was a farmhouse at the end of a dark desolate road, pulling right up in front, Otto parked the car and let Zeke out commanding him to sit and stay outside. I had no inclination as to where we were, but I trusted Otto. The place was faintly lit, and I noticed a small kitchen area with an icebox, stove, and an old wooden table and two chairs as we entered. Further inside was a sitting room that had a couch and several more chairs arranged in a circular pattern.

There, I was introduced to a room full of eleven individuals. Quickly taking a glance around, I noticed people of many different ages, men and women alike.

Some arrived here in the southwest as Otto did, answering a 'calling' and some were originally from these parts. Either way, they were somewhat surprised by my presence, until Otto stepped in and vouched for me. Among them, was a former archeological student, a retired army nurse, a writer, a welder, a couple of widowed housewives, an elderly couple, and various others who did not disclose their occupation or position in life.

They took umbrage at me being from back east, where dismissing the highly publicized incident as a miscommunication on the government's part was a typical response. They were displeased with the fact that I, like so many other Americans accepted the weather balloon story. But having been accepted by Otto did give them some encouragement about my character.

As I spent the night hearing their stories, each one took pride in telling, or re-telling them, as I believe they must have given several recounts by now. They not only wanted to convince me of a true government coverup, but all of them believed that evidence of alien life was more than this one occurrence. They believed it to be the genesis of human life itself. That we were derived from alien ancestors and that their power and intelligence, far superior to ours, is somehow embedded in our DNA. The potential, they believed, was one which is incomprehensible to our own, possessing the ability to create world peace, to forge highly technological advancements, or cure disease and illness, and even overcome death.

This speculation, this set of beliefs that they have now entrusted themselves with, had, in essence, become their religion, their church, their cornerstone. I have always considered myself as non-judgmental as they come, but given the testimonies I had heard that evening, I didn't know how to comprehend it all. I didn't know if I was surrounded by an unconventional set of philosophers or a group of individuals, like Otto, who just needed something different to hold on to, something other than the norm to believe in.

There I sat on a worn and sagging green satin couch, listening respectfully to each one of them as Otto brimmed with delight. Their tales ranged from being at the original site to seeing the actual explosion of the crash itself. Most astonishing to me was hearing the retired army nurse tell how her best friend was there to see the bodies that were recovered, alien bodies, which were never mentioned in any newspaper printing.

I had taken in their stories one by one and tried to be as open-minded as possible. I could tell they were a close-knit bunch, they supported each other and sympathized with the fact that they were set apart from the general public. They were guarded against the outside world and had a general distrust, even anger towards the government.

Eventually, each said their goodbyes and by the end of the evening, they were shaking my hand, thankful to make my acquaintance. Seemingly comforted to know that there was a community they belonged to, each exited and made their way out in various directions. Some in automobiles, one on horseback, a couple walked quietly off into the desert night and another loudly roared away on a motorcycle.

Along the highways, there were many road signs referencing Roswell and flying saucers and spaceships in general, but I never really paid much attention to them, dismissing them as purely tourists attractions. But now, after a night such as this, I started to think, perhaps there may be something more to it. Were they onto something? Was it possible that so many people who bore witness to it could be caught up in a hoax? And what of the folks back in town? I have never really heard any mention of it there. I thought this to be odd, the proximity and the interest that rest of the state seemed to be caught up in was glaring, yet no one in town seemed to discuss it. Perhaps the next time the moment presented itself, I would strike up a conversation about the subject.

Back in Otto's Chevy, things were quiet at first. Driving at a slower pace this time, it felt good to have the breeze run past us as we cruised our way down the darkened highway. I looked over at him, he seemed at ease leaning towards one side of his seat with his left arm hanging out the window in the warm night air. Zeke barked twice at something, most likely a jackrabbit, as Otto looked back at him to keep him quiet.

"You think me and the rest of them are crazy, don't you?" He finally said.

"Honestly, Otto.... I don't think any of you are crazy, I will admit that I am amazed and skeptical about what I heard tonight, but crazy, no."

"Do you believe any of it? Do you believe any of it all?" He asked in a warm tone.

"Frankly, I don't know what to believe anymore. I was brought up to believe in certain things, and I think I still do. I mean, I know I do, but, ..." I paused.

"You're talking about God, Vincent, aren't you?" Otto genuinely asked.

“Yes, I am," I said as I stared blankly out the window into the passing landscape.

There was nothing but silence until we arrived back at the *GAS+Plus*, where I thanked Otto for a mighty interesting evening and patted Zeke on the head, before heading for Denise.

“Hey Vincent,” Otto said, as I sat in my car with the window open and the motor running.

“Don’t stop believing in whatever it is that you really believe in.”

“And I’m not crazy!”

I could hear him shout and laugh loudly, as I watched him, and Zeke retreat around back towards their lodgings.

Otto and his friends gave me much to contemplate that night, I needed not to question my own beliefs any further than I already had done. He was a straightforward earnest guy and I did enjoy his company. I felt sad for him at times as I think he had been generally misunderstood his whole life. He found solace in this place and in his own personal beliefs. And since he had been open enough to reveal all to me, perhaps it was time that on my next visit, I should explain more about my belief system, my upbringing, and my faith. I was never to get the chance; I never knew that would be the last time I would see Otto again.

4

It was the most amazing night of my life. A five-minute standing ovation, an image that will last forever in my mind. The show went off without a glitch. We were in perfect unison, 74 individuals working together as one. And looking tremendous as well, as each of us did, it's funny how different, how mature, formal wear can make you look. I would go so far to say that even Oppenheim looked distinguished in his own awkward way.

Lizzy was astonishing, a look of true elegance in her gown, my heart melted when I saw her. Z Klein was in his glory acting like a proud parent, taking bow after bow in front of that packed boisterous crowd. The activity backstage was as chaotic as it was out front. Family and friends crowded around performers as they exited into the hallways, getting congratulatory hugs and accolades. Bouquets abounded in all directions, the air was celebratory. And I, well, Johnny was right, and Lizzy too, I came off looking and sounding like a star. My parents were overwhelmed and speechless. I don't think they ever imagined their son winning over a crowd of that size. I even surprised my self during the encore, my voice transcended power and emotion. I felt as if I was elevated further than ever, the experience was exuberant and surreal. And at that moment, I loved life, appreciating everything my family had ever sacrificed to get me here, and I thanked them several times over for it.

Through the crowded hallway, I could see Johnny heading right for me, he was emphatic in getting through the mass of people which stood between us. Closing in on me he lunged and hugged me at the same time. I introduced him to my parents, as they had heard me talk about him practically every time I called home.

"Kid, I told you! I knew it, that solo was incredible, and the encore, I never heard you any better! Did you hear that crowd? Ok, level with me, what the hell, did you take your vitamins before the curtain went up?"

"Holy cow Johnny, you were amazing too, I could hear you strumming the whole time, you were just fantastic!"

Then, leaning over I whispered.

"Johnny, I almost didn't make it, I have to tell you all about it later."

He gave me a momentary baffled look of disbelief. But it was immediately swallowed up by the electricity of the mob surrounding us.

The crowds began to disperse ever so slowly as many celebrations were planned for the evening. Z Klein had made it known that he wanted a quick word with us backstage before we went our separate ways. This was not only the culmination of our musical majesty, but it also marked the end of the semester, most of us would be leaving for a well-deserved three-week-long winter break. For me, it was bittersweet, and even though I thought about Lizzy dating that sax player, I still wanted to be here, in Boston, close to her.

I left my parents waiting for a short while as we all gathered backstage. You could just feel the comradery that takes over on nights such as this. We formed a large semi-circle in two double rows as Z Klein stood towards the middle.

"I'm not used to doing this, but I just wanted to say."

He pulled off his glasses and wiped them with a handkerchief which he retrieved from his vest pocket.

"I just wanted to say……this was one of the best performances that I ever had the pleasure of conducting."

I looked around at some startled expressions, two flute players on my right began to get teary-eyed as he continued.

"So, rest up over the break. I hope to see everyone in the new year, and we can all do it again in the spring." He stated resoundingly as he wiped his brow with the same handkerchief before leaving.

I was told those were the most admiring remarks that Z Klein had ever made. And we embraced them feeling proud of what we had accomplished, especially because at this point most of the orchestra was made up of underclassmen. We hugged each other, said our farewells, and went off from the spotlight to find our families.

Mine had made a reservation at a top-notch seafood restaurant on Boston's Southside, one that I had told them about, one that little Jim had recommended and one that we rarely frequented. Johnny's family had not been able to make the trek from Chicago, work obligations kept them there, or so he claimed.

Out into the cold New England air, light snow had begun to fall. My parents, dressed in their Sunday best and I, in a formal black suit, walked across a lighted parking lot as the snow created a serene white landscape. Off in the distance I saw a familiar figure and expressed my concern to my father. Without any deliberation, I ran over to Johnny and passed on an invitation to join us for a dinner celebration. After several moments of coaxing, he accepted.

We piled into my father's Buick, with myself and Johnny, of course in the back seat. Now, being chauffeured through the streets of Boston we were finally able to sit back and relax, with the energy we had expended over the last several weeks coming to a slow retreat. Several moments went by as we both stared out the window watching a misty snowy night develop. Johnny turned to me when a thought suddenly occurred to him as he leaned over and whispered.

"Uh….hold on a minute kid, what did you mean in the hallway before, when you said, you almost didn't make it?"

As my parents were engaged in conversation, mostly about tonight's performance, they were paying little or no attention to us. With my head leaning back on the seat, I began to wearily tell him of an episode that added to this remarkable evening.

"Oh man, Johnny, I was in the hallway before the curtain went up pacing back and forth. I was a total wreck and my throat was as dry as the Sahara. I didn't know if I was going to pass out or what. I was really beginning to panic. Then something happened." I said, lowering my voice even further.

"Whoa, baby……. I thought something wasn't right," he interjected., continuing on.

"I was looking for you backstage and couldn't find you anywhere. So, what the hell happened? Because from the sound of things on stage, you fooled me and everyone else in that hall, you really killed it tonight boy."

Just as I was about to give Johnny the lowdown, we came to an abrupt halt, as my mother turned and said joyfully,

"We're here boys, bundle up its cold out there."

And with that, the front doors of the car swung open as Johnny looked at me with annoyance. He wasn't used to having to wait to get the scoop on things, no matter how trivial it may have been.

Entering, *The Top of the Mast* restaurant, both of us noticed many other families celebrating there as well. Towards the far right were the two teary-eyed flute players (they were sisters) sitting at a large round table with a half a dozen or so of their relatives and friends. Following the hostess, we passed by them as they waved eagerly. There was Tony Matone with a couple of other percussion mates and their families sharing a long table, and several other small tables filled with students and families, scattered about partaking in the festivities. And all seemed to acknowledged our presence as if we were some kind of celebrities, as we made our way through the dining room.

"Boys, order anything you like, the night is yours!" my father said resoundingly.

And we did just that, sitting there at a spacious corner table for four, and having full view of the entire place, we ordered as two ravenous growing boys would. We devoured a basket of homemade biscuits, forcing my father to promptly ask for more. We each consumed a large amount of shrimp, scallops, and fried flounder, before ending with the best Boston cream pie the city had to offer.

"Okay, feeling good now kid?" Johnny said with a smirk, as we both sat with our stomachs feeling fully content.

"Yep, feel real good," I slyly answered back, as I knew where his questioning was heading.

"So, you're feeling good, right?"

"Yep, sure am," I said curtly.

"Nothing bothering you, everything cool, daddy-o?" He became more intense.

"Yep, everything is real cool," I stated as I leaned back in my chair, looking in the opposite direction, fighting off the laughter.

Johnny waited for the correct timing, both of my parents had left the table to visit the restroom and go over to the bar for an after-dinner drink, leaving us alone. Classmates were moving about, and some stopped for a minute or two to say a quick word. When no one had ventured over for some time, Johnny grabbed my forearm, squeezed it tightly, and said.

"You are going to tell me now, or I will throw you out into the back alley and beat you silly in the snow!"

I couldn't hold it, I laughed uncontrollably, it wasn't often I could get under his skin. And I knew if we were not in a public place, he would find a way to beat it out of me.

"Okay, okay," I said as I leaned in on the table.

"Like I was telling you. I was in the hallway, behind stage, pacing. When she showed up."

"You mean.........."

"Yes," I stopped him before he could finish his sentence.

"Lizzy was there, this time sipping on a cup of cool water. She came over to me and asked if I was alright. I told her I thought I was dying. Johnny, she calmed me down, and thank God she had water with her because I had extreme dry mouth going on."

"So that's it, she saved your life with a cup of water?" He answered surprisingly.

"Well, not really. After I calmed down, she wished me luck, and then she........she.... moved in closer, and I couldn't hold back, I went for it man, I don't know if it was all the nervous energy I had at that moment, but I kissed her. A long meaningful kiss."

"You did what! Wow, now that's crazy man, wasn't expecting that." He stated in total delight.

"Yeah, me neither." I agreed.

"Okay look, kid. I know you're on the hook for this girl, but you gotta cool it down. I don't know if she is playing both sides of the street here." He advised.

"I know Johnny, she just seemed so sincere, and I guess I got three weeks away from our place to think about it, anyway."

"Yeah, you do that, think about it, just think about it." He said, as his tone became firmer.

With my parents returning to the table, we knew that this spectacular evening had come to an end. My father graciously paid the check and left a tip as we headed back through the dining room. It was half empty by now, as most families and patrons had called it a night. My suitcase was already packed and in the trunk, ready for the trip home, then it was one last stop back to the dormitory to drop Johnny off.

Outside the car, we stood in the dim light of the dormitory parking lot as the snow continued to silently fall. Johnny and I became close friends right from the beginning of that first semester and now this was our first goodbye. Knowing that three weeks would be over in the blink of an eye, made it less dramatic.

"So, I'll see you soon kid," he said, as he punched me sideways in my left arm.

"Are you leaving for Chicago in the morning?" I asked.

"Nah, kid, not going home. Got me a paying gig downtown, you know, with those guys I've been jamming with. Besides, who else is going to keep this place warm for you?"

"Oh, so that's where you disappear to all the time?" I said with a worrisome look.

"That's right daddy-o, and when you get back, they want to meet you, told them all about you. And here's another surprise, a couple of them were here tonight and heard you blast off."

He went on.

"It's cool, man, they're a little older, but real hip, and we can make some dough in the meantime."

I returned the punch to his arm, not nearly as strong, and got back into the idling car. Pulling away, I could see him standing in the veil of gently falling snow, waving as we made our way off.

* * *

It was a picture-perfect Sunday morning in Mara Del Santos, and as Sundays go, discreetly quiet. Shops, schools, ranches, and some say, even the livestock take the day off. I awoke from an interrupted night of sleep with my thoughts that were surrounded by the events of Otto and his friends. Several times I got up and sat by my window staring out into the night sky, wondering and more so, waiting for some tangible evidence to come streaming by before I eventually hit the sack and dozed off.

Feeling a bit dazed from the previous night's encounters, I hastily got myself together with the beckoning urge for several cups of strong coffee. A bit ruffled and not too concerned about it, I promptly made my way to the diner. The streets on Sunday were practically barren, so the need to be perfect in my appearance was secondary. The was no one sitting on any of the benches along the way. The general store was locked up tight. And the only few people I would see would be the sheriff riding by occasionally, or one or two stray souls heading right for the same place I was off to. As I took my usual route through the center of town, I couldn't help but rehash to myself some of the stories and testimonies I had recently heard.

With my focus elsewhere, I plodded up the wooden stairs which I had become so accustomed to doing, then pulling open the screen door and sitting at my usual booth, I tried to straighten myself up and look semi-presentable. Just as expected the place was empty, I counted only three people scattered about, none of which I knew all that well. I sat staring blindly out the window for several minutes, as the typical sounds of mumbled voices and kitchenware clanging around could be heard in the background. I hadn't noticed the waitress presiding over me until she cleared her throat not once, but twice before she was able to get my attention.

"Hello stranger," she said with a soft voice and a smile to match.

Sitting up seeing Frankie standing right before me, caught me by sheer and utter surprise. I can only remember feeling that way one other time in my life and I had done my best to put that out of my mind. But now, here she was waiting for my order just as I remembered her on my first night.

Sometimes in life, you come across someone or something that grips you in an unspoken way. You get the feeling that it is innate, but you really can't quite put your finger on it, that was the feeling I had not only about this place but also about Frankie. I had only met her one other time but felt something implausible, something I couldn't ignore.

"Well hello yourself," I responded with a smile of my own.

It was as if we had known each other for many years and were having some sort of reunion. And although she looked tired and troubled, which was not surprising knowing what she had been facing in her life, I still thought there was a true and simple attractiveness to her. We both halted momentarily as there was a noticeable awkward pause in the air. Trying to speak at the same time, we cut off each other's sentences as we laughed.

"Should I take your order, Mr. Vincent?" she said politely.

"Oh, uh I guess you know my name? And Just Vincent is fine."

"Well, you have made quite an impression around here, I have heard many nice things about that 'gentleman' from the east, who looks like he may have decided to settle down here?" She continued.

It felt good to see her again and to know the townspeople had reinforced my standing as a good guy. I wanted to talk with her more, I wanted to have our conversations become more than just a passing inclination between waitress and patron. I wanted to tell her that I knew of her hardships in caring for her brother, and most of all, I wanted to offer my help. I wanted all this the moment I saw her again and knew I had to find a way to show my sincerity without sounding like others who had shown shallow interest in her.

"Well, it's good to hear that folks are saying good things, I do try my best. And yes, I have taken a liking to this town, so I am staying, or at least trying to. I am going to have to find a job real soon and a place to live of course. If you hear of anything suitable.........I mean, I don't have a lot of skills to brag about, by I am a hard worker."

"Yes, well, that I can do, I hear many things in this place, you know, if walls could talk and all, and if I do come across anything, you will be the first to know."

She smiled again as she turned and took my order over to the kitchen window.

I sat there wishing I had made a more presentable appearance that morning, but it didn't seem to matter much to Frankie, she gave off the impression of being a down to earth southwestern girl trying to earn a living and care for a family member. Nevertheless, a clean shave could have helped matters. We exchanged glances several more times as I sat, purposely eating slow, while I tried to find the right words to come up with next.

She returned to my table twice and each time we exchanged small talk. Finally, when I had nothing left on my plate and had consumed my fill of coffee, she dutifully came over clearing the table.

"All done for today? Anything else you might like?" She asked.

"No, think that will be it.......... I think." I clumsily repeated continuing on.

"That is, if you, uh, might like to go for a ride with me and Denise some night?"

"Denise?" She asked.

"Oh, Denise is my 1954 red rambler," I quickly responded.

"You named your car Denise? You fellas from the east are a bit on the strange side, aren't you? But yes, I would like to go for a ride with you and......and..... Denise." She chuckled.

"Great, how's tomorrow?" I promptly asked.

"How about Wednesday, I get off early, make it then and it's a deal."

"Okay, Wednesday it is, where shall I pick you up?"

"I get off at 7, is that ok? I'll see you here."

"Seven it is then." I eagerly replied as I made my way out.

It had been a very long time that I had felt any type of meaningful connection to any one of the opposite sex. After leaving the east coast as abruptly as I did and making my way cross country, I had several pointless encounters in the months that followed, each of which gave me no great desire to stick around in any of those places. My only solace was that I did continue to send a letter or two, back home to my mom from every location I eclipsed.

In Springfield Ohio, there was a dancer named Rosie. In Whitestone, Indiana, I met a transplanted Canadian maid named Arlette at a quaint motel there. In Mount Vernon, Missouri, there was a cashier with beautiful blue eyes named Joanna. My brief stay in El Reno Oklahoma introduced me to Liza, a nurse, and in Canyon Texas, I met Denise, a pretty, petite bank teller. Yes, that

Denise, who I eventually named my car after and who came as close as anyone, in convincing me to stay. I guess each of these women played a role in my life, but the fact remained, I wasn't ready, I wasn't able to give of myself again. I considered myself damaged goods……. extremely damaged goods.

Wednesday arrived as I had waited with great anticipation, I even avoided going to the diner, so I wouldn't see her preemptively. Managing to borrow the hose from the Winchester's backyard spigot, I decided to give Denise a good cleaning. It had been nearly a year since I had done so and getting off the grime that accumulated from many miles of travel was to be no easy task. I made it a point to stop at the general store to see if Mr. Martinez carried any car polish, but alas there was none to be had. So, with some Lestoil and water and good old-fashioned elbow grease, I did my best to bring Denise up to snuff. I also thought about making a quick run to Otto's to get the new tire I needed but didn't seem to have enough time to do so.

When I had finished, I stepped back and was satisfied that she looked rather spiffy. Now, I needed to concentrate on myself. It was off to the barbershop for a trim and a shave, and then over to the haberdashery for a new shirt, perhaps something of color, rather than my usual white. Choosing a smooth light blue one, I hastily made my way back to my room for a refreshing shower as the late afternoon sun had begun to recede.

The seven-pm hour was approaching, and I needed to make one last stop. Pulling up to the front of the general store one more time, I left the engine running while I ran in and purchased one yellow rose, a couple of cheese sandwiches wrapped in wax paper, and two colas. Mr. Martinez always had an array of fresh-cut flowers in water along his front counter, albeit they were a little wilted most of the time. Placing the flower on the passenger seat I drove slowly over to the diner. It was a clear and thankfully more forgiving humid night than most, I approached with my radio tuned into Ricky Nelson's hit, *Poor Little Fool* pouring forth. Parking right in front, I sat listening for a moment as Frankie came bopping out the door and down the stairs right over to me.

"Right on time." She said with a smile.

"Hi." I simply stated while rushing over to the passenger door, opening it for her.

She paused before getting in, seeing the yellow rose occupying her seat.

"Um, excuse me, but there is something on the seat." She said displaying an infectious grin.

"Oh……. Oh……yeah, sorry. Let me get that out of the way."

Reaching in to pick up the rose, I turned to her and continued.

"Oh, I'm sorry, did you think that was for you?" I laughed.

"It is!" Laughing again, I handed it to her.

Giggling along with me, she slid into the passenger side giving the flower a whiff as I shut her door.

"So where are we headed?" She asked politely.

"I thought we could take a drive out onto the 007 (CR-b007 was the main highway or just the 007 for short). I have an idea if that's ok?"

"You're driving, so it's fine with me," she exclaimed.

We headed north for only about three miles where I turned off the main road and into the desert for another 300 yards, there I pulled Denise onto a slightly elevated hill surrounded by a concave rock formation and several oversized cacti. I turned off the engine and left the radio playing with the volume slightly turned down. Our surroundings were beginning to become illuminated by the light of the moon and as I looked over at her. I could see her tanned skin glistening. It was awkward at first, but with each passing minute, our conversation expanded. I got out of the car, walked around to the passenger side, and opened the door, and extended my hand.

"C'mon, the view is better out here."

She gently took my hand as I led her over to the front of Denise where we sat on the hood as I continued.

"This has become my favorite place in a short amount of time, sometimes I just come out to listen to the sounds of nature and watch the stars. I thought it might be a good spot where we could talk privately and maybe get to know each other a little better."

"It's beautiful here, I have been living here for about eleven years now and never really have ventured out this far at night. Think I was just afraid to come out here alone, I guess." She responded, as we both were taking in the sky above.

"Well I must say, I'm glad you decided to let me give you the grand tour of these majestic night heavens, it's nothing like the view I've seen in my travels from back east." I stated, as I turned my gaze towards her before continuing.

"Did you ever feel as though you've met someone before, like you have known them? Call me crazy, and I hope you don't think this very forward of me, but I must admit, for what it's worth, that's how it felt when I first met you."

She smiled intently and nodded approvingly as she stared upwardly taking in my ramblings along with the stars above.

"Hey, are you at all hungry? I did manage to grab a couple of sandwiches from Mr. Martinez's place, they're on the back seat of my car." I interrupted as I motioned to jump off and retrieve the brown bag inside.

"Oh, that was thoughtful of you, but I ate on my break just two hours ago, and I'm not very hungry right now. But thank you anyway. And besides, He does run a tidy store, but his sandwiches may be a bit lacking, if you know what I mean."

"Oh, ok, thanks for the info, I'll remember that next time.

I wasn't very hungry either, I think just the anticipation of being out there curbed my appetite. From the start, the mood was friendly and relaxed. And maybe it was a natural attraction, or simply the idea that the moment seemed comfortable enough to open up about life. Our discussion ranged from her current situation of caring for a sick brother(whom she advised was doing much better on her recent visit) to her job at the diner. But, like any two people wanting to know more about each other, what we were both most inquisitive about, was our personal lives. She hinted that her life was rather uneventful and conceivably did what every mid-western girl growing up in the suburbs of Santa Fe was supposed to do.

Go to school, get a job, get married, and so on. In high school, she showed unprecedented athletic ability as a track star, but women's sports in the late '40s were just a side attraction. She admitted that her love of running and her continued desire for it, gave her aspirations of chasing an Olympic dream which was never to come to fruition. Her parents died at an early age leaving her and her younger brother mostly to survive on their own.

She had been married but after three years her husband just up and left with a burlesque performer headed to find a more glamorous life on the west coast. But from my immediate observation, the trait which stood out to me, was her sense of independence. Frankie was atypical of a woman living in 1940's America. She possessed an inner strength, marched to the beat of a different drummer, and politely didn't care much of what others thought of her. She had a closeness to her father, and being a bit of a tomboy growing up, he tutored her in the art of marksmanship. A discipline she excelled in, earning her many awards at county fairs throughout the state and garnering her a reputation of a sharpshooter. She came to be well-liked by the townspeople who had come to accept her as she was.

I sat and listened intently for much of the time and didn't mind seeing her striking features, white smile, and beautiful facial contours highlighted by the rays of the evening light. She ventured on to tell how her time in Mara Del Santos was only supposed to be temporary, it was only going to be a stopover on her way out to Los Angeles.

She lived in a nice neighborhood in a modestly small home in the easternmost corner of town. The last house on the left, pale yellow, it was situated at the end of the block and was bordered by typical desert landscaping. She had originally lived there, taking care of an elderly spinster of means, Mrs. Adele Williams, and surprisingly was bequest the home after she passed on, as the deceased had no known family to speak of. As time went on, she became content living in Mara Del Santos, and months easily turned into years. She described it as a stirring, uncanny feeling which just made her want to stay, a feeling that I had been able to relate to.

As the night drew on, we just sat with our backs up against the front windshield listening to the radio. It was refreshing to spend moments with someone who I could communicate with, without any obstacles or heavy intentions. She presently lived alone, admitted dating a couple of gentlemen callers who stayed a short while before moving on.

"Well, I think I have said enough, maybe too much about myself, so what's your story? Or are you just the mystery man from back east?" She said as she hopped off the hood and paced slowly in front of the car.

"What makes you think, I have a story?" I said trying to avoid the question itself.

"Oh, I don't know, it's just that most people coming into our little town usually find it as a convenient stop as they are passing through to wherever it is, they are eventually headed to? Same for you?" She politely prodded.

"Honestly, not entirely sure yet. Got a good feeling about this place, think I'm gonna be here for a while."

Quickly trying to divert the attention from the question at hand, I went on about my travels across country, giving her an abbreviated version at best. The subject of my past was not one I wanted to approach and one that I felt was best served by small installments. Seeing my hesitation to go into any detail, she alluded to how she worked a long shift and thought it better to call it a night. I agreed.

Driving back into town she had grown noticeably weary, being on your feet all day will have that effect. Looking over at her, I admired what I perceived to be a strong resourceful woman. It takes courage to be on your own, not having to rely on someone else for your happiness. She began to doze off as we made our way back towards town. Gently nudging her as I made my way down the main road, she awoke, groggily, and immediately apologized for nodding off.

"No need for apologies," I reassured her.

"But I do need to know where I'm taking you."

She sat up more alert and after a series of left- and right-hand turns, directed me to the front of her house.

"Thank you for a really pleasant evening," she said while trying to cover her yawn with the palm of her left hand.

"Thank you too, it was nice.... maybe we could do something again sometime?" I sheepishly asked.

"I would like that....... you know where to find me." She said as she held onto her flower looking at me with tired eyes.

We sat for a moment, not knowing what to do or say, but with both of us glad that this night had finally taken place. Then sliding over rather quickly on the black, now clean and slippery vinyl front seat, she gave me a peck on the cheek and wished me a good night as she scurried out of the car.

* * *

As expected, three weeks vanished before my eyes. I was on the 8:06 train inbound for Boston, with luggage in hand. I couldn't wait to see my friends again, I couldn't wait to hear all those musical notations reverberating all around me. And with the initial semester under my belt, I felt more empowered, more self-confident than before. I spoke to Johnny a couple of times over the break and although it was difficult to hear him over the noise of the club payphone he would call me from, he let me know that his playing career was working well. I thought about Lizzy many nights while I was at home and wasn't sure how I was going to address the situation when I got back. But for the most part, I spent quality time with my family and rode the vitality of the recent performance.

The chilling temperatures were now in full swing as I arrived back at school. The New England winters were notorious for being at least 10-20 degrees lower than in my home state of Jersey. It was a seven-hour train ride and the sun had already begun to set as we pulled into the station. Not a soul in sight, I was one of three passengers to step out into the frigid night air as a single streetlight lit our passage. A taxi shortly arrived to pick up the two other passengers and luckily, they agreed to let me share the ride as our stops were near each other.

It felt good to be back in my dorm room. I began to unpack the clean clothes I had returned with, turned off the light, and stretched out on my bed. Falling into a tranquil sleep, I was soon startled by a knock and a beam of light streaking in from the hallway.

"Hello.........Hello," the voice repeated.

I knew it couldn't be Johnny, it wasn't his style to make such a subtle entrance, and with the light shining directly in my eyes, I really couldn't distinctly see who was there. Jumping off my bed, still, in a sense of slumber and fully dressed from my commute, I made my way over to the door and opened it further.

"Hi, it's me." The voice said again.

"I thought I saw you getting out of that taxi in front." She said.

It was Lizzy, unexpectedly, she was right at my door, looking innocently attractive, wearing a powder blue sweatshirt, tight jeans, white Keds sneakers, and her hair pulled back.

"Oh, hey there, sorry, I must have dozed off," I said, first rubbing my eyes and then trying to adjust my hair.

"How was your break? Mine wasn't so exciting, I got here early this morning and it doesn't look like everybody is back yet." She rambled on without letting me get a word in.

"Do you have a few minutes? I need to talk to you about something."

"Uh, sure, come on in." I finally responded.

Leaving the door wide open as it was the gentlemanly thing to do, I pulled out the chair from under the small desk in my room and offered it to her politely, as I sat across from her on the bed.

"So, what's on your mind?" I calmly asked.

"Well, I didn't get a chance to talk to you after the show and you left rather quickly, but I just wanted to say that, I ......I.....like being with you. I mean those practices we had....... well I miss them. And I thought we shared a real moment just before the curtain went up?"

I sat there with a blank look on my face as if I had still been asleep and the reality of what she was saying was simply not registering. I liked her from the moment I met her. Maybe I was infatuated, but maybe, just maybe it was something more. All I knew was how I felt at that moment, no one had ever made my heart melt as she did. I wanted to grab her, hug her, and kiss her again, but I thought it best to play it cool.

"Okay, but let me ask you a question. But what about your sax player boyfriend?"

"He's not my boyfriend, yes, we dated for a while and he made more of it than it was, anyway, that's all over with now, it's been over for a while."

"I don't know what to say." I answered with a certain amazement.

"Don't say anything. Just think about it, Vincent Scardosa from Jersey," she said flashing that playful smile of hers, as she got up and walked over to the door.

"Hold on, hold on, I mean don't go, I mean I don't have to think about it. I like you to Lizzy."

I blurted out and with my sudden statement of conviction, I gently tried to pull her close.

"Calm down boy, just think about it some more and we will see what comes from it."

She stated as she slinked away looking back at me with a sultry grin leaving me in an utter state of bewilderment wanting more.

"Oh, and by the way, I told you, you were going to be a star!"

My mind raced; I didn't know how to comprehend the gravity of what just took place. Lizzy Brundige, yes, the girl I was awestruck with from our first encounter was just here, in the flesh, in my room, telling me that she LIKED being with me. And I had kissed her once already, making a point to know I would love to repeat that performance. My heart raced furiously with each passing thought.

What seemed like hours were only minutes, sitting on my bed in a darkened room, locked in place. The sound that was so familiar, wasn't even able to pry me from the position I was in. Johnny was back, but instead of going right to his room, he noticed my door partially opened.

"Kid, you in here?" he asked as he slowly opened it further.

"Yeah, I'm here." My voice slowly rose, emanating from the darkness.

"What the hell you doing sitting there with the lights off? You ok?"

"I'm great Johnny, I'm just great." I softly answered back.

"Good, it's great to be back and all but, have I got news for you, buddy boy!" He announced as he turned on the lights and shut the door behind him.

He pulled the chair closer and turned it around sitting on it backward with his legs straddling each side and leaning forward on its backside.

"Ok big news, number one. Your little girlfriend and Mr. California saxophone player are splitsville. Yep, over and done with. I got the word, she never really was serious about him anyway." He said excitedly as he continued.

"And big news number two. You, me, and a couple of the other guys are going downtown. We got our first audition and it could lead to a paying gig for all of us at The Raven's Nest, our try out is day after tomorrow."

Still being gripped by a slight feeling of incoherence, I turned to him, hearing the words come out, but not fully focusing on their meaning.

"Wow.........what?......Johnny, the world is suddenly moving too fast, I'm spinning out of control here. I know about Lizzy.........She was just here!" I sputtered.

"What, here......she was here?"

"That's right daddy-o," I said with more clarity.

"She came to tell me all about it, and Johnny, she said she liked being with me!! I couldn't contain myself as I jumped up off the bed and started pacing frantically.

"What do I do?.......should I....... Johnny boy, I'm in Love!!!!" I continued, on and on.

Johnny was always the voice of reason and of course, in this instance, he would be no different, besides, he was much more experienced in this area than I was.

"Whoa, cool down buddy boy. Cool down! You got to get a handle on it and take it slow. I know she is one hot number and talented on top of it all. But just cool it down and we'll see all about it."

Sound advice and I needed it. This was my first bona fide experience of being attracted to someone, with that feeling being mutually returned.

"Ok, now that we got that out of the way, we got even faster hotrods percolating and ready to roar! And one has your name on it down at The Ravens Nest."

The Ravens Nest was an underground jazz club located on what was the seedier side of Boston. It was known for its progressive style of entertainment which not only included sultry jazz, but also the newest movements in an upcoming sound called rock and roll. It was owned by a guy approximately 12 years older than any of us and with a notorious reputation of being self-indulgent and a womanizer.

Dexter DeMarco, spent two years in the navy before being dishonorably discharged, married, and divorced a couple of times, had a live-in girlfriend, and was expecting a child with his former wife. He stood a little less than six feet tall with a big bushy hairdo, and biceps that looked like he worked out frequently. He had several tattoos that made him a look even more imposing. He was a smooth talker, slippery at times, and liked to believe that his demeanor was one of self-confidence. I saw it more as just plain arrogance. He had no reservations when it came to exercising his authority at the club. To his credit, he did possess a good singing voice which he utilized on certain occasions, to his advantage of course. And Johnny, unknowingly, had set us up for a collision course, one that would change our lives forever.

The next few days were filled with the kind of energy that comes with friends and acquaintances returning together. The fervor that took place about a month ago was still ever-present as we all reunited in joyful form. Classes were beginning again and the sights and sounds of the conservatory were steadily getting back in full swing. Our crew was intact and eventually, we made our way to the usual lunchtime spot at the back tables. Lizzy and her female counterparts joined us there as well.

Things were somewhat different this time around, we garnered more respect and our presence grew more obvious. We were ready for the new semester of work, but more so, we were ambitious about the next level of our abilities which was about to crossover from campus life into the 'real' world of entertainment.

We met on a Tuesday for a rehearsal of sorts. Our goal was to show Dexter DeMarco our versatility. We ran through jazz collaborations and of course newer type rock and roll renditions which we were somewhat familiar with from our Thursday night roustabouts. The challenge of perfecting various tunes was secondary to that of making sure that none of our teachers were to find out what we were up to. They not only frowned on this type of activity, but they also discouraged it emphatically. And there were also the likes of Z Klein who wouldn't think twice to have us suspended for such an infraction.

So, we covered our tracks and worked late at night, in the orchestra hall. I managed to recruit my friend, Little Jim, as a lookout in exchange for a meatball sandwich from the cafeteria. Gaining momentum and coming together as a band, Johnny set up an initial audition at The Raven's Nest and we were off to the races.

From the very first time I was introduced to Dexter, I had an uneasy feeling about him. I had heard he attended our Conservatory year-end performance but left in the middle of my solo. The Ravens Nest was in a lower level basement setting. It was dark and dingy with a strong smell of stale cigars and liquor. The stage was slightly elevated and was large enough to hold up to fifteen musicians at any one time, with an upright piano set at one end. It was surrounded by a sea of small tables and chairs for its patrons. The usual hours were anywhere from ten p.m. to closing, which could be anytime from two to three in the morning.

We arrived around six o'clock in the evening, after classes and dinner were well over with. The club was closed to the public and the only ones in the joint were a smattering of bartenders cleaning glasses, and cocktail waitresses aligning cigarettes and cigars for the evening crowd. A set of drums had already been set up for the house band and we headed right for them and the stage. It was during our soundcheck that non-other than Dexter hopped up on the platform to formally meet us. Johnny coolly made the introductions.

An unlit cigarette was perched behind Dexter's left ear as he sized us up, shaking hands with each one of us. You couldn't help but be slightly intimidated, he was not cut from the same cloth as any of the teachers we had known and was streetwise with an aura that projected it.

We poured it on from our opening number with the Hank Williams rendition of *Movin' On Over* and slid right into *Rocket 88* by Jackie Brenston. The bartenders along with a strong-arm individual, who's main job was probably to keep order in the house in case things got dicey, stopped right in the middle of their conversations and took notice. In front of the stage was an area of approximately 20 square feet which was the designated dance floor. It was where all the newly self-proclaimed bobbysoxers would migrate to on any given night. We were so in tune, that the two cocktail waitresses came over and began to dance. Dexter couldn't help but nod his head in approval and immediately booked us.

From that moment on we were known as 'The Conservatory Cats', Dexter thought it a bit lengthy, but it would suffice for now. We sported our Thursday nights four-piece band, Johnny on Guitar, Tony Matone on drums, Jake P. on sax, Joe West on bass, and of course, me, on piano and vocals.

Life was on the upswing. My God-given talent had catapulted me to a level I never thought I would reach so rapidly. I was beginning to establish a relationship with the girl of my dreams and my future at the conservatory and beyond looked to be on the right track..................... or so it seemed.

5

Frankie and I had many more nights together, our friendship was growing, but at the same time, it was teetering on something more, playfully resisting the next step. It was a game of cat and mouse that was worth being a part of.

When I decided to set roots in the south-west, I never realized that I would gain a wealth of knowledge regarding American history, science, or any other conventional subject. My formal education didn't have much focus on such academics, it was mainly concerned about developing my specific talents. But Frankie, being as bright and intelligent as she was beautiful, filled me in with a crash course of the comings and goings which took place here. She had in her possession a couple of old-time history books which were left in the house when she obtained it, along with some other assorted items and in the nights that ensued, my inquisitive nature had us going through them quite extensively.

"You know honey, I was never really much of a history buff, but I would love to know more about this town of yours, in fact, I find this whole area of the country intriguing. Mind if I borrow these books of yours for a spell?" I asked as I retrieved one of her textbooks from a shelf on the living room wall.

"You could if you like, but I like to think of the history of our town is better off learned from eye-witnesses."

"And are you one of these eye-witnesses? Or maybe you could just come over with this book and, uh, read me a bedtime story?" I jokingly said with a mischievous grin.

"A bedtime story, why, Mr. Vincent are you flirting with me?"

I kept my grin going for several minutes as she came over and nudged her forehead right up against mine as she took the book from my hands, closed it, then tucked it under my arm, while giggling and slipping past me.

I had lived through a tumultuous era growing up and never really understood the concept of war, except for what was tuned in on the radio in my parent's house. My Father returned home earlier than expected from serving in the navy after receiving a purple heart. He didn't speak much of any events during his enlisted time and I never really asked, as I felt his silence was his way of dealing with the memory of it. And even though certain instances, such as my piano lessons coming to an abrupt halt when my aunt Nell went to work in a parachute making factory and cousin Tommy not returning home after serving on the front lines, had me aware of the ongoing wartime situation.

For the most part, I was sheltered from it all, my parents continued to make family life as normal as possible, with music, of course, being at the forefront. But now in my new hometown, I was surrounded by a rich and sometimes disturbing chronicle of its past, which I was quickly becoming engulfed by as I read Frankie's textbooks each night before drifting off in bed.

In 1945, New Mexico had become the proving ground for the first-ever atomic bomb. It was a project dedicated to ending the war and hypothetically saving millions of lives in doing so. In the badlands, some 20 miles from Mara Del Santos, a makeshift temporary town, housing more than 1600 scientists, Nobel prize winners, laborer's and families, was erected. It was called the Manhattan Project.

The war in Europe had all but ended, but in the Pacific, (where my father's ship, the aircraft carrier, the USS Yorktown was dispatched to), it furiously waged on with Japan. Thus, a gathering of some of the most brilliant scientific minds, from Einstein to Fermi, banded together here in this region of the country, to create a weapon that would have no equal. But it came with a hefty price. In the secluded picturesque town of Los Alamos, in 1942. It was there that a military camp was assembled, complete with laboratories, 4-family dwellings, and concrete bunkers. And it was there that the atomic age was born.

This boomtown sprung up from the desert floor in such a secretive manner that the state's capital across the Rio Grande, Santa Fe, was not aware of what was actually taking place, and neither were any of the residents for hundreds of miles around. After several years of perfecting their creation, this formidable invention was ready for its final run-through. The site that was chosen for the actual test was located 27 miles from the nearest town (and approximately 50 miles from Mara Del Santos), it was christened; Trinity site.

After three years of working nearly sixty-hour weeks, it was completed, and science would be put to the test. Nearby communities were evacuated and in the early hours of a cool New Mexico morning at approximately 5:45, before sunrise, detonation had arrived.

Trinity site was besieged by an intense flash, as if the sun itself had dropped to the earth's floor. The heat from the explosion was like none ever felt. The age of destruction, in one fell swoop, had now been recognized.

The world would never be the same again.

In its aftermath, this idyllic area of nearly 54,000 acres was irradiated with dust, debris, and nuclear fallout. The native Indian tribes which were plentiful in these parts referred to it as the 'scorched earth that would never be healed'. Many old-timers within a concerned radius described the following years as a travesty to the natural land. They claimed that the soil had been tainted and the earth itself would one-day rebel. Forestry, wildlife, and crops suffered for many seasons. This land of pure and fruitful scenery had taken steps backward without knowing the true long-term effects of what was propagated that summer.

In any event, the bomb was delivered, and the war had ended.

In the weeks and months that followed many inhabitants from surrounding areas claimed to have become mysteriously become ill with chronic breathing disorders, headaches, and unnatural ailments, and in turn, began to outrightly blame the government. Some even insisted that during the late-night hours, in the radiance of the moonlight they would see the landscape possessing an eerie glow. For all the pomp and circumstance that was associated with the end of the war and the GI's returning home victorious, in this part of the country, the military became an unwelcomed friend.

Life in Mara del Santos, continued without much interruption, although several residents decided to pack up and move further west. As time went on, the memory of it all seemed to diminish as peace and prosperity engulfed the post-war country and migration of a new populace began to arrive.

I wanted to get Frankie's firsthand take on the historical perspective in her own words but thought I should learn all I could from the history books before I ventured to coax her in providing her rendition.

Each Friday night after Frankie was off the early shift, I would spend the evening at her house watching our favorite show, *The Honeymooners*, starring Jackie Gleason and Art Carney, on her small black and white RCA television set. Most families now had one, and those who didn't were always welcomed at someone's home who did.

Frankie's home, located at the end of a row of houses that were similar in construction, was a modest 2-bedroom structure, possessing a decent size kitchen, with an icebox, stove, and five piece white vinyl dining set, the bedrooms were of equal proportion and a living room, which contained a sizable couch along with her television set in full view made up its interior. It had an open back porch neatly aligned with two solid wooden chairs overlooking the never-ending terrain and the mountainous plateaus in the distance.

Most often as we cooked dinner together, she would introduce me to food specialties which had a Mexican flair and I, in return, would bring out some of my mother's Italian favorites(albeit, I had to improvise on several ingredients that were just not available in the southwest). We would then settle in to watch our programs for a short while usually ending up on her back porch talking for all hours of the night. On occasion, we would fire up Denise and take that moonlight ride back out to the place where we first embarked too.

On several occasions, I would work all day filling in at the Winchester, checking guests in, as the regular daytime front desk person had been home in bed with a cold. The hotel owner was starting to take a liking to me and began to trust me with added responsibilities. The timing couldn't have been better with my funds becoming critically low. And on any typical Friday night, after finishing up my tasks, I would routinely get myself cleaned up before heading out the door and over to Frankie's.

"Hey there Vincent……Vincent….," I heard a raspy voice screech over to me before getting to the front door.

The night manager, Charlie beckoned me to come over with a wave of his hand and follow him. His sparse gray hair and round-rimmed glasses combined with a slight limp gave him the appearance of being much older than he was.

"Did I forget something, Charlie?"

"No, no, ……. well maybe you did, come around back with me to the storeroom," he requested as he slowly led the way.

Pushing open the door to the storage room located far behind the check-in counter, I followed him in as he bent over. Opening a large cardboard box which had been sitting on the floor, he withdrew a dark bottle of red wine.

"Here take this," he said handing it over to me.

"The boss said we could each take one. I think it was a gift and he can't possibly drink it all. I figured you were headed over to that sweet number of yours, and the two of you could enjoy it."

"What 'sweet number', are you referring to?" I asked, knowing exactly who he meant.

"You know, that girlfriend of yours from the diner."

"She's not my girlfriend, Charlie." I adamantly stated.

"But I'll take the bottle with me anyway, we can have it with dinner, thanks."

Placing the wine on the front seat, I drove over to Frankie's for another relaxing evening. The stars were brightly twinkling, and the air was not as steamy as it had been in recent days. Frankie knew when I would exactly arrive. Each time I drove up and parked in her driveway, I would intentionally turn up my radio to announce my presence. This time it was *Only You*, by The Platters. Being one of my favorites, I sat there in her driveway listening to each note and fighting off the temptation to sing along. It had been a very, very, long time since I exercised my vocal cords, and I had vowed to never do it again in public. I sat there reminiscing for a moment, using every strand of restraint to hold back.

"You having fun out here?" she asked, as she came out from around back and stuck her head in the passenger side window.

She looked especially radiant, with her hair tumbling down around the right side of her face and wearing an orange sleeveless shirt, blue jeans rolled up to her knees and bare feet. Noticing the bottle sitting on the front seat within reach, she went on before I had a chance to say anything.

"I have an idea, are you really hungry? If you're not, let's eat later. I'll be right back." She said before retreating inside.

In a minute she returned with a large woven canvas bag, opened the car door, and in one motion, grabbed the bottle and slid into her bag as she jumped in.

"Well, don't just sit there, let's go, drive on, man." She eagerly stated while gingerly folding her legs under her torso.

I loved her spontaneity. Backing the car out of her driveway, I shifted into gear and hit the gas, then sped out of town heading for the 007. We felt free, unencumbered. That's how it was each time I was with her. With the radio blaring and the wind flowing wildly through our hair, I hit the road without any consideration.

We pulled into our usual spot, by now, my tire tracks had carved out their signature there. A small herd of antelope was grazing by as we exited the car. Leaving the parking lights on was a necessity for making sure there were no snakes or vermin in the area, and besides, they also gave off a nice amber glow. Retrieving a plaid colored blanket and spreading it on the ground about four feet in front us, she began to stake out a comfortable area for the evening . We sat as she reached into the canvas bag and withdrew two glasses. I, on the other hand, oversaw opening the wine, which I promptly did. She then also removed a basket full of homemade empanadas of her own recipe.

"Ok Mister, here is my idea." She said with a big grin.

"For the last month or so, we have been getting to know each other pretty well, haven't we? Or should I say, you really have gotten to know me.........but you are a real mystery, and its time you answered some of my questions....... directly!"

As both of us sipped on our wine, I knew by the look in her eyes that I didn't have a chance of escaping many of her inquiries much longer.

"Okay, Okay, but hold on just a second." I pleaded.

"Hold on nothing......" She tried to respond as I cut her off abruptly.

"Listen, you were the first one I met when I got here, and honestly, I felt like there was something about you immediately. So, I will tell you everything you want to know. I just don't know if it will be before this night is over. My story is not an easy one for me to get out. I want you to know everything, I do. I trust you, and when the time is right, I will tell you, promise I will."

* * *

My first official date with Lizzy was in the spring of 1948. Her parents gave her a car for her birthday, which she immediately drove up to school. It was a beautiful white Chevy Cabriolet 2-door convertible with a black roof, and it suited her to a tee. Being that she had already obtained a driver's license and was a year older than I, she did all the driving. Asking her to a movie downtown was one of my few options, and having that car of hers available made many other venues accessible.

We scoured most of the city of Boston, visiting museums and examining old buildings became a favorite pastime of ours. Lizzy was particularly fond of looking at architecture, an interest she acquired at an early age from her parents, and educated me quite thoroughly on the subject. Our time together was steadily increasing and everyone at school began to know us as a couple. Johnny took a liking to her too and began to accept her friendship as well. I was proud to be seen with someone of her caliber, especially when we were in social settings and holding hands. We would walk the corridors together, study, practice, and yes, many times disappear between classes for a quick make-out session (the small tucked away practice rooms were more than useful for just practice). I had gone on a few dates before in my past and could probably count them all on one hand. But for the first time in my life, I had a real girlfriend, I was happy, immensely happy, and knew without a doubt that I was falling in love.

Classes became more intense, rehearsals more concentrated, and some of us were assigned a personal mentor to work with towards perfecting our craft. These were the best of the best, instructors who had an undeniable resume and who were getting paid to push us to a higher level. Students assigned to such a program were chosen randomly and at the discretion of a faculty committee. And of course, I was one of them. This meant spending an additional 2-4 hours a day working with one individual, when schedules permitted, without interfering with your other courses. It was a rigorous agenda, but each of us knew that this was a benefit not to be taken for granted. If you want to be the best at what you did, there is no substitution for the effort and work that needs to go into it.

I was holding my own, delivering my best at school, and enjoying a wonderful relationship with Lizzy. I had even finally joined the church choir, after all, what better way to serve God than to use the talent he gave me to the best of my ability. And as a bonus, I was pulling in some cash as well, at The Ravens Nest.

It was the latter that made me feel independent, as I let my parents know there wasn't any need for them to send me money. Not being completely honest, and wanting to be as small a burden as possible, I told them how I had a part-time student job at school. And I didn't think they would approve of me being in some smoke ridden after-hours club to all hours of the night.

Our gigs at The Raven's Nest started very sporadically. Dexter would get word to Johnny when he wanted us on stage, which usually occurred about once a month at first. He said people got a kick out of seeing us perform, we were a much younger age than the usual suspects and therefore considered a novelty of sorts. Wanting to stay on top of the changing music scene, we rehearsed and kept adding new material to our sets as often as we could. What began as mostly jazz numbers, evolved to rhythm and blues and were quickly moving to rock and roll. It was a true transition from what I had learned in my formal schooling, but it was liberating to feel as though I could express myself in a new and inventive way without the rigors of academic standards hanging over my head.

We began to develop a following, people came to hear our soulful sound as we delivered the newest hits covered from the current radio play. The dance floor was filled each time we took the stage, they were out there doing anything from the jitterbug to the lindy, and any improvisation in between. As we gained in popularity, Dexter was more than pleased than ever, his door receipts were bringing in good amounts of cash, not to mention the tobacco and liquor sales he was profiting from. And as far as our personal effects were heading, members of the band were meeting women much older, much to their amusement, and of course, Johnny, with his unmistakable guitar play was amassing a fan club all his own. I was not without invitations myself, but being true to Lizzy, had no interest.

The scene at The Raven's Nest was worlds apart from where I came from. The very first time we took the stage it was not only nerve-racking but electrifying. This was an entirely different crowd than I had ever performed in front of. Patrons of various ages, some dressed in swank suits and ties on most occasions, while on other nights a hard-looking crowd in black leather became the scene. The place was always smoke-filled and hazy. The waitresses, mostly dressed in tight short skirts did their best to act flirtatious and play along with the crowd to keep them from getting unruly.

Like anyone else, I enjoyed the attention, but what I loved more, was simply, just making music. When you are passionate about something, when that something literally stirs your soul, not much in life can compare to it, with maybe, with the exception of finding true love.

Knowing my buddies and I could swing from classical to blues, to rock, then back again, so seamlessly, was most gratifying and just plain fun. At times, we felt like we were living a double life as the Conservatory walls would be beckoning upon us when we awoke each following morning.

Every time the semester ending spectacle would come around, we became more aware of what to expect. Having experienced and conquered such, sometimes it was even comical to sit back and watch the newer students stress level rise to manic heights. In time, we grew accustomed to each other and became aware of what was necessary for success. I believe we eventually got used to the strict nature of Z Klein and almost felt like we had graduated to his good side, that is, if he had one.

Each performance felt more magnificent than the previous one, and the crowds blossomed to excessive proportions. The local papers began to take notice and reviews were printed, including an interview by Z Klein with quotes from several of us. If was a time where bonds were formed, where mutual respect abounded and the idea of pursuing our passions was as joyful and innocent as it was during one's childhood.

The more time I spent at the Conservatory, the more it became a part of me. I had now considered it my home away from home and the people there were my extended family. It became slightly more difficult each time a semester would end, knowing that I would have to leave, even if it was just for a short while.

The summers were especially hard, being away from the gang in Boston for three months felt endless. My biggest consolation was that Lizzy was not very far away, in New York City, and we had several chances to be together. Johnny, on the other hand, was a different story, he only ventured back to his home in Chicago just once, choosing to stay in Boston and continue his playing career whenever and wherever he could. And I knew that his female fan club would miss him dearly, and he, in turn, would miss them.

As the demand for our group became exceedingly prevalent, Dexter was requesting us to take the stage more often, once during the week, and twice on weekends. Up to that point, we had been rehearsing continuously, when life at the conservatory allowed us to. The strain on my vocal cords was beginning to add up and I do believe Johnny began to take notice. Also, I wasn't especially happy knowing that I wouldn't be spending Saturday nights with Lizzy all that much.

"Kid, there is something I want to talk to you about." Johnny said as he put his arm around me while strutting down the hallway between classes.

I just looked at him in a partially drained state. I was physically feeling the effects of all that I had been undertaking.

"You have been keepin' one helluva schedule these days, and man-o-man, I don't know how you are you are doin' it, but." He paused for some time.

"I think you need to take a break."

"A break, I don't need a break!" I immediately quipped back.

"Everybody needs a break sometimes, Kid."

"So, what are you saying, John? Should I quit the choir? Maybe tell Z Klein I need time off from his rehearsal? Or is it that you guys want to play the nest without me?"

I had never been short with Johnny before, nor did he ever take me to task either, but with my energy level running low, I became momentarily frustrated with the idea that anyone should insinuate that I needed a 'break'.

"No way, kid, couldn't go on without you. But here's what I'm thinking. How about us adding a fifth, someone to spell you from singing every number, someone that can play the piano too, and give us a different sound from time to time……. someone with a higher falsetto, uh you know, a softer……. well…. FEMALE sound? Someone you know really well, of course it's up to you, but, whatya' think, kid?"

"If I think I know what you are saying, and I think I do, it may not be a bad idea, but let me talk to her and see what she thinks," I said with some trepidation in my voice.

"Ok, thanks for being onboard kid. We all know she is one hell of a cellist, but I have heard her belt out some tunes in the hallway while she sings along to the radio. I mean I heard her the other day and….."

"I know Johnny, I know alright, she has surprised me too at times in our practice sessions, and she is pretty damn good on those ivory keys too. I'll run this all by her tomorrow."

The thought of Lizzy joining our band sent me to my room with mixed emotions. I agreed that it would add a dimension to our sound, and she was a very good piano player as well, with a quality voice, but I wasn't sure if the environment we were exposed to would benefit her. In any event, myself, as well as Johnny would be there to keep an eye on her. And at least, for the most part, I would be seeing more of her.

The following morning, Lizzy and I met bright and early for breakfast and I decided to run last night's conversation with Johnny, by her. I laid out all the pros and cons, I described everything at The Raven's Nest in all its slimy décor, including the patrons. I accentuated the risks of being caught and the ramifications it would have in our standing at the school. I was sure that there wasn't any way that her parents would approve either. She had been sheltered most of her life, like me, her innocence was evident. She hadn't had many other boyfriends and was a little naïve when it came to men.

I cared about her tremendously and felt the need to give it to her plain and simple while protecting her in some way. I could see that that idea of playing in public, in a different kind of arena excited her, and I couldn't say I blamed her, this was real life, this was the true limelight, a spotlight like no other. It excited me too and I wanted her, I wanted us, to be successful together. I loved her, I loved having her near me all the time, but my gut instinct was responding differently, cautiously. (Sometimes in life, you just gotta go with your gut!).

She listened to what I had to say, clinging to my every word. Throughout my whole rundown, I could see the highs and lows in her expression, and in the end, she sat back in momentary silence.

"That's a lot to digest, are you sure you will be ok with it if I say yes?"

"Yes, if you're ok with it, I will be too."

"Give me a little time, I'd like to think about it."

Two days later, the band's late-night rehearsals continued with the same routine, one of us would show up with our payment of a meatball sandwich for Little Jimmy and off we would go to get our rhythm down. It was late on a Friday, I think we were all just about out of gas trying to work on our latest number called *Rock This Joint*, by Jimmy Preston, when out of nowhere, the doors clanked, and we watched as Lizzy strolled in. Haired pulled back in a pony-tail, tied with a strand of pink yarn, wearing a tight-fitting white sweater, sleeves rolled up and a loose silk scarf flowing around her neck, along with white wedge shoes, she was ready to jump into her part.

"Let's go boys, I'm in. Where do you want me?" she confidently stated.

She smiled and came and sat beside me at the piano to view the sheet music. I quickly explained the chord progression and she ran with it, not missing a beat, as the rest of the guys joined right in. We sang together using our harmony, even though it wasn't meant to be a duet. I took the lead on the next song, *Good Rockin' Tonight*, by Wynonie Harris, while she moved along on the tambourine, swaying to the beat. The feeling was right, she added a dimension to the whole mood of the band that wasn't there before. And being as close as I was to her, I felt an even deeper connection as we would consistently make eye contact with a sense of approval abounding from both our directions. A connection that belonged to just the two of us while we were on stage.

Johnny was smiling from ear to ear as he and his guitar were grooving right along. She sounded fantastic, looked tremendous, and suddenly, this element was about to help us catch fire. With each tune we did, Lizzy was right on key, she was a quick learner musically and vocally. All that had to be done now was to concentrate on the lyrics. And even though we had jammed on these songs before, to be playing in a public atmosphere, was much different than anything any of us had experienced, the scene was very far removed from Bach, Beethoven, and Handel. As a band, we were already musically tight, but we knew that it would take a little time to perfect our sound with our new addition, and decided that we would not introduce her to the crowd at The Ravens Nest, not just yet.

* * *

The sound of coyotes howling in the background usually signaled our time to retreat. Driving home, Frankie was somewhat quieter than usual. I knew she wasn't very happy with me holding out yet again on her questioning. I knew that I would have to find a way to get past my reluctance or risk losing whatever relationship we had established thus far. We got to the town limits and instead of making the required left turn towards her house, I veered right and sped up.

"What are you doing, where are we headed now?" She sat upright and suddenly inquired.

"I'm taking a shortcut, hope you don't mind."

"This isn't a shortcut, and we shouldn't be here." She said in a frantic sounding whisper.

There we were, not a soul in sight, parked silently with the engine turned off, looking down that row of abandoned dwellings just outside of town. The lost neighborhood of structures which captured my curiosity a short time ago. I had to find out, I had to take the chance that Frankie would give me some answers.

"Vincent, we really shouldn't be here," she repeated, as she turned to her left then back to her right looking out the rear window to make sure no one had seen us.

"So, you do know what this is all about?"

"Yes…. I mean sort of, its…its… 'bathtub row'…. but please let's go back to my house, I'll put on a pot of coffee and tell you what I know about it."

I didn't know if it was the wine that had her so startled or just my abrupt decision to descend on that location. Being a bit light-headed myself, I revved the engine as the wheels spun a blanket of dust in my rear-view mirror and sped off. Not a word was spoken until we got to Frankie's. Parking Denise in her driveway, we both got out and headed right inside. Turning on the kitchen light, she went directly over to the cupboard took out a small sack of ground coffee, filled the stainless-steel percolator, and lit the stove. We sat at her table across from each other silently, before the subject was addressed.

"Bathtub row?" I finally said with a look of confusion.

With the coffee beginning to brew, she rose and retrieved two adobe clay looking cups and a bowl of sugar, placing them on the table before us. Then, taking the pot from the stovetop, she filled them both and sat in a more relaxed state.

"It's all part of it, it's all part of the military camp that began at Los Alamos and continued here."

"You mean, the atomic bomb testing, the real atomic bomb, that Los Alamos!"

"Yes Vincent, the camp at Los Alamos was for the scientists and their family members, we aren't that far from there and they needed another place for their security detail and their families, so they came here to build more housing for them. They came rolling in with their bulldozers and even an army tank. It was a frightening scene."

"Well, what happened, why is everything left abandoned like that, seems like good strong buildings just going to waste."

"Yes, those buildings have been there some years now, just as you see them, and from what I have heard from the town-folk, there they will remain as they are."

"So, you were here? You were here when it all took place? Did you see it? I mean did you see the explosion?" I asked with a sudden spurt of energy.

"I was a much younger version of myself but can remember the day it happened, and I can remember it clearly. It was just shortly after I got here. I was the new waitress at the diner, I just started working part-time on the weekends while I was taking care of Mrs. Williams during the week. It was a quiet Sunday morning. The sound they made rumbling in and tearing up the ground, it also tore up the peace, things weren't quite the same after that. When the construction was finished, families moved in, real families, women, and children. It was a big boom for the town and many of us tried to look at it from the positive side of things. I mean businesses were flourishing, we had to hire extra help and sometimes had people waiting for a table. The general store had its shelves stocked high and those families spent a lot of money, the government's money."

She continued.

"Each time the train came in, more people showed up, there were fresh faces practically every day. The Winchester had a no vacancy sign hung for a couple of weeks, I don't know if we will ever see that again! The only thing that wasn't full was the church on Sundays, Father Tom over at San Sebastian's was disappointed, all he ever wanted it to be was a packed house. For a while we believed, we wanted to believe, that this town was going to be a thriving suburban site, an alternative to Santa Fe itself."

"Hold on, if there was this population explosion like you say, why would Father Tom be disappointed?" I asked with mild curiosity.

"Vincent, you are a naïve at times, aren't you? Those people have their lives based on science. To them, science is knowledge, and knowledge leads to creation and healing. Religion doesn't have much to do with it. I'm sure they are good people, and I am not being critical, but science and God didn't really mix for them, so they weren't church-going people at all, and as you can bet. They must have been pretty preoccupied with what was going on up there."

"Anyway, as I was saying, they left as quickly as they came, it was like, soon as their testing was a success, trucks rolled in to whisk them away. And it was unnerving too, we heard the thundercrack of truck after truck come through late into the night and by morning, it felt like a ghost town. And to answer your question, no, I did not see the explosion."

"Wow that is some story," I said shaking my head in disbelief.

"You know living back east, we only read about this stuff in the papers or heard about it on the radio. But out here, you have lived it."

"Yes, that we have." She stated in a much lower tone.

"I still think someone should inquire about turning those buildings around and making them useful. People always need places to live, don't they?" (I couldn't help but think of myself just then).

"The people around here are proud Vincent, the army and the government have left a bad taste in their mouths. They don't want anything to do with it, and if it was up to them, they would tear it all down. The aftereffects of that bomb testing have lingered, and many people still remember it, very clearly. Ask any of the elders around here, they believe that the radiation has caused unexplained and unnatural occurrences. They just have a lot of animosity for it all."

I thought about all that she had said, it made things much clearer, I thought about that wrinkled elderly woman I met in my early days here. The one who had sold me my straw hat with the frayed edges, and how her attitude changed towards me when I saluted her in military gesture, yes things were beginning to become clearer. Frankie went on solemnly to tell me many other details through the night. How no one ever ventures to that part of town, how people are still leery about the governments promise to come back and modernize the buildings and eventually turn them over to the town itself. And how there is just a general mistrust for the entire situation.

I sat there, soaking it all in, not knowing how to respond with only one thought left lingering in my head.

"What exactly did you mean when you said, the elders blame the fallout for unexplained and unnatural occurrences?"

"Well, not sure, no one ever really asked them for a detailed explanation. I'm sure it's just their way of coming to grips with things. It's all part of the folklore around here."

"One last thing."

"Yes?"

"Why bathtub row?"

"Oh that, there were just a few houses up at Los Alamos that had bathtubs in them, it was considered the original bathtub row. They belonged to the top scientists, you know the cream of the crop. So, when they built these here, they included bathtubs in all of them for their top security and high-ranking officers as well, hence the adoption of bathtub row."

The night began to take its toll, Frankie and I had spent many evenings together. Those had been generally filled with laughter, television, and radio play. I wasn't sure if I had regretted taking that bottle of wine from Charlie, to begin with, but this was probably the most serious of conversations that we had so far. As we sat there sipping on coffee, that had now turned luke-warm, I noticed that in rehashing such tales, she had grown weary. I still wanted to hear more, the first-hand approach that I had just received was electrifying, and Frankie, even in her tired state looked as enticing as ever, maybe even more so.

"Well, I think I've said all I could tonight, Mr. Vincent," she said as she covered her mouth during a huge yawn.

"Why don't we go inside and watch the late show for a while, to wind down a bit."

"Now that's an excellent idea, no more talk about abandoned buildings, or scientists, or even Father Tom, the late show it is," I answered as I gave her my hand and gently helped her up from her chair.

Making our way into her living room, I turned on the TV set and we took our usual place on an old brown sofa directly across a 2-foot wooden table where the television was resting. An old Charlie Chan movie was on, *Dead Men Tell No Tales*. Within five minutes, Frankie had her head resting on my shoulder and was out cold. It felt good to have her that close, but I knew I couldn't hold that position for very long. Not wanting to wake her, I slowly moved over as she slid down onto the sofa. I then gently picked her up and carried her into the bedroom where I eased her down on the bed. Removing her shoes, I covered her with a blanket and gave her a slight kiss on her forehead. She was fast asleep and looked so content. Shutting off the television, I went back to her room for one last look.

"Until tomorrow, my dear, until tomorrow."

* * *

The Conservatory made us musicians, but, The Ravens Nest turned us into professionals. The knowledge base and expert tutelage we received in school had enabled us to continue to higher evolutions with each passing year. We perfected our instruments and our craft. At times it was painstaking, we were pushed to our limits and often beyond, but to excel, we knew it had to be the case, and no one dare complain. With each passing semester, our ability was tested, and our goals were thoroughly achieved. The place that we had grown so fondly of, was priming us for the next level. That first memorable year lapsed quickly, becoming year two, then three. Each of us had grown and matured not only in musical comprehension and skill level but also toward the brink of adulthood. We were taking the city of Boston by storm.

The world of an eighteen-year-old music virtuoso was a complex one. It was my world, one which I grew accustomed to and one where notoriety was coming at me at a rapid pace. But in life, just when it feels like everything is falling into place, just when you think that aspirations are becoming a certainty, just when you feel that your highest goals are within reach, you are faced with the true notion that reality suggests nothing is guaranteed.

Summer break was fast approaching, our recent year-end show was a hit once again, and we were taking it all in stride, after all, three years of steady standing ovations will do that. I was headed home once again, but this summer was going to be different. This time I wasn't going home alone.

Lizzy received an internship tutoring and performing at the New York School of Music Composition. An institution on the rise with the hopes of one-day rivaling Julliard. She would be staying in a one-bedroom flat on the lower east side, provided by the school. It was only a 30-minute train ride from my home and hopefully, we would be seeing each other more frequently than past summers. But as wonderful as that news was, it matched my excitement to know that Johnny would be visiting his aunt for an extended stay in New Jersey, about a one-hour drive away. This was to be the first time in my three years at the Conservatory that I didn't mind leaving Boston.

The plan was to escort Lizzy to her summer surroundings before finding my way back to Jersey. I accompanied her to her new living quarters in New York, helped her get settled in, and after a long kiss, a very, very long kiss goodbye, I headed right over to the nearest subway stop, made my way uptown, and boarded a train homeward bound. My father was there at the station to pick me upon arrival. He greeted with a big hug and a showering sense of pride as I took my place in the passenger seat of his Buick. At home, my mother was preparing a big welcome back meal as she always did each time I returned. I looked forward to getting some rest and spending family time together in the next several months ahead. Deciding to make it a slow and easy summer, I gave my voice a chance to rest by choosing not to sing in my local church choir this time around.

I spent much of my time, doing chores around the house, going to movies with my sister, and taking driving lessons with my father. I even obtained a part-time job, stocking shelves at a local liquor store in the center of town as a means of adding to my future savings. And when her schedule allowed, I would get together with Lizzy as often as possible. Spending time in New York City was an adventure in itself, but discovering new things with the one you love is the best part of it all.

On occasion, she would come out to Jersey and mingle with my family, they all easily accepted her and treated her as one of their own. The same went for Johnny, my mother especially regarded him as a surrogate son, and my sister, and her friends became infatuated with him. Some evenings he would serenade them softly with his guitar on the screened-in porch of our house. Our bond became even stronger as he seamlessly fit into my family life. And many a night he and I would spend hours under the hood of my father's car, as he instructed on the importance of varied auto parts and their function. My father also became fond of him, they together shared an interest in cars and sports among other things, and would spend hours sitting on the back step involved in discussions about such, while having a smoke or two. Cigarettes were not the best thing for my singing voice and my parents discouraged me from the start. But my father enjoyed his Lucky Strikes and having Johnny around allowed him to share his indulgence with someone.

It was a summer of relaxation and ease as we ventured down to the beach on several weekend jaunts. There were times when all six of us squeezed into my father's car and spent the entire day at the Jersey shore. They had become memorable times, and Lizzy, Johnny and I had become the best of friends. There was no mention of school, rehearsals, or The Ravens Nest as we enjoyed these special moments as young ordinary teenagers should. If only it could have lasted forever, if only times like this could be frozen in place.

But the peace and prosperity that I was living and enjoying were about to be altered, and it would become the first time that my world would be shattered.

It was an ordinary Sunday night, events of the day were winding down, Lizzy was spending the evening with us, bunking with my sister in her room as she did each time she stayed. Johnny had left for his Aunt's place earlier, and my mother, sister, and Lizzy were together gathered around the television getting set to watch a new variety show which was about to debut called, *The Ed Sullivan Show*. My dad was relaxing in his usual place in the backyard enjoying his smokes before the long work week was to begin again. I decided to go over to the evening church service which started at 7 pm. It was usually on the lighter side of attendance with most people of my age being present. In walking distance from our home, I set out around thirty minutes before its start and got there a little early as I would often do. I liked to sit quietly, contemplate, and pray alone before the scheduled mass had started.

No sooner had the mass begun, than I was quietly startled by a tap on my right shoulder, turning, I saw Lizzy, and immediately knew that something was amiss. It is one of those moments when the world around you turns completely silent and, in your gut, you know that the next sound you hear is one that is going to overpower you. Looking at her in a profound state of surprise, I immediately noticed a troubled look on her face.

"Angelo, you have to come with me, right now," she whispered as the sounds of Sunday mass continued around me.

Feeling an overpowering weakness run down my legs I immediately got up and followed her outside.

"What is it, what's the matter, what are you doing here?" I scrambled to put a cohesive thought together as panic began to set in.

"It's your dad," she said, as I saw the tears begin to develop in her eyes.

"What happened, what do you mean?" I said, now overridden with fear.

I followed her frantically outside as she had parked my father's Buick just at curbside. I knew in that instance the worse could be imagined, my father never let anyone drive his car. She fought off her emotions as we sped home. Pulling up in front, I immediately ran from the car leaving the door open as I busted into the house.

Finding my mother and sister huddled together on the living room couch, sobbing hysterically, I knew this was unimaginable. Seeing me as she looked up, my mother screamed as she pulled me into her arms.

"He's Gone……. He's gone……your father is gone!"

6

Destiny always seems to come knocking at the strangest times and I wasn't entirely certain if that was true in my case, but I was sure as hell determined to find out.

Taking Frankie's advice, I never ventured over to bathtub row again. I took into consideration all that she had described to me and began to understand the values and way of life of those I had now come to know and befriend. I now saw my surroundings in a new light, one that was not so serene as I had originally thought, and one that came with tremendous sacrifice.

The Winchester, originally seen as a stop-over for travelers on their way to Santa Fe, was getting a few more guests than normal lately. Travelers moving on through the cooler air of September always brought about more activity. I persisted in working as often as they needed me to, and never complained about anything I was asked to do. The morning desk clerk had returned after a long bout with some sort of ailment, which old Doc Coots attended to with concerned diligence. My employment there was nearing an end and I knew it.

There simply wasn't enough work to go around. If I didn't come up with something soon, the only alternative I had was to migrate over to Santé Fe, where jobs were abundant. I had picked up some skills during summers at home with my dad. He was very handy in doing all types of odd jobs from minor woodworking and carpentry to basic auto repair. Nothing too elaborate, but good enough when it came time to get things done. And granted, those indirect skills did afford me enough to support myself while traveling along, picking up some temporary work when the need arose, but this new life, in this new place, did not have many of those opportunities at present. My choices were either to take it on the road again, or give in and become a ranch hand at the Jaco spread, an idea which I still was very reluctant to entertain. The days began to run short and by three o'clock, most afternoons, my menial tasks at the Winchester were usually complete.

Taking siesta was a tradition for most in this part of the country and it was a concept I found hard to adjust to at first. But by mid-day with finding nothing to do with myself, I would eventually succumb to this idea and retreat to my room for a nap.

"Vincent……. Vincent……." A familiar voice called at my door.

Awakening slowly and groggy, I glanced at the small wind-up alarm clock sitting atop of my nightstand and realized it was only 3:45 in the afternoon.

"Just a minute," I answered back as I grabbed my trousers from the chair where they hung and pulled them on.

"Hi. I thought it was you," I said as I slowly opened the door letting Frankie inside.

"Come on in."

I continued as I inconspicuously tried to tidy up, grabbing some loose articles of clothing, placing them in a small pile at the foot of the bed.

"Are you ok?" I asked seeing her bent over as she was trying to catch her breath and gather herself.

"I'm…. I'm fine, I haven't run like that in quite a while." She returned as she straightened up and steadied herself before delivering her news.

"Sorry to barge in like this, but I was working my shift and Father Tom happened to come in for a late lunch. We got to talking and all, and he mentioned that he is looking for help to arrange, and set up the upcoming feast of San Sebastián."

“The feast of San Sebastian?” I curiously responded.

The Feast of San Sebastián was an annual festival of sorts, a celebration of the church, its patron saints, and the long history of the Spanish conquistadors who settled here and played a prominent role in establishing the town of Mara Del Santos. It was something that the whole community and the surrounding areas looked forward to, every two years. It consisted of music, food, dancing, lights, and more recently, a cavalcade of carnival rides that were trucked in from Texas.

“Yes, the feast is a big event around here and as soon as I heard of the job, I thought of you right away. But I have to get back to work, Tessie is covering for me, and I wanted to get to you first before one of those cowhands come in and grab it. You know how to use a hammer don’t you?”

“Of course, yes……...uh, yes I do.”

“Ok, pick me up in 2 hours and we can go over to the church. I’ll introduce you to Father Tom in a hurry.”

“Sounds peachy keen, I’ll see you later………..and thanks.”

Frankie hustled back down the stairs, as I, excitedly began to get myself cleaned up. In no time, I was showered and shaved, dressed in a clean shirt and trousers, hustled around back, climbed into Denise, and started the engine. It didn't sound much like permanent employment, but at this moment, I was willing to take whatever I could get. And besides, I had some knowledge of using tools, and this sounded like it could be an assignment of the enjoyable kind. My only concern was my recent dedication to the church, I didn't feel as though my faith, in general, had the same strength of conviction as it did when I lived back east. I hadn’t been as strong a churchgoer than my previous self. There were even times during long durations on the open road where I felt distant from my faith, focusing only on the painful memories which consumed me. I was somewhat apprehensive about meeting the Catholic priest who was the spiritual leader of this community, but I would keep my current feelings in check, seeing the necessity to find work was my first priority.

Waiting in front of the diner, I could see Frankie as she waved to me through one of the large glass windows overlooking the parking area. Moments later, untying her apron and leaving it behind, she was out the door and in my car.

“Ok, here’s the deal,” she said while frantically chewing on her gum.

"I'm sure he has heard about you, but I will make the formal introduction. I have known him for some time now, and he is very a nice person. Sound good?"

"Sure, sounds fine to me." I answered as I cleared my throat.

Father Toomas Velazquez (a. k. a. Father Tom) was a dedicated man of the cloth. He had been the primary priest in residence for the past 17 years, and the townspeople adored him. He was everything you would expect a priest to be, kind, consoling, wise, possessing an inner strength, and a devotion to his faith and the teachings of Jesus Christ. The community relied on him heavily at times and he, in turn, was always there for them. He was a fit individual, with dark hair, graying on the sides, and a goatee to match, olive skin, standing approximately 5 feet, 10 inches tall, with broad shoulders. He had taken over for a much more elderly priest, who had been there for nearly forty years prior, Father Mycale Ortiz, who was now residing in a convalescent home for the elderly in Alamogordo, Texas.

Driving over to the church, I suddenly realized that this was the building that I had curiously noticed during my first days here. It was the one building that I thought stood out as an oddity, even more than anything in bathtub row. And it was the one building that I had not thought about investigating further. But, once again, here I was, with Frankie heading towards a mystery that was about to unfold.

The church may have been small in size but lacked nothing in its grandeur. Its architecture was a contradiction to its environment. Typically, most houses of worship in these parts were generally mission style, but this had a design all its own. It was nestled in the middle of a dirt lot, without much landscaping to speak of. Parking right in front, all its structural details were clearly evident, and now standing close, I immediately noticed how the spires skyrocketed up towards to the heavens in full splendor.

It had a very large set of red wooden double entry doors, Byzantine in nature, which was rounded towards the top and peaked upwards in the middle. Trying to enter there, we found them locked and deciding to walk around back, stopping at the side entrance, we found that to be the same. A bit further around the rear of the building approximately 20 feet away stood a free-standing shack-like structure where we heard a knocking sound. There was Father Tom, in a pair of old trousers, boots, and a crumbled white collared shirt, hammering and sawing away at some wood. If I hadn't known better, I would not have guessed he was a priest.

"Hi there, Father Tom, didn't mean to interrupt." Frankie said politely.

"Oh, hello, no interruption at all." He responded as he took a rag which was hanging from his back pocket and wiped his hands.

"This is the gentleman I was telling you about, Vincent Scardosa." She said as she motioned towards me.

"Glad to meet you, Mr. Scardosa," he stated while holding out his hand.

"Good to meet you too Father, but please, Vincent is just fine."

"So, I hear you are pretty handy with all kinds of tools." He said confidently to me, as I glanced over at Frankie through the corner of my eye.

"Well, I'm, I'm..........."

"He is quite handy, you'll see Father, and reliable too!" She interrupted.

"Very good then, I have some commitments to attend to first, but after that, it will be full steam ahead, can you start a week from today? It doesn't pay much, and it is only temporary, say for about three weeks or so?"

"Sure Father, I can handle that."

"Great, see you in about a week then." He said, shaking my hand once again.

"Looks as if you are pretty handy yourself Father," as I gestured towards the wood he was working on.

"Truthfully, no, not exactly, I manage to do what I can, but a Shepard taking care of his flock has many duties my son, and getting things repaired around here is just another of my responsibilities I suppose."

Frankie and I left with a good feeling abounding. I looked over at her grinning.

"I'm very good with all types of tools, am I?"

"You better be buddy boy!" She said laughing wildly.

"I'll be fine with it.........but how am I going to thank you?"

"Well let's just say you owe me a dance at the feast, you can dance, can't you?"

I turned up the radio, *Kansas City*, by Wilbert Harrison was playing as I looked over at her.

"Don't you worry chickee, I've been known to have some rhythm at times."

* * *

It is when the people you are closest to, the people who matter the most to you, arrive at the hour of your grief, that's when your true emotions are set free. It is then, at that moment when you truly feel loved.

My father's death came in the form of a heart-attack, it was sudden and impactful, and without any warning. His wake was for two consecutive afternoons and evenings and Lizzy was with us every step of the way. Relatives I had not seen in years came flowing in as I stood tall. I held my feelings in reserve as I played the dutiful son. My mother and sister, on the other hand, sobbed intermittently throughout. It was two days of overpowering grief with the funeral to follow. But it was when Johnny showed up, that I lost control.

Standing at the foot of the casket where my father lay, several people were coming in to console our family and pay their final respects. Seeing Johnny walk in with the look of a heavy heart and concern for me, called on every fiber in my body to keep calm. When he finally was able to make his way past the crowd and over to me, I couldn't hold it in any longer.

He gave me a big bear hug and held on as I wept uncontrollably all over the shoulder of his suit jacket. It's a good thing he was wearing his dark glasses, as I think I saw the trail of a tear rolling down his cheek from beneath them. It was then that I felt the true severity of my loss.

"It's gonna be ok, Angelo, it's gonna be ok, we'll get through this." He said while gently rubbing his hand on my shoulder.

Calling me Angelo sounded odd, but the mood didn't dictate anything different. Rows of people continued to parade in, and the emotional, as well as the physical drain, began to mount. Standing by the casket in front of that room was like being in a dream state, I had a hard time trying to find a way to grasp reality. The only thing that kept me grounded was looking up occasionally to see Johnny and Lizzy sitting in the row behind my immediate family, as far as I was concerned, they were part of that too.

The Conservatory was fully represented, the guys in the band all found a way to make an appearance. Some teachers and other students who I had gotten to know fairly well, also showed up. Lizzy's parents came to give their support and condolences. But what made a full room grow quiet was when much to our surprise, Z Klein entered. There was something different about him that night, perhaps it was the suit he was wearing, perhaps it was simply the sincerity he exuded, either way, I was grateful for him coming all the way down to Jersey to pay his respects.

When the funeral and services had finally ended, after everything began to quiet down, I didn't know what to expect from life. My father had been a pillar of strength for our family, and losing him was a devastating blow to all of us. Life, as I had known it, would never be the same. Just one more year before graduation and I wasn't sure where this would leave me. But my biggest concern was for that of my mother and sister, and how we would all inevitably cope and carry on.

Getting my driver's license that summer made me a bit more marketable and I was able to take on a larger role at the local liquor store, not only stocking shelves, but also making deliveries. I was determined to contribute any way I could to the family household. The next few months that followed were difficult, dealing with the sheer absence of my father and seeing my mother struggle with the loss of the only man she had truly loved, became crippling at times. But I knew I had to stay the course, just as he had taught me to do.

I found myself going to church frequently in those days. I would sit quietly when no one was around, listening to the soothing sound of water trickling from the baptismal font. I would not give up on my faith, being thankful for the good people that God had put in my life. I was grateful for my friends who were there to pick me up, and I was comforted to know that I had found the love of my life and the thought that we would carry on together. I prayed for strength, courage, and wisdom in making the decisions that lay ahead.

With my newfound family duties, it became difficult at times getting out to New York to see Lizzy, but she did understand, and it was always fulfilling when we did finally get together. Johnny came down from his aunt's place as often as he could for the remainder of the summer, his moral support was much appreciated. My mother's best friend Rose was able to procure a more permanent job for her in the secretarial pool of a large insurance company in Newark, New Jersey, rather than work only during the school year and my sister began babysitting as often as someone needed her too. Myself, I did my part of doing chores around the house while trying to maintain as many hours as I could at my job.

My original plan was to graduate and pursue my career as a singer, whether it be with a world-renowned opera house, or simply as part of a band, or just making records, it didn't matter, I was determined to succeed in the world of music, no matter what the cost. I would ask Lizzy for her hand in marriage and we would live the storybook life together that I had dreamed of. Now given my new circumstances, that future vision seemed filled with uncertainty and the summer was fast approaching its end.

I was blessed in many more ways than I knew, and my father had seen to that even after he was gone. Coming home on a rainy night in August after making several deliveries, I was looking forward to getting into some dry clothes and sitting down to one of my mother's home-cooked meals.

"Angelo, sit down please, there is something I need to talk to you about." My mother said as she took a seat at the kitchen table.

"Sure mom, is everything alright?"

"I'm fine, but I wanted to talk to you about going back to finish school."

"Mom, it's ok, I know things have changed and I will stay right here if that's what it takes, I could ask for more hours at work and.............."

"Stop, just stop, please. That's not what I was going to say. Your father was a smart man, he made some investments which did well over the years, not to mention the insurance he set up. I want to let you know that there is enough money right now to pay your tuition and then some. He wanted you and your sister to have the best education possible."

Right then, I did my best not to break down in tears as I felt the rush of them come steaming towards me.

"There's something else too." She went on.

"He got a good deal on a used car that he was going to give to you as a graduation present. It's been parked in your uncle Rocky's garage, I called him and said I think you could use it now, rather than later, he is going to bring it by tomorrow."

That was it, I let loose, the tears came rolling down, I thought I had experienced my share of crying, but this was the icing on the cake. Missing my dad, these were not only tears of sadness, but also tears of joy, knowing and appreciating the man that he was. I vowed my best to make him and my family proud.

I phoned Lizzy right away. We would set up a certain time at night where she would go down to the corner phone booth to receive my call, there were no telephones in her apartment or the building it was situated in. We would talk for lengths at a time, sometimes at the expense of passersby waiting to use the phone. This night, I had told her all that transpired (except my plan for marriage). She was excited to hear about my good news and the fact that I would be returning for our final year together at school.

A day later, just as my mother had promised, I came home to find a bright shiny red automobile sitting in our driveway. A sense of excitement overtook me, there it was, twinkling in the late afternoon sun. Running right over to it, I ran my hand up and down its length, it was clean and smooth. With the doors unlocked, I immediately opened the driver's side and sat in it, playing with the knobs and just admiring everything about it. Inside my uncle and my mother were having coffee.

"So, what do you think, Ange?" My uncle spouted as I burst in.

"I love it, just love it, thank you," as I gave him a big hug.

Then going over I also embraced my mother in my moment of elation. It was good to see her smiling again.

"Now, it's not brand new, but it was a steal. She is only a few years old with very low mileage and in tip-top shape. Your father got a great deal on it from one of his friends at work. Oh, and she has a nice radio too."

I couldn't wait to get out on the road, he jingled the keys at me as I swiped them from his hand and went right back outside. I could barely contain myself as I started it up and turned on the radio right away. My first thought was to shift it into gear and drive right over to Lizzy. But, New York was a bit out of reach for the moment and my driving expertise only consisted of making local liquor deliveries in the store owners 1932 Ford model A delivery truck which was difficult to steer and backfired often.

My sister came dashing out and jumped into the passenger side becoming just as jubilant as I was. Off we went, driving all through the adjacent neighborhoods, both of us singing the tunes that continued to pour out of the dashboard. It was bittersweet, knowing that my dad was with me only in spirit, but I knew that I had to keep my thoughts focused to tackle my upcoming senior year.

After a couple of hours, back in my driveway, I parked head in so that I had an unobstructed view from my upstairs bedroom window. I must have wiped it down several times before I finally went in for the night.

"Angelo, just one more thing we need to figure out," my mom said before I fled into the kitchen to call Johnny next.

I couldn't imagine what else had to be said, so I proceeded cautiously.

"Sure mom, what is it?"

"Well I wanted you to have the car now, rather than wait an entire year, but there is another reason for that decision. Moneywise, we are going to be ok, I think, but keeping up this house, well, I may need your help."

"Sure, I understand, but what exactly are you saying, mom?"

"We are going to need you to come home a little more often, say on your winter and summer breaks from school. It doesn't matter if you drive or take the train, but having you here is going to be helpful.........for the time being of course, I mean until we get things sorted out."

I couldn't dispute what she was saying, and I knew that just being able to finish my schooling was a blessing in itself. If that's what my mom needed, then I would make it work. I knew I would have to sacrifice some things, and I believed that Lizzy would understand too, after all, if we had our way, we were going to have a lifetime to spend together.

* * *

It was closing time at the diner and I purposely swung by to surprise Frankie.

"Hi, what are you doing here, you know we are about to close."

"I know, I ate earlier, just wanted to see if you were up to taking a ride with me?"

"Uh, okay, sure.... let me just finish up and I'll be right out."

I sat out there watching her continue moving gracefully back and forth in front of the large overlooking windows as she finished waiting on tables. She waved with a smile and motioned with one finger to suggest she would be done in a minute.

"So where are we going?" she said as she pranced out to me.

"I have been putting off replacing that front tire on Denise," pointing to the right side of my car. "And since I am going to be working soon, thought I should go out to the *GAS+Plus* and get it now, while I have the time. Have you ever met Otto? And Zeke?"

"Met who?....... Otto? and who? Oh, the car guy, I have heard of him."

Making a sharp right turn and circling the diner, I headed out to the 007 and streamed down the highway to Otto's. It had been some time since our last meeting, but being with Frankie more often had pleasantly taken up most of my time. I just hoped that he would not take my absence as ignorance towards his beliefs or the friends he introduced me to.

Frankie had never stopped out to the *GAS+Plus* and never had any need too, seeing as she didn't own a car. Everything she needed for the past several years was within walking distance.

Down the darkened roadway we proceeded with nothing but my headlights cutting through the night and sound of the Del Vikings and their hit *Little Darlin* announcing our presence from my radio as we sped along.

"Oh, little darlin….

Oh, little darlin….

Oh-oh-oh where,

Arrr-are you………" Frankie sang along delightfully and a tad off key.

"C'mon Vincent, sing with me, I love this song, or at least do the background vocals."

I drove looking straight ahead, trying to seem like I was preoccupied and hadn't heard her request. All I wanted right then was to get to Otto's as fast as I could to avoid the moment. Part of me wanted to speed up and push the gas pedal to the floor, as the other part wanted to pull off to the side of the road and let it all out. Tell Frankie everything. Why I left, what my life was like back east, tell her about my best friend Johnny, who I missed terribly, and what the hell happened to me, but most of all, most of all, I wanted to tell her why I didn't want to sing! Thankfully she just continued singing and before we knew it, we came upon the *GAS+Plus*.

I noticed right away that something wasn't right, Zeke was not sitting outside in his usual position, like I would find him each time I showed up. The place was dark, and Otto didn't look to be in the garage, nor was he to be found sitting on the step outside. A northerly wind was blowing, and tumbleweeds were skirting by, making the place look like it had been vacant for some time. Otto had been in the habit of leaving his place for short spells from time to time and most people had become accustomed to his sporadic behavior, so seeing the place vacant as it was, wouldn't really alarm anyone. And as good as Otto was, the truth of the matter was that people would drive miles in the other direction in their pursuit of a more reliable mechanic.

"Are you sure we're in the right place?" Frankie asked as she viewed the area with her door partially opened.

"I don't understand. Otto! ….. Otto!" I yelled out.

There was no answer, the place was desolate. I tried the front door of his shop and it was surprisingly unlocked. Stepping inside, it looked like it had been ransacked. Fumbling in the dark, I managed to open the bottom drawer of a small desk that I knew Otto kept in the corner of his office for his receipts, I reached in and pulled out a flashlight. Frankie followed me as she stumbled over debris of some kind. Shining the light around the small storefront we could see that the place was in total disarray. I went further back towards the garage where the repair area was located, instructing Frankie to stay right where she was. I also found nothing back there, no sign of Otto, nor any sign of his Chevy.

"Vincent, Vincent!" I heard Frankie yell out.

"Frankie!" I said with concern, running back to the front of the building.

"I think I heard something outside, in that direction." She fearfully stated, pointing to the far side of the building.

Turning the flashlight beam outside towards the direction that Frankie indicated, there was nothing out of the ordinary. I maneuvered slowly around the building, shining the light ahead of us with Frankie following closely behind, holding a hunk of wood tightly in both hands. Then from around the side of the building, we both heard a rustling sound.

"There, over there, I heard something too." I stated, moving the light towards the direction of the sound.

We moved slowly, keeping our guard up. The sound became louder as we drew near, yet I still couldn't make out what it was. The brush was thick and for we all knew it could be a coyote or some other wild animal. Continuing closer, we could see the tops of the tall grass moving about as the rustling grew closer. Then suddenly with a scream from Frankie, from out of the dark underbrush, lunging directly at me, was……was……… Zeke!

He was wagging his tail frantically as I held him towards the ground. He was extremely glad to see me, and we stayed there for a moment just getting reacquainted. Frankie had bent over and was rubbing away at him also.

"Zeke, what are you doing out here alone boy……where's Otto, boy, huh, where's Otto?"

We kept petting and caressing him as I kept talking. Finally, on one knee with Zeke much calmer, I tried to ask again.

"Ok Zeke, where's Otto, boy, can you help us find Otto?"

He paused for a moment as his ears rose slightly upon hearing his owner's name, then he darted around the building, then back towards us, then around the building again, prompting us to follow him.

"Come on, this way, I think he wants us to go after him." I stated with enthusiasm.

Frankie and I ran after him, around to the rear end of the building which led only to an open field where Zeke had stopped about 20 feet away. When we caught up to him, I looked out into the darkness with my flashlight and saw nothing but a wide field of flat brush ahead of me.

"Zeke, is Otto out there Zeke, is he boy?"

And in the oddest of gestures, Zeke sat there for a moment looking up into the night sky as he began to bark. He then trotted around in a tight anxious fashion while barking repeatedly with his gaze remaining overhead.

After several minutes, and not knowing what to make of the whole ordeal, we made our way back to the car, Frankie, Zeke, and myself stopping and spying one last time around with the same results.

"So……..do you want a new friend," I said to Frankie as I patted Zeke on the head.

"Are you thinking about taking him?"

"Well, yes, I can't leave him here, he looks like he hasn't eaten in days. And I will come back when its daylight to get a better idea of what happened. I find it very odd that Otto would leave without any notice, mind you, he has done this before but never has left Zeke here on his own, they have been inseparable."

We decided it was the right thing to do, I opened the back door of my car and Zeke hopped in without hesitation. Frankie, on the other hand, was still holding on to that hunk of wood she had picked up from the debris in Otto's office.

"What's that?" I asked curiously.

"What's what?"

"Oh, I don't know, I tripped over it inside the office."

Shining the light on it, I could see it was the plank that Otto had hung in his shop. It was part of the sign that read 'Found from the alien ship in Roswell, NM, 1947 which at one time had the piece of a shiny silver object attached to it. Only now it was fractured and there was nothing attached to it.

The next morning, I wasted no time reporting the information to the local sheriff and filing a formal report. He assured me they would have someone out there to investigate although he didn't seem too concerned given Otto's relaxed reputation. Afterward, it was a quick stop at the general store for a supply of dog food, for which Mr. Martinez gave me a quizzical look about, then over to Frankie's to see how she was managing with her new housemate. As I arrived, she was having a grand old time of it, playing fetch with a rubber ball in the backyard. When I appeared, Zeke welcomed me playfully as well.

"Wow, it looks like you guys are just the best of friends out here."

"Yes, that happens when you have eaten your share of hamburgers, three to be exact. And then slept like a baby on my back porch."

"Oh, ok, well I feel like I have a six-month supply of dog food in my trunk. Are you okay to keep him for a while? Or at least, until we can find out about Otto?"

"I guess so, Vincent, but he is going to be here alone a lot, especially when I work a double shift."

"I know Frankie, I know, it's a lot to ask, but I would gladly take him to the Winchester, only I know that wouldn't go over so well. I need to find a place of my own right away."

"Uh, you do realize that I have two bedrooms here, and, well……if you……. "

“Frankie, we have come to know each pretty well in a short time, but if I entertained your offer, what kind of light would that put us in, I mean put you in? I mean people would talk, wouldn’t they?”

"Vincent, first and foremost, we are friends and friends care about each other, no matter what anybody has to say about it, and I only meant it as a last resort. Besides, it would be temporary, until you do find something else. And you know I don’t get so concerned about what people think anyway."

"Thanks for the offer, but, right now I am going to try and search for another alternative, I just think that would be best."

I could see a slight look of dejection come over her from my response, as I was feeling a bit of the same myself. Here I was, with an offer from a beautiful, caring, intelligent, strong woman and I didn't dare to accept. Friends or not, I just hoped that I wouldn't regret it someday.

* * *

The final year of school was considered to be the most enjoyable and at the same time, the most stressful. It was a time when the inevitable would be approaching, saying goodbye at this interval would have a sense of finality which we all were fully aware of.

Departing from my family was difficult without my father’s hardy farewell looming over me. I knew the course ahead would be a long one without his guidance and reassurance, but I believed that my extended family in Boston would help me survive. That’s how it came to be, that’s how we were known to each other. Four years of struggling together for the same goal creates something that binds you, forever. With Lizzy by my side and Johnny’s grit and watchful eye seeing me through, I felt secure.

We had staked our claim at The Conservatory; this graduating class had developed a designation that raised the bar for all those who were to follow. The underclassman looked up to us and the faculty had admitted several times that they hated to see our tenure come to an end. Our musical prowess had grown to extraordinary proportions and most every one of us was being recruited for different ensembles across the country. We had dedicated ourselves not only to this great institution, but also to the idea of becoming the best we could be. It was about passion, and the energy which fueled it became contagious.

Each time there was an extended break in the curriculum, I headed home, just as promised, often leaving after my last class on a Friday to return to Jersey by midnight. My routine continued and at times I was saddened to miss the extracurricular activities that all seniors were partaking in. Lizzy was attending parties with her girlfriends and there were many event invitations from other nearby colleges which were ongoing as well. I continued my part-time employment as often as I could and certain nights, when I would get home on the later side, I would call the dormitory payphone just to hear her voice, and for the most part, someone would always answer and let her know that I was on the other end of the line. Thankfully, the semester breaks seemed to pass rapidly, and I would return to the gang without missing a beat.

Up in the Boston area, things were progressing at a furious pace. New clubs were opening rapidity and students from the immediate area and beyond were coming into town. The economic atmosphere was changing, President Truman enacted the GI bill which allowed tuition grants for soldiers returning home to attend college. Thus, more patrons were frequenting the city nightlife and club owners like Dexter were cashing in.

As far as The Ravens Nest went, it had to keep in stride with the upspring of new venues, and Dexter was very adept at giving the audience what they wanted, as long it lined his pockets. And one of the main attractions that were hitting the heights was 'those youngsters from The Conservatory'. With competition heating up around the nightclub scene, we were more in demand than ever. Johnny was a master when it came to juggling our schedules between our daytime lives and the after-hours demands. But for me, things were about to take on yet another twist as wc were approaching the moment to introduce our newest addition.

“So, are you ready? Tomorrow, it’s your big debut.”

“I know, I know Angelo, I am a little scared.” Lizzy whispered timidly.

"It's a real different scene, but I know the crowd is going to love you, and besides I'll be there right beside you."

“I just can’t help but be a little nervous, what do I wear?”

"You always look good, just wear what you are wearing now."

She had on a pleated skirt down to her knees, a tight blue sweater (she filled out all her sweaters very easily, making them look tight) buttoned up to her neck and white wedge shoes. It was a look that I had grown accustomed to and she wore it well.

We went in like any other night, ready and confident. Our setlist was a combination of rhythm and blues with also the trendiest rock music we could come up with. We met on the north side of the building in the alley, it was our ritual that we would all make our entrance together through the back-stage door, in unison. Tonight, it wasn't just me and the boys, tonight she was with us. Her makeup done just right and looking adorable, she was going to steal the hearts of this crowd and we knew it. Once inside, we filed in, right in step, Johnny led the way, as always, then the rest of us with Lizzy in front of me as I brought up the rear.

Dexter, taking notice that we had a new member with us sauntered over to get the low down from Johnny.

"So, this is a surprise, who's the chick?" I overheard him say.

"That's Lizzy, she is the added dimension I was telling you about."

Johnny coolly motioned Lizzy to come over as he introduced her. Dexter tried not to look like he was taken by her, but we all got the feeling he was.

"I didn't know they served such hot dishes up that at that school." He said with a grin as he took her hand and held it for a longer length of time than he should have.

"Oh, thank you, Mr. Dexter." She said softly, withdrawing a bit from him.

"Please, if you are going to be a fixture around here, and I have a feeling you are, the name is Dex."

Johnny stepping in between them, turned Lizzy around as he stated that it was time for us to get ready for our set.

The announcer brought us out to the crowd with a roar, it was a full house, although it was difficult to see through the amount of smokey vapor that filled the place. I opened with our noted first number, *Rocket 88*, that got the joint jumping right away. The women shrieked as they filled the dance floor in front. Looking over at Lizzy I could see she was somewhat tentative, but with each tune we introduced, she became increasingly energetic. This was raw and hard biting rock and roll that people responded to. It consisted of biting guitar riffs, bold drumbeats, and synchronized harmonies. It wasn't the auditorium life where we would jam within the protected boundaries of our campus, this was music that made people move, it was music that was appreciated in an entirely different way.

Lizzy began to swing to the beat, banging her tambourine against the side of her leg as she delivered background vocals right on cue. Johnny gave a nod of acceptance as he drove that guitar from one hit into another. Next up was, *We're Gonna Rock, We're Gonna Roll* by Wild Bill Moore, which featured long solos by our sax player. Then it would be Lizzy's turn to strut her stuff.

I was nervous for her and secretly kept my fingers crossed. *Hole in the Wall*, by Albinia Jones, a top hit of 1949 was Lizzy's to reproduce. She started with apprehension missing the first queue, Johnny picked up on it and covered it quickly with an impromptu guitar lick. I looked at her and motioned.

"It's ok, keep going........"

In minutes, she came to life, dancing around her corner of the stage, blasting the lyrics into the microphone. Looking down, there wasn't an empty space on the dance floor. The lights were hot, the music was loud, the drinks were flowing, and we were having the time of our life. By the time we had completed our standard set and a roof-burning rendition of Billy Wards, *60 Minute Man*, we were drenched with sweat and exited out immediately into the back alley to cool off.

Johnny came out with ice-cold Pepsi's for all of us, and we chugged them down before we could look up.

"Guys, we blew them away tonight, we were frantic and disastrous, they loved us. And you (pointing to Lizzy) why did we wait so long to get you here?" He said as they both laughed.

It was a jubilant moment and we were feeling our oats. I stood there with my arm around her soaking it all in, as Johnny continued.

"Alright, gents, and gal, I have news for you, Dexter wants us booked every weekend, semester breaks and especially during the summer months when the out of towners roll in. We are going to be the regular act, no more opening up for someone else. And that means more bread too!"

The gang was filled with joyous emotion as everyone started clamoring around.

Everyone that is............ besides me.

7

I was ready, yes, I was ready to tackle whatever Father Tom was going to throw at me. After breakfast, I made my way over to the church to seek him out. I had on an old pair of trousers, work boots, and a white tee shirt that was slightly stained with car grease on one of the sleeves. I thought of it as, my working attire. The church doors were locked once again, so I followed the same path that Frankie and I took the last time we were here.

Out in the workshop, in back, I found no one there either. I hoped that I wasn't mistaken, and Father Tom hired someone else. I was sure I had gotten my days right, it was precisely one week from our last meeting. Taking the time to look around, I saw several workbenches that were terribly unorganized, tools were strewn about everywhere. There was scrap wood piled in every corner of the place and sawdust and debris randomly scattered about. In the far-right hand back corner was a shabby old pick-up truck with a wooden flatbed attached to its backside. And a decrepit old ladder that looked as if it was the very thing that Father Tom had been working on when we first met.

"Good morning Vincent." A voice exclaimed behind me.

Startled, I turned suddenly with a jerk.

"Good Morning Father."

This time he looked quite the part, wearing the customary black shirt and pants with the traditional white collar. It was a look that I was very used to seeing and respecting in my youth.

"Didn't mean to sneak up on you like that, but I just finished locking the doors after morning mass."

"Oh, that's quite alright, Father, I didn't know where I should find you, so I just came around back, hoping that was okay."

"Yes, perfectly fine, since this is where we…… I mean you, will be doing most of the work, building sets for the feast and all."

"Uh, what is it exactly that I will be building, what do you mean 'sets'?"

"Ahhh, we will go over all that soon enough, but maybe it would be a good idea to start by getting this place in order. I'm sorry it's such a mess, I just don't have the time to keep up organizing everything back here."

"Great idea, Father, I will get this place cleaned up in a jiffy."

I worked all day and well into the night, past the five o'clock hour that was predetermined. Throwing myself into the task at hand, I lost track of time. Four oversized wooden crates on the left side of the shack were now filled with scrap wood, broken parts of tools, fragments of concrete, and general debris. Finding a bucket of old nails, I took the liberty of using them to hang and arrange all the working tools on the back wall. After completely sweeping up the entire place, I turned my attention to the old pick-up truck. On the bed lay matted piles of hay and small wooden boxes of nails, screws, and rivets. Organizing those, I managed to clean out the bed and the inside of the truck itself. It was littered with old soda pop bottles and candy wrappers. Behind the front seat, I found an old shotgun, with some of its parts, dirty and rusty, most likely used for hunting or scaring off wild animals. Having never fired a gun in my life, I left it there, making a mental note to let Father Tom know about it. The keys for the truck were nowhere in the vicinity, so trying to start it up and move it out of the way would have to wait for another day, although seeing it in its current condition, I doubted it would start at all.

"Vincent, I see you are still at it." Said Father Tom as he stood there viewing the job I had done.

“I can’t remember when I have ever seen this place looking as good as it does now.” He continued with his hands on his hips and a look of astonishment.

“Uh, thank you, Father.”

I was exhausted, grimy, and drenched with sweat as I sat on one of the more stable benches nearby.

"It is nearly half-past six, you didn't have to do this all in one day, but I must say, I do appreciate it." He resounded, as he sat down next to me.

"I’ll be back tomorrow Father and start working on fixing these benches, by the way, is that the only ladder you have available?"

I asked, pointing to the splintered and battered-looking one leaning up against the side of the pick-up.

"Oh, that ladder is going to be the death of me yet, it's been around for ages and needs much repair, if you can get that in better shape, it would be a wonder. Three years ago, I fell from it when one of the rungs broke. Thank God, I was only about five feet up, landed right on my elbow, Doctor Coots had me in a cast for two months."

"I'll give it a try and see what I can do with it when I get the chance," I responded.

“Go home now Vincent, have a meal, get yourself cleaned up and get some rest, I’ll see you in the morning.”

Just what I was thinking too, but I didn’t want to mention that home for me was a hotel room. In any event, I climbed into Denise with weary legs and drove slowly over to the Winchester. Too tired to eat, I went upstairs, peeled off my dirty clothes and took a long, much-needed shower. A few minutes later, I was in my bed, out like a light.

As Father Tom said, there was much work to be done for the festivities to be successful, it was not only a big event for the community, but it would also, hopefully, raise money for the church.

The next morning, I reported to my new assignment, as promised. Father Tom was out in the workshop waiting for me with two cups of coffee and a brown bag filled with hunks of corn skillet bread, lightly dusted with sugar. He also had with him a stack of plans that, in some fundamental way, resembled blueprints.

"Good morning, I thought you might like a traditional town favorite." He said as he held up the bag in my direction.

"I was out early and stopped at the diner, your friend Frankie made sure that I was to deliver these. Nice girl that Frankie. Come sit down, have some, then we will get a look at these plans."

We sat there for several minutes enjoying our Mara Del Santos breakfast, compliments of 'my friend' Frankie at the diner. And it was comforting to know that she was thinking of me.

After we had our fill, Father Tom spread out the pile of papers he brought with him. We discussed each one and what I needed to do, more importantly, the time frame I had to accomplish it in. There were to be deliveries of donated raw materials that were scheduled to arrive each day for the next week or so, that would allow me to continually work as planned. The diagrams included a dunking station, a kissing booth, and several smaller structures that were to be used for various food locations.

But the largest job, much to my amazement, was building a bandstand for the announcer and speechmakers, and, of course, the musical performers. Sometimes the irony in life catches up to you when you least expect it. I had spent many hours standing on a stage, now it was something I had to construct for others. I knew right then and there, I had my work cut out for me. This was to be no easy undertaking, and I would have to draw on my experience, knowledge, and memory from some of the things my father had taught me. Looking over at it all, I silently hoped I was up for the job.

"Just a couple of questions, if I may Father?"

"Sure, ask away."

"That old pick-up in there, it would great if we could move it out, it takes up a lot of room. Are there keys? Does it run?"

I secretly wished that my friend Otto were around, I knew he would be able to get it going and bring it back to life.

"Well, it's been here a long time, I would think it needs a new battery to start with. As far as I know, it was last used by Father Ortiz. He lived in the small house about a quarter of a mile from here and would walk over most of the time not utilizing the truck too often. If you look hard and squint your eyes you can see his house on the horizon towards the south. I will be going there this week to pack up the rest of his belongings to send off to him and his family, and while I'm there, I will look to see if there are any keys."

And you said a couple of questions, "What else is there?"

"I was just wondering why the church doors are always locked?"

"Oh, I see you've noticed. It's been a necessity for some time. There have been some attempts of theft here, and since I'm the only one around, I have no choice but to lock everything up tight, in between church services."

"Thefts? Why would anyone want to steal anything from here, Father?"

"You haven't been inside yet, have you, Vincent?" He said rather suspiciously as he continued.

"I think we should study these plans right now and get started on the construction as soon as possible, perhaps in a day or two, we'll go inside. Or you could always attend morning mass if you feel inclined to?" He stated as I noticed a tiny semblance of sarcasm in his voice.

I didn't think much about what he seemed to be alluding to and set my focus on the pile of papers in front of me. I knew that he was depending on me and so was the entire town. The Feast was the biggest event for miles around, and everyone was abuzz about it. Even the school children were talking about it months in advance.

And as word spread of my endeavors, each time I found it necessary to make my way into town, someone would stop to ask how the construction was coming along. Frankie, herself, knowing how important the feast was, didn't expect me to be around as much, although I would try and make a quick visit at times to check up on how she and Zeke were getting on, and to let her know how I was progressing.

I worked from sunrise to sunset for many days. I had dedicated myself to this chore and vowed to see it through to completion. At first, my novice skills had left me in a bit of a quandary, but as many things in life go, the more you do of a certain activity, the better you become, and sometimes, the more you learn in the process.

There were times where I struggled with the old tools that were provided me, and when things didn't turn out as plans dictated, I improvised to the best of my ability. Stepping back, and seeing what I had accomplished each day, sometimes, I even managed to impress myself. I knew what it took to satisfy a crowd, I knew about the pressures of deadlines, but this time I was working strictly from behind the scenes, and I not only enjoyed it, I began to prefer it. At this juncture in my life, I thought the spotlight would be better off directed elsewhere.

* * *

The memories we created during our time together were those which we would forever cherish long after we would leave. The Conservatory had served as a major influence in our lives and the days towards graduation were winding down. There were no more unmitigated jitters regarding our final performance, we had matured beyond the level of average stage fright, we had become accomplished musicians.

For Lizzy and me, we had discussed several times having a life together after graduation, and now, the possibilities were becoming a reality. We both had extremely promising futures, and when the news came that I was invited to try out for the Boston Pops Orchestra, I couldn't contain myself. The Pops had never really incorporated vocalists within their fabric, so when the invitation came, it was something I was extremely proud of and at the same time, excited for. It was for the position of a junior intern to start, but it paid a decent wage and was an opportunity that very few received right after completing school.

Lizzy, on the other hand, was being recruited on the academic side of life. Two separate universities had scheduled interviews for her to become part of their prestigious faculty. In any event, if we both landed our respective positions, we would be able to support a comfortable life together. Johnny too wanted to stay in the area, he had established a reputation as a talented, popular, and well-known guitarist with a following, and many bands and clubs were trying to sign him. But what he wanted to do was to cultivate our band, the one which he originally had roots in and one which had now grown in recognition as a local favorite.

As far as the Raven's Nest went, it was gaining a character for drawing some of the biggest acts around and packing the house almost every night. And we were fast becoming one of the better-known headliners. The more we played together, the tighter we became, and with each gig, we sounded more professional. With our popularity rising, Johnny was approached to see if we were also interested in playing outside private events such as occasional weddings and private parties. It was a bit tamer, and more social an environment, but the money was extremely tempting. And in the music scene, you have to strike while the iron is hot.........and we were hot!

Scheduling was difficult and it became a balancing act especially for me, as I was leaving for home during each school break. The thought that the band may have to turn down jobs due to my absence, weighed heavily on my mind. It was then that a solution began to emerge, one that would have far-reaching implications.

As my stints at home sometimes lasted a day or two longer than expected. The trips became more frequent as my concern for family grew. And on most Sunday Nights on my return trips back to Boston, I would end up taking the late train back and head straight to my room where I would fall right into bed.

"Kid, you got some time, I gotta talk to you," Johnny said as he came sauntering in.

"Sure, Johnny, I'm all ears."

"I know it's been hard for you, with your dad gone and all, and you having to pick up the pieces at home, and you know I love you like a brother, right?"

At that point, I sat up more alertly, having a bad feeling to where this conversation was headed.

"Ok, let me have it, it's about the band, isn't it?"

"It is, kid, it is. You know I would never do anything behind your back, but something happened the other night when you were gone. Dexter called me in a pinch, his scheduled act got hit with a stomach bug or something and he needed a fill-in, on the spot. I rounded up the guys, and yes, Lizzy too, and we shot over to the Nest."

"Holy Cow, I'm sorry that I couldn't be there Johnny, really sorry." I said in a dejected tone.

"But who took the lead on my numbers?" I continued looking puzzled.

"That's where it gets overcooked, kid. We just raced down there expecting to do whatever we could when he caught us by surprise, just before we went on."

"Who caught you......what happened?"

"Dexter! He just grabbed the mike, and went right into the set with us, he seemed to know the lyrics and took the lead automatically."

Stunned, I sat there not knowing how to react. Part of me felt anger beginning to rise, part of me felt regret for not being able to be there for my friends. I somehow knew that Dexter would capitalize on our success whichever way he could. I was in a state of bewilderment as I tried to comprehend it.

"So……. how did it go then?" I asked, trying to keep calm.

"Of course, it wasn't anywhere as good without you kid, that much is true. But it wasn't that bad, and I think the crowd had a lot of alcohol in them already, anyway."

I knew this was inevitable ever since Dexter proclaimed that we would be a lead act in his place. I feared the worse and now it all began to unfold just as I thought. Johnny went on to explain as respectfully as he possibly could and tried to emphasize that it was only a temporary fix. Nights and weekends were crucial in the music industry and because I didn't have the freedom to be there at times, it would be necessary for them to adjust the best they could. He even said that they all agreed to hand over to me a share of whatever they earned. I refused, I didn't believe in accepting anything I wasn't pulling my own weight for.

We decided that for the time being it was the most convenient scenario for all involved, and I would still be there for most gigs anyway, although Dexter would now have to come and join in our rehearsals.

With a feeling of helplessness and disbelief, I did the best I could trying to deal with this new wrinkle as I continued to look towards the future.

Lizzy came to me the next morning as I was getting ready for class with a strong feeling of apprehension knowing that Johnny had discussed with me this new strategy.

"Hi Angelo, you in there?" she whispered outside my door as she gently knocked.

"Hi honey, yeah give me a minute, I'll be right out."

And closing the door behind me, I greeted her with a morning kiss in the hallway.

"It's kind of early, and I was wondering if we could get a quick practice session in if you have time." She asked.

"As a matter of fact, I do, let's go."

The practice rooms on campus were rather small, approximately six feet by six feet with an upright piano occupying most of the space. We had ventured in them often between classes, to go over sheet music, not to mention these were convenient places to take advantage of being alone.

"Hold on Liz, before you say anything, let me do the talking here.......... Let's go, right now, I mean let's just go and do it." I blurted out with a tone of unexpected enthusiasm.

"Do what? What are you talking about?"

Smiling with nervous energy and directing my gaze directly at her, I held on to her, while I continued wildly.

"Let's take off and go get married, I mean today, I mean right now."

The silence became deafening as we just froze together.

"I mean, I know how I feel about you and you feel about me, so why wait, let's just get the hell outta here and find a way to do it right away!"

She stared at me in a state of total bewildered and surprise. I had blindsided her with my request and at the same time, this unplanned proposal had caught me in a sudden condition of amazement. It was out of the blue, and without any consideration. I let an overwhelming air of affection decide what I was suggesting, something extremely out of character for me, something I had never let happen before.

"What!......... Angelo, don't joke around like that."

"I'm not, I'm serious let's go, right now!"

"Have you lost your mind? We can't do anything like that. What about your mom, my parents, school? You know I love you but think about what you are asking. Let's get through school first, there will be time for that later. Just you wait."

She smiled and kissed me intently calming me from my hasty outburst, before the discussion turned back to the matter at hand.

We both knew what had taken place over the weekend and it was up to me whether to accept it or create a stir. I, of course, chose to do what was best for the evolution of the band and took into full consideration the benefits of my bandmates. Besides, I had an invitation looming from one of the most well-known orchestras forthcoming and should regard the band only as a secondary notion.

Rehearsals with Dexter ran smoothly in the beginning. Surprisingly, he was laid back and went out of his way attempting to become everyone's friend, including myself. I wasn't sure how to accept him and always kept my guard up. Lizzy, on the other hand, showed her naivety at times, Dexter would try to come across as the big brother, guardian type, as he tried to gain her confidence. He would sit in the background watching and studying all we did, expressing his opinion just on certain occasions. Knowing that he was some ten years older than any of us, he would be persistent in trying to portray the impression as the wiser, more astute soul and that his experience in the music world was incomparable to what we had learned through our formal education.

As the days marched on, graduation was in full view. The final performance we were about to give was well in hand. And for the last time, family, friends and the general public were going to fill our concert hall. School rehearsals were going strong, with Z Klein showing a sense of confidence never displayed before. There was no doubt that this was going to fill the expectations of everyone in attendance. And once we had laid it all to rest, all that was left to do, was to complete our Conservatory curriculum and move on to the opportunities which lay around the corner.

Lizzy returned from both her interviews in high spirits and within a few days, she got offers from both universities. Looking at her options she chose the one that allowed her to live off-campus, in the heart of Boston, a decision I was very happy with. Myself, I gloriously handled my audition and was given notice directly afterward of my acceptance, requesting me to begin my internship immediately. This meant working double duty, maintaining my school schedule, and participating at least one day a week in my new position. As usual, I accepted the challenge.

Sharing our incredible news, we planned a romantic dinner, in downtown Boston to celebrate. It was there that we decided that once school was finished, we could conceivably tie the knot, look for a flat which was convenient for both of us, and start the next phase of our lives together.

* * *

With each passing day and with each nail I drove into the wooden structures now surrounding me under the heat of the arid New Mexico temperatures, certain configurations began to take shape. One after another the plans that were laid out began to materialize with only some minor deviations. As each construction came to completion, I would arrange them around the outside perimeter of the workshop area. It looked like a carnival itself could have been held right there behind the church.

I was so particularly fond of what I had been accomplishing, I felt inclined to swing by Frankie's, pick her and Zeke up and drive them over to see what was materializing.

"See. I knew it, I knew you were handy with those tools, just like I told Father Tom." She said excitedly.

She walked around the entire area with a childlike look of amazement, touching and climbing on each structure as she came upon them. Zeke jumped and climbed up and down sets of stairs which led to platforms, he also seemed to be completely enjoying himself.

"I guess you were right then, but I must admit, I wasn't sure I had it in me. And the best part is, I'm ahead of schedule....... I think."

"Has Father Tom seen this setup yet?"

"Not yet, I haven't seen him in a few days, I think he has been out at Father Ortiz's place to finish packing up and clean everything out."

"So, it seems you do have hidden talents, Mr. Vincent!" She stated as she playfully jumped off the ramp she was standing on.

"What! what do you mean?"

"I mean, who knew that you are one hell of a carpenter, what did you think I was referring to?"

"Oh......... Oh, yeah that, right, who knew."

I continued to set my sights on finishing all I could earlier than scheduled, as it would give me more time to spend with Frankie and Zeke. In the meantime, I would stop at the sheriff's office occasionally to see if there were any new updates on Otto, but my efforts were to no avail.

The excitement level began to grow throughout town as the date of the feast was nearing. I had come to know that feeling of anticipation quite well in the past and for a moment, now, found it a bit stimulating. The women were planning their menus, the Sherriff and other authorities had recruited volunteers to work the different booths and local merchants were set to do their part lending a helping hand to complete the final set up.

The sight for the festivities was the open-air pavilion centrally located, and access could be gained from all directions. With the assistance of several townspeople, the bandstand was moved into place. Then the format of the other structures was set around it. Lights had been strung from end to end, covering the circumference of the entire pavilion. I found myself acting as a foreman, directing the entire operation, and shouting out orders as positively as I could. Cars would circle and slow down to witness what we were doing, even the set-up became a spectacle to an awestruck viewing audience as they passed by.

A hot and sultry August night was scheduled for the opening festivities. The crowd in attendance outnumbered anything that Father Tom had expected. It all began with the signal of lights, a firework display, which the children were most fond of. A traditional Spanish-American band from the neighboring county, complete with mariachis handled the introductory music, as Father Tom took the stage for a moment of prayer and welcoming remarks.

In the air were consistent odors of delectable foods, barbecue pits with smoke emanating from them delivering the nonstop aromas. There were balloons of all colors, bright lights, and girls adorned in their fanciest dresses.

I could hear the sounds and see the sights from my window at the Winchester. I had spent the last two and one-half months hammering, sawing, and drilling and the callouses on my hands were proof enough of that. Now sitting at this vantage point, it was fulfilling to see the work being enjoyed by so many, perhaps the carpenter inside was the vocation that was meant for me.

Not wanting to receive any accolades, I was reluctant at first to make my way down and join the crowd. But as I sat there watching the activity in the distance, I knew Frankie would be there, we had planned to meet around eight o'clock and if I didn't show up on a night like this, I might as well call it quits with her. So, without any further hesitation, I proceeded to get myself looking respectable, put on some clean trousers, a brand new green shirt, which I was holding out for a special occasion, and worked up the courage to make my way out towards the celebrations.

I strolled through the grounds, mingling about, seeing many faces that were not familiar to me. Everyone there was quite distracted with all the activities taking place at once. There was an oversized gazebo that was brought in to cover the makeshift dance floor set up near the bandstand. Wandering over towards it, I spotted Frankie with the two other waitresses from the diner, Tess and Rita.

“Hello ladies,” I said as I addressed the three of them.

"Hello, Mr. Vincent." Giggling, they responded almost in unison.

As I drew closer to them, Tess and Rita, intentionally moved slowly off in another direction leaving myself and Frankie alone. She looked beautiful, displaying a vibrant look of youthfulness. She was wearing a blue poodle skirt with a white blouse and white Keds sneakers. Her hair was pulled back in a ponytail, tied with a small blue silk ribbon.

“You look like you are ready for these celebrations tonight.” I stated.

“I am, and I sure hope you will be able to keep up with me buddy boy!”

She took my hand as she smiled openly and pulled me energetically towards the tilt-a-whirl. As we stood in line amongst a much younger crowd, I felt like we were a couple of teenagers ourselves. It was a moment that I had never really experienced before. Sometimes, you get to make up for lost time, it may happen very infrequently, and it may occur in a brief instant, but when it does, you need to recognize it, hold onto it, and embrace it. At that moment, I owed her a debt of gratitude.

That feeling continued throughout the evening, Frankie had me take part in the full experience of the feast, from the food, to the games of chance, to the various booths, (except the kissing booth, she steered me away from that one quite conspicuously). It had been a long time since I let loose and enjoyed myself as I did that night. I even managed to win a stuffed animal for her, it was a gray plush monkey, Curious George by name, wearing a sewed on red shirt and a baseball cap to match with a large white letter G on its chest. Frankie paraded around all night with it cradled in her arms. As far as the musical acts went, there weren't any there that struck me as being as good as I hoped for, but I suppose my standards would never be the same. Then it was one last ride, as the night began to dwindle.

We sat together on the Ferris wheel as it began its backward climb. Stopping at the top for several minutes almost had me drifting into a daring state of mind.

The night had already been unforgettable, and as we sat there with the car rocking gently, the thought of leaning over and kissing her became more evident than ever before. And just as I pondered the idea, the great wheel began to turn and slowly lower us to the ground as we heard the music from the bandstand echoing in the distance.

"Okay, Vincent seems as though we have only one thing left to do here tonight." She said with a gleam in her eye.

"And what would that be?" I responded knowing full well what was about to transpire.

"C'mon'. " She said as she gently tugged my shirt. It was off to the gazebo where many folks were dancing in the moonlight.

There was a five-piece band transported from Texas. It was made up of mostly middle-aged men and consisted of two guitarists, a saxophone player, a lead singer, and a drummer. We got to the edge of the crowded dance floor when they were attempting to play Frankie Avalon's, *Venus*.

"Well then, you know why we are here, I think you still owe me a dance?"

"Yes, I suppose I do," I said hesitantly.

In the next minute, as the drummer counted four, we were out on the dance floor moving like two people who had danced together, forever. The melodies changed in several stretches and our steps right with it. The crowd noticed as we put together some unexpected swing moves. Frankie's look became one of wonder towards me, while we went on for at least three more songs before the tempo turned to something much more mellow again.

We started dancing slowly as I held her in my arms.

"Who are you, Mr. Vincent?" She whispered in my ear, as she caught her breath.

We moved together in harmony as I was holding her closer than I ever had before. The thought that crept in, while we were on the Ferris Wheel was moving upon me again, only this time my courage was on the rise. I looked at her intensely, and she seemed to reciprocate, the moment felt right, I placed my hand gently behind her head.

"Well, there the two of you are!" Father Tom called out as he approached us.

"Oh hi, Father", we both said, acknowledging his presence as we stopped in our tracks.

“I have some very important news, may I have a minute of your time Vincent, and ah, Frankie, you may as well come along too.”

“Um, any chance it could wait until tomorrow Father?” I said, as I still held Frankie’s hand in mine pressed to my chest, while the other was now wrapped around her waist.

“NO, NO. my son! ……. It is of the utmost importance for me, and for you, especially for you! I need to speak to you right away, while the representative from the bishop’s office is still here.”

With great concern, I took Frankie’s hand and followed Father Tom at a quickened pace. He moved hurriedly along as we made haste through the crowd to a quieter, darkened area, away from the bandstand and the bustling crowd.

My alternating duties at home, combined with my new internship and finishing up my course load, left me little or no time to practice with the band. Dexter took the lead as I suspected he would. The more they practiced together, the more he gained their confidence. They were not only playing to packed crowds at The Ravens Nest, but the weekends were now filled with well-paying gigs throughout the wedding scene, as well. It was then that I began to notice a change in Lizzy. Perhaps I should have seen the signs sooner, but with the chaotic schedule I was keeping, I was too distracted.

It was subtle at first, her dress style became more contemporary, and provocative at times. Her sweaters and blouses became low cut, while her skirts got tighter. Dexter had one of his cocktail waitresses take her shopping, at his expense of course, for a new wardrobe. And the more time she spent at The Nest, the more indiscreet her look became. Each time I brought up my concerns, she would argue that it was in the 'best interest of the band and that Dexter knew what he was doing, and his experience knew just how to 'win over an audience'.

Practice sessions, without me, were lasting longer than usual. And when I was present, I started to feel as though Lizzy began to look up to him or even admire him. I was told that her and Dexter were even spending time together during breaks, between sets, at those weddings. And he had (conveniently) comprised a list of love songs which were primarily duets, geared for the two of them.

They began rehearsing, many times, apart from the rest of the band, just the two of them. Dexter would have her come to his flat on Saturday afternoons while his live-in girlfriend was at work, to go over, as he put it, 'their harmonies'. One Saturday became two, then another and another, their personal practice sessions went on for several weeks in succession.

I tried to ignore the thoughts that were running through my head, I tried to keep my fears from becoming an obsession and leaned on the primary fact that I trusted Lizzy. Besides she had come from a very wholesome upbringing and I knew she was level-headed and always exercised good judgment. We had already been through much together and soon graduation would lead us away from The Nest anyway.

And when Johnny also made his mind up that he would be staying in the area after school was over, the three of us decided that after Lizzy and I got married, we would look for a 2-bedroom flat that would accommodate the three of us. The plan seemed infallible and I was banking on it.

Sometimes in life, we are sent messages. We may not know where they come from, or who exactly is trying to tell us something, but they are there. We may not want to believe in them or may even try to deny their existence, but they are still there.

Mine was in the form of dreams. Dreams, not of the fulfilling type, dreams that had me confused, dreams that were subtly tormenting, and became difficult to endure. Maybe it was my deep concerns entering my subconscious, or maybe I was just becoming paranoid. In any event, the vividness of my dreams was persistent and clear. They were dreams of Lizzy and Dexter.

They started slowly, at first. I would see visions of them together, very close together, kissing, hugging and laughing, in isolated places. They would only last briefly in the beginning, like watching scenes from a movie that faded out quickly. But as time went on, the growing scenarios became more intense with a longer duration.

I had heard it said that dreams are infrequently remembered, but these, would vividly awake me in the middle of the night with a racing heart and an immersing cold sweat. I couldn't help but remember every detail of them the next day. During my studies, practice sessions, or any part of my daily life, I had a tough time focusing, my thoughts would always wander back to Lizzy and Dexter. Feeling like a fog had enveloped me, many people, including Lizzy, and of course, Johnny, began to take notice.

"Okay, what the hell is going on with you these days?" Johnny inquired as the two of us sat at the cafeteria table before anyone else arrived.

"Johnny, I think I'm going out of my mind!" I said in a severely panicked state.

"Whoa, let's get outta here kid, c'mon, take a walk with me outside."

Once away from the cafeteria crowd, I told Johnny everything that had been running through my head, I told him about the dreams, how I saw the two of them making out in the back seat of her car. I told him how things between me and Lizzy seemed different and how I felt like I was not only suddenly losing her, but also a grip on reality.

"Slow down, slow down kid, you better calm down before you break a blood vessel! Yeah, you are losing it! Look, kid, I have been there at those weddings, I have been there at The Nest, and I have been there at all the practices. Yeah, Dexter has gotten a little chummy with her, but he does that with every woman he comes in contact with. And he always says how he wishes you were there, so he could get a break from all the singing he's been doing."

"Johnny, I can't help it, it's driving me crazy, I can't sleep right, don't feel like eating and I'm really having a rough time concentrating!"

"Kid, I think you are overreacting, from what I can see, nothing is going on. Everybody knows how Dexter is with women, but do you think Lizzy would fall for that?"

"No, uh, well I sure hope not," I said rather reluctantly, backing down a bit as we headed back inside.

"I don't know any more Johnny, maybe your right. Call it intuition, but I can't see things straight. I feel like when they're together, well I just seem to sense something happening between them, it's the way she's been acting around him, giggling, laughing, almost in a flirty kind of way. And he, well I just have suspicions that he is leading her on somehow. Maybe it's all just building up in my mind, and those damn dreams don't help either."

Johnny went on trying to calm me down and reinforcing the fact that I was making too much of it. We both agreed that the best thing for me to do was to confront Lizzy at some point and tell her how I felt.

Facing Lizzy with such thoughts was a situation I was not looking forward too, but the dreams kept haunting me and I knew I had to put the subject to rest one way or another. It seemed like the perfect opportunity as we had plans to catch a movie that very night. We were headed to the old Arlington Theater down on Tremont street where they were screening '*The Bachelor and The Bobbysoxer*, starring Cary Grant and Shirley Temple.

Parking the car about a block away, we strolled hand in hand just as we had always done. There was a slight chill in the air, and I put my arm around her as we approached the theater. A small crowd was milling outside underneath the brightly lit marquee.

"Hey, before we go inside, there is something I have to talk to you about?" I said as I moved us slightly further away from the entrance.

"Uh, okay, what is it, Angelo?"

It was then I told her exactly what I confessed to Johnny. I went on about my dreams and my suspicions. I explained it all in grave detail and how it was doing me in. I pleaded with her to tell me the truth, even if it wasn't what I wanted to hear.

"Angelo, please! Nothing is going on with me and Dexter, that's just crazy talk." She managed to say very abruptly as if she was angry at me for even hinting at such a thing.

"I don't want to hear another word about that, now can we please go in and see the movie?"

Not fully comprehending her reaction I wasn't sure if I should have been relieved or puzzled, I decided to not pursue it any further that night, Lizzy was my love and my life, I had never felt this way about anyone else and if she said nothing had happened between them, then I should believe her, after all, what is love without trust?

Two days later things began to fall apart.

Once again, a three-day holiday weekend found me back home in Jersey, still with an unsatisfied resolution in my gut and a heavy heart notwithstanding. I wanted nothing more than to believe her, I wanted nothing more than to know that our lives were about to continue in the most loving way possible, yet something continued to eat at me.

It was the end of another stay, away from the gang in Boston, I began to pack up the day before, to get ready for the long trek back. My car had been parked in the driveway for some time, as was riding the rails more often, yet this time, I elected to drive back rather than take the train. There was only about a week left before graduation and I could a head start by loading up my trunk with belongings from my dorm room. The plan was to get a good night's sleep so that I wouldn't tire behind the wheel. That good night's sleep was never to come.

This time the dream was unrelenting, this time it was more than I had envisioned before. This time they were bearing it all, and I was there to witness the entire scene as I saw them, clearly, in my bed, Dex and Lizzy, together! At that moment, it sounded as if a gun went off and I was shot in the back. Startled, I arose, my tee-shirt drenched with sweat, it was three o'clock in the morning and I found myself pacing in my room with my heart beating uncontrollably.

Staring at the ceiling for much of the night, I tried to remain as calm as possible, I tried to think about Johnny's words and Lizzy's rebuttal. What else was I able to do at that moment? In times of turmoil, I had always been able to turn to my faith. It was the only thing that gave me reassurance that I would overcome any trial or obstacle I was confronted with. And making up mind, I decided this was to be no different.

Blurry eyed and with a pounding headache, I packed up my car the next morning, said goodbye to mom and sis and headed out. My first stop was church, before any morning mass had started or any of the congregation had arrived, I sat in the back, in solitude and prayed about my hunches, those dreams, and for an answer, a truthful answer.

8

I drove frantically, running mostly on adrenaline and the three cups of coffee I consumed before hitting the road. It would take me nearly six hours to get back to Boston and I knew there was much work left to be done when I got there. Trying to keep my wits about me, I concentrated on the final week of school and my pending assignments. There were two final papers and my senior recital which needed to be completed, not to mention the final school extravaganza which was to take place in three days.

Each time the thought of Lizzy and Dexter entered my thoughts, I would do my best to fight it off using any means possible. Turning up the radio, singing at the top of my lungs, visualizing being on stage, or just picturing having a peaceful married life with her, would prevent my consciousness from falling into a deep abyss. I was determined not to let those thoughts become the ruination of all I strived so hard for.

Trying to adopt a new attitude, for the time being, I went in for my last hurrah with guns blazing. Buckling down, I worked feverishly to complete my music theory paper and my composition proposal. After being satisfied with those results, I knocked my senior recital out of the park and got ready for the last and final performance. My relationship with Lizzy had been strained by continually questioning her with my suspicions, so I thought it better to hold back for a while, or at least for a more opportune time to discuss it further.

The band continued rocking the joint at The Ravens Nest and were persistently being booked on the wedding circuit every weekend. In doing so, they were pulling in a good amount of cash. I stood back in the shadows thinking that my future with Lizzy would soon lead us off in another direction completely. But with the band's ongoing success and its popularity growing, I learned through my bandmates, that Lizzy had hinted to continue with it after graduation. With the lasting effects of my last dream still lingering, my instincts took over and I decided to confront her one last time.

Back in my dorm room, I had not seen or heard from her since I returned. This was an extremely stressful week and I chalked it up to the fact that she was also scrambling to finish things up. Besides she was also spending much time getting set up at her newly acquired university position. It was a demanding post and required her to be there for informative meetings several times a week. She was even given a small office of her own, furnished with a desk, bookcases and a phone. Lizzy made friends quickly and had established a rapport with two other female faculty members, who I was introduced to, and was accepted by immediately.

The school was on the emptier side of things; many students had completed their work and were already packed up for the summer. I hadn't seen Johnny for nearly three weeks as he was extremely entrenched himself in his ongoing guitar play all about town.

Taking a well-deserved nap, in an abnormally quiet dormitory was something I wasn't accustomed to, and for the first time in four years, I welcomed it. But sleep for me was not to be peaceful and the dream I had experienced only a couple of nights ago was now repeating itself. Lizzy and Dexter, again, holding each other like lovers do, in my own bed! This time I awoke immediately, I needed to get to the bottom of this. For weeks, I had felt like I was going insane, everyone has their limits and I had finally reached mine.

Out of my bedroom, it was half-past three in the afternoon when I dashed down the hall, wearing only a pair of old khaki pants, I headed directly for

Lizzy's room on the girl's floor. Not caring too much about the implications, I went straight to her door and knocked several times emphatically. After several minutes, the door across the hallway slightly opened with Nancy, a clarinet player and a good friend of Lizzy's leaning her head out.

"She's not there, or didn't you get the hint by now?" she said in an annoyed manner over my persistent knocking.

"Any idea where she might be?" I ask exasperated.

"I wasn't keeping track today, but you may want to try her new office, she has been there a lot lately."

Acting on her information, I ran back up to my room, grabbed some loose change from my desk drawer, and proceeded back down to the hallway payphone located in the front vestibule. Dialing her office number with a purpose, it rang several times before she answered.

"Lizzy, it's me, I need to talk to you right away!"

My voice displaying a sense of urgency that she had never heard before.

"Ange, what is it, what's the matter?"

"I need to know, I can't take it anymore, these dreams are killing me, I am losing my mind, if you love me like you say you do, then PLEASE.........PLEASE, just tell me the truth. Has anything happened with you and Dexter!"

I stood there bare-chested and shoeless as students passed by through the entrance doors looking at me strangely. On the other end of the phone line, waiting for Lizzy's response, I heard nothing but silence, dead silence. Saying nothing in return, I stood there waiting for her to answer.

Several moments passed in what seemed like an eternity.

Then quietly and steadily, she began to cry.

In stunned silence I held the receiver slightly away from my ear, her sobbing became more predominant. Slowly, saying nothing, I hung up the phone.

Staring out into space, I made my way sluggishly back to my room. There, I laid on my bed, staring at the ceiling trying to comprehend the entire situation. I reviewed the dreams, examining every detail in my mind. Then, being as naïve as I was and in a state of dour disbelief, I sat up with one more dismantling thought.

Finding my way back down to that payphone, I dialed her number once again, she answered right away.

“I just have one more question.” I sternly stated.

"Yes?" She said, as I could still hear her sniffling between tears.

"DID YOU SLEEP WITH HIM?" My voice was now filled with a wave of quiet anger.

Again, nothing.............then a stream of loud tears followed which told me the entire story.

“DID YOU SLEEP WITH HIM?” I repeated louder as I knew I needed to hear her answer.

Then hearing her voice, in a very soft and terrified whisper, she responded.

“Yes.”

The events which followed were some that I was not proud of, nor defined the person I truly was. Maybe it was the recent loss of my father, maybe it was the pressure of having to live up to all the expectations which surrounded me, or maybe it was just the nature of the situation which led me to it, in any event, for one night, I acted out of pure passion. I acted irrationally.

I pulled on some socks and shoes, threw on a tee-shirt, grabbed my keys, and busted out the front door of the dormitory with an uncontrollable rage silently building inside. First, making my way to the cafeteria, I saw the workers there in a harried state, prepping for the upcoming dinner rush. Many of them had gotten to know me over the years and stopping by in the late afternoon to pick up a carton of chocolate milk or two was not uncommon. Generally, I would just venture in, open the icebox, take what I needed, and leave payment by the cash register. This time my intentions were much different.

Not noticing any drastic change in my demeanor, they went about their business. There on a serving table nearby, sat a carving knife, a very large carving knife. Without anyone noticing, I reached for it and tucked it under my shirt as I darted out the door.

I got to my car, placed the knife on the passenger seat, and drove right to the campus where Lizzy's new office was located. As time drew near for her to file out, I pulled into the parking space next to her car and waited.

Saying goodbye to one of her colleagues as they got to the parking lot, she immediately saw me as she approached with an alarmed look on her face. She came towards me and tried to give me a hug. I moved away from her immediately.

"I WANT HIS ADDRESS AND I WANT IT NOW!!" I shouted as I pounded on the trunk of my car.

She stood nearby, trembling, with an expression of fear on her face.

"Why? What are you going to do? Please Ange, can we just go somewhere and talk about this?"

Her alarms worsened when she noticed the knife sitting on my front seat.

"I WANT HIS ADDRESS AND I WANT IT NOW!" I repeated loudly, pounding again.

Then reluctantly with tears streaming, she recited it me.

1201 Orient way was a six-story apartment building located on the lower south side. I had never ventured down there, but I knew the general vicinity. I was determined to find it this night.

As dusk approached, I drove through the streets, deep into that southside neighborhood. I had no idea what I was going to do when I got there, and my mind was in a state of turmoil.

It's funny how sometimes when we least expect it, before making what could be the biggest mistake of our lives, a twist of fate seems to intercept the events at hand. Some people are put in our lives for a reason, and when they show up at that exact moment, divine intervention seems to have taken place.

I was approximately seven blocks away and stopped at a red light. It was an intersection that had small businesses and shops on all four corners. A tailor shop and a women's dress store to my left. A newspaper stand on my right and diagonally from where I sat, a small tiny hole-in-the-wall bar called The Penny Stop Pub. The drinks were mostly watered down there, but they were extremely cheap and were noted for practically serving anybody who had a pulse and money to spend. As I waited for the light to turn, I picked up the knife in my right hand, while keeping my left on the wheel. The thoughts of Dexter and Lizzy were escalating as I gripped it even tighter before resting again on the seat next to me.

Then, there out of the darkened streets, a familiar profile was crossing at the intersection right before me, on his way to the Penny Stop. It was Johnny. He turned, stunned, to see me there, as he approached.

"Kid, is that you?" He said leaning over and poking his head in the passenger side window.

It had been almost three weeks since Johnny and I had seen or spoke to each other and now with a fleeting look, he saw me in a state he never had witnessed before. Glancing down and seeing the knife in full view, prompted him to open the car door and slide in immediately. Picking up the large blade by its wooden handle, he looked at me stupefied. The light turned green and I began to drive away.

"Kid! Kid! What the hell is happening and what are you doing with this?"

He stated in hysteria as he held the knife with its blade occasionally glistening from the reflection of the passing streetlamps.

"He did it, John, He did it! And now he is going to pay!" I screamed without looking in his direction.

"Who? Did What?"

"That son-of-a-bitch, Dexter, that's who. He had sex with Lizzy!!"

"No, no……. calm down kid, calm down, how do you know that?"

"She damn well told me, John, she finally admitted it! I'm going to kill him!"

I drove frantically until I reached the street sign which read Orient Way, Dexter's apartment building was towards the middle of the block and I was going in, regardless of the outcome. We pulled up in front, the street was quiet, no one seemed to be around. Johnny sat there with knife in hand and tried strenuously to talk some sense into me.

"Okay kid, if you're going to do this, I'm coming in with you. Only, we are not taking the knife, let's just leave it here."

With that, he slid it under the front seat. Somewhere in the back of my mind, I knew it was the right thing to do. I sat there in utter silence, listening to Johnny's voice, but not fully hearing it as I kept staring straight ahead in a catatonic-like state.

"You calm right now?"

I shook my head yes.

"You're not going to do anything crazy, right?"

I shook my head yes.

"We are just going to go in there and talk to him, Right?"

I shook my head yes.

Out of the car, we made our way through the glass door entering the foyer of the building. Apartment 4c was located upstairs as we quietly climbed.

Reaching the hallway and then his door, Johnny tried to reassure me one last time.

"You're just going to talk to him, right kid?" he murmured.

I shook my head yes, yet again. Then knocked.

Never expecting to see me there, and not having any inclination of what Lizzy had just told me, Dexter tried to greet me, smiling, gesturing to shake my hand.

"Hey, look who it is, it's Angelo himself coming over.........."

And before he could finish his sentence or mutter another word, I found myself lunging at him with both hands grabbing his neck,

"I'M GOING TO FUCKING KILL YOU!!!" I screamed.

My hands held tightly around his throat as we both fell to the ground, with myself landing on top of him. We wrestled there for several minutes, as his live-in girlfriend was screaming over us in disbelief. Here was mild-mannered Angelo Vincent Scardosa, from Jersey, thin with a slight build, taking on big bad Dexter Demarco in the most uncharacteristic way. Johnny grabbed me from behind and pulled me off with all his might, while Dexter laid there momentarily catching his breath.

With Johnny, dragging me away, the both of us found ourselves rolling down a flight of stairs, I could hear almost every apartment door in the building opening to see what the commotion was. In the distance, the sounds of police sirens were beckoning.

Johnny pushed me out the front door, as the sirens drew nearer. We ran straight for the car in a moment of clarity. He jumped behind the wheel after forcibly throwing me into the passenger side and hit the gas with the tires screeching as we sped off.

We drove around for a spell, as I ran the gamut of emotions, from hurtfulness to anger to sheer uncertainty. After a while, Johnny invited me back to the Penny Stop bar, his original destination, for a drink, I declined, wanting only to see Lizzy with an ultimatum in mind.

"What are you going to do now kid?" Johnny asked with great concern as he remained in doubt over the events which just took place.

"Don't know, John, maybe I should fill the tank and head west, you ever been out west John?" I responded in a sullen and withdrawn state.

I went back to the dormitory with the specific intent of confronting her in person this time. Entering, I received many strange looks from other students, who, by now, had heard the rumblings of my actions. I went to Lizzy's room and knocked gently. She opened the door with that fearful look upon her face yet again. Not knowing what had just taken place between myself and Dexter, I asked her to come outside.

It was cooling off and the night air was chilly. She was wrapped in a knitted brown sweater and pulled it tightly around her like a security blanket. Her gaze was swollen and puffy and with no makeup on at all, her innocence looked forthcoming. Not considering the scope of my actions, I believed that somewhere in my heart this would all pass, I didn't want what we had to end.

"So, here's how it's going to be. It's me or the band. Tell me right now, it's either me or the band." I said sternly.

She looked at me with those red, teary eyes.

Angelo, I don't know what to say, I'm.........I'm sorry." She whimpered with a stream of tears traveling down her cheek

"It's you, it's you, I will quit the band."

"Ok, let's go, right now. Go upstairs and tell them you quit." I stated in my suppressed state of anger.

"Right now?"

"YES, Right now!"

And doing exactly that, she followed me back into the dormitory as we went directly to the third floor, knocked on the drummer, Tony Matone's, door, and gave him the news. Then proceeded to each other band members' room and did the same. Johnny would receive the news in the morning.

Given the recent circumstances, the next several weeks went on as normally as could be expected. Graduation came and went, as did the Conservatory's grand finale. It was all very anti-climactic for me. The spark which once burned so fiercely had now been extinguished. I did my best to put up a front, but there was a void that I couldn't seem to recover from. Our thoughts for the next phase of our lives went on as scheduled. We ended putting a deposit on a flat on the north side, with a small piano included, which was subsidized by Lizzy's parents. It was an opportunity in a rent-controlled building that Lizzy's Father had connections too and couldn't be passed up. The plan was for me and

Johnny to occupy the place while waiting for wedding plans to come together. And being near Lizzy's job, she could conveniently visit at any time.

For me, although, I couldn't seem to escape it, my vision felt as if it had been shattered. I went through the motions the best I could, but each time I was close to her, each time the door opened for any kind of intimacy, each time we kissed or at the least, touched, I could not free myself from thoughts of Dexter. I was a different person now, I knew it, she knew it and Johnny could see it. The entire event had transformed me somehow and I was sinking fast. Weeks turned into months, my performances became sub-par and my desire completely diminished. I would spend several weekends away from Boston, back home in Jersey, putting in extended hours at the liquor store, where I would sometimes leave with a pint or two of Guinness, for my own consumption.

The years which had led up to this point in my life were filled with dedication to my faith, my music, and eventually Lizzy. Now, I felt soulless. When love has struck you so deeply at a young and impressionable age and then it is torn from the very fabric you believe in, the consequences to the heart are irreversible. Once trust is compromised is there ever a chance that love can exist again?

So, without forewarning, without any notice, after sitting at the piano for some time, alone in our Boston flat, on a sultry Saturday afternoon, I got up, grabbed three suitcases from my closet, packed my clothes and personal effects and drove home to Jersey, leaving only a crumbled sheet of hand-written notepaper on the piano bench which simply read, 'GOODBYE L'.

Whether my decision was the right one or not, I didn't immediately know, I just knew I needed some time to think.

My mother knew that I was struggling, I had only told her that Lizzy and I had broken up, never offering any further details, no matter how many times I was questioned. Nor did I tell anyone else exactly what had happened, I mentioned nothing about her and Dexter, I protected Lizzy and her reputation, somewhere, my love for her still ran deep, despite the inner turmoil and pain I was experiencing.

I escaped to the comfort and memory of the most reassuring place I knew, home. I didn't want to think about Boston, or a singing career, or anything else that came close. I just wanted to live on and forget. My internship was in jeopardy and Johnny tried to cover for me the best he could, but eventually, it was inevitably withdrawn. He tried calling several times, but I refused to come to the phone. Lizzy tried also, but to no avail, I just wanted to be left alone.

Over the next several months, I tried to make sense of it all. I couldn't understand how this had happened and most of all how Lizzy could fall for such a creep like Dexter. In our last month together before leaving, I couldn't help but question her many times over and again about the entire situation. My trips to church became severely hindered, I prayed for an answer, but none came.

Almost a year to the day, my journey was to take a definitive turn. The comforts of home could not close the wound which still openly existed, and knowing not where to turn, I decided it was time to venture out elsewhere. My only recourse was to put as much time and the distance between myself and the memory of what once was and what could have been. I packed again, perhaps for the last time. I couldn't explain, I couldn't say a word about my plans, I really had none.

It was a bright sunny morning when I loaded the trunk of my car, the contents included my three worn out suitcases, and an old electro-voice microphone, wrapped in a felt blanket. It was a goodbye present from my janitor friend, Little Jim, which I just couldn't let go of. My mother made a large breakfast for both of us, as my sister slept at her girlfriend's house the night before. We sat at the kitchen table without a word being spoken. It was as if she had known, (mothers always know). She could see the pain that I had been suffering all along, she could tell that the light that shone within me had grown dim and she knew I was leaving, not knowing if, or when I would return.

Outside, I stood next to the open door of my car as she gave me a long hug, then she handed me an envelope, and kissed me on the cheek.

"Mom, I need to just go and figure………"

I began to let her know what I was feeling, but before I could get any more out, she stopped me.

"Angelo, you're a man now, but you will always be my son. I know you have your reasons and I believe in you. I love you, and I will always be proud of you, no matter where life takes you. Just remember, you always have a home here." She said as she wiped a tear from her cheek with her apron while I began to pull away.

* * *

Father Tom's sense of urgency had both Frankie and me puzzled, and it could not have come at a more inopportune moment.

"Vincent, I just had a rather lengthy conversation with the chief advocate from the bishop's office in El Paso. He was very impressed with the construction and organization we accomplished here tonight. And it is all because of you, and you too Frankie. We would not have had all this wonderful work done if you did not introduce me to Vincent here."

With excitement in his voice, he continued as Frankie and I listened intently to his every word.

"And to top it all off, we have already surpassed the donation amounts from the last feast, and the night is not over yet!"

"That's all well and good Father, but I still don't understand what this has to do with me?"

"Well it seems that the bishop himself may require someone of your talents to refurbish the main chapel there, that is if the plan is approved."

Frankie looked at me with a sense of dismay and at the same time, great concern.

"Hold on a minute Father, are you saying what I think you are saying, this would all take place in El Paso?"

"Yes, my son, as it stands right now, the project would be scheduled to take about eighteen months, it pays extremely well, and you would have beautiful living accommodations at your disposal."

Frankie turned her back and looked away as she heard the proposal.

"When would you need my decision?"

"I'm sorry to say, but that is why I interrupted you so hastily, the advocate is leaving shortly, and he would like an answer tonight, so he can bring the news back with him."

"Tonight! He needs my answer tonight?"

"I'm sorry, yes. These types of appointments are quite scarce and if you turn it down, they will move quickly to the next candidate."

Turning to Frankie, I asked if I could speak to Father Tom alone for a few minutes.

I have never really thought of myself as much of a carpenter, designer, or construction worker before, but perhaps this was an honorable profession that I had now stumbled upon. I discussed the pros and cons with Father Tom for a short time as I could hear the music and festive sounds continuing in the background. This turn of events came as a total surprise, and sometimes some of the best opportunities present themselves that way. I would be earning, as Father Tom put it, a 'very decent' wage, and have a place to live. Also, the possibility of growing a reputation as a builder would be limitless.

It didn't take long for me to know exactly what my decision would be.

"Father, I am honored to be considered, but I must respectfully decline."

"Are you sure my son?" He said as he put his hand on my shoulder.

"I am."

He looked me right in the eye almost with a sense of relief, as if to say, I'm glad you will not be leaving so soon, there will be something else which comes your way, something better. And just before he turned away, I thought I could see a concealed smile flash across his face.

Getting back to the crowded and the lighted area nearby, I could see that Frankie strolled further off, alone. I came up behind her and stood directly next to her.

"So, I'm glad that's over with." I said without even looking at her.

"When do you leave?" she asked, also peering straight ahead.

"Oh, in about an hour."

"WHAT!" she exclaimed now turning to face me head-on.

"Yeah, in about an hour. ....I think the feast should be over by then and I'll be leaving alright, leaving to go back to my room at The Winchester.......... where I will be, as long as they let me stay." I stated as I began laughing aloud.

"Oh.... Oh ...you think you are sooooo funny."

She went on smiling and began pummeling me with the stuffed animal in her possession as I tried to flee her attack.

The feast ended up being a tremendous success. Everyone I had met, even days later had nothing but flattering things to say, it was the talk for miles around and my efforts did not go unnoticed. In the end, the church benefited the most, the gate receipts were triple what anyone expected.

But much to my dismay, my work would be nearing an end. The job I had been given was not only to construct and manage the set-up of the entire operation, but it also included the dismantling and storage of it all. And a day later, I was out there working just as hard to restore the town's pavilion by removing all reminders of the prior celebration. It was no more an easier task then the construction itself and it would take days to disassemble. At first, I had several volunteers who assisted me with the larger structures, but for the most part, I was to finish up alone.

Frankie and Zeke would come out to bring me lunch whenever they would get the chance, and it did allow me to take a break and spend a little time with them both.

"Do you regret not taking that job in El Paso?"

"Not for one minute," I said with reassurance as I sat enjoying the tamales she delivered.

We both knew that the reality of it all was about to return, my work here would soon end and the need to find a steadier income and stable place to live would come into focus once again. The thought of moving in with her and Zeke crossed my mind several times, but I was persistent in trying to find another alternative.

I had made up my mind, maybe I could even say, I had matured, but I felt as if I was done running. The thought of leaving this new town of mine and the people I came to know and care about didn't appeal to me. But it wasn't just that, it wasn't just the relationships, it wasn't even Frankie, my gut told me it was something more. Maybe it was as simple as the peace and serenity that was evident here. My intuition had given me an inkling from the beginning, and I trusted that feeling. And maybe, just maybe, the instinct that I felt when Father Tom's look pierced me just nights before, was telling me that something better was about to come along.

Sometimes, when you think you've reached the end of the road, you come across a detour that takes you in another direction entirely.

I broke down each unit just as I assembled them. The plan was to organize, stack, and store them in the garage workshop so that they could be easily accessed for future use. In the past the constructions were left out in the elements to their own demise, and inevitably became unsafe. My one impediment was that old flatbed pickup truck which was still taking up most of the room.

Before the volunteers returned to their daily lives, I convinced several of them to help me attempt to push the truck from its current location and park it around back. There were four of us stationed at the back end with a thirteen-year-old boy manning the steering wheel. But try as we would, it would move only about halfway. After about an hour with the same results, Carlos, the thirteen-year-old, muttered something in Spanish and ran off. Ten minutes later he returned with a mule in tow, tied a rope to its harness and the other end to the front bumper, and within minutes we pushed and pulled that clunker out, positioning it around back. The foresight of the youth caught us looking foolish, but we were all amused by the entire situation, laughing over it for a while.

The next couple of days saw me complete my tasks, everything had been stored as it should be, and all that was left for me to do was to clean up any loose debris. Father Tom would be there to make sure it was to his liking and give me my final pay.

Over at Frankie's, I had dinner and took the time to relax after weeks of long hours and sometimes difficult labor which had me worn out by days end. It was a beautifully clear September evening as we sat on her back porch enjoying a cold beer, with Zeke perched on the smooth clay floor beside us, and her small transistor radio playing in the background.

"So, I guess everything is about done at the church."

"Yep, you could say that."

"You know, I wasn't going to bring this up, but, my offer is still open about coming to stay here, I think Zeke would really love it."

"Oh, Zeke would really love it?" I said with a grin.

"Yes, that's right Zeke and ONLY Zeke would love it." She responded with a sheepish smile of her own.

Being with Frankie was a joy. We seemed to be on the same wavelength, and I wanted so much to say that I was going to move my belongings from The Winchester to her place tomorrow. But she didn't know the real me, she didn't know anything about my past, and it was purely because I didn't tell her. I had skirted the subject each time she had tried to bring it up.

The events that struck me at such a young and tender age diminished my capacity for love. For years, traveling about, I felt I was incapable of ever knowing that feeling again. The damaging effects it had, not only hindered the passionate side of me, but also made me question my faith. A belief system that I had been so strongly reared with, had now become a something I questioned.

I never shared my story or those feelings with anyone. Sure, some had been there and heard the rumors afterward, but no one fully knew the devastating consequences it had on me. Now, as I sat here with someone who I finally felt close enough to, I pondered baring it all and letting the chips fall where they may.

"Frankie, there is something I want to tell you."

I said seriously as I moved to the edge of my chair and looked directly at her. She Put down her beer and looked at me knowing that something meaningful was forthcoming.

"Hello……Hello….is anybody home?" A voice at Frankie's front door beckoned.

"Vincent, hold that thought …please!" She said as she got up to see who it was.

I sat there with Zeke, feeling a bit relieved at that moment. Hearing voices from inside her house, I also got up as Frankie came out followed by Father Tom.

"Looks like I've done it again, haven't I? Sorry for the interruption, but I had a feeling I would find you here." He stated upon entering.

"I must say, you have impeccable timing Father, but it's quite alright. What brings you out this way on such a glorious night?"

Frankie pulled out a chair and place it near us, then also offered Father Tom a cold beer, which he gladly accepted. After Zeke made an introduction of his own by sniffing him and being petted until he was satisfied, we all sat curiously waiting to see what Father Tom's appearance was about to bring forth this time.

"Well, first I wanted to say once again, what a fine job you have done with the feast. I went by the workshop tonight and it is in outstanding order. Second, I brought you your pay."

He continued as he handed me a large white envelope.

"Thank you, Father, but you didn't have to make a special trip, I could have gotten it from you tomorrow morning."

"And that's where the third issue comes in. I didn't want to wait, I was too excited to hold off until then."

Now he had both our attention. The last time he had news like this it wasn't so beneficial. We quietly hoped for something of a different sort this night.

"As you know, the feast pulled in more money than we could have imagined. Everyone including the bishop himself was amazed. And we also know that it was mainly due in part to your talents Vincent, that is why they wanted you in El Paso."

He took a swig of his beer as he went on.

"And this brings me to the third point. We now have enough money in our budget to hire someone for a new position. It will offer you an honest day's pay, but the best part is, room and board are included."

We looked at each other with a stunned sense of elation. I was going to accept this new post even before I knew exactly what it was.

"I don't know what to say Father, and its right here in Mara Del Santos?"

"It is, I will go over all the responsibilities and duties, they are more than meets the eye, but I have faith in you, and you can move into Father Ortiz's old house should you accept."

"I ACCEPT!I ACCEPT!"

"Well then, it is my honor and privilege to formally offer you the position of……. THE CUSTODIAN."

9

I had no idea what laid next for me, I supposed that my construction abilities would be useful once again, and here I was, the product of an ill-fated relationship which drove me from a lifelong vocation of glistening lights and constant ovations, to a job hoping to preserve and upkeep a small church in a vastly unknown town, in the middle of nowhere.

With Father Tom's exit, and receiving the news that I would be undertaking this new position, Frankie and I went inside and turned up the radio, loud. The Coasters, *Poison Ivy* was playing and we both began to jump and dance around with Zeke doing the same as he barked away. It was Friday night and after several beers, each of us was ready to buckle down for the evening. I said goodnight and drove back to the Winchester knowing that in a day or so, I would have a new place to call home.

Wasting no time, Saturday morning came rolling in with a bit of a hangover. Frankie and I made plans to get over to Father Ortiz's house, where the key had been placed under the front mat awaiting our arrival. It was a small adobe and wooden house, apart from the main rectory. This was where Father Ortiz resided for most of his days, but after he had diminished duties at the church, due to his age and failing health, he was eventually forced to move into a retirement home. I believe she was feeling more excited than I, wanting to do some re-decorating right away. I was sure that after so much time, the place could use a woman's touch, after all, Father Ortiz lived alone for nearly forty years.

The climate had been extremely arid and dry the past several weeks, and everyone was in anxious anticipation of the rainy season which was just around the corner. Frankie, Zeke, and I drove over to my new house leaving in our wake a large cloud of dry dust as we sped along. Father Tom was correct in saying that it was approximately a quarter of a mile from the church, within walking distance for sure, if need be.

On the approaching horizon, the house quickly came into view. It was a basic one-level style construction, that looked like the original design was reminiscent of a log cabin. Driving up and parking right in front, two large windows were evident on each side of the main door which had a pronounced overhang above it. We immediately got out of the car and went right for the front mat retrieving the key. Zeke was sniffing and wagging his tail at the entrance as I jiggled the lock to let us in.

As expected, a musty, heavy aura hit us as we entered. Frankie shuffled right over to the windows to open them, but needed my assistance in doing so, the wood around the frames had warped, making them difficult to lift. Consisting of a total of five rooms, it was deceiving, looking much smaller from the outside. There was an oversized bedroom, a bathroom, a living room, and a very large kitchen that was desperately in need of painting. We planned to paint the entire place as soon as we had a handle on things.

The furniture was covered with old dusty sheets and rugs of the same nature. We looked at each other knowing that we would be spending much time here before I was able to move in. As we began to pull the sheets off, it didn't matter how slowly we tugged on them, the dust was overwhelming, creating a small cloud and forcing us outside. Managing to remove as many as we could, we dragged them outdoors and shook them vigorously loosening the grime into the air around us.

The furniture, severely outdated, was still appropriate for my needs, but Frankie insisted that we also move some it to the yard to air it out. There was an enormous paisley sitting chair, circa 1930s and a small cream-colored sofa which we dragged out with much effort. We went on in this fashion for most of the day and by the time we had gotten most items moved and cleaned, we were both covered with a film of gray soot. Zeke would enthusiastically shake himself off several times with his own personal swirl of dust cascading from him.

The kitchen needed the most attention, especially the refrigerator. Opening it, a foul odor emanated, and I had no choice but to slam it shut right away.

"I think we better save this one for tomorrow," I said holding my nose and motioning to Frankie.

Calling it a day, we brushed off as much filth from our clothes as we could, got back into Denise, and headed to Frankie's.

I was grateful for finally being able to call a place my own, regardless of how much cleaning or painting or repair it needed. Father Tom knew just what condition it was in and gave me enough leeway to get things in order, two weeks to be exact, before I started my duties as custodian.

Back at The Winchester, I gave my formal notice to the night manager letting him know that in a week, my patronage there would come to an end. The news came as no surprise and I would venture to guess that most everyone in town already heard about it. The whole scenario was a bit daunting, in my excitement, I accepted this position so abruptly that I still had no understanding what it entailed. I kept repeating the words that Father Tom mentioned during his offer, 'I will go over all the responsibilities and duties, they are more than meets the eye'.

I was uneasy about the whole prospect of spending so much time alone in a church, ashamed to admit that my faith had been jolted in recent years. Now, I had just one concern in mind, to be the best I could be at this position, not only for myself but for the people who truly did believe, for those whose faith did remain strong and for those who considered this place their own.

We took the entire two weeks to straighten up the house and get it in the best condition possible. We cleaned, painted, and polished every room and together had it looking more than acceptable, including the refrigerator. I think Frankie was even a little envious, wanting to move in herself.

Carlos, the thirteen-year-old, who outdid the rest of us with his mule while moving the pickup truck, didn't live too far away and on many occasions, he would show up offering to help. I gave him mostly small jobs, like feeding Zeke or sweeping up after us and would generally reward him with a charitable payday and something to eat. He didn't speak English too well, but I would try to teach him a word or two, as he would try to return the favor in Spanish.

Shopping day came along, and with the money I had earned during the feast, I picked up a decent-sized Zenith television that came with a stand, a red Phillips transistor radio that reminded me of the one that Little Jim and I used to listen to Boston Braves' games on, and a load of curtains, linens, and towels, that Frankie of course, picked out. After those essentials were taken care of, it was off to the general store, which was now modernizing with a couple of refrigerated cases, to stock up my food pantry and fridge.

The final chore ahead of me was to pack up my clothes and personal belongings and say goodbye to the hotel room which accommodated me so generously since I arrived. The staff at The Winchester prepared a large frosted cake with a candle in the center and the words Goodbye Mr. Vincent, written on top. The entire crew was there, from the night manager to the young enthusiastic morning clerk, to the housemaids. I was flattered as they all partook with a big slice while wishing me well with hugs, handshakes, and smiles.

With my suitcases already loaded in Denise once again, I revved my engine, shifted into gear, and headed straight for my new home.

The first night in a new place always seems a bit uncomfortable, but here, I felt right at ease almost immediately, perhaps it was all the personal touches that Frankie had been responsible for, maybe it was knowing that I would be staying in one place longer than a month or two, but whatever it was, it was certainly a tranquil feeling that I couldn't deny.

Most of the houses built in this area included a back or front porch, sometimes both. That was done to take advantage of the majestic sunsets and landscapes which surrounded them. This house was no different. I sat quietly on the back wooden porch in an old rocking chair that we found in the living room. It was more comfortable having it out here, where I could relax and take in the night view. And for once, without a care in the world, I rocked myself for a long while, dozing off into a peaceful somber sleep.

Daybreak came upon me in a dazzling array of sunlight creeping over the horizon. Still, in that creaky chair, I awoke not realizing how long I slept or what time it was. Needing to shower, I learned that the water pressure must build before it can do any good, so heading into the bathroom, I turned on the spigot while I proceeded to get my morning coffee going.

Cleaned and dressed, I prepared some eggs and country bacon, as I listened to the news broadcast over the airwaves on my new radio. I was scheduled to start my job this very morning, everything had gone as planned and Father Tom and I would be meeting at the church.

I arrived a bit early and parked Denise around back near the workshop. I decided to take a tour of the outside of the building and get a closer look at its unique design. The detail was exquisite, each spire looked to be masterfully carved and the stained-glass windows were even more magnificent with the sun shining upon them. I remembered for a brief second how we used to examine buildings such as these back in Boston, only this one had its peculiarities and seemed much older than any other I had seen before.

"Ahhhhh good morning Vincent." Father Tom said in a resounding voice as I came around the corner, meeting him at the west side entrance.

"Morning Father."

"Come with me, this way Vincent."

He turned and led me towards the back of the church, where we entered through a rear door. Following him down a narrow corridor, we arrived at a room that was designated as his office. It was brightly lit and one of the stained-glass windows stood about 8 feet high on the left wall, letting in an immense array of colors. There was a large oak desk positioned towards the middle of the room with a very comfortable looking high back chair in tanned leather stationed behind it. He took his seat there and motioned for me to sit in one of the two cushioned chairs in front of him.

"Well Vincent, I think I should explain what all this is exactly about."

He reached down and taking an old brown leather-bound journal from the bottom drawer, placed it in front of him as he clasped his hands over it.

"We have not had a custodian here for some time, in fact, I never met the last one, he worked primarily for Father Ortiz many years ago. Most of the history I have learned about our little church was passed down from the good father himself, so I am not entirely sure how accurate it is."

He sat back in his chair as it swiveled to the right a bit.

"This journal is the best source we have containing information you may find helpful. It is something I found here when I first arrived. The writing is faded and is incomplete in most parts, but it may come in handy someday. I don't think it will be too useful yet, so I will keep it locked in this draw for the time being."

"I don't get it Father seems all a little mysterious to me."

"Mysterious, no, my son, we just need to be protective of this place." He said with a chuckle.

Locking the journal back in its place, he got up from his chair, as I did the same. Placing his arm on the back of my shoulder, we walked back down the corridor to another door with a small window in the middle of it. Unlocking it, he pushed it open and led me into the main church itself.

"Wait here a minute, I need to put the lights on."

The only illumination at the moment was coming through the sun-drenched stained-glass windows, entering with theatrical fashion. I stood in a quiet corner as I heard him switching the lights on from somewhere behind the entry door. With each coming on in succession, I could see that the interior of the building was as dramatic as its exterior. It had a vaulted ceiling constructed of wooden rafters, that rose at an extremely steep pitch and looked as if it was hardly able to support itself. The floor plan mimicked the shape of a cross, a set of pews on the left and right side of the altar with the main seating area elongated in front. There were several statues, and an empty tiered bank of candles with red votives set before each of them.

"Now, I can give you the grand tour." Father Tom proclaimed as he returned.

We explored the entire building, first walking down the left-hand side aisle towards the back of the church where the main entrance was located, then up a set of stairs to the choir loft. Here, affixed in place, was a large ancient-looking pipe organ that took up a majority of the entire area.

"Does that thing work?" I asked pointing to the behemoth towering in front of us.

"That it does, my son, that it does." He responded shaking his head slowly with a proud look abounding.

The choir loft gave a view that oversaw the entire seating area and the altar itself. It was there, as I looked out, that a first noticed it.

Off in the distance straight ahead, hanging on the front wall behind the altar, I could see the outline of an image that was immensely familiar to me. My vision not being as good as it should (never bothering to get the correct eyeglass prescription), I squinted mightily to try and get a better assessment of what I was seeing. I stood there in silence, not noticing that Father Tom was doing the same, as he watched me diligently. I turned twice to look at him and then back again at the image, I felt as if I couldn't turn away from it, it held my gaze steadily.

"What do you see, Vincent? What is it that you are looking at so intently?" He asked as if he already knew the answer.

"Uh.... Uh.... I'm not sure Father, but there, down there, can we go down and take a closer look?"

"Of course, but first let us continue our tour and we will make our way around towards the front."

Back down the choir lofts stairs, we passed through a set of double doors and into the vestibule. This was a small area where usually the entrance procession for mass would begin. It was also where parishioners would get a chance to say a few words to the celebrating priest afterward. There was a locked closet on the right, which he aptly opened to show me supplies located within, mainly boxes of votive candles in several sizes. At the other end was another room which he referred to as the cloakroom. It stored many garments worn by himself or, on a rare occasion, visiting priests, and altar servers.

As we made our way back towards the main seating area and up the right aisle, I kept squinting as we got closer upfront. He then led me through a final door that took us to an area behind the altar itself, where more supplies were stored including a small refrigerator that kept the wine and communion hosts from spoiling. Beyond that was a stairway that led downstairs to the basement.

Slowly descending, I could see rows of chairs stacked upon one another, sections of pews and other miscellaneous items scattered about which needed mending. This is where I thought the bulk of my work was to come from. Finally, returning close to where we began, was a single door with the word C U S T O D I A N , printed on it. This was to be my room, it was small, no bigger than 10 by 8 feet. It had an undersized wooden desk, with draws on one side and an old padded swivel chair to match and was surrounded by shelves on the left wall and towards the back. There was a toolbox with a minimal amount of hand tools in it, also a broom and a mop with a bucket. A much-needed sink with a faucet that produced hot and cold running water was mounted to one of the walls. It wasn't much, but it would suffice.

"It is a wonderful church you got here Father, but I would like to, I mean can we go back out to........"

"Yes, we can." He said cutting me off.

We walked out from behind the altar and there I stood mesmerized.

I think Father Tom was curious about my reaction more than anything, as he watched me with glee. I had seen many artistic works in my younger days. I was blessed with having the opportunity of visiting many museums in better times, whether it was in the Boston area, or New York. I had experienced countless great works first-hand, some of which left me astonished at the level of craftsmanship and their attention to detail. I was also fortunate enough to see just as many famous works in books and publications. But what I saw hanging on the wall before me, at that moment, could not compare.

The image mounted approximately 20 feet up on the wall behind the altar, facing out towards the seating area, was one of the most magnificent representations of the human figure in all its suffering, in all its physical presence, that I had ever witnessed. The life-like feeling of this sculpture was uncanny, and it was displayed there for all to experience.

"Father, it has taken my breath away, literally, there are no words for me to describe it." I whispered.

"Now you see! This is what brings the people here, and this is what continues to bring them back."

"Where did you get it, Father? I mean where did it come from?"

"I wish I could give you an answer. It was here when I arrived, and it spoke to my heart immediately."

"I mean, who made it, it is perfection."

"AHHHH these are the questions that many have asked for years, and these are the questions I don't have any answers for."

"But Father, someone must know its origin, what about Father Ortiz, surely he must know something about it?"

"That is a long story my son, and I have never been able to fully extract all the details. Each time I asked him, he would just simply say that God delivered it to our doorstep, and we shouldn't question it."

"With all due respect Father, that's not a logical explanation, is it?"

"Depends on what you believe, Vincent, depends on what you believe."

"But, what about the archdiocese, wouldn't they have any record of it?"

"You are sounding just as I did when I was a younger man. I researched the same path, even went to the archdiocese office myself, but found no record, no information about it, and I must say, I was frowned upon for inquiring so much. The only record I can tell may be in that old journal I showed you earlier and I'm not so sure about that either. So, I just accepted it, just as everyone else who comes here does."

We remained there for several more minutes, silent, before Father Tom turned to me.

"And this, my son, will be the greatest part of your duties." As he raised his right hand and pointed to the Crucifix hanging before us.

I wasn't sure what he meant, and I sure didn't understand the impact of what he was referring to. All the custodians I had ever known in my lifetime, were more like Little Jim, sweeping the floor, perhaps mopping once a week, or even handling slight repairs when necessary. But my instincts were telling me that this was something more, something very different than just ordinary custodial duties.

Back in Fathers Tom's office, I was staggered over the mysterious content which surrounded this building and the statue I had just encountered.

"Vincent, do you have any questions for me?"

"Questions? I think that is an understatement, Father."

"Well then, here is a list of your duties which I feel may need immediate attention. Let's focus on them for now, then I want you to think about everything you saw today and come up with any other concerns you may have for me."

He handed me a handwritten sheet which listed all that needed to be done, from dozens of repairs to listing inventory, to general de-cluttering and cleaning. But nothing on that paper made any mention of his previous comments and before I could bring up the subject again, he locked up his desk, handed me a set of keys, and advised me that I should get started right away. He had a scheduled meeting that he was off to and we would continue matters as we went along.

I proceeded to my new 'office' to get a feel for it and organize it. An odor of mildew seemed to be entrapped within it, which prompted me to move all the contents out into the hall, so I might be able to give it a thorough cleaning. Hours later I had an uncluttered dirt-free space to call my own. The only thing I would need now is to bring over my transistor radio which would go nicely on my desk.

As the end of my first eventful day approached, a feeling of satisfaction came over me. Following the notes that Father Tom had scribbled, I made sure that all the windows were locked along with the supply closets, and both our offices. Then returning to the main chapel area, I promptly checked all the entrance doors to be sure they were locked up tight also.

Here I was alone, in this place when it dawned on me just how quiet it can be. Each time I closed a door or made some kind of unassuming sound, the echo which stirred would last several moments, making it a bit unsettling. On my way out, passing in front of the altar, I couldn't help but look up at the Crucifix again. Moving past it, I turned twice, before shutting the lights and locking the door behind me.

Arriving home, I was met with a surprise. Frankie was there cooking up an incredible dinner to celebrate my official first day at work. The aroma of roasted chilis permeated the air as I drove up. Zeke came running out the front door the minute I got out of the car, it almost felt like I was having a glimpse of what family life would amount to, and I didn't mind. I wanted so much to go inside and kiss her hello and tell her she was the best thing to happen to me in a long time. But I still owed her an explanation, one whose immediacy had died down for the time being. Still, I felt like I had reached some semblance of happiness and a life that was moving in the right direction.

“Hi, I thought you wouldn't mind if we came in before you got home, I'm making something special.”

"Not at all, it smells wonderful," I said, entering the kitchen with Zeke in tow.

“Sit down, would you like a beer?”

“You better stop, a guy could get used to this.”

"Well then, I hope you're hungry." She said as she placed two plates on the table.

We ate deliberately making pleasant conversation throughout, then retreated out to the back porch which had become a routine that we both enjoyed. Two chairs, the stars, a beautiful dry night, and the company of someone special, the simple life, who could ask for more.

"So, it seems that Tess at the diner has come down with a case of gout in her left foot, and she will have to stay off it for a while, doctor's orders."

"Oh no, will she be alright?"

"Yes, she will be fine, but, it looks like I will be working double shifts for a spell. And I was thinking about Zeke........."

"Yes, he can stay with me, you would like that wouldn't you Zekey boy?" I said as I rubbed his snoot vigorously.

Zeke wagged his tail and plopped down by my side, I knew it was only a matter of time, but I welcomed the thought of it. I always wanted a friend like Zeke and besides, I owed it Otto (wherever he was) to take care of him.

"Oh, by the way, I found something in the back of one of the kitchen drawers when I was cooking, we must have missed it earlier." She stated as she went inside to retrieve the items.

"Here you go, I don't know how on earth we could have overlooked these."

She handed me a set of two keys connected together on a small piece of rusty wire and a roll of old yellowing newspaper with something wrapped inside

"Wow, I think I know what these are, these must be the keys to that old truck that was in the workshop." I stated excitedly.

Proceeding to unravel the discolored printed paper, I opened it to find a dozen shells that most likely were for the shotgun which I found behind the front seat of the pick-up. The paper itself was the front page of The Roswell Daily Record, dated Tuesday, July 8, 1947. The headline read, RAAF Captures Flying Saucer; On Ranch in Roswell Region. Catching my eye, I read it out loud to Frankie and gave her the entire rundown regarding Otto and the night I was introduced to his friends. The talk of alien sightings was not surprising, and Frankie dismissed it as a forgone news article which she took in stride, although we both agreed that his disappearance was yet unnerving.

"Have you ever fired a gun, Vincent?" She asked as I rolled out the shotgun shells onto the kitchen table.

"Can't really say that I have," I said almost shamefully.

"But I would love to try it someday, you never know when it may come in handy." I continued.

"Well, as I mentioned, my daddy taught me when we lived out in farm country in the Midwest. Think I was seven years old, we used to go out back and shoot old cans off our fence. I first learned with a pistol, then graduated to a rifle. I like rifles better. I could hit a can dead center from fifty yards out by the time I was thirteen."

"You are just a woman of many talents, aren't you?"

"Yes, I am, and maybe someday, you just might find out what other talents I have, that is, if you play your cards right."

She smiled even wider as she began to rock her chair back and forth. I began to do the same.

Owning a gun in this part of the country was not uncommon at all, in fact, just about everyone out here did. Frankie was a darn good shot and her reputation was well known. Being surrounded by open land, with wildlife having access to roam free, it was a necessity at times to scare off any unwanted visitors that might venture too close.

The next morning, after a quick shower and breakfast for myself and Zeke, I was excited to get back to work wanting to try the keys to see if they did indeed belong to the pick-up truck. Leaving Denise and Zeke at home, I decided to walk over, coaxing Zeke to stay back as he tried to follow me a couple of times. Once there, I went right over to the truck, now moved to the outside of the workshop where weeds had slowly begun to grow around it.

Trying the first key, it fit right into the door as I turned it locking and unlocking it several times to be sure. Then, sitting inside and rolling down the window to clear the trapped stale air, I tried the second in the ignition, that one also slid right in. Of course, as I suspected the engine wouldn't crank at all, not even a slight sound, the battery was surely dead. Then, reaching in the back of the front seat, I removed shotgun, wrapped it in a nearby soiled cloth, and left it in the workshop to take with me when my day was over.

Now, with my own set of church keys in hand, I proceeded to the back door, which was already opened as I noticed the sounds of morning mass taking place inside. Peeking through the window of one of the inner doors, I could see a small congregation engaged with Father Tom's words as they looked upon the altar. I quietly proceeded to get to my office and go over the notes that outlined what needed to be worked on next.

Around the back of the altar, through the hallway and down the stairway into the basement, I got a close view of what was waiting for me. The windows were the casement type, set in the upper part of the wall, and only about 24 inches wide. Standing on my toes I could reach up and attempt to tilt them open. Most were difficult to release, and I needed to stand on a crate to get enough leverage to maneuver them free.

With air now circulating through the dense space, I began to move the stack of chairs and broken bench sections to create a workspace. In doing so, about three-quarters of the way through, I could see another door on the furthermost wall, hidden behind a pile of these stacks. Pushing my way around the pile and moving it as much as I could, I squeezed in closer, as I came upon a thick solid wooden door with rusted hinges which was bolted and padlocked shut.

"Vincent, are you down there?" I heard Father Toms voice calling from above.

"I am, just taking a look at what's here Father."

"Can you come up, I would like to talk to you for a minute."

Leaving the basement mess to be dealt with later, I hurried up the stairs to his office.

"Splendid job, on the custodian room, Vincent, looks great."

"Thanks, Father, and I am going to tackle the basement and the candle set-up next."

"Yes, yes, that is all well and good."

He proclaimed as he got up from behind his desk and walked over to shut the door to his office. And with a concerned look about him, he ventured to continue with our previous conversation.

"Vincent, you must now know the rest."

"Uh, the rest, Father?" I responded, not knowing exactly what he was referring to.

"Yes", he stated as he swiveled in his chair looking away from me.

"You see, as you have keenly noticed, the church doors are always locked when I'm not here. There have been attempted thefts, as I have mentioned. But now all that is going to change. The people want to come in during the day and sit silently and pray. They want the freedom to come and light a candle when they feel the need to. Now that you are here, now that we have an official custodian, I intend to leave the doors unlocked until nightfall."

"Ok, by me, Father, but these attempted thefts, what exactly were they?"

"What did you see here yesterday my son, what was it that you could not turn away from?"

He said as he swiveled around clasping his hands together on his desk and leaning forward looking more intently at me.

"You mean............the Cru...." I said stopping in the middle of my sentence.

"YES...... The Crucifix. Not everyone who looks upon it sees it as you did yesterday, that is how I know you have a purpose here. There have been many rumors, and stories that have led to local lore over the years which may explain the attempts to steal it. The sheriff is aware, and several reports have been filed. Although it is our most valued resource, it is not a substitution for faith, it is still faith that keeps bringing our followers here, it is faith that ultimately remains."

"But, what am I supposed to do about it Father?"

"I don't know exactly, but you are here for a reason, whatever that journey was that you experienced, whatever led you here, the time is now. You must understand Vincent, this is more than just a statue to us, we are not a rich and thriving city, most of our residents are on the poor side. This statue above everything else is regarded as a local treasure to them.........and me. Look after it Vincent, guard it, protect it!"

His words were transcribed in my thoughts all day. I went about performing the duties on my list, but each stray moment led me back to stop what I was doing and think about the significance of what was being asked of me.

I never gave any regards to being 'chosen' for anything, even when the spotlight shone so brightly in my past, even when success came so effortlessly, I hadn't thought in those terms. Was this the path my life was supposed to take? Did it all boil down to me looking after a mere statue? Each time I walked through the church, I paused to look at it, all-day, I questioned the very thought of it.

That night, after stopping at the workshop in back to retrieve the shotgun, I took a slow and ponderous walk home. I thought this job was perfect for someone who wanted to just exist, it made me invisible, and I liked being invisible, or so I thought. Here I was, practically out in the middle of nowhere, asking myself whether being here was just a knee-jerk reaction to a broken heart or a way of dealing with tragedy or just escaping the mounting pressure of living up to expectations. Was I just running away from situations that I should have stood up to and addressed?

And on this night, surrounded by the unending borderless New Mexico landscape, a sense of melancholy seemed to pass over me, the feeling of missing my family, my friends, my hometown slowly crept in as I took a deliberate saunter back to the house. Father Tom believed that my purpose was here, and from my very arrival, I would have agreed just on a hunch. Just twenty-four hours ago, things seemed very clear, now I wasn't so sure. For the first time, I questioned my decision to abandon my talents which had me rise up, so quickly and so fiercely.

Was this place, this time, really supposed to change all that?

10

Awakening to the sound of immense rain cascading on my roof, I knew that the drought-like conditions that we had been experiencing were finally over. It had been a dust bowl for weeks and many of the farmer's crops were on the brink of retreating. Getting out of bed with Zeke by my side, I went directly out in the yard and stood there in the drenching rain in nothing but my underwear, bent slightly backward with my hands raised to the sky, with both of us becoming completely saturated. It felt cool and refreshing as it came flowing down over my body. After several minutes, getting back in the house, I turned on the shower and finished the soaking that I started outdoors.

Zeke shook himself off while I grabbed a towel and dried him further. Having awoken earlier than expected I had a little extra time before heading to work. I took the shotgun now laying on my kitchen floor where I left it the night before, unfolded the cloth it was tangled in, and began to inspect it the best I could. It was especially dirty, and I had no idea how to go about cleaning it, but I would bet that I knew someone who did. Grabbing a rag, I started to wipe around the handle and trigger, but it didn't seem to make any difference. As I glanced up at the clock, I decided to place it in the hallway closet and get back to it when I had more time.

The rain continued at a steady hard pace with the pounding becoming louder as the morning went on. Scurrying to get myself ready, I hadn't noticed that leaks from above were causing small pools of water to accumulate in the kitchen and living room. In my haste, as I was about to find a clean pair of socks and shoes, I slipped on the wet floor, falling straight down on my buttocks. I laid there for a few minutes as I could feel the hard thump stinging the side of my hip. Zeke, of course, ran to my aid and was licking my face as I began to laugh and playfully roll alongside him. Eventually, I got myself up and set two pots beneath each drip, knowing I would have to address them later also.

Finally getting myself together, I picked up the cloth that the shotgun was covered in, wrapped it around my tabletop radio, and ran out through the pouring rain to Denise jumping into the front seat in one fell swoop. I headed over to the church with my windshield wipers on high speed. Visibility was at a minimum, but I was told that rains such as this were to be expected.

It was a deluge, and the first real thunderous storm I had experienced since coming here. Slowly driving over to the back of the church, I parked in the vacated spot left by the pickup truck in the workshop. Then grabbing my radio, and a brown bag lunch which I had prepared, I ran as fast as I could for the back entrance. It was teeming, and it didn't matter how quickly I made it inside, I was soaked to the bone.

Getting to the custodian room, I unlocked the door to find two new work uniforms neatly hanging from an exposed pipe in the ceiling. They couldn't have come at a better time. I quickly stripped down and changed into the welcoming dry clothes. Each set included khaki-colored pants and matching long sleeve shirts. I assumed Father Tom placed them there. With the pants being slightly larger than expected, I had to adjust my belt a couple of notches to keep them up, while the shirt seemed to fit fine.

I placed my radio on the desk, plugged it into the wall socket, and turned it on. The volume was turned down low while I could hear static as I fished around for a station with better reception. I still loved listening to music even if I chose not to create it anymore. *Theme from A Summer Place* came in clear as I slowly turned the dial and let it settle there.

The rain sounded even more ominous as it danced loudly on the vaulted ceiling above and I thought it best to inspect for leaks right away. Mass was over and once again, I was alone to do my work. I believed it would be a while before people got used to the idea that the doors would no longer be locked, and they could come and go as they pleased.

My fears were correct, there were several pools of water throughout the building and I could hear the drip in certain places continuing at a quickened pace. Three buckets from my office had now been set up, one at the very back of the church, one towards the side entrance, outside the confessional booth, and one on the altar itself, somewhere below the crucifix. As I dashed around with my mop getting the wet spots under control, I hoped that it would only amount to these three, I really wouldn't know how to repair a leak which was located so high above my reach.

When the rainy season starts it usually lasts close to two or three weeks, and I would have to make do with my bucket brigade until it resided. Somedays it would let up just enough to settle down to a steady pace, other days, it could feel like a floodgate had opened.

The number of chores that needed my care ranged far beyond just emptying buckets. With so many other issues that needed attention, my days were sure to be completely filled. It was no fault of Father Tom's, nor anyone else's for that matter, it just came down to what the parish could afford, and now that they had it, I professed to make things better.

Settling in, I tried not to question any major life decision, past or present, I was intent on focusing on the moment, and the undertakings that were set before me.

Many times, knowing that I was alone, I would turn up my radio and the music would echo throughout the building as I went about my business, it was a welcomed distraction and didn't make my surroundings feel so eerie. I started to become familiar with all the creaks, groans, and subtle sounds of the empty building and soon recognized where they would come from.

Deciding to leave the basement work for last, I concentrated on preparing the place to be as welcoming as possible for the general public. Each statue, other than the Crucifix was thoroughly cleaned and primed (I would need a sturdy ladder and a greater amount of attention and time to focus on the Crucifix later). I then set up the tiered candle stands with varying sizes of brand new votives, along with thin wooden lighting sticks, carrying out box after box, until they were all filled. I worked methodically, while continually monitoring each bucket as they randomly filled with rainwater.

A clanking noise at the back of the church turned my attention towards the entrance where I heard the main door open, temporarily letting in the sounds of the teeming rain. Pausing, I saw a small figure perched in the doorway. I didn't think that anyone would be out during the monsoon-like condition which was taking place but being familiar with the size and shape of the person standing in the vestibule, I approached. Carlos stood there shivering, soaking wet.

This young boy seemed lost, with nowhere else to go, solitary and alone. He would come around my home for frequent visits and now has proceeded to follow me here. I took him directly to my office and told him to wait while I got a towel out of the cloakroom and dried him off.

"What are you doing here? Its terrible weather, shouldn't you be in school or home or something?" I asked as I ran the towel over his rather full thick head of black hair.

"Señor, I come to be with you, I come to help you here." He responded displaying his gleaming white smile as he innocently grinned and shrugged his shoulders.

He followed me around for nearly the rest of the day and I allowed him to assist me whenever I could find something trivial for him to do. In any event, between him and my radio, it did make for some welcomed company.

"Hello Vincent, I see you have a new assistant with you today." Father Tom said as he came up behind us.

"I do Father, this is Carlos."

"Oh yes, we know Carlos very well around here." He said to my surprise.

"When you have a moment, why don't you let Carlos empty the rain buckets and come by and see me."

"Sure Father, let me tell him what to do, and I'll be right with you."

Our language difference, as much as it was getting better, still created a barrier. It took me time to try and explain my directions, and as I attempted, Father Tom stepped in and easily stated our instructions in Spanish. Carlos was off in a flash to fulfill the request.

Sitting in Father Tom's office, he went on to tell me all about Carlos. Both his parents died when he was but an infant, and he lived with his grandparents who had been raising him since. He didn't have many friends and preferred to be alone. Unlike most boys his age, he would rather hang around here than be on the playground and would usually show up the minute school was out for the day.

"I think, sometimes he looks to me as a replacement, or how do you say, um, 'father figure'. But it looks like you have gained his admiration rather quickly, from what I can tell." He said in a rather jovial tone.

"He seems like a good kid, and I don't mind him coming around, if you don't either, Father."

"He is a good boy, and it is fine with me. School does tend to get out rather early, before the heat and humidity take over, and it is better him being here then off getting into trouble somewhere, I guess."

I was beginning to make some headway on the list of the most immediate chores, and Carlos would randomly show up with each passing day. The rain began to subside somewhat and slowed to an easier pace, making our bucket emptying system a little less of a priority. The pews were all cleaned and polished, a fresh coat of paint was given to the lower interior walls, and I even managed to clean up the landscape around the outside, making it look more inviting. Some days, Carlos was there lending a helping hand and the best part of it all was seeing his expression while sharing my lunch with him. Whether Father Tom was right about me now becoming a strong support figure or not, didn't matter, I became used to having him around, and well, if he thought of me that way, so be it. I thought of him as a friend and I believed he thought the same in return.

With the church looking like it was getting a new facelift, and with the word spreading that the doors were open more frequently, a continuous flow of people began to come and go. Most of the time, when I was working in the public view, I would get a friendly nod or gesture in passing. There were some faces that I began to recognize and many others I didn't know at all, but each came to accept me as the quiet man who cleaned and maintained their prayer building.

Home became a welcome sight after spending longer days than expected at work. The rain had now greatly diminished and was down to a light gray mist.

The air had become cooler and walking to my house was relaxing. The most comforting sight I could imagine had become seeing Zeke laying on my front stoop with one paw tucked under his chin as he awaited my return. Otto was truly lucky to have found a loyal companion such as he. Like a guardian at the gate, through the foggy mist at dusk, he would see me, sit up and start his tail wagging furiously, as I approached.

This night I decided that after a good dinner, Zeke and I would just take it easy, plop down on the couch and watch some television. No hammers, no paint, no water buckets, no shotguns, and no statues. Frankie was continuing to work double shifts and we hadn't spent as much time together as we had on prior evenings. But the weekend had arrived, and I knew that I would be seeing her tomorrow, that is after I had the chance to start repairing the leaks from my own roof, (The large bruise on my left hip was a reminder to address that issue right away), bright and early the next morning..

"Anybody home.... Vincent.........are you here?" A voice called out in the early hours, penetrating the silence from below.

"I'm up here!" I responded as I looked down from my rooftop.

"Up here, where?" the voice continued

"I'm up on the roof, come around the back so I can see you."

"There you are, and I bet I know what you're doing up there."

Looking downward I could the simple beauty of Frankie's features smiling up at me.

"I thought you had to work a double today?"

"It was slow, so I was able to get some time off and thought I would pop over to see what you were up to."

'Popping' over for her was nothing short of about a two-mile walk. She walked wherever she went, within reason that is, and she was in fit enough shape to do it. I climbed down slowly from my roof at it shortest point, ten feet from the ground, where I stacked a couple of wooden crates to ease myself downward. Roofs were leaking all over town and Frankie's was no exception.

"That's one hell of a ladder you have working there." She said pointing to my boxes.

"I know, I know, but it was the quickest way I could get up there before the rain breaks out again. I got a couple of leaks, but I think I have fixed them, for the time being."

"That's great because now you have to come and fix mine!"

"Alright, how many do you have?"

"Rough estimate, oh, about half a dozen.... I think."

"What! six, six leaks. Let's go. Gee, you know, you are lucky I like you."

Getting into Denise, under some very threatening cloud cover, we stopped at the workshop, where I picked up a box of leftover roof shingles from the feast's gazebo, a pail of nails, and the old, very shaky ladder, that I still had not fully repaired yet. It had seen better days, it was rotted in a few places with traces of green paint showing and rusted bolts holding it together. There was one very noticeable broken rung, and I had to make sure not to step on it with my full weight while climbing. Father Tom did order a new one, but it was out of stock and would take weeks before it arrived. So, gathering some rope, we tied it to Denise's roof, and off we went.

I worked as quickly as I could while Frankie held the ladder each time I climbed or descended. I not only did what I could to fix her roof, but we ended up salvaging most of her neighbors and a handful of others as we drove through town. All told, we repaired over fourteen roofs that day just before the rain steadily increased once again.

With each repair I made, word circulated that 'the custodian' was coming around to patch up as many roofs as he could free of charge. And working out of genuine concern, I didn't ask for any payment either. Many folks handed us fruits and vegetables that they grew in their yards, some gave us baked goods and others fully cooked meals, I even received a box of hand-rolled cigars. By the time we had ended, somewhere before nightfall, a persistent drizzle had begun, and we were headed back to my house with a bounty of food that would last for weeks, maybe longer.

"Hey, I had a thought," I said reservedly.

"And what might that be?"

"It's getting late, we have plenty of food here, and I think Zeke.......and ONLY Zeke wouldn't mind if you stayed here tonight, we do have a freshly painted, clean and dry second bedroom you know."

"You think you are soooo funny, don't you Mr. Vincent? Oh, Ok, Zeke and only Zeke, wouldn't mind?" she said with a large grin on her face.

"I have no idea what you mean honey," I responded, doing all I could to contain my laughter.

Knowing Frankie would be in my house, right in the next room was something I found comforting yet distracting. I wanted to find my way to be by her side but resisted enough to try and wait for a more appropriate time. I tossed and turned for most of the night before passing out from exhaustion.

The next morning with the rain continuing on cue, as expected, I awoke to the smell of coffee and fresh bacon and eggs. Zeke, usually at my bedside was nowhere to be found and I presumed he was already in the kitchen alongside Frankie.

Making my way there, she was at the stove, looking quite adorable, wearing my old worn out Boston Braves sweatshirt which was much too large and hung down very low. Her hair was pulled back in a ponytail with her bare legs and feet exposed. Watching her there, smiling, and getting breakfast together, brought me such a feeling of warmth and adoration. I stood staring for several minutes while she continued. It was just the three of us, sitting around the kitchen table enjoying a slow Saturday morning while the sounds of the television hovered in the background.

"I had another idea," I said with a more serious note.

"Another idea, Mr. Vincent?" She responded as she took a sip of her coffee.

"Yeah, and I think it may be a good one too."

"Okay, you sure it's your idea? Or did Zeke put you up to it?"

"Very funny, but here's what I was thinking."

She listened to me intently as we got into Denise, choosing to leave Zeke at home for this trip. Out on the 007, I powered through several large puddles that had formed in the crevices on the highway. The sky seemed to be clearing and an elongated rainbow had appeared off in the distance. Both of us noticing it simultaneously looked at each other and contently smiled, while I quickly informed Frankie what todays plan entailed. A short while later I pulled off the road at the *GAS+Plus*. Much to our surprise, it was now boarded up with signs indicating that new owners had taken over and it would be remodeled and reopening shortly.

We parked on the side of the building so that we wouldn't gain any attention from passersby's.

"Let's go, follow me," I said as I quickly got out of the car and headed around back.

The back of the building was not boarded up as the front. I knew Otto would always leave one of the windows unlocked just in case he forgot his keys and I was hoping this was still the case. Frankie gave me a boost and thankfully it was. Pushing it open, I climbed in and tumbled to the floor.

"Are you ok." She whispered.

"Yeah, I'm fine," I said as I brushed myself off and looked down at her from inside.

I groped around until I found what I was looking for and within minutes I was back at the window lowering a small, but heavy box, down to her. Then grabbing four quarts of oil from a nearby shelf, and a two-gallon container that Otto generally had filled with gas, I handed them out to her as well, before climbing back out and down to ground level. We made our way hurriedly over to Denise and placed our goods in the trunk before heading out as fast as we arrived.

The rainbow was still visible, but now fading. I cranked up the radio, rolled down the windows, and sped off towards home. In the trunk was now a brand-new battery along with battery cables and fresh oil. I would return and pay for everything once the new owner was in place, but for now, this was my only recourse to put my next plan into action.

We went straight over to the workshop and parked Denise directly in front of the old pick-up. Then removing the box from my trunk and retrieving a wrench from the toolbox there, I opened the hood of the truck and took out the old corroded battery. Cleaning off the connectors the best I could, I replaced the battery with the new one and attached the cables from the truck to the battery in Denise. Emptying the gas container into the truck's tank, Frankie looked on with hopeful anticipation.

"Ok, start her up, and when I tell you, rev her engine."

I climbed into the truck, placed the key into the ignition, and gave Frankie the signal. Hearing Denise's engine roar, I turned the ignition and the truck's engine began to make a whirling sound. I tried it again, and after several waning moments, it turned over and started up, bellowing large puffs of white smoke from its tailpipe.

We sat there and let it run for a while, feeling victorious. Looking at the engine, I could see that there were many worn down parts, which I didn't know much about, but for now, the best I would be able to do is try and change the oil and see how it drove out on the road.

"We did it!" I said as I removed the cables and shut the hood.

"Now all I have to do is change the oil in this baby and see where it goes!"

"Oil changes, batteries, car repairs, and you said I had many talents. Where did you learn all this, Mr. Vincent?"

"Oh, this is nothing, it's just basic stuff. But I had a friend once, a great friend, who was pretty good with this kind of stuff………..his name was, was……., Johnny."

"Johnny? Now that's the first real thing I have ever heard you tell me about your past!"

Frankie stood close, I wiped the grease from my hands with a rag as I quickly changed the subject.

"So here is what I was thinking, I never really let anybody drive Denise before, but now that I got this old jalopy working…. well……. Maybe you would like to keep Denise in your driveway. And I guess……you can use her whenever you need too."

She said nothing, looked at me with a sense of admiration, and just threw her arms around me giving me the biggest hug I could imagine. We stood there like that, for what seemed like an eternity.

"Uh, are you alright?" I said as she held onto me tightly.

Our embrace separated as I noticed her wipe a tear from her eye.

"You are a kind and gentle man Vincent, and I…...I…..."

She stopped abruptly as we just looked silently at each other. The moment was deeply intense. I knew how I was beginning to feel about Frankie. And it frightened me.

I pulled away, unintentionally.

"What, what is it, Vincent? Is it that you just don't think of me that way? Because I do think of you that way, and sometimes I think you feel the same."

"That's not it, that's not it at all, honey. It's just that…. a long time ago…...I, uh…. well, I have a story to tell you. But not here and not now. It's long and it ain't pretty. Tell you what, I will come by one night this week and we will sit down, and I will spill it all, I promise."

"Okay, okay, I will be looking forward to that." She said lowering her voice with silent concern.

"Well, you may want to have a bottle of wine ready for this one."

Now that Frankie had access to Denise, she would show up more often. It was a pleasure to see her come humming up from around the bend. Most days I would be working diligently in the workshop, but every so often, she would unexpectedly meander into the church to see what I was up to.

I knew she was patiently waiting for me to get to her house as promised. This time, there would be no avoiding it, this time there was no way out, I would have to come clean, and now, I cared and trusted Frankie enough to let it happen.

I spent the entire next day attempting to bring the pick-up truck back up to full working order. Doing my best with the oil change and lubricating most of the moving parts, I went on to give it a thorough washing and cleaning. Letting the engine run for a while as clouds of white smoke continued to be sporadically released from its exhaust.

I knew it was time to give it a test run. The tires were low on air and worn down, but they would have to do for now. Just before I was about to give it the gas and release the choke, Carlos appeared out of nowhere and I motioned him to jump in. We drove around the church several times with loud backfiring noises popping free. Carlos was laughing with glee and yelling things out in Spanish as I tried to keep up with him in English.

It wasn't a very smooth ride, we bounced from our seats every time we hit a bump, but circling several times, we were having fun. The radio didn't work, but I noticed several loose wires hanging down and would address them later also, but for now, I was content just getting this thing moving again. It was a project that Carlos and I would continue working on together.

With the rainy season heading to a close, the evening sky seemed more illuminated than usual. Sitting out on my back porch with Zeke, puffing away on one of those hand-rolled cigars I was gifted, it was as if we had our very own light show taking place. The clouds were parting and moving further from us, giving way to the most alluring brilliance of colors cast onto the horizon. Every once in a while it looked as if a shooting star would cross our field of vision and I couldn't help but think of Otto. It was a thankful way to relax before a new week of chores were to begin.

The first and most important thing I learned from all the rain and roof work that just occurred was the importance of a dependable ladder and the one at my disposable, surely did not fit the bill. Knowing that I needed to get up high to clean the Crucifix in the upcoming weeks, I was intent on repairing it the best I could. The broken rung had to be replaced and many others were in a much-weakened state. The bolts holding it together were badly rusted and I questioned their strength. I would have to disassemble most of it, replace several sections with new wood, and attach it all back together using the strongest nails and screws I had.

As the days continued forward, I became quite comfortable in this solitary working environment and basking in the serenity of each day. Being generally alone gave me a sense of inner strength, one that I thought had completely disappeared. And seeing the faces of those who frequented this place was intriguing. Some were joyful, some were troubled, and some were just trying to cope with life. But they came here to find peace also, they came here, if only for just a few minutes to gain some conviction in their faith, something that I felt was stirring within me once more. They started to see me as another constant in their lives, if Father Tom was their inspirational leader, then I was their standard-bearer, keeping watch over this sacred space.

"It looks like you are going through something." I whispered with concern.

I approached a younger man somewhere in his teens, kneeling in the front row with his head down, sobbing quietly.

Being caught off guard, he looked up at me as I unexpectedly drew closer. Not responding at all, with a trail of tears running down both of his cheeks, he simply nodded yes.

"You see that statue up there? I'm going to light a candle for you, right there."

I continued, pointing to one of the larger votive holders hanging on the wall, below and to the right of the Crucifix. He wiped his eyes with his shirt sleeve and shook his head once again. I didn't need to know what his trouble was, I just knew that he needed consolation right then and there, and it felt good to be able to offer it to him.

"My mother.......she sick.........gracias, gracias......." He quietly responded as he pointed towards the candle holder getting up slowly, bowing his head, and making his way out the door.

At that moment, I was transported back, seeing his pain and knowing what it was like to endure such a hardship at a young age. But if I could offer any kind of compassion, no matter how brief it was, or how insignificant it might have seemed, then I felt like a better person for it. It was these kinds of circumstances, that I encountered frequently and those which began to teach me what I valued as my role here.

After spending several hours each day working on it, the ladder was in the best possible condition that I could manage, or so I thought. It didn't look very sturdy or appealing, but I hoped it would hold up long enough for me to find my way up to the Crucifix. It now resembled a combination of old faded and splintering dark wood, screwed tightly with sections of bright new wood, all held together with roofing nails, large metal bolts, and industrial tape.

At least one day a month, I was allowed to lock all the doors for a couple of hours to allow me to perform certain duties that were better suited to be done, for safety reasons, away from the public eye. These included such tasks as changing light bulbs over the seating areas, repairing pews and kneelers and other duties involving work in open areas.

Knowing I was to be alone, I brought in the raggedy looking ladder and decided to give it a trial run for just such a job. Light bulbs first, and many needed changing, and then the Crucifix second, taking as much time as needed.

In my office, I turned up the volume on my Philco radio, it echoed loudly throughout the building and could be heard to the back of the church. Not a soul in sight, just myself and that Crucifix staring out at me. Sometimes I felt as if its glance was piercing and wanted to drape a cloth over it while I worked so it wasn't so glaringly intimidating.

The light stations were set about ten feet apart from each other for a total of twenty in all, with each housing four bulbs. I started towards the front of the church, propping the ladder up against the wall and replacing bulbs in each station as needed. Every time I climbed up the ladder I could hear it creak in certain spots making me very uneasy as I reached the highest point. But with no other immediate work to be done, I worked slowly and methodically. The sunlight looked like it was back in full swing as the stain glass windows were streaking colors throughout the interior of the church. It all seemed to coincide with the music resonating from my radio.

Halfway through, I decided to take a break. Wandering up the back stairs, I found myself in the choir loft spying out towards the front of the building. I leaned on the railing with both my forearms gazing ahead. The Crucifix's vision seemed to be directed right at me, even from that distance. I turned, faced the mighty pipe organ, walked towards it, and sat before it. Its sheer presence overwhelmed me.

Sometimes a moment of courage overtakes you when you least expect it. (and when nobody else is around). But I sat there and gingerly placed my hands on the keys. I slid them ever so gently over the entire keyboard, barely making contact. Then I paused. Breathing slowly, I reached down under the right side and switched it on. It hummed strong and steady as it began to go to work.

One note, then two, I stopped. Another deep breath, and a few more notes. It was a rush of feelings, invigorating, monumental. My heart raced as I played a portion of Bach for ten minutes. Stopping again, I got up and was overwhelmed with a feeling of anger.

"You….. that's right, you there, hey, you down there, I'm talking to you!! I yelled out pointing my finger at The Crucifix.

"Is this what you want me to do?"

I paced back and forth in the empty choir loft, with both my arms spread out in opposite directions, fighting back the tears and kicking the bench once as I walked by.

"I had a voice and now it's gone, why? So I could end up here, cleaning a statue…. Oh….. and excuse me……. Guarding you!!" My words echoed loud throughout the emptiness of the building.

My heart pounded. And I felt a sweat begin to rise. I sat back down on the bench facing that immense organ once again. In the background, echoing louder than ever I could my radio playing, it was, the Sonny James hit which sold millions of copies a couple of years earlier, *Young Love*. I could remember singing this many times in my travels. Now, alone again, I began to play along on the organ.

Then in an instance, uncontrollably, after nearly years of silence, I began to sing………...

They say for every boy and girl
There's just one love in this whole world
And I know I've found mine, I've found mine.
The heavenly touch of your embrace
Tells me no one could take your place
Ever in my heart…….

Young love......... first love
Filled with true devotion
Young love........... our love
We share with deep emotion..........

I stopped playing the organ, stood up, and acted as if I was on stage once again. This time I faced an empty audience, I faced the crucifix, smiled and sung as I had never missed a beat. My voice, as far as I could tell, was still in perfect pitch and as youthful as ever. It was exhilarating!

Suddenly startled by a sound just below me, I stopped immediately. All the doors were locked, I was sure of it and yet it sounded as if the side door entrance just below the choir loft had just slammed shut. In a nervous dash, I ran down the stairs two at a time, stumbling as I reached the bottom.

It was unlocked!

How could I have made such a tremendously foolish error? Opening the door and bolting outside I heard the unmistakable sound of a slant six engine motoring off in a cloud of dust. Catching a glimpse, I knew the shape of those rear headlights all too well, they belonged to the only car I have been driving since I was nineteen years old.

11

Back inside with a dejected spirit, I went straight to my office, shut the radio and sat at my desk, and pondered what I was to do next? Why did she leave without confronting me right here and now? I contemplated my next move for several minutes with confusion abounding. I need to first finish changing the lightbulbs, turn off that damn infernal organ, clean up, and then think about what to do at this point.

Leaving my office and hustling about to lock up, I was startled as I found Carlos standing silently in the altar area, most likely, also finding his way in through the unlocked door. He was staring intensely, stoically, at the Crucifix, as if he were being held captive by its gaze.

"Carlos…. Carlos!" I said as I shook him back into awareness.

"What are you doing, what's the matter? How long have you been here?" I continued frantically, feeling quite unnerved by his sudden still stance.

"Sen ore……Sen ore, el se movio…. el se movio." He said, mumbling something incoherently in Spanish, pointing overhead.

"What? I'm not sure I understand what you are saying, but we have to go home right now. I will see you tomorrow, Ok?"

In my haste, I paid no mind to his rambling, I had little time to concern myself with a young boy's imagination. My immediate plan was to gather him along, drop him off at home, and continue my pace to secure the church before I was to move over to more pressing matters.

Leaving the ladder propped up against the wall, very close to the Crucifix, I decided it would be best to come back early tomorrow and start with its cleaning. Right now, I better get over to Frankie's and try to explain all of this. Perhaps the time had finally come, she had become as dear a friend to me as Johnny was, and friends of that caliber deserved honesty. And if we were ever to become more, I had to come clean.

I made my way out early, it was only three o'clock in the afternoon, but feeling like this was a priority, I didn't think Father Tom would mind me leaving. Climbing into the pick-up, it started up slowly, backfiring a couple of times before I could get good gas flowing through it. Dropping off Carlos, then stopping home for a moment and feeding Zeke, I gathered my thoughts as I headed over to Frankie's.

"Stay Zeke, I think it's better I handle this one alone tonight, buddy." I said while petting his head and snoot a few times as he tried to follow me onto the front seat.

I still hadn't managed to tinker with the radio or its loose dangling wires yet, so the ride over was a silent one. I had been to her house hundreds of times, sure sometimes I did have butterflies, but today, it felt more like crows. I didn't know what to expect, nor did I have any idea how I was going to address this. Closing in on her neighborhood, her house came quickly into view as I came around the corner. The driveway was empty, no Denise, and no Frankie I presumed. Parking out front, I decided to wait.

The sky grew overcast again, as tepid stray showers fell intermittently. I sat there fidgeting, trying to look under the dash at the loose radio connections. About an hour later Frankie pulled up. Seeing Denise was comforting, and at the same time nerve-racking. Frankie parked her right in the driveway and went immediately inside, not acknowledging me at all.

I knew I had a lot of explaining to do, so biting my upper lip, I garnered up my courage and headed towards the front door. Knocking twice, I wondered for a moment if she was even going to answer.

She did.

The look on her face was not the usual happy, smiling one, I was accustomed to. Instead, she stared sternly at me, opened the door, then turned and walked inside. I followed her slowly debating with myself on the best way to approach the subject.

Making our way into the kitchen, I sat down across from her at the table where she also abruptly took a seat. Looking at me with certain skepticism, whether it was for my singing, or holding out so long about my past, I couldn't tell for sure, we sat there awkwardly for a while in silence.

"Sometimes, things don't go the way you plan in life……and well, I guess I have a story to tell you," I said rather embarrassedly.

"I'm listening."

The sound of despair was clearly evident in my voice as I gazed down at the table. Then looking up at her and into her eyes, I continued.

"Listen, I can honestly say that I have never met anyone like you. You are the one person who I've come trust right now…...and I trust you with my life."

"But not your heart?" She interrupted.

"Oh No……., especially my heart, and that scares the hell out of me! I have had this wall up around me for so long, I don't know how to let it down. I have met other women before I arrived here, but…...…you……you are different."

"What happened to you Vincent?" she said now with a bit of compassion in her eyes as she reached out for my hand across the table.

For the next several hours, I proceeded to tell her the truth about everything. It had been years since I buried all those memories, from Lizzy to The Ravens Nest, to Dexter Demarco, to the tormenting dreams, to the unexpected death of my father. Now as I sat across from the most sincere, gentlest, caring person I had ever met, a rush of emotions came swarming back. Tears began to well up in my eyes, and she couldn't help but notice.

"I am so sorry Vincent, I am so sorry you had to go through all that." And I'm so sorry about your father."

I held her hand tightly as she looked sorrowfully at me.

"It explains a lot, I can see now that you haven't got over all of it yet, did you ever talk to anyone about it? What about your friend Johnny?"

"My father's death was difficult in itself, and I guess I harbor a lot of anger over it, but my other situation, it just compounded things. As far as telling anyone, well, no one, not a soul, not really. Sure, some people were there when it all came down, but no one knew what actually took place, I continued to protect Lizzy and her reputation. No one knew how much it destroyed me. I kept it all inside.............until now, that is. And Johnny, well he was there with me, he saved my life."

She withdrew her hand from mine and slowly rose from the table. Moving over to the kitchen counter she leaned back and looked at me with some confusion.

"Okay, Okay.... wait a minute, yes, that does explain a lot, but I couldn't believe what I heard today! Was that you? Was that really you, I heard?"

"Yes, honey, that was me."

From there, pacing back and forth in her kitchen, I went on to tell her all about my singing abilities. I filled the next hour with stories of sensationalism regarding my talent. I told her about my days at The Conservatory, my experiences with crowds, and being a child prodigy. I even told her about Oppenheim and Z Klein. And of course, the band Johnny formed and the audiences we won over at The Raven's Nest. I went on about Johnny, how I loved his style, especially how he wouldn't go anywhere without his guitar, and how he always wore it strapped around his back, and how he was known for wearing dark sunglasses and slicked-back hair. And how he exactly 'saved my life' on a fateful night in Boston.

I explained in detail all the good moments as well as the bad, and how I just picked up and left everything behind. Filling her in, I ventured to tell her that the only connection I still had back home were the letters I continued to write to my mother, keeping her abreast of my travels and each city or town that I stayed in for more than a couple of days. I told Frankie how I arrived here, the night I met her, in this place, with a strange and uncanny feeling that this is where I belonged.

I think by the time I was done, Frankie was as emotionally drained as I was. She shuffled around the kitchen and sat back down at the table.

"Well now you know, you know it all, at least I think I haven't forgotten any of the important stuff. No one else in this town knows any of this, especially the singing part, and please honey, I am trusting you to keep it that way."

She looked puzzled. I laid a lot of information on her in a short amount of time. She always thought of me as a mystery man, but I think I gave her more than she bargained for.

"I.... I.... won't say a word, I promise. But Vincent.........uh......uh.."

"What?"

"I...I... don't know what to say right now....... I...I...need...."

"Honey, I understand, no need to say anything, it's a lot to think about."

The hours had dragged on and before we knew it, the moonlight was bearing down on us through the window. She stood there stoically, looking into space as I walked over and gently kissed her on the forehead.

"I'll see you tomorrow?"

She shook her head yes, slowly, not saying anything further, as I turned and headed out the door.

I was angry with myself for leaving that side door of the church unlocked. I had every intention of telling Frankie about my past, but this wasn't the way I foresaw it. As I drove home, I felt some strange sense of relief, knowing that, for good, bad, or worse, she now knew it all.

The rainy season was at its official end and so too, the bucket lineup I had going at the church. We were headed into the fall and a cooler air had migrated in. I continued with my duties, becoming more adept at them each day. Carlos showed up more frequently after school as I became accustomed to seeing that familiar eager look emanating from beneath his wide-brimmed straw hat. Our bond seemed to be getting stronger, not to mention his appetite and physical appearance as well. I had forgotten what a growing young boy can consume daily, as I would often save part of my lunch to share with him later in the day.

"Buenos Dias, Señor Vincent."

"And a Buenos Dias to you my young friend. And, uh, hold on, I think its.........Como estas hoy?"

"Ahhh, muy bien......I mean, eh, very good, Mr. Vincent, very good."

"And wait a minute Carlos, uh, I can say.........Ladder, escalera." I motioned as if I were climbing.

"Hammer, martillo." I motioned as if I were hammering something.

"And, truck, camion." I motioned as if I were steering an automobile.

Carlos began laughing out loud as he pointed up at me in delight. My Spanish was getting a little more understandable, while his English was also becoming better at a rapid pace. He was learning other things as well, and I was proud to be the one teaching him.

From minor wood-working skills, to handling all sorts of tools, and occasional driving lessons in the old pick-up, we continued to seal our friendship. We also went as far as to build a wooden enclosure which was attached to the back of the open flatbed of the truck, it came in handy keeping supplies on board. We managed to get the radio wired up, although the speaker was so old that it cracked consistently making it hard to understand it clearly at times.

I was comfortable going into town for provisions while letting him drive, which he was more than happy to do. He was a bright young boy and picked up things very quickly. Father Tom also noticed that exact thing as he saw him progressing by my side. There was even a standing joke between us, that Carlos could replace me someday.

I hadn't seen Frankie in almost a week and feared that my confession harmed our relationship. But keeping my wits about me, I thought it best to give her some time and space. Staying busy in my work, I did my best to resist running over to her and seeing if her reaction had changed at all, but the more I resisted, the more difficult it became.

Now that I had a kitchen of my own, I hadn't eaten at the diner in quite some time and trying not to be too conspicuous, I thought that maybe I would just happen to stop in for a quick meal.

With my usual booth being available, I sat myself down, noticing that Frankie had her back to me as she waited on a table at the opposite end of the row. Seeing me as she turned, she stopped to have a word with the other waitress, Tess, then walked behind the counter and into the kitchen.

"Haven't seen you for a while, whatya have?" Tess said as she chewed a mouthful of gum.

"Hi Tess, listen, nothing personal, but do you think I might have the 'other' waitress take my order?"

"Uh, I dunno." She responded quietly as she looked back over her shoulders at the kitchen entrance, twice.

"Please, I would consider it a personal favor," I said very politely, trying to turn on the charm.

"Oh, hold on, let me see."

She turned and went right into the kitchen where I heard some chattering before Frankie came out with her pad in hand, right to my table.

"Ok, make it quick, I get off in 15 minutes, what would you like?"

"You look good, I haven't seen you in a while and the last time we talked, well, I was just wondering........."

"Vincent, did you come here to eat or for something more?" she said sounding somewhat short with me.

"I thought we could maybe catch that new John Wayne flick, *Rio Bravo*, tomorrow night?"

"Like I said, I'm off in 15 minutes, meet me by my ...uh I mean your car around back."

Not particularly liking the tone in her voice. I folded the menu and took my leave, going around back as she instructed. There, Denise was parked, and I went over and leaned on her with my back against the driver's side door, waiting for Frankie to come out.

"You know, I have been doing a lot of thinking. You're not the only one in this world who has had their heart broken Vincent." She said coming right towards me as I stood there motionless.

"Yes, I know it was a terrible thing that happened to you, but I think you haven't gotten over it. I think you may still need a lot more time to heal, and I just don't know if I want to be involved with all of it right now, Vincent. It's been years and you still are carrying it around with you! Furthermore, I don't know how you could give up such a talent, a God-given talent like the one you have!"

She turned and walked away, opening the door to the car, as I was brushed aside, then pausing for another second, she looked at me with sadness.

"I'll bring your car back by the end of the week if that's ok?"

"Frankie, that's not necessary, wait.........I think we should talk .... Frankie."

I tried to make some sense out of it, trying to reason with her, but she got into the car, shut the door, and drove off. Left standing there in the parking lot, I never felt so alone. I wasn't even sure what had happened between us, but I knew I had to find a way to make it right.

That night, sitting on my back porch with Zeke, I felt a sense of loss that hadn't come over me in years. The last time it happened it was for many different reasons, this time I felt fully responsible. I thought about all she said in those two minutes behind the diner. Maybe she was right, maybe I never really dealt with the pain and humiliation. I just buried it and ran.

My work, and the church, became a haven for me. The hours passed quickly as I kept busy, but Frankie occupied most of my thoughts. If this was to be the end of our relationship, I didn't know if I could stick around, maybe they still needed my talents at the bishop's office in El Paso, maybe I should pack up again and take Denise and head further west. Whatever the resolution was to be, I was feeling disjointed over the whole situation.

Sometimes, things need to be done, tasks need to be addressed, and I had recently learned that waiting isn't always the best solution. It was that very way when it came time to finally clean the Crucifix. I don't know exactly why it took me so long, or why I was so hesitant, perhaps I wasn't so keen on getting up close and personal with it, or it could simply have been because I wasn't looking forward to climbing that old ladder again. Whatever the circumstance, I couldn't put my finger on it, but I sure couldn't put it off any longer.

Having left the ladder parked right on the back wall behind the altar for the last two days, Father Tom was a bit perturbed having to say mass with it in full view.

"Vincent, I take it you plan to get up there today and remove the ladder when you are done?"

"Yes, sorry Father, it will be done today, I promise, but I am going to lock the doors and tend to it later in the day when I'm sure no one will be here."

Making my way to my office, I prepared a solution of pure milled soap and luke-warm water in a small bucket, one that was handy enough for me to maneuver and carry up with me. I then plucked a clean white rag from a burlap bag and started towards the altar.

Turning on all the spotlights and ceiling lights, I proceeded around the corner, then, struck by a moment of panic, I couldn't believe what I was seeing.

There at the base of the ladder was a body lying on the ground, unconscious. It was a small familiar frame, wearing a typical white shirt and pants, with a straw hat laying close by.

Dropping the bucket of cleaning solution, I ran straight for him. And began to call out frantically.

"FATHER TOM! FATHER TOM! ANYBODY! HELP!"

I knelt over him, my heart racing fiercely, first checking to see if he was breathing, thankfully he was, but at a slow pace. I patted his cheek lightly calling his name.

"Carlos……Carlos……come on buddy, wake up!"

There was no response.

"HELP! HELP! ANYBODY!" I yelled out again.

Taking the rag from my back pocket I mopped up some water which was in a small puddle behind him and tried to use the wet cloth to revive him wiping his forehead and then his face. It trickled down his chin, still no response. In a moment of sheer urgency, I picked up his limp body and ran for the pick-up truck parked out back. Laying him on the back bed and closing the gate, I raced at top speed to Doc Coot's office.

Busting through the doctor's front office door, Milly the receptionist-nurse sprung up from her chair and immediately let me in.

"Bring him in here!," she screamed as she flung open the door to an examining room.

"DOCTOR!, EMERGENCY IN ROOM TWO" She called out.

The doctor came running in, as I placed Carlos down on an exam bed face up and still unconscious.

"What happened?" He asked as he opened Carlos's shirt and placed his stethoscope on his chest.

"I don't know doc, I found him lying under my ladder, laying there. I don't know if he tried to climb it and fell, or what."

The nurse quickly escorted me out of the room, closing the door, while the doctor took over.

I sat in the waiting room, struggling to figure out what happened. What was Carlos doing there in the first place? He usually comes in and finds me right away, this time he took it upon himself to be on his own. Then I remembered what he was mumbling the other day, 'el se movio', perhaps his wild imagination got the best of him, or perhaps I should have listened to him more closely.

After nearly thirty minutes, the doctor came out putting on his jacket, looking very concerned.

"Vincent, we have to get him over to Our Lady of the Roses hospital in Santa Fe, right away. He is unconscious, but his vital signs are stable, I need to be sure there is no internal bleeding."

"Doc, what can I do? I'm coming with you!"

"Well then, let's go, I called the sheriff and he is going to escort us."

The hospital was a good fifty minutes away at top speed, but with the sheriff clearing our path, we made it there in nearly thirty.

There was a gurney waiting for him the moment we pulled up and a team of interns wearing white, rushed him off. Moments later, I found myself in a waiting room, pacing nervously and migrating from chair to chair, while I hoped for some positive news.

It was hours later when Doctor Coots appeared with a weary look about him.

"Doc! what is it? Is he okay?" I said jumping out of my seat.

"Well, it seems as if this goes a bit deeper than just a fall. The boy has a brain tumor, a fairly sizable one, pressing against his optic nerve also affecting his pituitary gland. It is probably why he has never grown to his full capacity like other boys his age. He must have had it for some time. But he also looks like he had a fall, evidenced by the lump on his head. He is in a coma. We are doing all we can right now."

I stood stunned, and helpless.

"Doc, can I see him?"

"Not now Vincent, he is getting the best of care, let's go home and get some rest, maybe in a day or two. We will have to see how his condition progresses."

Back home, I just wanted to get into a hot shower and my bed. I knew the news about Carlos probably reached everyone in town by now and I didn't feel much like giving any explanations.

Getting to work the next morning, I was overcome with a feeling of uneasiness. I had grown accustomed to having Carlos around. Too tired to make the walk, I drove the pickup and parked it in the workshop. Then going around through the back door, I remembered that the ladder must still be where I left it and Father Tom would not be very happy seeing it there. I hoped that under the circumstance he would understand.

Mass had already begun, but this time as I peered through the window, I could see that the place was full, it looked as if it were a Sunday, rather than just a weekday. I noticed an elderly couple sitting right in front, with Father Tom addressing them directly. I recognized right away having met them once before, they were Carlos's grandparents. Everyone here had come out to pray for him and it was a moving sight.

I busied myself with other responsibilities as I waited for the place to clear out. In the hallway headed downstairs, Father Tom and I inadvertently met.

"Hello, Father." I said in a rather dejected tone.

"Hello Vincent, how are you doing?"

"Seen better days.... I guess."

"I know you are worried about Carlos, as we all are. It is out of our hands. Stay positive my son."

"Trying to Father.......... Oh and I will finish cleaning the statue, I mean the Crucifix this morning and get the damn ladder out of the way.... oops sorry, Father."

After the crowds had finished filing out, I later returned to complete what I started before I was derailed by Carlos's incident. Again, mixing a cleaning solution in a small bucket and gathering a clean rag, I made my way to the back of the altar where my ladder still stood. Before even attempting to find my way up, I noticed once again that there was a small puddle of water at my feet, it was there the other day when in my moment of hysteria, I wet my cloth and wiped Carlos's head and face, and it was there yet again today.

The leak in the roof must have been bigger than I thought. Getting my mop and bucket I cleaned up the area and set them aside. Looking up at The Crucifix, with mixed emotions, I began a slow steady climb, holding the bucket by the wire handle attached to it and the rag hanging from my back pocket. Halfway up I could feel that loose rung as I gently stepped over it, making sure not to exert my full weight on it. Five more feet up and I was there

There are times in life when I had questioned things, everyone at some point does. My faith was not as strong as it used to be, with past situations having shaken me, but here I was, standing face to face and eye to eye with an image that I knew all too well. A mild sweat came over me.

I reached into my back pocket, pulled out my cleaning rag, dipped it into the bucket, and began to wipe in a circular motion. My hand traveled up and down as I could feel the actual anatomy, every rib, muscle, and bone. This sculptor, this creator, whoever it might be, was magnificent. Being this close made me realize that the features, and those eyes, especially those eyes were more realistic than I have ever imagined. My sweat turned into a subtle chill.

Cleaning the wounds sent an odd feeling throughout my body, almost as if an electric current was emitted, causing me to almost lose my footing momentarily. Grasping the ladder tighter, I paused for a moment and taking a deep breath, I pressed on.

"So, I finally made it here, I'm just going to clean you up, it looks like it's been a while, there is a nice film of dirt all over you, but I'll be done in a flash." I quietly stated.

"Hey, listen, please don't take it personally, I didn't mean to yell at you the other day, I was just remembering things that I shouldn't, but you probably already knew that."

I continued wiping and ringing out my rag with each pass I made.

"You know, I haven't been a strong church-goer recently, but, well, if there is anything you could do for Carlos, a whole lot of people around here would appreciate it……...uh, yeah even me. He is only a little boy ya know."

In about an hour I was done, the statue looked even brighter and more realistic than it had looked before. My bucket water was almost brown, it must have been years since someone had gone up there. Getting down from that ladder was quite a relief, but there yet again, a tiny puddle had formed near the base at my feet. I would need to find a way up to the roof in the days ahead to check the condition from the outside. The other leaks did not continue as this one had, and the steady rain had stopped some time ago. A passing shower or two could be the culprit, especially if there were timbers or slates up there that needed replacing.

I spent the next two days in Santa Fe at the hospital. Father Tom had granted me time off so that I could be near Carlos, even though he wasn't aware of my presence. The whole time there, I didn't venture out to see the sights of the city, I stayed mainly by his bedside, talking, and reading to him. I was told that although he was comatose, the sounds of my voice, or anyone else's for that matter, could make a difference. So there, I sat, going on about it.

The nurses let me sleep in the chair next to his bedside, it wasn't at all comfortable, but it allowed me to keep my vigil during the night. And each time a doctor came in to check up on him, I would begin my rant of a dozen questions, and each time I was told the same thing, 'no progress to report'.

Finally, as afternoon approached, I was getting set to leave when Doc Coots made an appearance.

"Doc! Man am I glad to see you!"

"Vincent, how long have you been here, you look like something my cat dragged in."

"Yeah, I suppose I do doc, but I needed to be here for him, you know when he wakes up and all."

"Come with me, Vincent." He said as he took me by the arm and led me out into the hallway.

"Ok doc, give it to me straight."

"There has been no major change in his condition. The tumor looks to be inoperable and the size is a big concern. We don't know if he will come out of this. That's all I have, Vincent. I wish I could tell you more, I sincerely do."

Shaking his head, he turned and made his leave down the hallway to the nurse's station.

I returned to Carlos's bedside one more time and grabbing onto his hand, I leaned over and kissed him on the forehead as I fought off my emotions. I proceeded down an empty stairwell and out to the parking lot. I drove slowly away thinking that perhaps I would never see my young friend again.

Getting back to Mara Del Santos, I headed straight to the workshop to park the truck there and take a slow walk home. Father Tom had agreed to feed Zeke and look in after him while I was in Santa Fe, so I was confident that he was alright. It was dusk as I approached my house, then suddenly, from nearly three hundred feet away, I heard what sounded like gunshots in the distance. Moving in closer, they became louder and were coming from right behind my home. And with each shot I heard, I could hear Zeke barking away.

I broke into a full, all-out sprint, skidded, and nearly tripped on some loose gravel as I turned the corner of my yard getting to the back of the house.

Lined up on a log about a hundred-foot distance or so, were a bunch of empty bottles and cans, from Dr. Brown's Cel-ray soda to Moxie's orange crème. And there was Frankie, taking shots with her rifle, firing steadily and knocking them off, one by one. I stood there frozen as I watched her take aim with uncanny proficiency.

"Well don't just stand there, if you want to learn how to shoot this darn thing, then come over here." She said pointedly.

I walked over to her with the biggest smile I could muster as she handed me her rifle. Then without any incidental discussion, she positioned herself behind me, placing her arms around my shoulders, as she correctly instructed me to hold, aim, and fire. It felt good to be that close to her.

"Wow, you are as good as everyone says you are, I mean you are one hell of a shot!" I said as I turned to her, breaking the rhythm in my lesson.

"Okay, Okay, but look down the barrel of the rifle not at me. Or you might hurt yourself when you pull the trigger."

"Oh and by the way, I cleaned your shotgun over there, it looks like to were trying to do the same, but it would help if you made sure it wasn't loaded first, because it was." She quietly said in my ear as she repositioned me to again aim ahead.

Our lesson went on for much of the night until I was able to finally hit a couple of bottles, shattering them to pieces. With darkness encroaching, we ended our shooting spree and headed over to the house.

"How about a drink?" I congenially asked.

"Sure, I'll take a root beer if you have one."

A few minutes later I came out with two ice-cold root beers as we sat in our usual rocking chairs on the back porch.

"How's the boy?" she asked concernedly.

She had heard all about the entire incident just as I had suspected.

"I don't know, I was with him for the last two days and there has been no change."

"You know, I'm praying for him, we all are, Vincent."

Things became quiet for a while as we looked out into the sunset at an array of yellow and orange streaks in the sky, slowly sipping our root beer.

"I'm glad you're here," I said, finally turning towards her.

"Well, Mr. Vincent, I did a lot of thinking and I'm glad you're here too. I don't just mean here tonight, I mean here in Mara del Santos. And you should take all the time you need to completely heal.........because.........well because…... I decided, I'm not giving up on you, or on us."

She looked out into the night sky, rocking slowly in her chair, lifting her bottle to take a big gulp as she tried to hide her smile behind it.

12

She appeared one day, a normal ordinary day. A woman of means, she was wearing expensive clothes, a fur coat, dark glasses, white gloves, and a scarf wrapped around her head. Not from around here and conspicuously out of place, she entered through the front door of the church. Outside, there was a large shiny black, 1959 Lincoln Continental, parked with its engine idling. On the driver's side sat a robust man dressed in black with a chauffeur's hat on. Perched in the back seat, was a child, approximately eighteen months old, also donning fancy clothes, but partially concealed beneath a large blanket which he was wrapped in.

I walked close enough to see the occupants, and as I passed, the child squirmed in his safety restraint to get a glimpse of me as well. The driver's eyes followed me with a look of caution. I usually didn't get around to the front of the church on my way in, but this day, I heard his engine running (there weren't many cars that drove up that early), and out of curiosity, I had to investigate.

Going in through the main entrance myself, I saw no one at first, but as I headed up the side aisle, there she was kneeling in the front row with her hands clasped together in prayer. With her head down, she looked up slightly as I walked by and around through the side door leading down the hallway towards my office. Wearing my custodian uniform gave me a sense that I had some kind of authority or knowledge, or in the least, just gave me permission to be there and move about freely.

As I came back out, with my set of keys slightly jingling, I noticed she was wiping her eyes from just under her glasses.

"Excuse me." She said as I began to pass by her.

"Yes, ma'am, can I help you with something?" I cordially responded.

"Would you happen to know if there is a priest around? My driver took a wrong turn off the highway and for some reason, I couldn't help but notice this wonderful old church of yours and had to stop in. But I would love to talk to someone, a priest if that's possible."

"Uh well, Father Tom isn't here right now, would you like to leave a message for him?"

"No, that won't be necessary". She responded disappointedly.

I went about attending to my business, and the first order was to again pull out my mop and clean up the recurring puddle which accumulated towards the back wall behind the altar. Once I had that dried up, I needed to find a way up to the roof to investigate the source of the leak. Needing to change the mop head, I made my way into one of the storage rooms.

Upon my return, the woman who had been kneeling, was now steps away from being upon the altar itself with her child in her arms, praying, or talking, or mumbling something as she stood directly in front of the Crucifix looking right up at it at a sharp angle.

I immediately left my mop behind and hurried up to the front where she was.

"Excuse me ma' am, you really shouldn't be up here, this is just for the priests and well, us workers only."

She continued with her ramblings, almost ignoring me.

"Ma'am, please, you need to come away from here," I said politely while stepping in front of her trying to gain her attention.

"It's my baby, you see it's my baby, sir, he is not well."

"I'm sorry to hear that, but why don't you come over here and sit down."

I slowly escorted her to the very front pew, where she sat cradling the child in her arms. Noticing his forehead was wet most assuredly from the drip in our ceiling, I pulled out my clean handkerchief and patted him dry as his mother looked on. Removing her scarf and glasses, I could see she was an attractive young woman who looked very troubled.

"Are you ok ma'am?"

"I'm fine. It's just that my son, well we have taken him to so many doctors, all over the country, and they all say there is nothing they can do."

"I'm sorry, may I ask what's the matter with him? He looks like a very happy baby." I said, as I reached over and caressed his cheek.

"What's his name?" I ventured on.

"His name is Samuel. He is so young and so innocent, and you are quite right, he is very happy. But he was born with a defect in his head and spine and will have to spend the rest of his life in a wheelchair, or so they tell us, I don't know where else to turn." She continued as she began to weep.

"I wish I could do something for him….and for you, I will pray for you both."

I think that was the first time I uttered these words in my adult life, but it was heart-wrenching to see the distress in her eyes and it was all I could do at that moment. I placed my hand on her shoulder to try and console her, while the child, continued to look about in all directions. After a few minutes, she wrapped the scarf once again over her head, put on her glasses, and got up.

"You have been very kind, but I better get going, my driver will start to wonder what happened to us."

She then reached into her coat pocket and took out a long white leather wallet, opened it, and generously handed me a fifty-dollar bill.

"Ma'am, this is not necessary, please forgive me, I can't accept it."

I gently nudged it back toward her and she knew I meant it, taking it, she returned it to her wallet and snapped the clasp closed.

"Before I leave, may I ask your name, sir?" she quietly inquired.

"Sure, it's Vincent, I'm the custodian here."

"Well thank you again for your kindness, Vincent. Goodbye."

She exited just as abruptly as she came, and placing the child carefully back into his seat, securing him thoroughly and covering him with his blanket, she climbed in herself and off they went, making a full turn, disappearing into the distance.

Mara Del Santos was used to strangers passing through and had become known as a stopover for many travelers on the way further west. And it also had seen its share of inquisitive sightseers going over to Roswell to satisfy their curiosities. Over time it maintained a slow steady growth and with each year that passed, progress slowly made its way here.

The town was abuzz knowing that the governing council had finally accepted a deal from the government to take ownership of 'bathtub row', and with all political decisions, it had its supporters as well as its detractors. In any event, the town would now become proud owners of an abundance of abandoned housing, with a government-funded project to remodel and renovate the entire area.

The construction was to start within two weeks and fresh faces had already been seen arriving. The Winchester was getting the brunt of the action and the diner was seeing much more activity as well. Two new waitresses were hired which suited Frankie just fine, preventing her from having to work double shifts. The general store was expanding and with it, a name change, to Martinez's Groceries. And of course, the nightlife centered around The Daisy Mae began to heat up.

As for myself, I spent my weekends driving out to Santa Fe as often as I could, I had an attachment to Carlos which I couldn't deny, and, on several occasions, I was glad to have Frankie's company along with me. We would spend a few hours at his bedside, including him in our conversations as if he would respond at any minute.

"I'm going down to the cafeteria, you coming?" she asked.

"No, I think I'd rather stay here if it's ok?"

"Sure, I'll bring you back something, would you like anything special?"

"Surprise me." I said yawning, leaning my head on Carlos's bed.

Moments later, as I sat forward, I heard a groan, or at least what I thought was a groan. My head sprung up and I saw his hand move.

"NURSE……. NURSE!" I yelled out into the hallway.

"What is it?"

A tall slender nurse wearing a crisp white uniform and matching hat appeared.

"I heard him moan, I think he moved his hand!"

With the nurse exiting quickly and reporting my observations, the on-call doctor came rushing in a few minutes later. He pulled a penlight from his white coat pocket, held Carlos's eyelids open with his thumb and forefinger and shone the light into his right eye, then the left. Then looking at his chart which was affixed to the footboard of his bed. He shook his head.

"Are you the boy's father?" he asked looking at me.

"No, I'm just a friend, a very close friend, and I think I heard him groan and move his hand doc, I was sitting right here."

"Well you see, sometimes the body responds involuntarily, a twitch here or a sound emanating doesn't mean anything but just that. According to his chart, he is scheduled for another CT scan in a couple of days, hopefully, we will know more after that."

He looked at his watch, made some notations on the chart, replaced it at the foot of the bed, and walked out, leaving me with yet another empty feeling.

Frankie returned with two cups of hot coffee and turkey sandwiches, as I went on to explain what just occurred. She looked at me sadly, while we sat at his bedside for the next couple of hours before deciding to call it a day. As we were getting ready to exit, an elderly man and woman arrived, I had seen them before, in the front row of the church, just the other day. They were Carlos's grandparents. Having met them only once, they addressed me right away and seemed excited to see me out of my working environment. Not speaking English too well, and not progressing on my Spanish lessons as much as I had wished, I was only able to pick up slightly on what they were saying.

Once again, Frankie stepped in, she was somewhat fluent and did her best to translate.

"They are so used to seeing you at the church each time they are there, and are saying that the boy would talk about you all the time. They are very grateful for what you have done for him."

I was getting that warm feeling once more and didn't want to have an emotional outburst, so shaking their hands and nodding politely, I graciously thanked them and eased my way out the door trying to keep up a smile.

Back in town, the sounds of machinery and construction equipment could be heard from far off. The revival project at bathtub row had begun and there was a certain sense of excitement being generated. Once completed, the town could offer living spaces at very affordable rents, benefitting everyone involved.

Life returned to an ordinary state for the time being. Frankie was back at the diner handling the now busier crowd of workers, as well as her regulars. And me, I was determined to find the source of that leaky roof, I would find a way to get up to those rafters no matter what it took.

Laying the creaky ladder against the outside of the building at its shortest point, and securing it with some rope onto one of the spires about a third of the way up, I climbed. Getting as high as I could, I stood on the top rung and was able to reach the roofline, where the rain gutter was connected. This was a dangerous position and not the smartest idea I have had, and if Frankie saw me now, she would give me a tongue lashing for sure. I expected her shortly as we had plans to have a late lunch together out back and I hoped to be done before she arrived.

Reaching up as high as I could, I grabbed onto the gutter and pulled myself up onto the roof. Slowly, I rose and ever so carefully, managed to walk over to the area where I presumed the leak to be. This location would put me directly over the center of the back wall, behind the altar, directly over the Crucifix. I got down on my knees and examined the entire area. The slates were intact, there were no visible holes or cracks. It was as solid as could be. Circling without finding any evidence of possible leakage, I was baffled.

I turned and sat on the roof for a moment catching my breath, and looking out, I could practically see for miles in every direction. It was then I noticed a vehicle coming towards the church at high speed, leaving large swaths of dust in its wake as it approached. Closing in, it was a brown convertible jeep. At first, I thought it may be a military vehicle, but at second glance, I could see three ominous-looking individuals wearing cowboy hats, carrying rifles across their laps as they headed this way.

My first instinct was to get the hell down from where I was and meet them head on to see what their intentions where. I began to panic, thinking that all the doors were unlocked, and no one was down there to question them. Almost slipping once in my haste, I collected myself and maneuvered slowly. I could hear voices below and the next thing I knew, they were already inside.

"HELLO……. HELLOooooo…down there!" I yelled, hoping they would know someone was here to deter them.

Then, realizing I should take a different approach, I shimmied over to my ladder and eased my way down. Still hearing voices speaking quite loudly with no regard for where they were, I knew trouble was brewing.

In a moment of either courage or stupidity, I ran into the workshop and grabbed the shotgun and some shells from where I had stashed them. I came around the south side and slowly entered through that door (I knew it was the quietest). Then silently creeping in, I hid behind a row of pews to see what was unfolding.

There were three men and there was something familiar about two of them. Each had a rifle slung over their shoulders and the third was swinging a rope, a lasso over his head as they stood upon the altar. He was trying to throw it over the Crucifix to pull it down!

With my heart pounding in a fast fury, I knew I had to act right away. I ran, up the side aisle without being noticed until I was within 10 feet of them. Never really firing a gun in anyone's direction before, I cocked the shotgun, pointed it away from them, and pulled the trigger.

The echo screamed louder than anything I ever heard. And it startled them as well.

"HOLD IT RIGHT THERE!" I said quickly reloading and pointing the gun at them.

It was then I knew who it was. The two cowboys I met when I first arrived, Mic and Jake with a third man.

"Well, it looks like college boy has some nerve after all." Mic squibbed with a devilish grin.

"If you leave now, nothing will be reported, just go, take your rope, and go home," I responded shaking slightly as I held the gun aimed right at him.

"You sure you know how to shoot that thing, college boy? Looks like you already missed once. And well there are three of us and I only count one of you."

The truth was, I didn't know how to use a shotgun with any kind of accuracy at all, and pulling the trigger was not what I initially intended to do, especially in a church. My hope was only to try and scare them off.

"Maybe you should count again?" a voice sounded from out of the shadows, from somewhere above.

Frankie had come in and taken a stance high up in the darkened choir loft above. There she stood looking down the barrel of her rifle pointed right at the three of them.

"Oh, hey there girl, is that you up there? I thought I recognized that voice. Now we don't want any trouble, we were just havin' some fun with college boy here and were just about to leave." Mic mockingly stated in return.

Tipping his hat, he motioned to the others to take their exit through the side entrance. I cocked the shotgun again holding it up to my side as he turned before leaving and looked at me.

"And don't call me college boy. I'm.............. THE CUSTODIAN!"

I heard their Jeep spin its wheels and peel away as Frankie ran down the stairs meeting me half-way, towards the middle of the building.

"You are just a regular Annie Oakley, aren't you?" I yelled out trying to make light of the situation.

"But, how in God's name did you show up here at the perfect time?" I anxiously asked.

"Things were slow at the diner, I got off early and thought I would surprise you, and lucky for you I did. I saw that jeep of theirs as I came around back. Those characters never had a need to be at church and I became suspicious right away. Then when I heard a gunshot, I grabbed my rifle out of the trunk and came in the side door. I decided to get up into the choir loft, my daddy always taught me to get the best vantage point as possible and well, guess he was right."

In reality, I was flushed, shaking on the inside and yes, slightly visible on the outside too. I had never been in a situation quite like that before, this wasn't the cultured streets of back east, it was more like the wild west. Firing that shotgun was much different than the rifle Frankie had given me lessons on. The recoil itself knocked me back a couple of steps and my aim was thrown off enough that I put a huge hole in the sidewall near Father Toms confessional booth, nearly 20 feet from where the three were standing.

"You could have hurt someone with that thing, including yourself," Frankie said as she came up behind me easing the shotgun from my grip.

"Whatever do you mean, I had it under control, I just meant to intentionally scare them anyway."

"Yes, I can see that by the crater you 'intentionally' put in the wall over there."

We weren't so sure of why they would want this statue in the first place, anyone could go and purchase a Crucifix if they wanted one that badly, why this one? Yes, it was life-size and the magnificent handiwork of some unknown artist, but was it worth coming in here committing armed theft? I knew the statue had a certain allure to it, I had seen it (and felt it), first-hand, but it was still just a statue, a symbol, right? But according to Father Tom, there were similar incidents in the past, although I never imagined anything such as this. We chose not to report it to the sheriff's office, not just yet, anyway, we thought it better to explain the incident to Father upon his return and see if he could shed further light on the matter.

It was something left for us, left for me, to ponder.

I set out to patch up the hole almost immediately, but each day began with my routine of first taking a rag and wiping up the wet spot which continued relentlessly. No one in the congregation knew of the threat which had recently occurred, the sentiment here was quiet and serene as usual, and I resumed my life of looking after things and greeting people as they came through.

There were still many times when the building was empty, and I found myself alone with just the faint sound of my radio in the background. And now that I confessed all to Frankie, it became easier to sing along at times, provided I was sure no one was listening. It had been years since I exercised my vocal cords and if felt good to open up at times. And in doing so, the bad memories had diminished. In the past, every time I turned on the radio, usually while I was driving a long stretch of highway, singing along would always bring me back to a hurtful place. It seemed different now, maybe because I did finally get it off my chest, maybe it was this protective environment, or maybe because that statue, that gaze, was constantly upon me, keeping watch over me.

The town had most definitively increased in its activity, each time I ventured over to pick up something at the diner, Frankie was always twice as busy waiting on tables. That never prevented her from coming over to the counter where I would be sitting to share a tender gesture or a smile.

Waiting for my order, not only gave me the chance to see her, but also the opportunity to observe the many new faces which had arrived. Some were not as congenial as others, and several times someone would make a pass at her, but watching Frankie, she always knew how to disarm a tricky situation and keep a customer politely at bay.

Most of the new clientele were part of the construction crew working over at bathtub row. They looked to be experienced personnel, some independent contractors, and some, government workers. It was not only interesting to hear them discuss the project, but also helpful. It was then that I overheard two gentlemen discussing a water leak problem.

"Excuse me for interrupting gentleman, I couldn't help but overhear what you were saying about a constant water leak?"

"Yeah, it's the way these buildings have been built, there are gaps below the slate roofs where water accumulates and stays for a time," said an older looking man, with rough skin and calloused hands.

"You mean like a basin where the water just sits?"

"Yeah, that's right, it could be up there for weeks before it dries up."

"Hmmmmm, I see......... thanks for the information," I said, stroking my chin as I pondered this new thought.

I may have just solved the mystery of the water leakage that had me puzzled all these days. If that was the case, given the fact that we hadn't had rain for over a week now, my leak would soon subside.

"Here's your order sir, " Frankie said handing me a small brown bag.

"Sssshhhh, I added some empanadas, that you like." She whispered partially covering her mouth with her hand.

"Thanks a bunch, I'll see you later."

Taking the bag, I paid at the cash register and made my way hastily into the truck. I felt relieved to know that I wasn't the only one stymied by a water problem, this gap situation between the roof slates and rafters had to be the cause for mine as well. I couldn't wait to get back to work to get a good look above, now knowing what the source must be.

13

The Church of San Sebastian was considered the home parish for three neighboring communities, thus Father Tom's duties ran him thin at times. He spent many days consoling widows, bringing communion to the handicapped and homebound, and administering to the sick. After two days of being on the road, he was completing reports and paperwork in his office when I knocked on his door.

"Father, sorry to interrupt, but, you got a minute?"

"Sure, sure, Vincent, I always have a minute for you. Come on in."

I proceeded to tell him what took place in his absence, how the vandals came in toting guns, and tried to steal the Crucifix. I went on to let him know how that hole in the wall came to be, and the repair job that I was in the middle of completing. I let him also know how Frankie luckily came in at the right time and how we turned them away. He sat there staunchly listening as if it was no surprise to him at all.

“Vincent, I believe they have tried this before without success. Mr. Jaco who owns the Jaco estate and much land from here to Texas is a very wealthy man, he has approached me in the past wanting to make a very sizable ‘donation’ if I was to make him a gift of the Crucifix, naturally I declined.”

“Why would a man of his wealth want it so bad, Father? With his money, can’t he just go get another one similar, or hire the best sculptor around to make one just like it?”

“Vincent, it is what I have been trying to tell you, there is none other like it. Our congregation comes from one of deep faith, but there have been many here who believe in such things that I cannot simply explain as just pure faith, local lore has survived for many, many years.”

“Are you to tell me that, the statue is responsible for …for ………”

"Vincent, I'm not trying to tell you or condone anything other than being a symbol of the most holy for the people here, you can translate it any way you like."

And reaching down, he took his key and unlocked his bottom desk drawer. He pulled out that old leather-bound worn notebook and flipped it up on the desk in front of me.

"Here, take this, I was told by Father Ortiz that it was found in the lower storage room, if nothing else, you may find it interesting in its antiquity alone. I have looked at many times, and am not even sure what all the scribbling is saying, but, here, it is yours, I will leave it to you to figure out if you like. It may be the only documented history of our Blessed Crucifix's origin."

Dismissing it nonchalantly he relaxed back into his chair as if to see what my reaction would be.

From outside his office, echoing through the hallway, several voices suddenly could be heard, we were startled by them as they went on excitedly. Looking at each other we both stood up and headed out to see what the commotion was. I alertly grabbed the notebook before leaving and tucked under my arm.

There, by the back entrance were several individuals, two people conversing primarily in Spanish, both wearing traditional white clothing and straw hats, and Doc Coots himself. They seemed to be bickering about something and their voice levels were getting louder. We headed right for them to see what the turmoil was about, and to quiet them down.

“Sssshhhhhhh, calm down, what’s going on out here?” Father Tom inquired as he moved right up to them.

“Es un milagro……un milagro………...a…a…miracle !!” One of the two men blurted out.

“Father, something has happened, these two men are relatives of Carlo’s and they just came back from the hospital, they are saying that he is awake. I just spoke to the doctor there, who has confirmed it. We came here because I knew that you and especially you (pointing at me), would want to know. I’m on my way over there right now.” Said Doc Coots resoundingly.

I stood there speechless, turned to Father Tom with a look of pure astonishment as I felt the blood drain from my face.

“Go……. Go now!” he alertly said to me.

Taking the notebook and locking it in my desk, I ran outside and got into the passenger side of Doc Coot’s car where he was waiting with the motor running.

“What does this mean doc? What happened? Is he ok?”

“Slow down Vincent, slow down, or you’re going to end up in the bed next to him with a heart attack.”

“You know as much as I do right now. He had scans two days ago and the neurologist called me this morning, saying I better come out and take a look for myself, that’s all he said. Then those two cousins of his showed up at my office in an uproar.”

We sped off at top speed.

Arriving at the hospital nearly an hour later, I went immediately to Carlo’s room, while Doc Coots stopped at the nurse’s station, looking for the neurologist that summoned him. Carlos was sitting up in his bed, wide awake, but still a little groggy.

Recognizing me right away, his bright white smile appeared. I walked over to him, stooped down, and gave him a big hug, almost lifting him right out of bed.

“Carlos! I missed you, my friend! How do you feel, como te sientes?” I said as I released him slowly.

"Feel good señor Vincent, I feel good." He responded with a certain tiredness.

Doc Coots came in a minute later and began to examine him thoroughly, paying much attention to his eye movement, speech, and hand coordination.

"I don't understand this, it's absolutely amazing." He said shaking his head looking over at me.

"Come outside for a minute with me Vincent."

After excusing myself to Carlos and assuring him that I would be right back, I promptly made my way out into the hallway where the good doctor was waiting.

"Vincent. I don't know how to tell you this, but.........I......I just reviewed the results of his last brain scan with the neurologist and we both have come to the same conclusion. We don't have one."

"What the hell does that mean, doc?"

"The tests are showing that the tumor has shrunk decisively. It has declined nearly seventy-five percent since he first came in."

"How is that possible? Is it any of the medications you have been giving him?"

"Not likely, they were basically administered to make him comfortable, they could not have changed his condition, especially so quickly."

"Well, whatever the hell happened here doc, I'm very grateful!"

Being so excited, I felt the overwhelming need to tell Frankie right away. Running down the staircase to the phone booth in the hospital lobby, I called the diner. They had just gotten a new phone booth installed, like most of the businesses in town.

"The Diner, Tess speaking." Said the voice at the end of the line.

"Tess, its Vincent, can I please speak to Frankie."

"Hold on." She said, hearing the thud as she laid down the receiver on the built-in stainless-steel shelf.

Frankie, not used to me calling her on the phone, in fact, this was the first time I ever did, picked it up with trepidation in her voice.

"Vincent?"

"Yeah, hi, it's me. Frankie!! He's awake! He's talking! He's going to be ok!!" I continued with uncontrollable enthusiasm.

"Who? What are you..............where are...........?"

She stopped in the middle of her sentence realizing where I was and who I was referring to.

"Oh my God.............. Carlos is awake! He's awake, he's going to be ok!"

I heard her yell out to the crowd in the diner, and whoever was there, strangers, residents, workers, it didn't matter, at the moment, they all broke out into applause, cheering and hollering. I felt goosebumps climb my arm as I tried to fight back tears of joy on the other end of the line, listening intently.

In Carlo's room, a gathering seemed to be taking place, not only was Doc Coots and a nurse there, but his grandparents had also arrived. Walking in, hugs were being exchanged and a feeling of jubilation was in the air. The elderly couple kept going on about it being 'un milagro'. And maybe, just maybe I was starting to believe them too.

Hours later, Doc Coots and I drove back into town in the middle of the night. Dropping me off at the back of the church, I started up the pickup, made a quick stop to feed Zeke, had a furious change of clothes out of my uniform, and sped over to Frankie's. The lights were out, and I knew she had probably gone to bed, but I didn't care. The moon was glowing especially bright and it lit up the entire neighborhood as I rolled in quietly and parked in front of her house.

Tapping lightly on her door, I waited with no answer. Tapping a little louder and softly calling her name, I heard her stirring about. The door opened, and I walked right in, standing there, hugging her so tightly for several long minutes.

"I know it's late, but I had to come, I just couldn't believe the news we got today."

"I can't believe it either, come and sit down, I want to hear all about it." She said taking me by the hand and leading me to the couch.

"No, get dressed, we have to go somewhere."

"Now?.............. Where? I'm in my pajama's."

"Okay, just come like that then," I said with laughter abound.

"Alright, hold on, give me five minutes, let me change."

She headed into her bedroom and a few minutes later emerged, wearing her standard blue jeans, a thick sweater, and Keds sneakers. Starting up Denise, she got into the passenger side, while I drove. It must have been half-past two and the streets were deserted. Not a word was spoken as I drove straight to the church. Looking at Frankie, I felt she knew why we were headed there.

Grabbing my custodian keys, we entered through the back. I turned on one spotlight in the altar section and also a couple of hallway lights to guide our way around. I then took Frankie by the hand, as we stepped up onto the altar area.

"I can't explain it, and you might think I'm crazy, I was up there (pointing high up on the wall where the Crucifix hung) the other day doing my cleaning, I spoke to him and asked him to help Carlos and I got a strange sensation throughout my body. Then today, they have no explanation why Carlos's condition has changed, practically overnight?"

"Vincent, perhaps it is just the power of prayer, I believe in that too, do you?"

"I don't know what to believe anymore, I feel like something strange is going on and I need to figure it all out," I said rubbing the side of my face as I went on.

"See, it was there, he was laying right there, that's where I found Carlos."

Walking over to the exact spot where Carlos's body had laid, I stood there looking down. For the first time in a while, I noticed that the floor was conspicuously dry. I stooped down on one knee and swiped my hand over the surface.

"What is it, Vincent?"

"Oh, nothing....... I think. I mean, I guess the construction guys I was talking to in the diner the other day were right. There was a leak here, but it must have dried up, just like they said it would."

We hung around for another few minutes as I held Frankie's hand tightly. We stood directly below the Crucifix, and at the angle which we were positioned, we could only see it from the bottom up.

"Hey, for what it's worth up there.........thank you!" I exclaimed rather loudly.

The next morning, the news had reached just about everyone in town, it was a bigger ruckus than the anticipation of the feast weeks ago. Over at the diner, many patrons were discussing it all morning, with Frankie gladly reciting the news over and over to anyone who inquired.

"Can I take your order?" She exclaimed to a stranger who ventured in not knowing anything about the latest fervor.

"How about the special up on the board there, please."

"Sure, be back in a jiffy mister."

This stranger seemed to stand out to her, even though she had never seen him before there was something oddly familiar about him. His hair was slicked back, and he was dressed in a black tee-shirt with the sleeves cut off, black trousers, leather jacket, black boots, and wore dark sunglasses. He barely looked around and didn't make much conversation at all, even when Frankie tried coaxing him. He kept to himself the entire time, sitting at one of the counter stools concentrating on the plate of food that was before him.

Parked outside, was his 1955 black Indian motorcycle with an elongated back seat and shiny chrome gas tank. Strapped to the tail end of the seat was a guitar case, in clear sight, with its neck end standing straight in an upward position. Frankie couldn't help but notice it and tried to raise a conversation with him.

"How we doing over here?" she said in her usual friendly fashion.

"I'm fine, everything was very good."

"That your bike out there?" she went on tipping her head towards the large window where it stood outside in plain view.

"Sure is, you like bikes?" He responded with slightly more interest.

"I do, but I see a guitar case on it too, you play?"

"You could say that."

"Say, let me ask you something, darlin', does this town have a church?" He continued.

She was taken back with his question, it was the last thing she would expect from a character such as this, her first notion was that he would be looking for The Daisy Mae, not a church.

"Uh…...yes of course we do." She stuttered.

"Could you point me in the right direction?"

With a puzzled look, she gave him instructions towards the church. Finishing his meal and taking one last gulp of his soft drink, he paid his tab and left a generous tip before he headed for the exit.

"Where you from anyway?" she said making one last attempt before he vanished.

"Back east…………see you around Darlin."

She stood frozen with uncertainty looking through the window as she watched him kick-start his motorcycle a couple of times before the engine turned over with a roar. In a second, he was gone in a cloud of dust. Her heartbeat fluttered faintly before beginning to pound emphatically. Her mind raced, could it be? No, she must be imagining it, just a coincidence, she thought. The longer she stood there the more she was convinced. He was from back east, he wore dark sunglasses and he had a guitar! And now, he was headed over to the church!

She ran for the phone and dialed Father Tom's office, it rang unanswered. She held on and let it ring continuously in the hopes that someone, hopefully, Vincent, would pick it up. After minutes of trying, she had to hang up. The lunch crowd had grown, and people were waiting to be seated. She thought about running out to the back, jumping into Denise, and speeding over, but it had gotten too busy for her to sneak out unnoticed.

Before mixing a batch of concrete and mortar to repair the hole I created with my 'flawless' aim, my daily morning inspection was first. This is where I would be sure that all holy water fonts were filled, candles burnt down to their wicks were replaced and just general clean-up was in order. Once again, just when I thought it was gone for good, that infernal dripping of water appeared, not as significant as before, but enough for me to wipe it up with the cloth I had hanging from my back pocket.

Feeling uplifted after getting the good news about my young friend, I had turned up my radio a bit louder. Playing was Dion and the Belmont's; *Why Must I Be A Teenager in Love?* I sang along softly.

It was then when I heard a voice from the back of the church, from amidst the shadows. I couldn't see who it was at first, but shivers ran down my spine as I knew all too well who it belonged to.

"We ain't teenagers anymore...........KID."

He slowly emerged, into the light, walking up towards the altar where I stood immobilized, my hands wet from cleaning up the water drip, I ran toward him and in one fell swoop, I gave him the biggest bear hug I could muster. He laughed loudly as I embraced his head with my dripping wet hands.

"Son-of-a-bitch! It's you, but how did you get here, I mean, how did you find me?"

And there he stood, it was Johnny, right in front of me, like a ghost rising from nowhere, to me this was a miracle in itself. I thought I would never see him again. My friend who I had missed dearly, one who I regretted losing touch with, was here and I couldn't comprehend how or why. We stood there giggling like the youthful adolescents we once were, caught up in the moment, not knowing where to begin.

"I can't believe this, it's you, it's really you!"

"It's me kid, here in the flesh."

"C'mon, let's go into my office so we can talk in private."

I led him through the side door, down the hallway, and sat him down in my office where the radio was still playing. Sitting across from me, I offered to get him something to drink, but he graciously declined. It was Johnny alright, same smile, same slicked-back hair, same dark glasses. I wasn't sure if age had caught up with him, or it was just the yellow hue from the lights overhead, but, up close, he looked a bit pale, yet here he was in the flesh.

"I can't believe that you are here! But how?" I asked again.

He reached into the inside pocket of his leather jacket and pulled out a wad of papers with an elastic band around them. He flipped them on the desk and motioned me to take a look. It was a stack of folded envelopes from the letters that I had been sending to my mother at each stopover I made while making my way cross country.

"You have seen my mother?"

"I have, I stopped in a couple of times asking about you. I knew she had heard from you, but she was holding out. I guess she wanted to respect your wishes for a while. Until one day, she finally gave in. She handed me these envelopes and I followed the postmarks as best I could. And by the way kid, she is doing alright, she and your sis are fine, and they miss you."

"This is just amazing, I can't believe you came up with a way to track me down, but I am sure as hell glad you did."

I wanted not to ask, but my curiosity got the best of me. At this point, it was in the distant past, yet one last urge pushed me forward, and against my better judgment, I relinquished.

"You ever see her again?" I said turning my eyes down towards my desk.

"Heard she got married, kid. Yeah went on to marry an accountant, had a couple of kids, moved to the suburbs and became a grade school principal."

"Huh, a principal? Didn't expect that from her, but I imagine she is happy." I responded dismissively shaking my head.

“Yeah, last I ever saw her was just after you left. I packed up my stuff about a week later and high tailed it outta there myself.”

“Johnny, I don’t know what to say. I had to go, it was like something telling me to hit the road and never look back.”

"I know you did kid and I don't think any less of you for doing it. I admire it, it was a gutsy move. But, I have to ask just one question………...a custodian? With your talent, you became a custodian?” He said pointing to the title on the door.

“I know, I ask myself the same thing, but for some strange reason, I’m happy here, and believe me it’s not as peaceful and quiet as you may think.”

We talked about the twists and turns that life had taken us through over the past several years, the places we had been to and the people we met. He told me how he followed my trail of cities and towns and even encountered some of the same folks while he was asking around about me.

In Springfield, Ohio he found the joint that I would frequent on occasion. There he met a shapely brunette dancer named Rosie. They shared a musical background, so while conversing and having a drink with her she advised him that I had passed through four weeks before he came into her establishment.

Coincidentally, in Whitestone, Indiana, while staying at the most desirable hotel in town, he crossed paths with a stunningly beautiful and equally desirable maid named Arlette, who he could not help but notice as he inquired about obtaining an extra towel from her. His charm led to a late-night conversation which quickly and inconspicuously referred to another stranger from the east coast, some prior months earlier.

And in Canyon, Texas, Johnny went into a bank to break a hundred-dollar bill and met an appealing looking bank teller named Denise. I didn't know if it was because he knew me well enough to know my 'type', but the two of them got to talking and she made it well known to him about me, and the short time we managed together. That's when he knew he was hot on my trail.

“What about you John, what’s life been like for you?”

“Well kid, it’s been great at times, I have lived the high life and then some, but I got something to tell you, it partly the reason I came all this way.”

He took off his glasses and I could tell by his eyes that things were not right in his world. They were bloodshot, and the whites had a slight yellowing tint to them.

"Look kid, I love you like a brother, always have, always will and that's why I had to find you. I'm headed to Vegas for one last hurrah. I got an audition out there to headline in a top-flight nightclub."

"That's fantastic, Johnny! I want to come and catch your act sometime."

"Hold on kid, there is more to the story. Seems about six months I started feeling tired. I mean all the time. I ignored it as far as I could, but when it started to affect my nightlife and my playing ability, that's when I knew I better get checked out. It was soon after that I got the news."

He paused as he caught his breath having a tough time letting me know what was happening.

"What is it John, you ok?"

"It's leukemia, kid………...and well, seems like its past the point of no return. Anyway, I'm going to go out in style, under the bright lights of Vegas. They don't know anything about it out there, and hell if I'm going to let them in on it before I can do my thing."

"How much time you got?"

"According to these so-called experts, anywhere from 4 to 6 months."

I didn't know what I was more shocked over, having him here with me, or knowing it could possibly be the last time I would ever see him. The room filled with an overwhelming silence as we both thought about what to say next.

In a moment's notice, the side door to the church flung open and Frankie appeared, out of breath, as she came bursting into my office.

"VINCENT! VINCENT! I had to get over here as fast as I could, I just waited on a stranger, wearing black glasses and he had a guitar, he was from back east……………………..."

She stopped dead in her tracks, still huffing and puffing, as she saw him sitting on the other side of my desk.

"Frankie, this is Johnny Mags……. Johnny, Frankie." I said slowly as I made the introductions.

"Hello Darlin, I had a feelin' I'd be seeing you again, and just Johnny is fine." He coolly said as he put his glasses back on looking up at her.

The three of us sat around for a short while as she and Johnny traded pleasantries while getting acquainted. I explained to him that I was living only a short distance from the church and invited him to come back home with me and Frankie to have dinner with us. I let him know that he could spend the night and was welcome to stay as long as he liked. He accepted the dinner invitation.

Stepping outside, he burst into a distinct roar when he saw Denise parked there. Running over to her he placed his hands on the hood and looked at her quite lovingly, like the memory that she possessed for him.

"Wow, I can't believe you still have this, and still runs, huh." He said surprised as he placed both hands on the hood.

"Yep, runs like a top."

The evening lasted more than several hours as we caught up on the number of years since we last saw each other. The topic of Lizzy never came up again and neither of us felt it necessary to even broach the subject any further. Some things are just best left where they should be, in the past, and I was understanding that concept more clearly with each passing day. Frankie listened intently relishing all the stories we shared about our escapades at the Conservatory and beyond. It was good to have him in my life once again, even if our time was to be short-lived.

I wanted to try and talk him into staying, I wanted to get him over to Doc Coots to see if there was anything he could do for him, I just didn't want to see him get on his motorcycle and ride off into the sunset like the end of some nondescript movie. I wanted a miracle, the same miracle that happened for Carlos, I wanted it to happen for him. He wasn't only a part of my youth, he was still my best friend and even though I knew this night would come to an end, I didn't want to let go of him, again.

The hours flew by, as is the case anytime you want something to last. And with dinner and long conversations coming to an end, we made our way over to the front door, Frankie gave him a big hug in saying goodbye. I knew she too was silently wishing that he would stay, but she turned and vanished into the kitchen leaving Johnny and me to our farewells, outside.

It was an awkward moment as we both stood there seemingly admiring his bike. Its black sleek lines reflecting the glaring moonlight were stark and bold. Goodbyes are difficult to begin with, but this was one I never expected to happen and one that I wished could have been avoided.

"Uh, I don't know what to say, John," I said trying to hold off the pit growing in my throat.

"Kid, just remember me. I'll give them one hell of a show in Vegas, then I'll be doing the same thing up there." He responded pointing to the stars above.

"And by the way, I had a feeling you had snagged that pretty little philly in there when I met her at the diner. She's a keeper kid.... I'm just sayin'."

He straddled his bike and gave it a couple of kickstarts, as myself and Zeke, who was sitting at my side, watched from a close distance. Then, with the engine rumbling, he pulled up the kickstand and slowly turned the bike around.

"Johnny, I love you brother, I'll be praying for you." I yelled over the noise of his motor.

"You do that kid!"

He revved the engine and shot out like a bullet across the terrain with Zeke barking and chasing him for a few yards before he disappeared over the horizon.

14

Without much time to contemplate the thought of Johnny's visit or his fate, I was unexpectedly awakened by the sounds of cars and voices coming from afar. Looking out my front window, I could see signs of much activity taking place in the direction of the church. Getting myself cleaned up as fast as I could, I devoured a quick breakfast, while retreating to the window several times to catch a glimpse of what looked to be a growing crowd.

Upon my arrival, I immediately noticed the parking areas in front and side, were full, and a chorus of voices echoed within the space inside. Entering through the back I decided to make haste right to Father Tom's office.

"Father? Father? You in here?" I said as I approached.

"Yes, yes, Vincent, please come in we have been expecting you."

There I found Doc Coots seated across from him, heavily engaged in what was a serious discussion. The good doctor had been making several trips out to Santé Fe regarding Carlos' case quite regularly. The prognosis was such that this young boy from Mara Del Santos was continuing to make remarkable progress and was gaining much attention regarding it as well. A team of neurosurgeons had been consulted and each one concurred that they had no real justification for the results. Carlos had improved so much that he was going to be released within days.

Upon hearing the news, I was overjoyed that my young friend would be returning home and hopefully would be joining me once again.

"We wanted you to know right away, given your relationship with the boy, Vincent." Doc Coots said with a cheerful tone.

"I have been discussing the entire situation with Father Tom here and we want to ask you a few questions, if that's ok?"

"Sure thing, doc, anything I can do to help," I stated, as I stood leaning in the doorway.

"Can you describe exactly what happened that day, you know the day you brought him in."

"It's like I told you from the beginning doc, I was closing up in the back and was planning to drop him off at home. I came to get him, and found him passed out at the base of the wall, underneath the Crucifix. My ladder was leaning there, and I first thought he had tried to climb up."

"Why would he want to climb up Vincent?"

"Don't know doc, just before I left him out there, he was mumbling something in Spanish, like 'it moved', or 'he moved'. But you know doc, the lights in here can play tricks on you when you're all alone here. It's happened to me as well."

"I see." Said the doctor as he contemplatively looked over at Father Tom.

"So, is he in the clear now doc, everything will be alright with him, right?"

"He is doing extremely well Vincent, and although he is coming home soon, we do have him scheduled for a final scan next week."

Brushing off the basis of the conversation as just incidental, I was elated to know that Carlos would soon be home and well.

"Father, uh, there are a lot of people here today, did I miss something?"

"Vincent, come in for a minute and sit down."

As I took the chair on the right of Doc Coots, he clearly felt as if the need for Father Tom and myself to be alone was upon us. Taking his leave, he wished us both a good day and made his exit.

"So, what's cooking Father?"

"Vincent, it seems as though Carlos told a story to his grandparents and cousins about the Crucifix, how he believed it moved and fell trying to climb up to get a closer look. They are calling the whole thing a miracle."

"But Father, I was trying to tell the doc how your imagination can run away with you when you're alone in here."

"Yes, I know, my son. But you must understand, these are people of very strong beliefs, as I am as well."

"Okay Father, do you believe it was a miracle that healed him then?"

"Miracle is not a word that I or the church use lightly Vincent. I believe in everything I preach to these people and the power of prayer. The question I have, is what do you believe, Vincent?"

With the town being abuzz not only regarding Carlos' story, but the construction project nearing an end at bathtub row, the number of travelers coming through had thoroughly increased. I wasn't sure if families had arrived to inquire about new living quarters or if they were coming to visit our Crucifix, or perhaps it was just a sprinkling of curiosity that attracted them. In any event, the energy level was steadily increasing, and with it, my responsibilities.

I was refilling burnt-out candles as fast as people were lighting them. Donations were being left in empty collection baskets at each entrance, which I promptly gathered and stored away in a lockbox. But the most trying part of my day became the duty of preventing people from venturing upon the altar platform. Many thought nothing of trying to get as close as possible and I found myself politely steering them away.

Amid all the activity that was swirling, Frankie was prompted to head out to Albuquerque for a short stay with her brother, and now that she had a car, it wasn't as much as of an inconvenience as in the past. She had planned to come over for a quick visit after I returned from work, but things were so busy, that Father Tom had asked if we could keep the church open an extra hour every night. She managed, however, to pop in just before she left and caught me in a quiet moment while I was filling out an order form in my office.

"Just wanted to stop and say goodbye, I'll be back in about three or four days."

"Okay, thanks for swinging by here, I was hoping to see you before you left. And I think you may even be back in time for Carlos' return."

"That would be great. You sure you don't mind me taking your car out there?"

"Of course not, but hold on a second."

I unlocked the bottom drawer of my desk and pulled out the old leather binder that I had tucked away there. I had been trying to understand the random sentences and words that were scribbled in it, but my efforts were of no avail. Some of it had faded and was ineligible and many words were in Spanish. With my meager translation ability, I had not been able to uncover anything of substance.

"Here is some reading material for you, if you get a chance."

"What's this?" She quizzically asked.

"I wish I knew, I can't seem to make much of it, and you know my Spanish leaves a lot to be desired. I figured you might be able to tell me something about it."

"It looks....and smells very old." She said picking it up and placing it up under her nose.

"Yeah, Father Tom gave it to me when I took this job, he said he studied it several times, but in the end, he didn't feel it is of much of importance, I get the feeling he thinks it just may be something of sentimental value."

"Does he know what it says?

"No, I think he gave up on it too."

"Oh, ok, I'll take it with me and give it a whirl. My brother goes to bed early, and well you know, I'm a night owl myself. I'll look at it when I have time before bed."

"Thanks, and don't knock yourself dead over it, I don't think there is anything so important in there anyway."

We gave each other a big hug and I walked her out to the car. Dropping the notebook on the passenger seat beside her, she blew me a kiss out the window, as she motored off.

As the days passed, I kept a diligent watch over the Crucifix and felt a bit anxious as many unknown faces came and went. My water problem had seemed to subside, and I felt assured that I had conquered it, knowing that there hadn't been any rain for days. And to be certain, I stayed late into the night, several days in a row checking numerous times, just barely making it home to take care of Zeke.

Walking through the cool fall night air made me feel serene and tranquil as I headed back after a trying day's work. It gave me time to think, about Johnny and what he might be going through, about Frankie, hoping she made it safely to her destination and about how the people who I had gotten to know stood their ground when it came to their faith. I thought about all that Doc Coots had said regarding Carlos, with his miraculous recovery, what it could mean for his and all our futures.

It seemed ages ago since I was that child prodigy. The memories of all those performances, the applause and accolades that came with it would sometimes haunt me in my seclusion. But now, they seemed to be gently losing their glamour and I wouldn't trade those former indulgences for any of the beauty and serenity that I was entrenched in. Looking up at the sky on such a clear night, I felt like I could see past an eternity of stars, up to the heavens themselves.

Getting to my front door, I could hear Zeke barking and yelping inside, most likely with his tail wagging uncontrollably, waiting for me to enter. I took out my key and just before I placed it in the lock, I noticed a large rock on my front stoop as if someone intentionally placed it there. Nearing closer to it, I could see something sticking out from under it. It looked to be the corner of a manila envelope.

It took two hands for me to remove the stone, tossing it aside into the yard, I retrieved the envelope from beneath. It was thick, very thick, but sealed. The words written on it, simply said: For Vincent, The Custodian, THANK YOU. I held it for a moment, turning it over and inspecting it further. Then looking around as if to locate any evidence of who might have left it, I took it inside. Dropping my keys on the kitchen table, and pulling out a chair, I sat and slowly tore the back-flap open. To my surprise, there was a pile of money in it, a lot of money! I initially fanned through it seeing a stack of hundred-dollar bills staring back at me. Zeke in his anticipation was pacing around the kitchen table waiting patiently for me to feed him.

"Hold on Zekey boy, I don't know what we have found here!"

I pulled out the wad of cash and noticed that at the bottom of the pile was a photograph of a toddler. He was running outside in a yard with his mother watching him dutifully, wearing a scarf on her head, white gloves, and the most emphatic smile on her face. At first, I examined it closely without understanding the significance of it, or who exactly the people in the photo were. Turning the photo over there was a notation on the flip side which read, Samuel – 2yr. 8 mo.

Then, suddenly I was astounded as I pulled the photo up close to my face and recognized the woman in the background. It was her, that mystery lady who showed up here some time ago, with her driver and baby. It was her, the well-to-do woman who was anguished about the doctors informing her that her boy would never be able to walk. It was her with her child, now walking, playing, and having a grand old time.

I sat still, looking at Zeke, then looking back at the wad of cash that was before me. I began to count, making piles of ten one-hundred-dollar bills in each pile. By the time I was done, ten even piles were sitting in front of me.

Ten thousand dollars in cash, here on my kitchen table, more money than I had seen in my lifetime and I didn't have any inclination what I was supposed to do with it. I let it just sit there, while I got up and proceeded to feed Zeke and then started preparing dinner for myself.

I turned and looked at it once as I began cooking. I looked at it again as I set my plate on the table, I looked at it a third time as I removed a knife and fork from a cabinet drawer. Then I went over and turned on the television where American Bandstand was being broadcast, an episode featuring Paul Anka, singing his hit *Lonely Boy* was airing.

I turned it up loud and looked at Zeke.

"There are ten thousand dollars on our kitchen table!!" I yelled out, with Zeke looking up at me, tilting his head as if he were cross-eyed.

And at that moment, I realized the extent of the enormous amount of money that had been left for me and started singing along with the television as loud as I could, not caring who could hear me. Zeke was barking along, I grabbed his two front paws and raised him on his hind legs as if we were dancing together.

As my jubilation began to settle down, I sat down eating dinner with the stacks of money lying on the table before me as if they were my dinner guests. I ate heartily trying to determine what I was going to do with it all. Lifting the photo, I became absorbed, I didn't who this woman was, I didn't know what her name was or where she was from, nor did I know how to get in touch with her, or exactly why she had left this for me. But sitting there in a moment of clarity it hit me as I dropped my fork to my plate. Her boy, the child that she came here to pray for, that same child who she carried upon our altar, was there in this photograph doing exactly what the doctors told her he would never be able to do. Walk!

My thoughts ran frantically in several directions at once, as I began deliberating out loud.

"Should I call Father Tom, donate it to the church?"

"My mom, I gotta send money to my mom and sis."

"What do we do Zeke? What the hell do we do first?"

Not knowing exactly how to react just then, I hurriedly found myself gathering up the piles of money with the photograph and tucked everything back into the envelope. Then searching for a secret hiding place to stash it, I remembered a loose floorboard under the throw rug in the living room. Flinging the rug to one side, I knelt down, pushed on the board in question with my left hand, and at the same time pried it up slowly with my right.

I placed the enveloped in the crevice, patted it down tight, then replaced the board and the rug. It seemed as safe a place as any, and thoroughly hidden out of sight.

As I lay in bed that evening, thoughts were spinning rapidly through my head. Did that woman also receive a miracle as everyone claimed Carlos had? Did her visit to our church have something to do with it? Was our Crucifix involved? After all, I did find her up close to the altar area where she was not supposed to have been. And wasn't that near to the same area that I found Carlos that fateful day?

I needed to talk to Frankie, she was the only one at this point in my life that could help make some sense of it all. It was late, I was tired, but the urge overtook me anyway. Getting dressed I took a slow jog over to the church with my keys tucked inside the pocket of my blue jeans.

In the dark, I fumbled for the door key and made my way inside, stopping briefly in my office where I kept a clipboard which included important phone numbers. I grabbed it and went right down the corridor without turning on any lights, to Father Tom's office. Thankfully, his door was unlocked. I stepped in, switched on a single desk lamp, and lifted the receiver of his phone. I dialed the first three numbers of Frankie's brother's place, stopped, and quickly hung up.

Thinking it over, I paused, wondering if I was just acting out of haste, perhaps it would be better to just show her the immense fortune when she came back. Besides, I would love to see her reaction in person. I sat there mulling it over with my right-hand sitting atop the receiver. The inclination surged over me again and I just had to call her. And in truth, I did miss her.

This time I dialed the entire number, it rang several times, and just before I was about to hang up, I heard her voice.

"Hello?"

"Frankie, it's me."

The connection sounded very staticky and her voice was fading in and out. Our conversation was fragmented into bits and she sounded very distant.

"Vincent, I'm....so...........glad..............."

"I think we have a bad connection."

"What?"

"I SAID, I THINK WE HAVE A BAD CONNECTION........" I shouted, raising my voice.

"I can barely...................."

"Listen, I have something to tell you, so just listen and I hope you can hear it. Someone left me a lot of money." I said with my heart pounding heavily.

"Vincent, I ....have been............reading the noteboooooook, and I'm nnnnnnot really sure but, the water....... It doesn't make sense........it says............"

She went on desperately trying to tell me something as if she hadn't heard a word of what I was saying.

"STOP, I AM GOING TO CALL YOU RIGHT BACK". I said rather loudly into the receiver holding it like a microphone.

I hung up hoping she heard me as I redialed the number once again, this time I only got a continuous busy signal. Dialing several more times, the results were the same. I sat there in frustration trying to comprehend the few words I heard her say. It sounded like she had read the notebook and was excited to have come up with something.

Outside, with the thunderclap of an impending shower approaching, I decided to head back home. But just before I turned off Father Tom's desk lamp, I happened to glance at his card files which were in a small wooden box located to my left. It was opened to a blue card that held the address of the convalescent home where Father Ortiz was currently residing. I wrote down the location on my clipboard.

The word had come down that Carlos was finally returning home in two days. On my way to going into town for groceries and other supplies, I first made it a point to cruise by bathtub row. It was a sight to behold. The major construction was nearly done, final details were taking place and it had been transformed from a desolate, weed growing wasteland to fully habitable homes. Then, deciding to make a quick stop at Doc Coot's office to confirm the reports I had been hearing, I took a chance that he would be in.

It was then that he not only let me know the news was accurate, but there was more that he wanted to share with me. Bringing me into his private office located in the back, I sat down as he shut the door behind me.

"Vincent, I suppose you are glad that your young friend is returning?"

He said as he moved behind his big mahogany desk and sat in a very comfortable looking leather chair of equal proportions.

"GLAD! That's an understatement, doc."

"Well, you must be asking yourself why I dragged you back here?"

"Come to think of it doc, yeah, it did cross my mind."

"Ok, here it is. Carlos just had his last scan and I have a copy of the results right here."

He tapped his right index finger on a stark white folder laying in front of him.

"And do you have any idea what it says, Vincent?"

"Not the faintest doc, but I'm sure you are about to fill me in."

"Vincent............... There is no trace of a tumor! Not one single centimeter. It has completed vanished!!"

"WHAT! How? How can you explain that, doc?"

"I can't, none of us can. I was hoping you could enlighten me somehow, because I just don't know what to say to anymore, to anyone. Just when you think you've heard it all, space aliens, atomic blasts, old Indian folklore, now people flocking to a statue. It makes me think, it may be time for this old bird to hang up his stethoscope."

"Doc, I don't have an answer either, why would you think I can explain any of it?"

"People around here are talking, Vincent, they are hearing rather wild stories coming from Carlos and of course, things get exaggerated and blown out of proportion rather easily. Still, it doesn't explain his recovery."

He scratched his head and arose, putting on his sports coat and adjusting his tie, he picked up his black medical bag and escorted me out.

I couldn't believe the news myself. Carlos was completely healed and without any explanation from the medical community. It was not only a mystery to those who attended to him, but to me as well. I had experienced some momentous situations in my life, but this time I needed to go further, I needed more information, I needed to find someone who could deliver an answer.

With Frankie not expected back for a few more days, I had time to kill on my day off. I decided to take matters into my own hands and venture out. Tearing the sheet off my clipboard which had Father Ortiz's address written on it, I hopped into the pick-up truck and headed for the highway.

First stop, the new *GAS+Plus*.

Pulling up in front, I noticed the transformation right away, what was once a small, quaint, filling station was now occupied by a large bright white building with red lettering. It had an oversized logo plastered right on top consisting of a huge letter T in red within a white star and the letters TEXACO spelled right below it. There were four shiny new red and white gas pumps and as I pulled up to one, three gentlemen wearing clean white uniforms and hats came dashing out to service my truck.

I politely asked to fill up my tank while I went inside. The manager couldn't have been more than twenty years old but seemed rather educated. I laid down fifteen dollars on the counter and advised him it should cover the gas, a road map which I removed from a nearby stand, and a debt I owed to the previous owner for a battery and motor oil. He smiled and reluctantly accepted the money ringing it into the cash register

After the three men completed pumping my gas, checking my oil, cleaning my windshield, and filling my tires, I was off and running. With a last look in my rear-view mirror, I wondered what Otto would have thought of his *GAS+Plus* now.

I followed the 007 for nearly ninety minutes until I came to a fork in the road. Unfolding the roadmap, I registered the correct turn and plotted a course out to 3129 Ocotillo drive in Alamogordo, only another thirty minutes or so south. I really did not know what I would say to Father Ortiz, or how I would present myself, or in what condition I would even find him. But once again, I felt some uncanny intuition to at least give it a try, besides when Frankie got back, we would have a heck of a lot to talk about.

The trail showed me nothing new, a long lonesome stretch of highway, with not much variation. It was beautiful, but typical landscape. Volcanic mesas in the distance, black rock formations hedging upward to the sky and dry lakebeds with the occasional herd of antelope scurrying by.

Soon I arrived in the town of Alamogordo. It resembled many of the same communities in this part of the state with the main street that held much of the town's businesses and activity. Following my map, I made it directly to my destination without any trouble at all.

The home was a large brownish brick building with beautifully landscaped gardens surrounding it. At first, I mistook it for a school building until I saw the framed sign mounted out front in the middle of a small yard, which read; Saint John's Restful Retreat Home.

Once inside, I found myself at a large semi-circle shaped receptionist desk with a matronly looking attendant stationed there.

"May I help you, young man?" She said as she peered up at me through the upper part of her oval-shaped glasses.

"Yes ma'am, I'm here to see Father Ortiz."

"And may I ask who you are, please?"

"Uh, my name is Angelo……. Uh, excuse me, Vincent Scardosa." I said clearing my throat.

"Are you a family member?"

"No ma'am, just a friend."

She looked thoroughly over a list of names on a pad which was among several on her desk, flipping the page once and running her forefinger up and down it, she shook her head accordingly.

"I'm sorry, I don't see you on the approved list and without prior authorization, I can't allow you in."

"I don't understand, you mean he can't have visitors?"

She leaned forward and took off her glasses which now hung down around her neck on a silver chain. If we had been anywhere else, I would have thought she was ready to play a game of canasta.

"Look, Father Ortiz has had a stroke some weeks ago and needs constant care, visitors are only those of his immediate family, or exceptions can be made if you have special dispensation from the archdiocese. And my guess is that you are not, or have neither? I'm sorry, sir, I don't make the rules around here."

I was just about to turn away and accept what she was saying, but I was determined to make my case. Sometimes in life, you just have to be persistent enough or you will never get what you came for.

"Well, I'm sorry to have bothered you miss, it's just that I came a long way from Mara Del Santo's, and I work at the church which Father Ortiz was from.

"Oh, you are from St. Sebastián?" She said surprisingly.

"And may I ask what you do there, you don't look like, or are dressed like a priest." She added.

"No, ma'am.........I'm just the custodian."

After a lengthy pause, she looked around, put her glasses back on, and told me to wait right where I stood as she disappeared down the hallway behind her. Two minutes later she returned.

"You have ten minutes, no more, if I look at my watch and see that it has been any longer, you can rest assured that I will send someone to escort you out."

Smiling, I thanked her repeatedly, as she looked at me sternly and fought the urge to smile back.

"Room 119, down the hall and to the left." She said extra quietly.

Ambling down the hall and through what seemed to be a very sterile environment of painted pale green walls, I followed the room numbers until I came upon 119. I knocked quietly, respectfully, as I slowly entered. There I found an elderly crippled man sitting in a wheelchair, perched in front of a window, staring intently towards the courtyard outside. He must have been nearly ninety years of age, with just a few strands of gray hair combed back on his head and gray stubble on his face where a beard once was. He had one eye barely opened and was slightly slouched over to the right side, wrapped in a brown blanket. I stood in reverence, knowing that this man had dedicated his entire life to his faith and to the church.

"Hello, Father Ortiz," I said as I walked over to him.

He gave me no response as I pulled over a vinyl chair from the corner of his room and sat right beside him.

"Hi Father, my name is Vincent."

Still, no response, as I could hear him toiling as he took each breath.

"I'm sorry to bother you Father, but I came a long way to see you. I came from Mara Del Santos……...you know, the church there, Saint Sebastián."

I began to get the idea that my trip was pointless, I wasn't aware that he had a stroke and was in decline, it was needless for me to be here, other than possibly to give this man some company for a few minutes. I laid my hand on his arm as I was about to take my leave.

"It was nice to see you Father, and just in case you were wondering, I am the custodian there."

At that moment he turned toward me, whatever had captured his attention outside that window was gone. He looked directly at me and formed a crooked smile and shook his head in an approving nod.

Speaking clearly for him had become difficult, but I was able to manage a conversation slowly and deliberately as best I could.

"You arrrr dah cuustodiannn?" He said stuttering.

"Yes Father, I am fairly new at it, but I'm trying to do the best I can. I was wondering if I could ask you a few questions, mainly about the crucifix?"

His eyes seemed to widen a bit further, even the one that was half closed tried to open slightly more.

"Father, do you have any idea where it came from? Is there anything I should know about it?"

"Noooooo." He said shaking his head from side to side.

"No, you don't know where it came from, or no, there is nothing I should know about it?"

"Yoooo must keep himmmmmm himmmmm him mm safe."

"Him? Who him, father?"

With his head and neck shaking, I did not know if I was causing too much excursion on him as he tried to continue.

"Ca….ca….carry him d …. down………. andddd da water……. wa…. watch da water."

I was totally confused and getting quite nervous as I saw him working himself up into a commotion. Within minutes, two burly men in white uniforms came in with a nurse who tended to Father while the other two asked me quietly and sternly to leave as they guided me out by both arms.

“Thank you, Father……..I will pray for you too.” I said as we made our way out.

Turning, I glanced over the shoulder of the larger of the two men, when I thought I saw Father Ortiz glancing back at me with that crooked smile of his, as I left his room.

Down the hall and out past the receptionist desk, I made my way through two double glass doors and into the open air of the mid-afternoon. The sun was bearing down and even in the fall, the temperatures rose quickly. I didn't find the direct answers I was looking for at Father Ortiz's expense, in fact, I now felt more confused than before. He said, 'him', but who exactly was he referring to? He, like Frankie, mentioned something about water. I was exasperated, but I had a long ride home to think about it. All I knew was that I couldn't wait for Frankie to get back, perhaps if the two of us put our heads together, we might be able to make the pieces fit.

15

I tossed and turned all night, going over what Father Ortiz said, or what he was trying to say. I tried to decipher all the possibilities I could conjure up, but nothing was making much sense. The fragmented phone call I had with Frankie just days earlier also passed through my thoughts as I jostled in my bed. It seemed like hours as I laid there with my mind entirely preoccupied while I tried desperately to will myself to sleep.

Getting up several times, going to the television and flicking it on, or wandering outside for a spell, the night lingered with continued anxiousness. Finally, with Zeke jumping up onto the bed from his usual place at my feet, I stroked his head gently as we both nodded off.

Within an hour, I sat up, startled out of a deep sleep, unable to explain what the cause of my awakening was.

"The water! The water Zeke……. they were both trying to tell me something about the water."

I arose and began to pace in my bedroom as Zeke watched me stride back and forth.

"That water, it's not coming from a leak in the roof, it must be coming from..........."

Stopping suddenly in the middle of my thought, I began to hastily get dressed. It was nearly four in the morning, but I couldn't wait any longer, I had to see if my theory, if what I thought Frankie and Father Ortiz were alluding to, was true.

"Ok Zeke, stay, you stay......stay Zeke. I'll be back soon."

I pulled on my canvas sneakers and locking the front door, I began to run. I ran at full speed towards the church with my set of work keys rattling loudly about me. My thoughts raced as I could see the church coming into view through the darkness and the late-night fog. The humidity could still be felt even at that hour as I could feel the perspiration mounting.

Reaching the workshop, I retrieved the old rickety repaired ladder knowing I would need it for my purpose. I had never inquired if the new ladder had arrived, my attention had been so sidetracked in the past several weeks that I hadn't taken the time to stop at Martinez's to see if it ever came in. For all I knew it was sitting in his back storeroom just waiting for me to pick it up.

Getting to the back door with the ladder hoisted on my left shoulder, I managed to maneuver the keys from my pocket and into my right hand to unlock the entrance. Clumsily balancing the ladder, I opened the door and made my way straight to the light switch box. I turned on only a couple of lights in the altar area, and the spotlight which was directed at the Crucifix. I took the ladder and leaned it on the back wall as close as I could, placing it next to the statue hung high above me.

I was alone. I had been here many times before, only this time it seemed different in a way I could not explain, as if I was summoned. I took several steps back and looked up and what I witnessed next, shook me to the core.

"NO.........NO.......NO...........I didn't just see that, right?"

I closed my eyes tight, placing both palms over each of them and turned away. I began mumbling and tried to convince myself that the lights, the shadows, and the utter stillness surrounding me were producing an illusion. I turned back, frightened, and looked more observantly.

"No...uh-uh....No way man, that's not possible, you can't do this to me!!!"

It was impossible, but there, as I came closer, studying it, I saw it move!

Pacing frantically on the alter trying to get a grip on myself, I remembered that fateful day, hours before I carried Carlos off in a panicked state of urgency. 'El se movio……. señor, el se movio!' Those words of his which I didn't comprehend at the time, those words which I easily dismissed as a young boy's imagination. But here I was, my sweat turned cold as I trembled below a statue, one that I now myself witnessed just as he had.

I climbed the ladder cautiously, one foot up, then two. It was about three feet and my eyes became fixed overhead, that I saw it move slightly again. This time it was as if the chest had expanded and retracted, creating a breathing motion, which I assuredly heard.

I froze where I stood, gripping the ladder tightly with both hands as I whispered to myself trying to muster the courage to go on. There, again, it moved, this time he turned his head and looked down at me.

I heard a soft moan. This wasn't a statue, this wasn't an inanimate object, there was life up there and I had to spring into action right away, forgetting my own emotions and sense of fear.

With my adrenaline kicking in, I regained my strength. Climbing down frantically, I slipped on a puddle of water below my feet catching myself as I grabbed at the ladder with both hands in a steadying manner. My heart pumped furiously as I ran, sliding haphazardly around the corner, almost falling once again as I got to my office. There, I pulled out the toolbox, which was tucked away under my desk, popped it open, and grabbed my hammer.

Sprinting wildly down the dimly lit hallway back to the altar, I tucked the hammer into one of the loopholes on my trousers and climbed, this time, without hesitation. I made it almost to the top, directly across from the figure and pulled the hammer out. Assessing the situation and getting to the correct vantage point, I slowly dropped down a couple of rungs where I began to go to work.

Reaching over, I first pulled a three-inch-long spike out of his feet. They dangled loose as the clinking sound of that nail hitting the stone floor below echoed through the building. Then I climbed up two steps again to continue. I stood even with him and looking into his eyes for that brief instant……………….. time stood still.

In that eternal second, I could see all the unimaginable pain and suffering that he bore for all of humankind. It felt as if a bolt of lightning had passed through my body. Then, he gently wept, and I watched as those tears fell to the ground below us, creating a slight pool of .... water.

It was at that precise moment, pausing ever so slightly, I knew. This is where I had meant to be from the beginning, this was my purpose. All the heartache of the past seemed to vanish in the blink of an eye. All the glamorous triumphs of years gone by felt unequaled, unimportant to where I stood right then. And I believed.

Keeping myself together, I knew I had to work fast. I would need to get him down as quickly as I could, carry him to the pick-up, lay him on the rear bed, and get him over to Doc Coots as soon as possible, just as I did with Carlos. I stretched myself over across his body as far as I could, hearing that old ladder creak again as I reached further out. Taking the hammer now in my left hand, I positioned the back of it to pry the nail from his right hand. Once again, it fell creating an echo. His arm slung free and I grabbed it, corralling it in and placing it over my left shoulder for support. One more nail and I would have him.

I could hear labored breathing, it reminded me of the sound I had heard just days before while I sat at Father Ortiz's side. And for a third spell, I withdrew a nail this time from his left palm, hearing the echo from below yet again.

Dropping my hammer and hauling in his now freed left arm in one motion, I lifted his body against mine. It was as if there was no weight to him at all or could it have been an unrecognizable surge of adrenaline that now fully encompassed me.

I held his body braced up against me as I began to maneuver my way down. Slowly descending I spoke to him with a sense of reassurance that we would make it to ground level, that I would get him down and everything would be fine. I held him tightly, carrying his broken and wounded body with as much care as I could generate.

Then, about a third of the way in our descent, with nearly twenty feet remaining between us and the floor beneath, I heard the ladder creaking louder and more steadily. Once again, I spoke to myself, asking, begging that old ladder to hold together for just a few minutes more. One more rung downward and the inevitable happened. It started to crack, loudly, with my forward foot braking right through the rung as I stood on it, we dropped suddenly to the next, the weight of the two of us began to dismantle the whole thing in one sudden unstoppable motion.

I felt the two sides of the ladder separating and breaking apart as we plummeted downward crashing through each rung in rapid succession. We hit the ground hard, but I held him on top of me using my body to cushion the blow. Lying there, I could hear his breath continuing and felt the warmth of his body as he slid off to one side. With my head resting on the cold hard floor, I could not move, I couldn't feel much of anything, as everything began to fade out.

Things started slowly and deliberately coming into focus as I knew people were standing around me, but with everything a blur, I wasn't sure of where I was. The first thing I felt was a severe shooting pain in my back as I tried to move, and my head felt like it withstood the blow of a sledgehammer. It was difficult to change positions with my hands or arms and the voices I heard around me were very muffled. I slipped back and forth into consciousness several times. I can't remember or even perceive how long I had been out for, but it felt like I had been gone for an eternity.

"Vincent…………Vincent…...it's ok, I'm here."

I heard that soft, comforting familiar voice whispering over me as I slowly began to open my eyes, squinting, they steadily began to adjust to the brightness of the white overhead lights. I could see Frankie bending above me, her face close to mine as I felt her lips kiss me on the cheek. Her smile slowly gained clarity as my sight began to clear.

"Welcome back mister, you had us worried there for a while." She continued.

"I…I…. where am I? What…...what…...happened?" I said with barely enough strength to complete my thought.

The next minute, Frankie moved away, two men were now standing above me looking closely into my eyes and asking me a barrage of questions. One of them was Doc Coots.

"Vincent, do you know who I am? Vincent?"

I shook my head yes, as my mouth was so dry it was difficult to get the words out.

"Doc................ Coots."

"Yes, good, do you know where you are? You are in Santé Fe General hospital."

I didn't have any idea what he was referring to, nor did I have any recollection of how I got there. All I knew was that something was wrapped tightly around my head which hung lower over my right eye, obscuring my line of sight and I could hear steady beeping sounds coming from somewhere behind me.

I felt the cold hard metallic disc of his stethoscope touch my chest as he examined me, then the second man joined in feeling my torso and legs. Within minutes, they moved away and began discussing something about my condition. Frankie reappeared, as well as a nurse checking an intravenous line which I now noticed was hooked up to my right arm.

"You have been asleep for a while, but everything is going to be alright." I heard Frankie say, trying her best to reassure me.

She picked up a small white styrofoam cup that was filled with cool water and a straw and leaned it over towards me as I took several long hard welcoming sips.

"Thank you. But what the hell happened?" I said in a state of bewilderment as the cool water briefly ushered in a moment of clarity.

"Honey, I don't know what you were trying to do, but lucky for you, Father Tom had come in early the other morning and found you, unconscious. He said the ladder was broken into bits and you were laying on the ground out cold. The doctor said that if they had not brought you in when they did, I might not be talking to you right now!"

The nurse moved in close again and let Frankie know that I needed to get rest, a lot of rest. I wanted her to stay by my side but was too weak to carry on about it and with my head pounding as it was, I didn't think I would be able to contribute much to our conversation.

In the days that followed, things started to take shape. I had formulated the notion that I had an accident, that if it wasn't for Father Tom, I would have been in much worse condition, or I might not even be here at all. From the constant visits I received from several doctors and nurses, it sounded like I was progressing steadily. And the daily meetings I was getting from Doc Coots, made it known to me just what shape I was in.

"Good morning, Vincent. Good to see you awake."

"Yeah Doc, I'm awake alright, but I still can't piece together what happened."

"Never mind that right now, it will come, but let me tell you where we stand."

I knew Doc Coots would give it to me straight, he wasn't the kind to beat around the bush.

"Here's the good news. You have suffered a skull fracture, three broken ribs, a cracked vertebra, and you broke the bone in your left forearm."

"I thought you said that's the good news, doc?"

"Yes, well quite frankly it is. Your fractures are healing well, and I suspect you will be up and about in no time."

"So, what's the bad news then, doc?"

"Long-term, that cracked vertebra may cause you persistent back pain, and I wouldn't rule out sporadic dizzy spells either, but these are things you may just have to live with."

"When can I get outta here Doc?"

"Oh, just a couple of more days should do, we just want you here for observation, just a formality, that's all."

It was difficult to conceive that I had suffered such trauma to my body, and even more difficult in remembering what led me here. Frankie came by as often as she could, but neither of us discussed the circumstances of my accident. She did make it a point, although, to let me know that many people back in town were asking for me and sending well wishes and prayers. And from the look of things around my room, there were plenty of flowers and cards scattered about attesting to such.

She had informed me that Carlos had returned and seemed better than ever. I had taught him so well that Father Tom had assigned him chores in my absence, even though they were both eager to get me back.

"Good morning Vincent, I brought a friend to see you today." Father Tom said entering my room with delight.

"Hey there Father, good to see you," I responded, not noticing who was following him.

"Well, I have been here many times to check up on you, but you were often sound asleep."

Then from behind him, Carlos appeared, smiling that impeccable white smile of his. He ran straight to my bedside, nearly climbed halfway up over the bed rail, and threw his arms around me, laying his head on my chest. I reached around with my good arm and pulled him in as tight as I could manage. Backing away after a few minutes, I noticed how well he actually looked. It had been several long weeks since I saw him, and it was as if he had grown several inches and even began to fill out that thin frame of his.

"Señor Vincent! I'm so happy to see you. So glad that you are okay."

"That goes the same for me buddy!"

"I want to thank you, you saved my life." He said as he wiped a tear from his eye.

"C'mon now, no need to thank me, after all, what are friends for?"

We spoke for a while as he reported on all the daily jobs he was doing at the church and asked my advice on completing many others. I was proud of him and his dedication at such a youthful age. I felt relieved to know that not only his health was completely restored, but he had taken in everything I taught him and was performing it to the best of his ability. I trusted him, and I believed that Father Tom had now come to do the same.

I had many visitors from town, the girls from the diner, Mr. Martinez from the grocery store, and others who I didn't know all too well but knew me as the custodian that cared for their church. But with all those that did manage to stop by, the one constant remained Frankie. She had taken time off from work and made it a point to be here, sometimes for many long hours, while the other waitress covered for her. Often, I would drift into a deep slumber but felt comforted knowing that when I awoke, she would still be there by my side.

"Huuuuuuuuh.........Frankie, Holy Cow...... Frankie!........... Where is he? Oh my God, where is the Crucifix????? I suddenly exclaimed startled from my sleep, propping myself up as far as I could in the bed.

Awoken in a cold sweat and panic-stricken, I called out again for Frankie as I tried to further pull myself out of bed, managing to drop the side metal guard rail down. Swinging my legs over one side of the bed, I continued, and tried to stand up.

In the chair, next to me, Frankie was jolted out of a slumber where she had peacefully nodded off and immediately jumped up to calm me down. Thankfully she was quick on her feet, as my legs were still very shaky and trembled, almost causing me to topple over.

"Whoa, slow down there, mister." She said as she held on to me by the waist guiding me right back into bed.

"Frankie, the Crucifix, where is it, I mean where is he?"

"Calm down Vincent, what are you talking about? The Crucifix is where it always has been. It's safe in the church, hung on the altar, where else would it be? Now please calm down."

"The Crucifix........... I carried him down, we fell, I remember now.......... but.... WHERE IS HE?"

"Okay, slow down, slow down, you must have been dreaming."

"Here, have some water." She paused passing the cup to me.

I gulped and swallowed deeply, as that feeling of confusion entered once again. Here I was, battered and bruised in a hospital bed and now, I fully remembered what took place. It was real. I experienced it, but why hasn't anybody brought it up. I mean Father Tom was here, he found me there, yet the subject had not been addressed, not even a question about it.

"Look, it happened, I was there, I remember the whole thing. Where is Father Tom? I need to talk to him right away!"

"Vincent, you have had an accident, there has been a lot of trauma to your head and the rest of your body and they have been giving you a lot of medication, it's understandable for you to............."

"STOP! Frankie, please, you just gotta believe me!!!"

"Vincent, this is not the time or the place, you need to stay calm right now, let's wait until we get you home.........please!"

I sat back breathing heavily, caressed by several pillows propped up on my bed. I didn't know if Frankie really believed me or if she were just pacifying me so I would get my rest. Laying there, it seemed hard to unravel the truth between reality and fantasy. It was just that the whole incident seemed so real and I couldn't imagine it any differently.

The nurse, hearing my voice becoming loud and agitated came shuffling in and handed me a tiny white pleated paper cup holding two pink pills.

"Vincent, take these, you need to remain at rest, these will help you sleep." She said rather sternly.

Taking the pills, I reluctantly swallowed them, shaking my head as I tried to continue telling Frankie my story, I slipped off into a deep immediate sleep.

With myself being out of commission, for the time being, things began to heat up back in Mara Del Santos. Word had spread like wildfire that miracles were taking place at our church and the crowds started to evolve, growing at an incredible rate. People came from miles around, all looking for some kind of relief, some answer to their strife or suffering. It didn't matter what class of people they were, they came looking for solace and expected to find it there. Father Tom was engulfed with the number of onlookers that came, and though Carlos was at his beck and call, the task of managing the crowds became overwhelming. He even got to the point where he enlisted a couple of volunteers from the parish to keep things organized and safe. Word had traveled so far and wide, that an entourage was scheduled to arrive from the bishop's office within the next week.

With my condition steadily improving, my release was imminent, but as much as I wanted to get back to the church and resume work, it would be some time until I was fully able. Approximately a week went by and I had recovered enough to have the bandages removed from my head, the intravenous lines were disconnected and I needed to take much less pain medication. My arm was in a cast, but I was able to move it about, occasionally resting it in a sling. Walking was a challenge at first, but with each passing day and each step I took, I became stronger. The only stipulation was that I had to use a cane for the near future.

"Okay, how is our patient doing today?" Said the day nurse as she entered pushing a wheelchair before her.

"Is that for me?"

"You betchya', got your walking papers at my desk and the doctor should be here any minute to sign you out. Is that pretty young lady coming for you?"

And no sooner had she had made that statement, Frankie came in behind her, flashing that wonderfully captivating look of hers, ready to escort me out.

The ride back home in Denise was reviving, even with a nagging pain pulsating through my spine, I managed to sit back and take in some fresh air as Frankie chauffeured me back to town. It seemed like things had changed practically overnight, the streets were more heavily trafficked than I remembered them to be, and passing through bathtub row, it looked like it was part of a thriving community which never lost its way. Frankie informed me that it was nearly ninety percent full, with most families coming from out of town. But at this point, I was more than happy to get back home to my own familiar quiet comforts.

We first swung by Frankie's place to retrieve Zeke, she had been taking care of him in my absence, and when he got a glimpse of me in the car, he couldn't contain himself. Jumping into the front seat as I opened the door, he licked my face profusely while I laughed uncontrollably.

"Frankie, there is more I need to tell you."

"I know Vincent, I wanted to wait to get you home. There are things I need to tell you too."

Purposely taking an indirect route, we avoided passing the church and having anyone see us. Frankie parked the car around the back of my house, out of sight. I walked gingerly, getting used to relying on my cane for assistance as we made our way inside. It felt good to back where I had a sense of safety within the confines of my own home. I immediately headed for the oversized chair in my living room and sank into it with a gasp of fatigue. Zeke sat, taking his dutiful place at my feet. I knew it would take time to fully regain my strength and would try to remain as patient as possible.

"Can I get you anything?" Frankie shouted from inside the kitchen.

"Okay, thanks, how about a cola?"

"Coming right up." She said as she entered with an open bottle of soda pop.

Taking the cold perspiring bottle in my hand, I gulped it down rather quickly.

"Ahhhhhhhhh, thank you, I needed that. Now come on, sit down, please, I want to talk to you."

I had ranted about my story to her in the hospital and even though she tried to dismiss it as imagination brought on by the adherent medication, I felt she knew it was more than just that. She understood me better than anyone and for some reason was reluctant to let the facts about my accident out in public.

"Frankie, before I get into anything that sounds stranger than fiction, there is something I have to show you. The night I called you at your brothers, I found something on my doorstep and was trying to tell you about it."

"Yes, well, Vincent, that is the night I think I may have learned something from that notebook you gave me, and I was trying to tell you about it too."

I slowly climbed out of my chair and got down on one knee.

"Uh, excuse me, mister, just what do you think you're doing?" She said with concern.

I quietly ignored her while leaning my cane against the chair and pulled over the throw rug with my good arm, exposing the floor and the loose board beneath. Lifting it, I reached down and grabbed the envelope hidden there. Then climbing back into the chair, I held it loosely, dangling it in front of her.

"And what is that, may I ask?"

I opened it, taking out the wad of cash and fanning it before her with a secretive smirk on my face.

"Oh my, Vincent. What?……… I mean, where did this come from? I don't think I have ever seen this much money."

She sat there with a look of amazement. Grinning, she took the money and began to count. I handed her the photograph that came with it, causing her to pause and study it. Then I told her the entire story of the mystery woman and her child who 'randomly' showed up here months ago.

"I can't believe what you are telling me…... what are you planning to do with it?........ I mean do you just keep it, or……"

I had gotten to know Frankie so well that it seemed I already knew what her line of questioning would be and how I intended to answer it.

"You know, at first, the sight of all this cash just bowled me over, but I have had plenty of time to think about it, and I think I should go to Father Tom with it."

She agreed, just as I thought she would. Placing the money back into its hiding place, our conversation then turned towards something I hadn't expected. The moment turned quiet as if Frankie wasn't totally surprised about this gift or the events that she had returned home to.

"Vincent, what happened that nearly got you killed? I mean I get home from my brother's and there is a note on my door from Father Tom that you were in an accident and I should get to the hospital right away. It scared the hell out of me."

I told her just how it happened, every detail, as real, and as powerful as it was to me. I told her all about my visit with Father Ortiz and what he was trying to say to me. And when I was finished, she looked down, not able to find the words to comprehend what I was describing. I sat back in my chair waiting to hear how I must have gone insane, how the tortuous stress of my past had finally caught up with me, or some underlying lingering effects of the radiation which tainted this land many years ago had affected my brain.

Instead, the opposite occurred.

"So, that's it, honey, go ahead and call me crazy, but I know what I saw and what I felt. I know statues don't come alive, I know they don't cry leaving a trail of tears. I know it all sounds irrational, but please tell me I'm not going crazy."

"Vincent, I believe you. You are not crazy" She said slowly looking up at me.

"What? You what? You believe me?"

"Well, I think I do...........if that makes any sense."

"Honey at this point, I don't know if anything makes any sense, but I'll take it."

"What I mean is, I cannot believe I didn't bring this up earlier, but with your accident and all, it slipped my mind. The night you called me at my brother's, I thought I found something interesting in that old journal you gave me, and well, I'm not an expert or anything, but....... wait, hold on a minute....... I'll be right back."

She swiftly left the room darting out the front door to the car. With the thud of the trunk slamming shut she returned, journal in hand. I moved over to the couch where she sat up against me, thumbing through it looking for a specific page.

"Here, look here, this seems like it's some sort of old-world Spanish dialect, I think, and I'm not sure I'm even interpreting it right, but look here. 'La agua', that means 'water'. 'Viene de los ojos', it's saying, coming from eyes."

She held the journal open, underlining various words and phrases with her index finger as she went on trying to translate them.

"It seems as though your water problem was never coming from a leaky roof, Vincent, it must have been coming from another source entirely, and I think it is saying from the statue itself!!! ....Now, do you know why I believe you!"

She continued.

"And that's only a small portion of it, there is much more encrypted here, but I am not a historian. It's so faded in areas, I don't know if anyone at all would be able to decipher it."

Terrified, I jumped up from my chair and grabbed my cane, as a spurt of pain shot down my spine causing me to wince.

"Frankie, we got to get over to the church, we just have to! If he is there, then I need to see for myself. I need to know this wasn't some sort of ill-fated dream or something."

"See who, honey?"

"Him......uh, you know.... I mean........the Crucifix."

"Oh no......we....... you, are not going anywhere like that mister, so just sit right back down. Besides, there is still a lot of activity going on over there and there will be plenty of time for it later."

Begrudgingly, I knew she was right, I gently fell back into my chair giving way to the signals my body was sending me. I had not the strength nor the courage to face my fears or convictions just then, that would have to wait, at least for another night.

16

Life began to take on some normalcy as my injuries gradually continued to heal with each passing day. I started to be less reliant on my cane. The pressure in my head had subsided just as Doc Coots said it would. The headaches and dizziness still remained, but gradually became less intense. The most difficult part of my day was looking out my front window and seeing the church off in the distance, knowing that I couldn't be there to do my part. I worried about the fate of the Crucifix and sometimes paced relentlessly trying to come to grips with my intentions toward it.

The word was out that I had been released and was recuperating at home, and on many occasions, I would get a knock on my door from a visiting parishioner who would stop, wish me well and drop off a care package of some sort, generally consisting of food. Carlos would often stop in, especially at lunchtime. I would most always have a meal prepared in anticipation and I enjoyed his company while he filled me in on the activities taking place. It was a joy to see him progressing and growing beyond my expectations. Some days

I would even give him lessons on shooting cans off the back log, just as 'miss sharpshooter of the county' did with me.

Frankie would assuredly stop by nearly every night, with our discussion ranging on topics from world news, such as Alan Shepard becoming the first American in space, to the election of a new young senator named Jack Kennedy becoming presidential timber or debating which was the best show on television, The Twilight Zone or Bonanza. But we always seemed to circle back to the same topic.

"You know, I'm feeling a hell of a lot better and I don't even think I am going to need this much longer," I said twirling the cane like a baton.

"It's so wonderful to see how you have improved so quickly, but, Vincent, do you think you are well enough to handle everything that's been going on over there?"

"I do honey, I need to get back there, if only for my own peace of mind. And as busy as he has been, I need to talk to Father Tom."

"Tell you what, I will make it a point to go over first thing in the morning before I start my shift and let him know you are ready. How about it?" she gently pleaded.

I was ready. I wanted to go out and walk over, yes, the whole quarter-mile, like I had done so many times before. Even with a tender leg and my arm still in a cast, the desire to get back to it was gnawing at me and if it wasn't for Frankie watching with a strict eye, I would have pushed myself without any consideration, but once again, realizing she was the voice of reason, I would just have to wait until sunrise.

"Good morning Vincent!" The voice on the other side of my door exclaimed.

"Just a minute….be right there," I shouted back as a tucked in my shirt and straightened my hair with my unrestricted hand.

It was only half-past six in the morning when Father Tom had made his presence known on my doorstep. I surmised that Frankie wasted no time in getting to him and letting him know that I had something pressing to discuss.

"Father! Come on in." I politely muttered opening the door.

"I hope I haven't come too early, but the demands at the church these days have me running in circles, especially without my custodian there to help." He stated, chuckling slightly.

"No, it's fine, my sleeping has been off, and I was up anyway. Just about to make a pot of coffee. Would you like some?"

"Yes, yes, that would be fine, Vincent. How are you feeling anyway, you look well."

"I feel great Father, ready to get back to work you might say."

Sauntering into the kitchen with a slight hitch in my step, I gathered two clean cups, a bowl of sugar, and a small container of milk and set them on the table. Father Tom followed, and after petting Zeke for a few minutes, he sat down.

"Coffee will be ready in a jiff, Father. But there are a few things I want to talk to you about. Give me a minute, I'll be right back."

Going back into the living room, I hastily thrust the rug aside, pulled up the floorboard, and grabbed the envelope of money, making more noise than I anticipated.

"Vincent, everything alright in there, can I be of any assistance?" He shouted from the kitchen.

"Uh, no, I'm fine, be right there."

Returning, slightly out of breath, I placed the envelope on the table, retrieved the coffee pot from the stove, and poured a cup for each of us. I then proceeded to tell him about the mystery woman and explained my theory, showing him the enclosed photograph, as I laid out the pile of money.

"This is truly an amazing story, my son, and a very extravagant gift to go along with it. What would you like me to do?"

"Father, at first, I felt fortunate to obtain this, but after thinking about it, I didn't do anything to earn it. I think maybe I should donate it?"

"Vincent, I cannot stop you from doing with it as you wish, but let me say something more. Healing comes in many forms. I don't know if you had anything to do with the changing condition of the boy in that photograph, but the fact that you comforted that woman and her child when they needed it the most, is in itself a form of the healing process. I believe she was so overcome with joy, that this was the only way she knew how to thank you and she obviously has the means to do it."

I listened to his words, they were profound and made sense. Recalling those events, I only did what any person in my position would have done, that was to listen and show a little concern and compassion. In any event, I knew, if that woman did receive a miracle, it wasn't from me that it came, it was from a higher source. One which hung behind me that day……...literally.

"I think I understand Father, still, I would like to make some kind of donation to the church, or perhaps to people of the parish who need it more than I do."

I took the stack of cash, counted out a set amount, and slid it across the table towards him. Then taking the rest, I placed it back in the envelope and folded it up. I knew that I would most assuredly be sending some off to my mom, but I had a stark inkling of what I wanted to do with the remainder.

"Thank you, Vincent, it is very noble of you. I will be sure it gets put to good use."

"Thank you, Father. Now I need to tell you a story……...…. about the night of my accident."

"Vincent, I will have to come back another time, there is a contingency coming tomorrow from the archdiocese office. I have a meeting scheduled with their deacon in twenty minutes and I need to get things in order right away, I'm not sure what to expect from tomorrow's assembly when the rest of them arrive."

He rose from the table, retrieved the cash and slid it into his pocket, then taking a last big sip of coffee, started towards the door.

"But…but……. Father, it's about the Crucifix!"

"The Crucifix is fine right now my son, I have two gentlemen watching it all day, and your friend Carlos is also there, he doesn't seem to want to take his eyes from it. So, do not worry, it is safe and awaits your return, I will see you soon."

And before I could explain any further, he shook my hand firmly and made his way out to his car.

I patiently waited all day for Frankie to get back, I was excited about my plan for the money and of course, wanted to share it with her. When she did eventually arrive, I met her outside, along with Zeke. As she pulled up in front, I walked over to the driver's side window and leaned in.

"Feel like going for a ride?" I asked with a sneaky grin on my face.

"Oh, I have seen that look before, you are up to something, aren't you?"

"I just might be," I said walking around the front of the car and opening the passenger door with Zeke lunging in back.

"Where are we going? I'm almost afraid to ask."

"Head out to the highway......and step on it, just drive baby, drive," I said smiling.

She shook her head grinning along with me and made a U-turn heading out at full speed. Frankie knew that whatever I had planned might not just be something exciting, but something unexpected.

"Ok, so where am I going?"

"Next stop, *GAS+Plus*.........uh, excuse me, I meant to say that newfangled Texaco station."

It was a clear afternoon and dusk was fast approaching as we motored along with the radio on. A warm wind was blowing through our hair, while Zeke, with his head leaning out the open window enjoyed the free-flowing experience as well. I knew Frankie had no idea why we would be heading to the Texaco station, but I wanted to surprise her, and I was almost sure that my next objective would.

When we finally arrived, Zeke began whimpering slightly and seemed agitated as he paced from window to window looking out keenly. At second thought, I should have known better to bring him along, after all, this was the location of his home for many years, and I believed his instincts were kicking in. We rolled up the windows more than halfway and thought it better to leave him in the car for the time being.

"I'm sorry boy, we will be right back." I sternly addressed him as he quietly whined.

Walking over to the office door I could tell that she was still very leery as to what I was up to. Once inside, we were approached by a very congenial young man adorned in the typical white and red uniform and matching hat. I advised him that if he would be so kind as to summon the manager, I would be much obliged. He disappeared in the back and a few minutes later he returned with a familiar looking gentleman by his side.

"Good evening, what can I do for you folks?" He said very courteously.

"Hello sir, my name is Vincent Scardosa, and this here is Frankie, we drove out from Mara Del Santos and I would like to inquire about purchasing a new car, like your poster hanging over there, states," I said, pointing to the placard on the wall.

"Ohhhhhh yes, now I remember you. You are that fella that came by weeks ago to pay for items you had gotten from the previous owner. I think you asked how the new car purchase plan worked back then."

"That's right, you have a good memory, and now, here I am ready to go ahead with it."

Frankie looked at me dumbfounded, while I could tell her excitement was building. The manager left for a moment then returned almost immediately carrying a shiny white catalog of cars that he would be able to order and have delivered to his location. He handed it over and offered me and Frankie a seat in the office, instructing us to take our time and look it through.

"You are too much." She whispered to me trying to contain her emotions.

We flipped through about three pages and stopped. Looking at each other we knew what our choice would be. There, jumping out at us was a photo of a brand new 1959 2-door Chevy Impala. It was jewel blue with a white stripe on each side panel. It was sleek and powerful with a V-8, 348 engine, two-tone split-bench seats, a four-on-the-floor shifter, factory radio, and airplane-inspired fins at its rear. We both pointed to that one almost in unison and called the manager over.

"That was quick, folks usually take much longer to decide. So, which one did you choose?"

We handed him the booklet folded open to the page containing our selection. He sat down with us and proceeded to discuss payment and ordering procedures.

"Ahhhhhh excellent choice. You're in luck, this car is in stock at our Houston location, I can have it here in two days, but it will require a sizable deposit and the rest upon delivery."

"Okay, that's fine. And as far as the deposit goes How much do need today?"

"Well, I would say, $1000.00 upfront and the balance of $1597.00 when you pick it up."

He paused not knowing how I would react, after all, I didn't exactly project myself as a man of wealth, and in reality, nor was I. But without hesitating I reached into my pocket and pulled out a nice sized bundle of cash as I began to count out ten one-hundred-dollar bills. He looked at me conspicuously with a sense of surprise.

"Very well, Mr. Scardosa, let me write you out a receipt."

Taking the money, he headed over to his desk, sat down, and pulled out a ledger from his top drawer. He shuffled some papers and came right back to us, handing me an order form with the specifications we required, and a cash receipt. We shook hands and he advised us that the car would be here in a couple of days.

Getting back to Denise, I knew I wouldn't be able to hold back Frankie's exhilaration once we were alone.

"WOW OH WOW! You are just non-stop full of surprises aren't you!"

"Honey, it's been a whirlwind of surprises since the day I arrived here, so I figured, what the hell, what's one more. And besides, I had a feeling you would like this one."

On our way back home, I told her about my morning meeting with Father Tom and the decision that was made regarding the money. It may have been a bit extravagant, but I never really had done anything like that for myself before. And given the fact that the old pick-up truck felt like it was on its last leg, parked back in its original spot in the workshop, I couldn't think of a better way to spend a portion of it.

As my general health continued to resume its path to recovery, I knew that I needed to get to Father Tom and discuss exactly what I experienced the night of my accident. But it wasn't just a simple feeling of apprehension which caused me to hesitate from making my way back to work. I found myself avoiding a return, due to the inevitable encounter I would have, seeing the Crucifix once again. I wasn't sure I was ready for it or what effect it would have on me.

Sometimes in life, the obstacles which prevent us from doing what we should do, are those which come from within, and those are precisely the ones we must find a way to overcome.

The morning was clear, and the sun shone brightly revealing the colors scattered throughout the desert sand. I knew the time had come. I picked myself up literally and emotionally, showered, shaved, and put on my clean and ironed custodian's uniform which had been hanging dormant in my closet for the past several weeks.

Getting through a hearty breakfast for myself and Zeke, and leaving my cane behind, I grabbed my set of keys and walked out into the morning dew, heading for the church. I wanted to get there as early as possible before any crowds gathered and much sooner than any mass would begin.

It was nearly six o'clock when I let myself in through the back entrance. The minute I entered, I could feel goosebumps emerging up and down my arm. I tried to treat it as any normal day, as if I had been on a vacation and was just returning to work.

At the breaker box behind the alter, I flicked all the light switches to the on position, illuminating the entire building. Then, without another thought, I came around the front where I knew the Crucifix would be in full view.

Looking up, I almost lost my breath, nothing like my last experience, this view stunned me in an entirely different way.

"Wait, what the heck.........hold on here. They told me you were here, they told me you were safe!" I spoke aloud in disbelief.

"The crucifix is gone, there's no statue, it wasn't a dream, I didn't imagine it. It really happened; did it really happen? And why hasn't anybody said anything to me?"

My thoughts raced as I stood there for quite a long time staring at a plain wooden cross, hung exactly where the Crucifix once was.

For a moment, I began to feel faint, then hearing the back entrance open and close in one swift motion, I collected my energy and headed right to Father Tom's office.

"FATHER....... FATHER TOM!" I shouted as I quickly rambled down the hallway.

"Vincent! What are you doing here, I didn't expect you for at least another week or two."

"Father.................Father...........The Crucifix........"

I said gasping for air, hunched over and holding myself up by my two outstretched arms as I leaned forward on his desk.

"Vincent, here, here. Sit down, you are not in the best condition yet and should not have come back so soon."

"But Father, The Crucifix.........It's GONE! And I know how!"

"How could you know my son, they just took it down yesterday, I haven't had the time to come and see you again?"

"THEY...... THEY, WHO?"

"I think I better fill you in on what has happened in your absence."

“Please Father, yes.”

“Three days ago, a delegation from the archdiocese office arrived. Vincent, the word of our little church here and the chatter of miracles made its way up the ranks. A special magistrate and his assistants were sent all the way from Rome to investigate further and compile a full report. And it seems as though we were ordered to remove the Crucifix, temporarily of course, and replace it with what you are seeing now.”

“But Father, how………...”

“Vincent, please let me finish. Your accident along with Carlos’ and well, the outbreaks of people looking for their own miracles have been a cause for great concern. Due to these recent events I have been instructed to keep our Crucifix in storage until further analysis.”

“Where, Father, where is it being kept?”

"It is safe, my son, I have personally seen to that. They wanted to export it away from here, but I fought persistently, and it is now lodged safely in the back basement storeroom, bolted under lock and key. That room at the far end of the basement was used to shield inhabitants during the atomic blast testing, it goes deep underground. No one has access to it, I am the only one with the key."

“Father, Can I see him, PLEASE!”

“Not now my son, the magistrate is still in town and hasn’t finished his report, you must trust me on this matter.”

“But Father, the water issue, I can tell you all about that too!”

“Easy does it, Vincent. Rest assured, the water issue also seems to be resolved, a couple of army engineers working at the construction site in town were recruited, they concluded that moisture was indeed trapped, not in the ceiling, but in concave hollow cavities within the wall, somewhere behind the Crucifix. Their findings have been officially filed and it has left me with no choice but to concur, despite any personal opinion I may have.”

I sat there in stunned silence. It appeared my story wouldn’t have any bearing on the outcomes which had emerged. Still, I felt compelled to tell Father Tom everything I witnessed, everything I felt, and if he determined that this was all some sort of dream, some sort of delusion, then I swore to myself that I would accept it, I would live with it.

In the next hour, I proceeded, indignantly spinning my tale to him. I told him every detail of what occurred that night, just as I had told Frankie. I watched him sit there at his desk, swivel his chair in the opposite direction with his back to me listening to my step by step account as it unfolded, up until the time I fell and blacked out.

Pivoting in his chair slowly, he turned back towards me and paused as if he was at a loss for words. He pulled himself close to his desk, clasped his hands tightly in front of him, and looked downward for several moments.

"Vincent, this story of yours is astounding. I cannot say that it did indeed happened or not, but that is not the most important thing here. I do believe that you had a spiritual encounter, one that does not frequent every person. You, yourself have said that you always felt an underlying reason why you ended up here, and frankly, I have always thought there was something different about you, and I don't mean that unique musical gift you possess either."

"What! You know about that Father?"

"I have known for some time. The echo in this building reaches far and wide, and I have enjoyed your magnificent serenades more often than you know."

"I guess I did get carried away at times, the place does have really good acoustics. But I didn't think anyone was around while I indulged. Why didn't you ever say anything?"

"Well, I believe that you have your reasons for keeping it to yourself and I wanted to respect that. You see Vincent, we all have our reasons for doing what we do. These people come here for their own deep reasons, they all have their personal views about it, and they will continue to come whether that Crucifix is hanging there or not. You must understand, my son, the figure which hangs there is a symbol of our beliefs, our faith. But what is most important, is where that faith comes from...................from within."

I needed some time to think about what Father Tom had said. I could accept the fact that there is power in prayer. I could accept the fact that healing comes in many forms, sometimes without really recognizing it. And I could understand that faith comes with blind trust, accepting something unseen and believing in it. But I still had a tough time dealing with the fact that what I saw and felt that night wasn't real? To me it was.

I suffered some terrible injuries on that fateful night, ones that could have even been fatal, but with them came healing, not in the physical sense, but one of the emotional and spiritual sense.

I took Father Tom's advice and decided to remain at home to finish my recuperation time. He was right in noticing that my energy level was not quite where it should be and besides, it gave me time to ponder, perhaps reason with everything that had taken place.

With two days having passed, I waited anxiously for Frankie to get off work and swing by as we had planned. Upon her arrival, she found me outside sitting on the front stoop.

"Looks like you're more than ready," she said spying me over a pair of sunglasses as she shouted out her window.

"Let's Go!" I responded getting into the passenger seat.

We were off to The Texaco station, in a short time, I would be cruising home in my brand-new Chevy. She had the radio turned up loud as we usually liked it on our high-speed jaunts, but this time I deliberately turned it down. She knew that was an indication that I had something important to tell her and of course she was right.

"Okay, mister, spill it."

"You just think you know me so well, don't you?"

"You know I do, so come on, out with it."

"Well.... it's not that important I guess in the grand scheme of things, but I went over to the church today. I went intending to go back to work."

"YOU DID WHAT!"

"I know, I know, and just hold on before you say anything."

I went on to tell her about the conversation between me and Father Tom. I explained how I felt going back and my trepidation of seeing the Crucifix again. And I told her how it had been removed with the authority of the special investigator from Rome.

"Wow, I had no idea Vincent, and you told Father Tom the whole story of what you saw and your accident."

"I did Frankie, yes I did. Now you and he are the only ones I have discussed it with."

"Well, where do we go from here?"

"I'm not sure, honey, his words made a lot of sense to me, but......but......"

"But what?"

"It's just that it seemed so real to me, even now when I think about it, I get chills down my spine."

Moments later we pulled into the Texaco parking lot and there at the end of a row consisting of new and used cars, was a beautiful, brand-new, jewel blue, Chevy, bubble-top, Impala. It was gleaming in the late afternoon sun, just waiting for us.

Not even bothering to go inside, we walked right over to it and just admired it up and down. Frankie was enthralled with its shiny sparkling paint and I wasted no time climbing into the driver's side and getting behind the wheel.

"Going my way mister?" She joked as she came up behind me.

"It's beautiful, isn't it?"

"Wow, it's the boss, Vincent, looks so much nicer in real life."

The manager, seeing us fawning like children over it came out grinning as he drew near.

"I take it you are satisfied?"

"I am…I mean, we are!"

"Wonderful, let's go inside and conclude our business, the sooner you sign the papers, the sooner you can drive off in it."

In a jolt, we were back in his office, completing the paperwork and handing over the balance due, and just as he promised the keys were given to me promptly and off we sped.

I felt like that youthful teen once again as I raced off the lot onto the 007. Frankie followed close behind in Denise, and at times pulled up right alongside me as we both couldn't contain our glee. It drove smoothly and comfortably and had power beneath the hood which I had not felt before. The pain in my back didn't even arise at all, sitting in that new well-padded driver's seat. I even had to keep it in third gear to avoid having Frankie disappear in my rear-view mirror altogether. Oh, if Johnny could see me now, he would have loved it. I thought of him frequently and wondered what condition his illness had progressed to and how he was doing. Pulling over only a short distance from town, I waved Frankie to come up alongside me on the shoulder.

"Whataya think?" I shouted over to her.

“It’s a blast! You like it?”

"You bet I do! I'll drive to your house, so you can drop off Denise, and then we'll take it for a spin through town together."

We spent the rest of the evening joyriding around like we hadn’t a care in the world. The radio blaring with both of us singing along at times. It was just the break I needed from the events which encircled my life over the past several weeks. I wasn’t sure if buying this car was the cure for any of my past indifferences, but cruisin’ with Frankie gave me a feeling of pride, and for the first time, in a long time, I felt happy.

It was more than just a car, it was something to be shared and enjoyed by both of us, something that could carry us off with ease, whenever the need to escape would arrive. And with plans I had been contemplating, I was now hoping that we could move forward to the next level. I didn’t think Doc Coots could have prescribed it any better.

17

With unanswered questions still rattling around in the recesses of my mind, I knew I had to search for something tangible, something explainable.

I had heard what Father Tom told me and though he was someone who I learned to admire and respect, I wasn't completely satisfied with his rationalization, I wanted more. There was something still gnawing at me, and I felt I had to get to the bottom of it. So, I scribbled notes to myself, I configured a timeline of the events which led up to my accident. I toiled on sheets of brown paper, scratching my remarks out for hours and in doing so, encountered many nights where I would fall asleep in the most uncomfortable places, whether it be sunken over my kitchen table, on the floor of the living room, or wherever my investigative process would find me.

The resolve came unexpectedly.

Awakening, I was suddenly jolted from sleep. I arose in a shudder, it wasn't the random twangs of pain in my back which caused it, this night, something more, something obvious, something abruptly lifted me from my slumber. In my darkened kitchen, lit only by the light of the full moon peering through the window, I discovered the obvious. After staring at my notes for quite some time, I looked up to the skies above.

"THANK YOU," I stated softly to myself. (and to whomever else may have been listening).

Sunrise was approximately 5:47 a.m. and I couldn't wait another minute. Barefooted and wearing a pair of old blue jeans and a white tee-shirt, I ran out to my car, started it up, and raced over to Frankie's. This time I honestly believed she would think I had lost my mind, and I may just have.

I skidded up to her house, right in front, the cacti growing in her yard were barely awake themselves, as I knocked rapidly on her door. Moments later, a light came on and she answered in her bathrobe with her hair pulled up.

"Vincent! Do you have any idea what time it is?"

"I know, I know, but it's urgent."

"What happened, are you ok? Is Carlos ok?"

"Yes, yes, I'm fine, he's fine, it's not anything like that. But I must go, and I hope to God that you say yes and come along."

"Hold on, come inside, there's a chill in the air, you are going to catch your death of cold out there, where are your shoes?"

"Frankie, I figured it out, but there is no time to spare, I have to leave, and I want you to come with me."

"Vincent, honey, you have to stop doing this. Figured what out? Where are you going now, and where is it that you want me to go with you to?"

I didn't have time to explain the details, and I wasn't sure if Frankie was open to what I was about to suggest, so banking on the mere hope and confidence in our relationship, I took a chance. Holding her out in front of me with both my arms, I looked more meaningful than ever into her eyes.

"Do you trust me?"

She stood there, not moving at all, her eyes not straying from mine, at that moment she knew I was more serious than she had ever known me to be. After several moments, she answered me with the same certainty.

"Yes, I do!"

I pulled her close, and kissed her on the forehead, releasing her, our eyes met strongly again as I was still holding her tightly by the shoulders.

"Can you get time off from work? Say, at least three days?"

"Uh, Yes, I think so."

"Okay, do it. Pack your bags and be at my house in three hours."

She looked puzzled, and I expected as much, but she had agreed, and I was hopeful that I would be able to put my plan into motion. My next stop was to see Father Tom.

Nearly three hours later, I found myself all cleaned up with my suitcases packed to the gills and neatly stacked in the trunk of my new Chevy. And as before, I was ready to follow the road. Only this time I knew what the exact destination would be, this time it wasn't random, this time it was a matter of conviction, and this time, I wouldn't be alone.

Father Tom, Carlos, and I, along with Zeke were out in front of my house chatting away as Frankie pulled up.

"Well the gangs all here, does anyone want to fill me in?" She curiously stated.

"Hold on darlin', let's get your bags out of your trunk and into mine."

"Listen, Vincent, I'm not sure what I have agreed to, but you've got to give me a clue or something here."

"Honey, I will explain it all to you once we get on the road, I promise."

The truth was that neither Father Tom, nor Carlos, nor Frankie, had any real inclination of what I was planning, and in reality, I wasn't even sure myself.

I transferred the contents of her trunk, including that old vintage microphone which little Jim bestowed on me years ago. I guess it was for memory's sake that I kept it, and it was still tucked away somewhere in the bottom of Denise.

Frankie got into the passenger side as Father Tom, Carlos, and Zeke stood together while I approached them. I crouched down on one knee and gave Carlos a hearty handshake, which he promptly thrust forward from and turned into a big heartfelt hug. I then handed him the keys to my house. He agreed to stay there in my absence and take care of Zeke, with Father Tom checking up on them, daily.

I stood up and thanked Father Tom for all he had done for me, for his support and his words of wisdom. His handshake also turned into a hug just as Carlos' did, only with much more strength and vigor.

"Whatever this is that you need to do my son, may God be with you."

"Thanks, Father."

Getting down again, this time on both knees, I held Zeke, petting and rubbing him zestfully while his tail wagged unstoppably.

"You be a good boy now Zeke, and take care of these guys, alright?"

Then rising, I looked over my shoulder at the three of them as I headed to the car.

"Señor!" Carlos shouted as he ran over to me one last time.

Holding me tight around the waist, I fought the tears from mounting up.

"Señor, you will come back, yes?"

"Oh, you haven't seen the last of me, buddy, I plan on it!"

Then getting behind the wheel, he gently pushed my driver's side door shut. I shifted into drive and just before I gave it the gas, I asked Frankie for the keys to Denise. She reached into the small moccasin purse which was slung around her neck and handed them to me. Leaning out my window I yelled over to Carlos, tossing them to him. Staring at the catch in his hand, he smiled like a kid at Christmas time.

"Take good care of her and she will treat you right!" I said to him motioning to where Denise was parked.

Off we sped, leaving the three of them in my rearview mirror waving goodbye through a cloud of dust.

Having already plotted our destination using the fastest route possible on the map, I knew exactly where we were headed and how long it would take to get there. We hit the highway in a couple of minutes, then shifting into 4th gear, I opened up the engine with all eight cylinders percolating. It was to be approximately a nine-hour trip and even though we had approached the cooler fall temperatures during the evening and early morning hours, the sun still blazed brightly and consistently during the day. I turned up the radio loud, as we powered our way through the desert landscape.

For the first couple hours of our ride, Frankie sat primarily quiet, looking out her window and nodding off for a while. But I knew eventually she would ask, it was simply human nature to want to know where we were headed. Hesitantly, I planned to wait for just the right moment before I divulged that information.

Three and a half hours into our journey, I noticed a small truck stop along the way and pulled into a parking space. Frankie had fallen into a deep sleep, most likely because I had awakened her at such an ungodly hour that morning.

"Hey, wake up, sorry, come on now," I said whispering as I shook her gently.

"Ummmmmm where are we?" she said yawning.

"I'm not sure, we haven't crossed the border yet, but this looked like as good a place as any, you hungry?"

"Crossed what border? Oh you better have one heck of an explanation this time mister."

Getting out of the car we found a small table in the corner, sat down where a waitress immediately approached us, poured two cups of coffee, and took our order.

"So, here we are in the middle of nowhere, are you going to tell me what this all about."

"Uh, not exactly, I want to wait until we get a little closer."

"A little closer to what, to where?"

"Hold on darlin', you said you trusted me, right?"

"I do Vincent, but can't you even tell me where we are going?"

"In due time honey.......in due time."

Our food appeared almost right away, we ate slowly and contently. I told her how I met with Father Tom briefly after I left her house that morning and he agreed to keep an eye on Carlos and of course Zeke, for as long as my quest was going to take. After about forty minutes, I paid our tab and we headed back out to the car.

I opened my door at the same time she opened hers, but before either of us got in, I looked across the roof and found her looking straight back at me, I smiled and simply said....................VEGAS!"

"What, Vegas? Oh, this is going to be a bash, Vegas, did you say Vegas?" she stated with plenty of enthusiasm.

"That I did, and I have a really good reason for it, so let's get it going!"

Sliding into her seat, she looked over at me with a wrinkle in her forehead and a perplexed smile on her face as she shut her door. We rode head-on into a dust storm and some fierce winds, in and out of rain showers and eventual clearing skies. The thought of stopping by nightfall and finding a hotel room crossed my mind, but with each of us taking turns driving as the other napped, it allowed us to press on without interruption.

Then in the wake of a crisp autumn evening, the lights of a big city appeared far off in the distance. I turned off the radio.

"Frankie, honey, you awake?"

"Yes, yes I am." She said softly as she sat up straight in her seat.

"It's time, it's time I tell you what I know, or least, what I think I know."

She perched herself up more attentively with one leg folded beneath her as she turned to face me.

"Okay, mister, you dragged me all this way, this better be good." She said gravely.

"I don't know how to explain this, so just let me get it out the best I can. You know how you found something in that old journal referring to the Crucifix as the source of the water leak, and you know how I said that Father Ortiz was trying to tell me something similar. Well, I traced back to each event, each time someone claimed to have received a miracle."

Things became eerily silent as I continued.

"Listen, see if this makes any sense to you. Let's take a specific instance, Carlos for example. When I found him lying there, there was that puddle of water on the floor and in my moment of panic, I soaked it up with my rag and patted his face and head trying to revive him. Then there was that mystery lady, at one point I found her with her child in her arms standing where she wasn't supposed to be, somewhere beneath the Crucifix, the child's head was wet from the dripping water, I remember it clearly because I wiped his head dry with my handkerchief."

"So, what you are saying? Is it what the writing in the journal described?"

"Honey, at this point, I can't be sure what I am trying to say or prove, I am merely stating the facts. And then the night of my accident, when I was up there getting him down, just before we fell, I saw those tears!"

I continued with excitement in my voice.

"Frankie, I don't care what those army engineers deduced about any hollow openings, behind any wall, where rainwater could have been trapped, I know now what I believe."

"Okay, Okay, I got it, I understand, but what does any of this have to do with your sudden sense of urgency to drive nine hours to get to Las Vegas in the middle of the night?" She inquired sharply.

"I gotta say, the night of my accident and the days that followed, not only opened my eyes but my heart. For such a long time, I tried to forget the hurt of the past and for the most part, I have, but I couldn't forgive, I couldn't let go of the pain, I couldn't let anyone else in. That night, that Crucifix, I mean all of this, has healed me in that way. It may not have healed me in the same sense that Carlos was physically healed, mine was an emotional healing, I have forgiven the past. I know I can move on from it now."

I pulled over slowly to the side of the road, it was quite desolate with just one auto speeding by as we came to a halt. Looking over at her, she was contently smiling. Moving close, our eyes locked, then I kissed her deeply and longingly for the next several minutes. It was tender and loving, she slid across the bench seat and moved right up against me. I wrapped my right arm around her while she nestled in tightly.

I maneuvered the car back on to the blacktop with her right at my side. Motoring forward, I forged ahead with my plan, as I went on with my conclusion.

"Honey, when my friend tracked me down at the church, I was cleaning up, my hands were wet and...........well, I didn't tell you before, at the time, it was just too difficult a thing for me to accept or understand. He was only given a matter of months, if there is any more proof necessary to my theory, I think it will be found there."

Heading down the welcoming road directly for the bright lights ahead, the highway was lined with numerous billboards advertising the casinos, glamorous hotels, showgirls, and nightclub acts.

The first one read in big bold lettering:

The Sands Hotel, featuring *The Rat Pack, Dean Martin, Frank Sinatra, Sammy Davis Jr., Peter Lawford, and Joey Bishop.*

Another read:

Debbie Reynolds, now appearing at The Riviera Hotel.

A third appeared, *Milton Berle and Ray Bolger with Dorothy Louden* at The Flamingo...... and so on.

They continued, on and on, one after another as I slowed down to admire each of them on our way.

Then, as I could see the city limits coming into view, I sped up, and in one quick moment, slammed on my brakes as hard as I could, I heard Frankie scream as the car spun off the side of the road onto some gravel into a 180-degree turn before coming to a dead stop.

With the motor still running, I flung my door open and jumped out of my seat. I hurriedly walked around to the front of the car where the headlights shone partially on me. I stood there awestruck. Waving Frankie to get out, she did the same leaving her door open as well. The radio remained on and in the background, the only sound we could hear was the voice of Bobby Darin singing his hit, *Dream Lover.*

Frankie came and stood next to me looking up at the same thing that had me frozen in place, her right hand covered her mouth.

We stood there mesmerized, as I took her left hand and held it tightly in mine. There in front of us, bigger than life was a billboard, brightly lit from left to right, top to bottom, it captured the image of a princely looking gent, appearing better than ever, with his black hair slicked back, sitting on a black and chrome motorcycle, wearing dark glasses peering out at us, with a guitar strapped around his back, it read:

*** NOW APPEARING AT THE DESERT SANDS ***

JOHNNY MAGNIFICO

AND HIS ELECTRIFYING GUITAR

THE END…………….?

Music Notes
(In order of appearance)

1. ***Sh Boom, (Life could be a Dream)***, The Crew Cuts, 1954, Writers; James Keyes, Claude Feaster, Carl Feaster, Floyd F. McRae, and William Edwards.
2. ***Move it on Over***, Hank Williams, 1947. Writer; Hank Williams.
3. ***Let's Have a Ball,*** Champion Jack Dupree, 1945, Writer; Jack Dupree.
4. ***Diana,*** Paul Anka, 1957***,*** Writer; Paul Anka.
5. ***Good Rockin Tonight***, Wynonie Harris, 1947, Writer; Roy Brown.
6. ***Rock This Joint***, Jimmy Preston, 1949, Writers; Harold Crafton and Wendall Keane.
7. ***Rocket 88***, Jackie Brenston and His Delta Cats, 1951, Writer Jackie Brenston.
8. ***Only You***, The Platters. 1954, Writer; Buck Ram.
9. ***Little Darlin***, The Diamonds. 1957, Writer; Maurice Williams.
10. ***Poor Little Fool***, Ricky Nelson. 1958, Writer; Sharon Sheeley.
11. ***Kansas City***, Wilbert Harrison. 1959, Writers; Jerry Leiber and Mike Stoller.
12. ***We're Gonna Rock, We're Gonna Roll***, Wild Bill Moore. 1948, Writer; Wild Bill Moore.
13. ***Hole in the wall***, Albinia Jones. 1949, Writers; Milt Gabler and Albinia Jones.
14. ***Theme from a Summer Place***, Percy Faith, 1959, Writer; Mack Discant.
15. ***Teenager in Love***, Dion and The Belmonts, 1959, Writers; Doc Pumos, Mort Shuman.
16. ***Young Love***, Sonny James. 1956, Writers; Ric Cartey, Carole Joyner.
17. ***Lonely Boy***, Paul Anka, 1959, Writer; Paul Anka.
18. ***Venus***, Frankie Avalon, 1959, Writer; Ed Marshall.

19. ***Poison Ivy***, The Coasters, 1959, Writers; Jerry Leiber and Mike Stoller.
20. ***Dream Lover***, Bobby Daren, 1959, Writer, Bobby Darin.

Notes

Cumming, Jack. "Seven Brides for Seven Brothers. "Metro-Goldwin-Mayer, 1954.

Sheldon, Sydney. "The Bachelor and the Bobbysoxer". RKO Radio Pictures, 1947.

Cooper, Merian C. "Rio Grande". Argosy Pictures. 1950.

Bonanza. NBC Network, New York, 1959. Television.

The Honeymooners. CBS Network, New York, 1955. Television.

The Lone Ranger. ABC Network New York, 1949. Television.

Howdy Doody. NBC Network, New York, 1947. Television.

Made in the USA
Middletown, DE
26 July 2020

13543592R00163